TONIGHT
YOU'RE
DEAD

ALSO BY VIVECA STEN IN THE SANDHAMN
MURDERS SERIES

Still Waters
Closed Circles
Guiltless

TONIGHT YOU'RE DEAD

VIVECA STEN

TRANSLATED BY MARLAINE DELARGY

SANDHAMN MURDERS

Previously published as *I natt är du död* by Forum in Sweden in 2011. Translated from Swedish by Marlaine Delargy.
First published in English by AmazonCrossing in 2017.

Published by AmazonCrossing, Seattle

Amazon, the Amazon logo, and AmazonCrossing are trademarks of Amazon.com, Inc., or its affiliates.

ISBN-13: 9781542048538
ISBN-10: 1542048532

Cover design by Kimberly Glyder

Printed in the United States of America

To Lennart,
without you I am only half

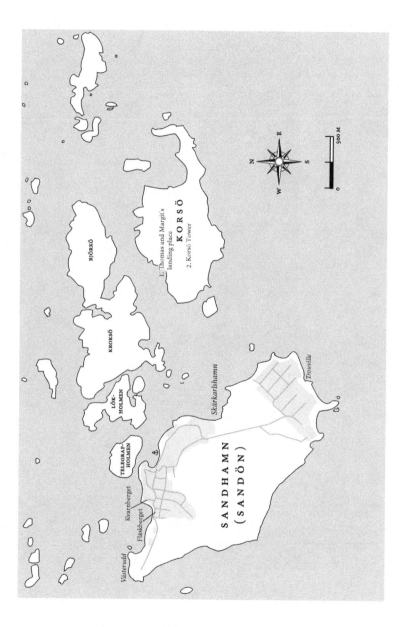

BJÖRKÖ

KORSÖ

1. Thomas and Margit's
   landing place
2. Korsö Tower

KROKSÖ

LÖK-
HOLMEN

Skärkarlshamn

TELEGRAF-
HOLMEN

Kvarnberget

Flaskberget

Västerudd

SANDHAMN
(SANDÖN)

Trouville

N
E
W
S

0   500 M

PROLOGUE

The splashing made him think of children playing in a bathtub. If he closed his eyes, he could picture a beach, with little ones running around without a care in the world.

One final splash, and the water slopped over the edge of the bucket and onto the wet floor.

The flailing arms grew still. The legs kept on twitching, like silverfish scuttling to and fro with no real purpose. Jerky, pointless movements.

Then they, too, grew still, and the slow dripping of the tap was the only sound breaking the silence in the white-tiled room.

He would remember that sound for the rest of his life.

The strong smell of soap filled the air, the odor of pine needles assailing his nostrils and making him retch. But he gritted his teeth; the fear overshadowed everything else.

Something warm trickled down his leg, and he realized he had wet himself.

It didn't matter. It was all too late anyway.

The tap continued to drip.

CHAPTER 1

Sunday, September 16, 2007 (The First Week)

The girl sounded terrified.

"You have to come now, right away."

"Can you tell me your name?"

The voice on the emergency line was professional without being unfriendly. On the screen, the digital clock showed precisely 10:03 in the morning.

"It's just terrible . . . It's Marcus."

"Can you explain what's happened?" said the operator. "Try to calm down."

"I'm at his place."

"You need to give me the address."

"He's not breathing. He's just hanging there." The response ended on a sob. "I can't get him down."

"Where are you?" the operator tried again.

She could hear the muted hum of conversation behind her as her colleagues took other calls. So far it had been relatively quiet; it was Sunday morning, and the events of Saturday night had been dealt with long ago. The operator had started her shift at six a.m., and she had already gone through three cups of coffee.

"Where are you?" she repeated.

The young person on the other end of the line calmed down a little.

"Värmdövägen 10B, in Nacka."

The words were almost a whimper.

"The student apartments." She hiccupped. "We'd arranged to study together."

"And what's your name?"

"Amanda."

"Your full name?"

"Amanda Grenfors." The voice was thick, dubious, as if she couldn't take in what she was seeing.

"Try and tell me what's happened, Amanda."

The operator had been making notes during the call. The address was no more than a stone's throw from Nacka police station; a patrol could be there in minutes.

"Marcus is hanging from the ceiling. There's a rope around his neck. His face is all blue . . ." The girl's voice broke. The operator waited, and after a few seconds, she heard a whisper: "I think he's dead."

The main door of the 1940s apartment building was ajar when the squad car arrived. The number of bicycles parked outside bore witness to the fact that this was student housing—one of the buildings that had recently been converted to meet the increasing demand from the capital's academic institutions.

The two police officers went up a flight of stairs and down a long corridor with a dozen or so doors on either side. They glanced into the shared kitchen, where a pile of dirty dishes filled the sink. A handwritten note had been stuck on one of the cupboard doors: *Clean up after yourself—your mommy doesn't live here!*

There was a carelessly knotted garbage bag lying in one corner; judging by the smell, it had been there for quite some time. No one was around.

At the far end of the corridor, one of the doors was wide open. Outside, an ashen-faced young woman was sitting on the floor with her back to the wall. She wore jeans and black sneakers, and her thick dark-red sweater seemed too big for her thin body.

"Amanda Grenfors?" said the officer.

"Yes." A tear-stained face turned up toward her. The officer crouched down and gently laid her hand on the young woman's arm.

"How are you doing?"

"He's in there." She pointed with a shaky right hand. "Hanging from the light fixture."

They followed the movement with their eyes. The sun broke through the clouds, and in the sudden brightness flooding through the window, they could see tiny dancing dust motes forming a shimmering halo around the body suspended from the ceiling. The drooping head and the angle of the neck confirmed what they already suspected.

Marcus Nielsen was dead.

CHAPTER 2

He was running across the dark, uneven ice just off the Sandhamn shore, and he could hear it creaking beneath his feet. Then the water swallowed him, and he felt as if his fingers and toes were being devoured by the cold. The icy seawater forced the air out of his lungs and sucked the oxygen from his blood.

Soon he would drown in the deep channel. No one would come to his rescue, because no one knew he was out on the ice.

He wept.

He didn't want to die, not like this, all alone, without the chance to say good-bye.

The water drove the cold into his body and drained his strength, and he bitterly regretted all the things he hadn't said and done.

How was he supposed to know that the clock was ticking?

As he rapidly lost feeling in his limbs, he realized that his heart was slowing, that he was on the verge of losing consciousness. Soon a false warmth would spread through his veins, he would give in, and everything would be over.

But he didn't want to die, not now, not without Pernilla by his side.

By now he was shivering so much that he had to let go. He sank back into the freezing water. He just couldn't fight anymore.

There was a ringing noise, shrill and insistent, an angry signal demanding his attention.

He opened his eyes and realized that he was lying in his own bed with Pernilla breathing evenly by his side.

He reached out and groped for his phone on the bedside table. His fingers lost their grip, and his phone fell to the floor. After a brief silence, it started ringing again; it sounded even louder this time. Pernilla stirred.

"Phone," she mumbled.

Her voice finally brought him back to reality. He swung his legs over the side of the bed, but when he lowered his left foot to the floor and tried to stand up, he almost lost his balance. He still hadn't gotten used to it. He bent down and grabbed his phone. He pressed it to his cheek, and immediately it was wet with tears.

His voice was scratchy as he said, "Thomas Andreasson."

CHAPTER 3

On the way to the car, Margit Grankvist thought about the sparse information she had been given over the phone. She had been at the breakfast table with Bertil when the call came through; both girls were still asleep. Bertil hardly looked up from his newspaper; he knew right away that she had to go.

He was used to the situation by now. Margit smiled as she pictured her husband, with his thinning hair. He taught high school English and Swedish. She knew that some of her friends didn't consider him the most exciting guy around, but they had stuck it out for over twenty years and had raised two fine daughters who would soon be ready to leave the nest. Anna was due to graduate from high school in the spring, and Linda a couple of years after that.

Margit got into the car. The chill in the air made it clear that autumn was definitely on its way. The late-summer weather that had held for several weeks would soon be replaced by cold winds and overcast skies. It was already getting dark noticeably earlier; the days would grow shorter and shorter until only six hours of weak daylight remained.

Before the year finally turned.

Margit was finding it increasingly difficult to cope with the long Swedish winters. Lately she had started to dream of renting a small apartment in southern Spain, a place in the sun for her and Bertil when the girls left home.

Her cell phone beeped as a text message came through with fresh information. The dead boy's name was Marcus Nielsen, and he was a student of psychology at Stockholm University. He had lived alone in the dorm room where he had been found an hour or so earlier.

OK, so he was twenty-two years old, but she still thought of him as a boy. Her own daughter Anna was eighteen . . .

Margit turned the key and backed out of the driveway. There was virtually no traffic at this time of the day, and it should take her only twenty minutes or so to get to Värmdövägen.

Margit parked in front of the apartment complex and locked the car. She nodded to a uniformed officer on the stairs and passed several students in boxers and T-shirts, peering out from behind their doors. She heard the familiar voice of Staffan Nilsson, the forensic technician, before she entered Marcus Nielsen's room.

The body was still hanging from a light fixture in the form of a hook on the ceiling, but it would soon be carefully taken down and sent to the pathology lab in Solna.

"Good morning," Nilsson said, inclining his head in Margit's direction. She moved forward, looking around and pulling on a pair of plastic gloves.

The room was surprisingly large for student housing; it must've been something like 645 square feet, at a guess. It was reasonably tidy, even though the trash can was overflowing with fast-food packaging and there was no sign that a vacuum cleaner had been used recently.

"We didn't have it this good when I was a student," Nilsson said from behind her. "We had to make do with rooms that were so small we could hardly turn around."

There was a neatly made bed immediately to the left of the door and a desk over by the window with an office chair pushed underneath. A white IKEA bookcase stood against one wall, the kind that was listed in *Guinness World Records* as the world's bestseller. A door opposite the bed led to a tiny bathroom; Margit could see several toilet paper rolls on the floor.

"There's his final message." Nilsson pointed to a piece of paper on the pillow.

"A suicide note?"

He nodded and read aloud: "Forgive me, but everything is so hard. Marcus."

Margit leaned forward. "It's a computer printout."

"Yes."

"And it's not signed."

"No."

"So where's the computer?" She looked at the desk, which was strewn with papers and several open books. "Have you already taken it away?"

"No, I haven't seen a computer."

"So what did he use to write the note?"

Nilsson shrugged. "Good question."

Margit went over to the desk and checked the drawers, then opened the closet and found a bunch of clothes, both clean and dirty, randomly stuffed inside. She spotted a backpack under the bed; she pulled it out and opened it, but it was empty.

"No sign of a computer here." She turned to Nilsson. "Do you know anyone of his generation who can live without a device of some kind?"

"I don't see a printer either."

Nilsson was right; there was no printer or computer paper in the room.

"If he'd been planning to take his own life for a while, he might have printed the note somewhere else—at the university, for example," Nilsson suggested.

"Possibly."

Margit went over to the body. The ceiling was unusually high, so her face was level with Marcus Nielsen's waist. He was wearing a gray hoodie and ripped jeans. A stench struck her as she walked around the back, and a stain on the denim showed that his bowels had emptied at the moment of death. She instinctively recoiled. Then she walked around to the front and moved a short distance away in order to get a better overall picture.

Nielsen's face had set in a distorted grimace. His eyes were half-closed, and there was a small amount of saliva at one corner of his mouth. His lips were parted, and Margit wondered if he had tried to call out as the noose tightened.

Had he changed his mind as his feet kicked out into thin air, or was it just some kind of reflex?

His hair was a strange shade of black, accentuating the deathly white pallor of his face.

"That can't be his natural hair color," Margit said.

"Probably not, but the autopsy will tell us for sure."

"How long do you think he's been dead?"

Nilsson scratched his nose.

"At least five or six hours; rigor mortis has started to set in."

Margit looked closely at the noose from different angles. It was deeply embedded in the neck, the skin discolored with livid shades of dark red and purple. The other end of the rope was firmly tied to the light fixture.

"How did he get up there?" she said, before answering her own question. "He must have climbed onto the desk, put the noose around his neck, then jumped off."

She gazed at the body; Marcus Nielsen was slim and not very tall, but still he must have weighed around a hundred and fifty pounds.

"I'm surprised it held," she said, half to herself.

"You mean the hook?"

"Mm-hmm."

Nilsson straightened up. "This place is solid; it's not like some of those buildings they threw up in the seventies."

"You mean if he'd lived somewhere like that he'd have survived?" Margit said.

She went over to the bookcase and picked up a framed photograph showing the deceased with a middle-aged couple and a teenage boy, presumably his parents and a younger brother. White letters in the bottom corner indicated that it had been taken on July 10, 2006—the previous summer. It looked like a holiday picture; they were sitting outside some kind of café, and the background consisted of white buildings with bright-blue doors. *Probably the Greek islands,* Margit thought. *A lovely family holiday. With no idea of what the future might hold.*

Marcus Nielsen bore a strikingly close resemblance to his mother, with the same narrow eyes and straight mouth. Her hair was light brown; perhaps her son's had been a similar color before he'd dyed it. Marcus's expression was open, and he looked intelligent. There was no sign of some inner torment that would make him take his own life fourteen months later.

His brother took after their father. They both had blond hair and were a little on the plump side. The father's arm was around his younger son's shoulders, and he was smiling broadly at the camera. Presumably they had asked the waiter to take the photograph.

"He looks like a nice guy," Margit remarked.

"Most people do. Before they die, that is."

The response wasn't sarcastic, merely a dry observation.

Typical black humor, Margit thought as she replaced the picture. A way of keeping tragedy at bay. She had found out that the father worked for the local council and the mother was a nurse. The younger brother was still at home; he was in his junior year of high school.

This might be the last photo of the whole family. There would be no more. The parents must be informed as soon as possible; Margit wasn't looking forward to that particular conversation.

Nilsson took something out of his black bag and headed for the bathroom.

"Any indication that we could be looking at something other than suicide?" Margit said.

He shook his head without turning around. "Not at this stage, but of course we're securing prints and other biological traces, if there are any."

"Where's the girl who found him?"

"In the kitchen with Torunn. She was in shock when we got here."

"Hardly surprising under the circumstances."

Margit took a final glance at the bookcase; many of the books had English titles relating to the field of psychology, and there were a number of what appeared to be textbooks on the desk.

"He was studying psychology at Stockholm University," she said. "I wonder if he had psychological problems of his own?"

Nilsson appeared in the bathroom doorway.

"You mean the kind that could make him take his own life?"

CHAPTER 4

Nora Linde wearily contemplated her son's messy room. Since she and Henrik had separated, Adam was spending more and more time on his computer. He'd let his clothes pile up on the floor, and he was always glued to the screen, chatting or playing games, as if he preferred the virtual world to the real one. He rarely answered when she spoke to him, and he could hardly bear to waste time sitting at the dinner table.

Nora tried to set boundaries, but it wasn't easy when she and Henrik had differing views on the matter. There wasn't much point in her insisting on a limit to screen time if Henrik let the boys do as they wished when they were staying with him. If it had been difficult to reach an agreement when they were living together, it was nearly impossible now.

Just weeks after Henrik's infidelity had been revealed six months earlier, Nora had efficiently submitted the relevant divorce papers to the court—she was a lawyer, after all. Because they had children under the age of sixteen, they were required to observe a six-month period of reflection before the marriage could be dissolved.

Nora didn't need a period of reflection. She was very clear about the fact that she didn't want to be married to Henrik any longer. They could barely exchange two words without getting into an argument, and whenever she had to call him, she'd put it off for as long as possible. However, sometimes she just had to bite the bullet; with a seven-year-old and a twelve-year-old, there were things that had to be discussed.

That didn't stop her from hoping that the answering machine would come on.

The worst thing was when Marie, Henrik's new partner, picked up. They had moved in together during the summer, and she had quickly made herself at home in the house in Saltsjöbaden that had been Nora and Henrik's home for so many years. Marie had a high, slightly shrill voice, and she spoke quickly and breathlessly as if she was constantly surprised at the way of the world. "MarieafGrénier," she would say in a single breath.

At least my ex-mother-in-law will be satisfied now, Nora often thought sourly. *At long last her precious son has found a woman who knows how to behave in proper company.* OK, so Marie was what you might call "lesser nobility." But still, her family was registered with the Swedish House of Nobility, and she had grown up in a manor house. She was just the type of woman Monica Linde had always wanted for Henrik. Nora might be a qualified lawyer, but she was also the first member of her family to go to university. Not exactly a point in her favor, in Monica's estimation.

It would soon be Simon's birthday, and somehow Nora would have to get through the celebration, whatever her opinion of her ex. The thought of the party made her stomach tie itself in knots.

She pushed at the heap of dirty clothes with her foot.

"Adam!" she yelled in the direction of the living room, where he was watching TV. "Can you come and tidy this up, please?"

A few seconds passed, and she tried again, a little more forcefully this time.

"Adam!"

The sound of footsteps told her the sharper tone had done the trick. Her son appeared, a sullen look on his face.

"Why do you have to keep nagging me?"

It was the last thing she wanted, but Nora could feel the irritation rising.

"I keep *nagging* because you leave me no choice. If you made more of a contribution, I wouldn't have to."

"Dad doesn't nag me."

Nora felt a stab of pure pain. With unerring accuracy, Adam had fired off the perfect shot.

"But right now you're with me, not your dad." She was already regretting her words, but she couldn't stop herself. "Besides which, your dad has a housecleaner, which we can't afford."

A look of contempt was the only response.

I want them to be happy here, Nora thought. *Why do I always end up starting a fight?* She caught a glimpse of herself in the mirror, which seemed to underline her gloomy thoughts.

She had always been slim, but now she was gaunt. If her diabetes didn't force her to eat regular meals, she would forget to eat at all; her appetite had completely disappeared over the past six months. Her shoulder-length strawberry-blond hair needed cutting, and there were dark circles under her gray eyes.

Nora knew she wasn't getting enough sleep, but she couldn't work out how to remedy that. Her briefcase contained a pile of documents from the bank that she needed to go through to prepare for the coming week; it was going to be another late night.

"I'll give you a hand," she said in an attempt to smooth things over. She bent down to retrieve dirty socks and underpants from beneath the bed.

"Mmm." He didn't look at her.

"Adam, please. I know this isn't easy, but we have to try."

"Mmm."

She placed a hand on his arm.

"Listen . . ." She took a deep breath. "I thought we might go over to Sandhamn next weekend? You can bring a friend if you like. Your dad's attending a conference, so you're with me two weekends in a row."

A faint smile appeared on the thin face.

Both boys loved spending time on the island, particularly now that they had moved into the Brand villa. It was perhaps the loveliest house on Sandhamn, and Nora had inherited it from her neighbor, Signe Brand, a few years earlier.

During the summer, they had worked together to redecorate the bedrooms and generally freshen up the place. Even Simon had learned to apply wallpaper paste with even strokes. He had concentrated so hard that he'd practically squinted with the effort.

They had also relocated on the mainland. Nora had found a light, airy two-bedroom apartment in central Saltsjöbaden, about fifteen minutes from their former home. The boys shared the larger bedroom, while she had taken the smaller one. The kitchen and living room were generously proportioned and flooded with sunlight on bright days, and she had managed to squeeze a desk into a small alcove in the kitchen so that she had somewhere to work.

Adam's voice brought her back to the moment.

"Can I bring Wille?"

William Åkerman had been Adam's best friend ever since they'd started junior high. The boys had grown even closer over the past six months as Adam tried to get used to switching homes every other week.

She put her arm around his shoulders and gave him a hug. When he was little, his hair had been white blond, but now it was a sandy brown. It wasn't as dark as Henrik's, but otherwise he was a carbon copy of his father.

"Of course you can."

"Thanks, Mom."

Adam's tone had softened, and Nora felt her heart lift.

Her thoughts turned to Thomas, her childhood friend and Simon's godfather. He had a summer cottage on the island of Harö, no more than ten minutes from Sandhamn. Should she give him a call to say they'd be coming over next weekend?

CHAPTER 5

As Margit approached the kitchen, she could hear muted sobs and the sound of someone speaking in a reassuring tone. She entered the room and saw a young woman sitting at a round table, with a police officer of about thirty-five years old sitting beside her. Margit realized that it was Torunn.

"This is Amanda," Torunn said, getting up to make room for Margit.

"How are you feeling?" Margit asked as she sat down.

"Not too good," Amanda whispered.

"I realize this is difficult, but can you tell me what happened?"

"We'd arranged to meet up today; we have an assignment that's due tomorrow, and we were going to finish it this morning."

Her eyes were huge, and the tears had made her eyelashes stick together like black straggling flies' legs.

"So you study together?"

"Yes, we're both in the psychology course." Her face crumpled. "I mean, we were . . ."

Margit placed her hand on the girl's arm. "Do you remember if the door was open when you got here?"

"I think it was closed."

"Was it locked? Do you have a key?"

Amanda shook her head. "It wasn't locked. I knocked, but when he didn't come to the door, I tried the handle."

She broke off as she remembered the sight that had met her eyes earlier. Her mouth twitched, and she pressed a clenched fist to her lips as if to stop herself from bursting into tears again. Margit waited; there was no point in trying to rush the girl.

"And when I walked in, he was just hanging there," Amanda said eventually. "Hanging from the ceiling. He was staring at me, even though he was dead. He kept on staring at me, the whole time."

She buried her face in her hands.

"Did you see anyone else in the corridor when you arrived?" Margit asked.

The girl looked up. "No—everyone was probably still asleep. I was pretty early."

Margit covered Amanda's hand with her own.

"Are you sure you didn't notice anyone?"

The sound of voices outside told Margit that the body was about to be removed; Nilsson should have done what he had to do by now.

"I don't remember anyone," Amanda reiterated.

"Were you close friends, you and Marcus?"

"Yes."

Amanda reached for a glass of water on the table and took several sips.

"We studied together; we've been doing that for a while. We started our course at the same time. But we weren't dating or anything like that."

"What were you working on?"

"We were taking a class on groups and group processes, and, like I said, we were working on an assignment."

"Do you know if Marcus owned a computer?"

Amanda frowned slightly as if she didn't understand the question.

"Of course he did."

"We can't find it."

Amanda thought for a few seconds.

"Have you checked his backpack? Or the bed? He often sat on the bed while working."

"He didn't work at his desk?"

"No, he just kept stuff on the desk."

"Do you know if he had a printer?"

"I don't think so; I've never seen one anyway."

"Are you sure about that?"

Amanda nodded.

"So how did he print out his work?"

A little color had returned to the girl's cheeks. She looked a bit more composed, but still she couldn't help tugging nervously at the sleeves of her sweater, which already stretched down to her knuckles.

"There's a printer at the university we can use. That's what most people do, including me."

Nothing strange about that, Margit thought. Suicides were often planned in advance. If Marcus Nielsen didn't have a printer of his own, he could have printed his suicide note elsewhere. He might have been planning this for weeks, maybe months.

The only thing that didn't make sense was the fact that he had asked Amanda to come over this morning. Perhaps he'd wanted to make sure that someone found him quickly?

"When did you arrange to meet up today?"

"Last Friday in the library, when we didn't get the assignment finished."

Margit straightened her back. The chair was hard and uncomfortable; no doubt it hadn't cost much. Then again, student accommodation wasn't known for its luxurious furnishings.

"Did you notice anything unusual about Marcus lately? Did he seem upset or depressed?"

Amanda shook her head.

"No, he's been the same as always. That's why I can't understand . . ."

Her voice broke, and the tears began to flow. Margit waited for her to calm down; the girl would be driven home in a squad car as soon as they were done.

"Had he ever talked about taking his own life?" she said after a while.

"Absolutely not."

The answer was instant and definite.

"You're sure about that?"

"Yes."

"And you were such close friends that you'd have noticed if something was worrying him?"

Amanda nodded with such emphasis that her dark hair fell over her forehead, hiding her face.

"Yes, we talked about most things."

Margit leaned forward.

"I have to ask you a difficult question. Can you think of any reason why he would want to die?"

"No, I already told you." Amanda's tone was suddenly stubborn, and she looked Margit straight in the eye. "Marcus wasn't depressed. He was a quiet person, but he wasn't unhappy."

Those who kill themselves don't always share their plans, Margit thought. The statistics told their own story; as a rule, friends and family insisted there had been no indication that anything was wrong.

A movement in her peripheral vision made her turn her head. A tall man stood in the kitchen doorway.

The blond hair, now lightly peppered with gray, was still tousled. It looked as though he had simply run his fingers through it. His eyes were puffy as if he had just woken from a deep sleep, and his broad shoulders were slightly hunched.

She sensed rather than saw the limp that was a reminder of how close he had been to losing his life on the ice off the island of Sandhamn last winter.

"Thomas."

Diary:

October 1976

Tomorrow it's time. I am to present myself at Rindö outside Vaxholm, at the Coastal Rangers training academy.

Dad has promised to drive me; I have to be there to register at eight o'clock in the morning. That means we'll have to leave at six.

Almost a thousand people applied, four hundred were invited for further tests, and only five percent were accepted. Usually around two-thirds of that small percentage make it through training.

Dad is so proud, he doesn't even try to hide it. He served in the army as a cook, and he actually seemed a little envious when I told him about my application.

Mom was worried more than anything when she found out I'd gotten in.

"Are you really going to do that?"

I just grinned at her. I could already see myself in the green beret with the yellow trident badge.

The emblem of the Coastal Rangers.

When I was ten years old, the family went to Stockholm. We visited the Royal Palace, and there were several military boats moored by Skeppsbron.

As we were leaving, a group of soldiers came along. They were all wearing green berets and marching in perfect time. They all looked exactly the same, with serious, focused expressions. But just as they were passing us, one of them winked at me. As if I were one of them.

I watched them pass, and when they had gone, I asked my dad who they were.

"Coastal Rangers," he said. "The elite unit."

"Coastal Rangers," I repeated, tucking my hand in his. "That's what I'm going to be when I grow up."

CHAPTER 6

Thursday (The First Week)

The woman sitting in the reception area at Nacka police station caught Thomas's attention as soon as he walked in. She was noticeably pale, and she wasn't wearing a scrap of makeup. Thomas guessed that she was around forty-five, a few years older than him. She was wearing a short black padded jacket and dark-blue jeans that were fraying at the bottom. It was seven thirty on Thursday morning.

"Thomas, this lady wants to see you or Margit," the receptionist informed him.

The woman immediately got to her feet.

"Thomas Andreasson?"

He nodded.

"My name is Maria Nielsen. My son Marcus . . ." She hesitated, then went on. "My son Marcus died on Sunday. You were there, you saw him."

Thomas remembered the dead boy hanging there in the sunlight. He remembered the bright autumn day and the stillness in the room when the team had carefully released the rope and taken him down.

Maria Nielsen's voice trembled as she said, "I need to speak to you."

"Come with me," he replied, leading the way to the elevators.

Thomas offered Maria a cup of coffee, and she accepted it without saying anything. She added two lumps of sugar to the steaming black brew. He showed her into one of the smaller interview rooms, and she sank down on a chair without taking off her jacket.

"I need to speak to you about my son," she burst out before Thomas had even sat down. "Marcus can't have taken his own life. It's impossible. Someone must have killed him."

"What makes you say that?"

Thomas fixed his gaze on the woman's ashen face, making an effort to keep his expression neutral. He didn't want to exacerbate her desperation by showing doubt.

"I just know. Marcus never said a word about taking his own life. He wasn't an unhappy person; he's never been depressed."

Thomas leaned forward. "Since Marcus no longer lived at home, is it possible that something could have happened, something you and his father weren't aware of?"

She shook her head firmly.

"I don't believe that. We got along very well, and besides, David would have known if something was wrong."

"David?"

"Marcus's younger brother. They're . . . they *were* . . . like twins. David is devastated. They were supposed to go skiing this winter; they were talking about spending a week in the French Alps after Marcus's exams in January."

She pulled out a crumpled tissue and wiped her nose.

"Why would he plan a trip with his brother if he was planning to kill himself?" Her tone changed from resigned to aggressive. "Why? Can you tell me that?"

Thomas held up his hand.

"You know the autopsy showed no evidence of anything that would indicate this wasn't a suicide? Have you received a copy of the report?"

Maria nodded, her expression grim.

"That doesn't prove anything."

"The CSI team has examined the scene, and they found no evidence to suggest that a crime has taken place." His eyes were full of compassion. "Unfortunately everything points to the fact that he died by his own hand."

Maria recoiled as if she had been slapped, and her eyes filled with tears.

"I'm so sorry," Thomas said.

"Someone must have murdered Marcus. You can't close the case. You just can't."

"I didn't say we were going to do that, but without signs of a crime, it's difficult to launch a homicide investigation."

Maria's burst of anger was replaced just as suddenly with despair.

"Please. My son deserves better than this." She leaned across the table and grabbed Thomas's wrist. He felt for her, he really did, but he also knew what the Old Man, the chief of the Violent Crime Unit, had said about cutbacks and understaffing at yesterday's morning briefing. The paperwork was piling up on his desk. A young student who appeared to have simply grown tired of life was unlikely to be prioritized under the circumstances.

"Do you have children?"

The question took him by surprise, and for a second Thomas didn't know what to say. He played for time by taking a sip of his coffee.

"Do you?" Maria repeated.

"No. Yes."

He could hear how lame he sounded. He remembered exactly how he had felt the day he'd woken up to find Emily lying stiff in her cradle beside the bed. When every attempt to revive her had failed, the paramedics had had to physically drag him away from her little body.

Her death had broken his marriage, and it had almost broken him, too.

"I had a daughter . . . but she died when she was very small."

At least he could say the words aloud now; it had taken a long time to get to this stage.

Maria Nielsen blinked, but the set of her mouth was determined. She fixed her puffy red eyes on Thomas's face.

"I'm sorry for your loss, but that means you can understand how I'm feeling right now." Her voice became even more insistent. "You have to help me. Marcus didn't take his own life. I just know he didn't."

CHAPTER 7

After showing Maria Nielsen out, Thomas made his way to the conference room where morning briefings were held. Her sorrowful plea remained with him.

The Old Man was sitting at the head of the table as usual, with their superefficient assistant Karin Ek beside him. Erik Blom was finishing off his coffee, his wet hair and flushed face revealing that he had come straight from the gym. His cell phone beeped, and he smiled as he read the message. Thomas had no doubt that it was from one of the many girlfriends who came and went in his carefree colleague's life. Personally he could hardly recall that kind of existence.

At precisely eight o'clock, the door opened and Margit walked in and sat down next to Thomas.

"Sorry," she murmured in the direction of the Old Man. "Traffic jam on Skurubron."

She received a curt nod in response.

As they went through the business of the day, Thomas couldn't stop thinking about Maria Nielsen. He had half promised her that he wouldn't drop her son's case—not because he had changed his mind about the cause but because he was moved by her despair.

Suddenly he realized the room had fallen silent.

"Are you with us, Thomas?" the Old Man said.

Thomas tried to pull himself together and look as if he was up to speed, but he had no idea what they'd been talking about. As so often happened these days, he had lost his concentration. It was as if his brain didn't want to cooperate. He might have one thing in his head, and then all of a sudden he was thinking about something completely different.

"Absolutely."

"OK, that's it for today," the Old Man said.

"Wait." Thomas couldn't help himself.

"Yes?"

"Marcus Nielsen." His tone was more challenging than he had intended.

"What about him?"

"Shouldn't we take a closer look at his death?"

The Old Man looked inquiringly at him. "He hanged himself."

"I spoke to his mother this morning. She doesn't believe it."

"I went to see his family on Sunday," Margit said. "None of them was willing to accept that he'd killed himself. The relatives almost always react that way."

"I'd like to spend a few hours on the case, if that's OK," Thomas persisted. He caught a glimpse of something that was difficult to identify in Margit's eyes. Sympathy, perhaps. Or worry that he was losing his grip?

On Sunday, he had arrived late to the scene. It wasn't the first time he'd shown up late; he was still sleeping badly, and occasionally he took a sleeping pill, even though it left him feeling drowsy the following day. Sometimes he didn't hear the alarm clock and missed the morning briefing altogether.

But the alternative was to wake up in the small hours, knowing he wouldn't be able to get back to sleep because of the thoughts going around and around in his head like a never-ending movie. Which left him walking around in a fog the next day due to lack of sleep.

"I'd like to visit the family, talk to them one last time."

He could hear the uncertainty in his own voice. He sat up a little straighter and tried again.

"I think we can afford that. The boy was only twenty-two."

"OK, but don't spend too much time on it," the Old Man conceded. "You're needed elsewhere, Thomas, now that we've got you back." He gathered up his papers and got to his feet. The meeting was over.

The Nielsen family lived in a whitewashed house in a northern suburb of Stockholm. The neighborhood was made up of similar small houses with tidy gardens side by side. Several of the properties had been renovated or extended, but it was clear that they all had originally been built to the same design.

The door was opened by a teenage boy who looked pale and strained. *David,* Thomas thought. Marcus's younger brother.

He introduced himself, and David stepped aside to let him in.

"Mom!" the boy called out. "It's the police."

Maria Nielsen came down the stairs. She looked as if she'd been crying; her eyes were red-rimmed. Her hair was caught up in a rubber band, but several strands had escaped.

"What are you doing here?" she said in surprise.

"I hope I'm not disturbing you. I have a few more questions. If that's OK, of course."

"No problem." She ran a hand over her hair in a nervous gesture. "Coffee?"

Thomas was ready for the question; most people automatically offered a cup of coffee when the police turned up, and it could sometimes be positively therapeutic. On this occasion he shook his head.

"I'm fine, thanks. I just wanted to find out a little more about Marcus."

He followed mother and son into the living room, which was dominated by a huge flat-screen TV. The Xbox told him that the brothers were into video games. But now there was only one brother left.

"When did Marcus move out?" he began.

"Last year, when he started at the university," Maria replied. "But he came home often—he was here on Saturday, for example." She looked down at her hands. "He used to bring his laundry," she went on, smiling bravely. "I thought he ought to be able to do it himself, but I couldn't say no."

She raised her chin, a defiant expression on her face.

"On Saturday Marcus was exactly the same as he always was, which is why it doesn't make any sense for him . . ." She gazed over at the window and whispered, "To have hanged himself that same night."

David made a small whimpering noise as his mother uttered those terrible words.

Thomas tried to be gentle.

"Do you remember what he did when he was here on Saturday? Did he say anything that struck you as unusual?"

She shrugged, a weary gesture that revealed the chaos within.

"Everything was just the same as always. Marcus had something to eat in the kitchen, and then he went up to his room."

Thomas turned his attention to David. "Were you here?"

"Yes."

"Did anything about your brother strike you as unusual?"

David's mouth trembled as he answered. "Marcus was just the same as always, like Mom said."

"Did you do anything special on Saturday?"

"No, he spent most of the time lying on his bed surfing the net."

Thomas recalled that Marcus's laptop and cell phone still hadn't been found. Strange.

"What device was he using?"

"His laptop, of course."

"We can't find it in his apartment. Are you sure he had it with him on Saturday?"

David was clearly taken aback.

"Marcus took his laptop with him everywhere. He carried it in his backpack."

"Could he have left it here?" Thomas asked. "Could it still be in his room?"

"I haven't seen it," Maria said, "but we can go and take a look if you like."

She led the way upstairs and opened the first door they reached. She stepped back to let Thomas in.

Marcus's childhood room wasn't large, no more than 270 square feet, and it contained a bed, a desk, and a shabby black leather armchair. The walls were decorated with a selection of posters and an old scout flag. Thomas went over and touched the faded fabric.

"Marcus was an active member of the sea scouts when he was a teenager; he liked being out at sea," Maria explained. "He was also a member of a canoe club; they used to go paddling around the archipelago."

Thomas turned to face her.

"That's something I enjoy, too. I have a house on Harö, not far from Sandhamn, and I often take my canoe out when I'm there."

Maria Nielsen's mouth twitched.

"Just like Marcus."

"How were his studies going?" Thomas asked.

Maria sank down on the bed and ran her hand over the soft sheepskin throw draped over the end.

"He was so pleased when he got a place in the program. His exam scores were excellent. It's not easy to be accepted; psychology is very popular."

"Why did he choose that particular major?"

"There was a teacher at his high school who got him interested. It's amazing, isn't it—one person can mean so much when it comes to the choices we make."

Her voice was melancholy.

Thomas glanced around one last time. There was no sign of a laptop, and nothing else struck him. Until his death, Marcus Nielsen had been like any other young student.

The familiar number glowed on the telephone display. If Nora didn't pick up, her voice mail would automatically take over, and she could choose when to listen to Henrik's message.

Or not.

But what if it was something important?

Reluctantly she accepted the call.

"It's me."

The nonchalant tone made her blood boil. They were separated, after all, and the divorce would soon go through.

After thirteen years of marriage.

"Yes."

Nora could be as abrupt as Henrik was casual.

"There's a problem with the midsemester break."

Nora bit her lip to stop herself from saying something foolish. She didn't know where all this anger came from, but it was like flicking a switch as soon as she heard him speak.

"Right."

"My schedule has been changed. I'm on duty all week, so I can't take the boys to London as planned."

"Are you sure Marie hasn't persuaded you to change your mind?"

The words had hardly left her mouth before she regretted them. When did she get so peevish? She really needed to pull herself together.

"Leave her out of this."

But Nora couldn't stop.

"Maybe the two of you would prefer a romantic break. I'm sure she can't cope with two demanding boys clinging to you the whole time."

"Stop it!"

Henrik's tone was like the crack of a whip.

Nora blushed. She took a deep breath and made an effort to lose the aggressive tone.

"The boys will be disappointed."

"I know." Henrik sounded more conciliatory. "It's actually nothing to do with me; another radiology consultant is off sick for two months, so we've had to revise everyone's schedule."

"I see."

She felt more than a little embarrassed.

"I thought we could maybe go later in November; I've got four days off at the end of the month."

"That would mean taking them out of school." Nora could hear how negative she sounded.

"Surely that's not the end of the world?" Henrik said. "It's not as if they have to take exams or anything—a few days won't make much difference."

Nora suppressed an acerbic retort.

"No, it should be fine. But you have to apply for leave of absence."

"How do I do that?"

The rage came surging up again. All these years she had taken care of everything, while Henrik remained blissfully ignorant. She had always dealt with the boys' nursery and then school; he had never even lifted a finger.

And still he had screwed a nurse at work.

"I'm sure you can call the school office and ask!" she snapped and slammed down the receiver.

The blue-and-white tape still stretched across the door of Marcus Nielsen's student apartment. Thomas carefully lifted it up and let himself in.

There was a musty smell, and the room was in semidarkness. The sky outside was overcast, and the bright sunlight he remembered from Sunday was gone.

He looked around without really knowing what he was searching for. Coming here might be a waste of time, but he had promised Maria Nielsen that he would try to find out what had happened to her son.

He would devote a few more hours to the case; it was the least he could do. He pulled on a pair of latex gloves and started to go through the books and papers on the desk. Most of the material seemed to be related to Marcus's classes, but under one of the piles he found several comic books with Japanese manga comics. They looked well thumbed, and one of them had a large grease mark on the front.

Thomas smiled. No doubt Marcus had needed a little relief from his academic texts.

Methodically he checked the bookcase, then the closet. He sensed Maria Nielsen's hand behind a stack of neatly folded T-shirts and sweaters on a high shelf, which provided a stark contrast to the mess below.

He found a red-and-white bag under the bed, with a shabby wetsuit inside. Presumably Marcus had used it when canoeing. If he had visited the waters off Sandhamn, he and Thomas might even have waved to one another, as canoeists do. Thomas had his own kayak and liked to go out early on summer mornings. Suddenly he longed to get out there; it had been a while.

He had spent an hour in the apartment, and found nothing.

With a final glance around the room, he switched off the light and left Marcus Nielsen behind.

DIARY:

OCTOBER 1976

There are eight of us in the group, and we all look exactly the same with our buzz cuts and green uniforms. Like a collection of paper dolls, all cut from the same pattern.

The transformation took place yesterday. I went to the barber as an ordinary Swedish boy with longish hair and came out with nothing but stubble. Then, clutching a stack of official clothing, I tried to find my way to the accommodation block.

There are twenty of us sharing the dormitory, with no more than three feet between the bunk beds. We're not even allowed to keep our first names; instead we are addressed by a number and our surname. My number is 103. The one stands for the first platoon, and the three is my position within the group. I'm the oldest in our group, and Andersson, whose bed is next to mine, is the youngest. His birthday is in December; maybe that's why he's a little smaller than the rest of us. He seems like a nice guy, even though he doesn't have much to say for himself.

Kihlberg seems pretty cool, as does Martinger, who is well over six feet tall and built like a barn door. The others are probably OK, too; the only one I have a problem with is Eklund.

Everyone seems nervous, but I've read all the material available, and I know that the training program to become a Coastal Ranger demands a strong mind and tip-top physical condition. Only the best will make it.

I'm ready.

I have slept no more than a few hours per night over the past week or so. We have ten minutes to shovel down our food and then run to wherever we're supposed to be. We move everywhere at the double. We are constantly being woken up, and in the end, we don't know whether it's night or day. It's like living in a constant fog due to the lack of sleep.

We do push-ups on our knuckles, and when someone collapses, we all have to start over. Everyone suffers when one person can't hack it. As soon as we do something wrong, we are punished, and everything we do is wrong.

I'm not sure if I can go on.

Everything is searched, over and over again.

Before I got here, I thought it was only the police or customs officials who do this kind of thing, but to me the word search *has acquired a whole new meaning. They go through our possessions over and over again, because we have to learn to put every item away in perfect order.*

We have to fold our clothes ten times so that they fit properly in the closet. Then the sergeant throws the whole lot on the floor, and so it begins again.

Yesterday we were just about to go to bed when he appeared in the doorway. That meant half the night would be spent checking our unit—again. I couldn't take it anymore. I felt a lump in my throat, and I squeezed my eyes tight shut so that no one would see the tears welling up in them.

My feet moved of their own accord, and I took my place in the lineup without saying a word.

"Order is key!" the sergeant yelled in my ear before cursing our collective incompetence. "This place is a fucking disgrace! Absolute discipline is expected, nothing less—do you understand?"

The sergeant joined only a year or so before us, but he has stayed on as a permanent member of staff. That means he's in charge. Whatever orders he gives, we must obey.

His word is law.

CHAPTER 8

Friday (The First Week)

Once again, Maria Nielsen was sitting in reception when Thomas arrived. She raised her hand in a hesitant greeting, as if she were embarrassed to be bothering him again. Without saying anything, she held up a small black cell phone.

Thomas went over to her.

"Hi, Maria. What have you got there?"

"It's Marcus's cell. After you left, I searched everywhere for his laptop; I turned the whole house upside down. I couldn't find it, but I found his phone in the gap between the bed and the wall. It must have fallen out of his pocket on Saturday when he was lying on the bed playing computer games."

"You're sure it belonged to Marcus?"

"Yes, I recognize it. It's definitely his."

Thomas weighed the phone in his hand; this was good news.

"Let's go upstairs and have a chat."

He led her to the elevators just as he had the first time, and they traveled up to the second floor. When they reached his office, he pressed the button to unlock the phone.

"The battery had almost run out, but I recharged it," Maria said.

Thomas brought up the list of recent calls. Marcus had made two calls on the last day of his life: one to "Home" and one to "Amanda." Thomas continued to scroll through the various functions and found an entry in the notebook app: *Dissociative behavior, repressed emotions, memories of traumatic events.*

He held out the phone so that Maria could see the screen.

"Any idea what this means?"

"I'm afraid not, but they sound like psychological terms. Maybe they had something to do with his studies?"

Thomas moved on to the calendar and scrolled through the final weeks of Marcus's life. He grabbed a notepad and jotted down a few details.

Marcus had entered his psychology lectures; there were also names listed under various dates. First came Jan-Erik Fredell, then Robert Cronwall, then Bo Kaufman. There was also a visit to a branch of the pharmacy Apotek Beckasinen at eleven o'clock on the Thursday before he died.

"Do these names mean anything to you?" he asked, showing Maria the notepad.

"No."

"Are you absolutely certain?"

"Yes, but I can ask my husband and David. Do you think they could be important?"

Her eyes were begging him for a positive response, wanting him to tell her that he had found something vital.

Should he be honest?

The names probably meant nothing; they could be friends, or tutors at the university. There was still nothing to cast doubt on suicide as Marcus's cause of death.

"I don't know, Maria. But I'll look into them, I promise."

She opened her mouth as if she wanted to continue the discussion, but then apparently she changed her mind. She got to her feet, and Thomas showed her out.

On the way back to his office, he called in to see Karin Ek.

As always, her desk was perfectly neat and tidy; even the pencils were freshly sharpened. Family photos were lined up in identical silver frames. She seemed very busy; her eyes were fixed on her computer screen, her fingers flying across the keyboard.

Thomas coughed discreetly to attract her attention, then held out the piece of paper with the list of names from Marcus's phone.

"Could you run a check on these people? See what you can find, and look for any possible connections to Marcus Nielsen."

He looked at the names once more, but he was none the wiser. There was still no explanation as to why Marcus's laptop was missing, and he couldn't get David Nielsen's words out of his head: *Marcus took his laptop with him everywhere.*

CHAPTER 9

Thomas had just finished writing a report when Pernilla called. It was after eleven in the morning, and he almost knocked over his mug of tea as he reached for the phone.

"When will you be home?" she asked.

Her voice sounded strange, and anxiety flooded his body.

"I won't be late—is something wrong?"

Silence.

"Pernilla?" Was that a sob he heard? "Has something happened?"

"I just want to know when you'll be home."

"Around six, I guess. Do you want me to do some shopping on the way back? Is there anything you're in the mood for?"

"Pick up something you like. It doesn't really matter."

Thomas ended the call and sat back.

Pernilla hadn't left his side during the months following February's events. He'd almost died when the ice gave way beneath him. The paramedics had had to use a defibrillator to get his heart going again when it stopped as a result of hypothermia.

He had spent almost a month in a rehab facility, and Pernilla had visited him every single day.

He could still recall the panic when two toes on his left foot had begun to shrivel and turn black from frostbite, but Pernilla had consoled him, reassuring him when he wondered if he would be able to continue working as a police officer.

The toes had to be amputated, and it was weeks before he could bring himself to look at his foot. He closed his eyes whenever he pulled on his sock.

Late one night, when the soft semidarkness made things seem more bearable, and he had had quite a lot to drink, he forced himself to look. He sat on the edge of the bed and slowly lifted his foot.

It wasn't as bad as he had expected.

An insert was fitted for his shoe, and he'd had to learn to walk in a different way. By now the only sign of the injury was a slight limp.

"You'll be able to run marathons if you want," the doctor had said, ignoring his skeptical expression. "It's just a question of training and determination. If you'd lost the big toe, it would have had a much greater effect on your gait and balance. And you should be glad that it was only your foot."

Thomas knew exactly what she meant. He had suffered severe frostbite in several of his fingers, too, particularly on his right hand, because he hadn't been wearing gloves.

During those early days after he regained consciousness, he had experienced night terrors. How would he survive without the fingers of his right hand? How would he cope with being disabled?

By some miracle, the hand had recovered. He couldn't even begin to deal with the thought that he might have suffered brain damage because of his heart stopping.

When he was discharged from the hospital, it was decided that he would take sick leave until the end of the summer. As if it were the most natural thing in the world, Pernilla was waiting in reception. With the same calm assurance, she collected his things from his new place in

Gustavsberg and installed him in their old apartment, which she had kept after the divorce.

They spent the summer in the house on Harö, where he had slowly recovered. It was as if the years they had spent apart, each mourning the loss of Emily, had never existed. He hardly dared believe that they had found their way back to one another, or that their relationship could possibly last.

What if something was seriously wrong? He'd have to wait until he got home to find out. His mouth was dry, and the little toe on his left foot had started itching furiously, even though he knew it was no longer there. The itch was so intense that it bordered on pain. He was about to bend down and scratch the phantom toe when someone knocked on his door.

"Thomas."

He gave such a start that Karin Ek couldn't help noticing.

"Sorry, I didn't mean to scare you."

He waved her into his office and gestured toward the visitor's chair.

"It's OK, I was in a world of my own."

Karin pulled the chair closer to the desk and held up a number of printouts.

"I ran a search on the names you gave me."

She put on her glasses, which were on a cord around her neck.

"I had no problems with the first two, then the computer began acting up as usual. Do you know how many times I've asked for a new one?" She frowned. "I'll try again in a while, but you can have this to get you started."

"What did you find?"

He took the papers and flicked through them.

"Jan-Erik Fredell has just turned fifty; he lives with his wife on Oxelvägen in Älta."

"Any kids?"

"A grown-up daughter at the University of Gothenburg."

"Where does he work?"

"Nowhere. He retired a few years ago."

"That seems pretty early, if he's just turned fifty."

"He retired due to ill health," Karin explained. "Before that he was a PE teacher."

"And Robert Cronwall?"

"He's the same age as Fredell, and lives in Lidingö with his wife. They have a son who lives nearby, and a younger daughter in Uppsala."

"What does Cronwall do?"

"He's a big shot on the council in Lidingö—director of finances. And he's well paid, judging by the annual income he declares on his tax return."

Thomas tried in vain to find any information that could move the investigation forward.

"Did you find any kind of link to Marcus Nielsen?" he asked.

"Nope. These two men live in different parts of Stockholm, they work or worked in completely different fields, and neither of them appears to be involved with anything related to Nielsen's studies."

"A dead end, in other words," Thomas said, almost to himself. But it had been worth a shot. He put down the papers. "Thanks anyway."

It was almost two o'clock by the time Margit got back to the station. Thomas had been waiting for her. His lunch had consisted of two hot dogs from the kiosk outside, and the taste of mustard still lingered in his mouth.

As soon as Margit had taken off her coat, he showed her Nielsen's phone and the pages Karin Ek had printed out. Margit studied the material for a few minutes, then sat back.

"Not much to go on," she said.

"I think we should go and see Jan-Erik Fredell and Robert Cronwall," Thomas said.

"Why?"

"Because I'm not quite done with Marcus Nielsen's death yet."

There was no mistaking the doubt in Margit's eyes. Outside the open window, the birds were singing at the tops of their lungs. For a moment, it was hard to believe it was the middle of September.

"We've got plenty of other cases waiting to be cleared up," she objected. "We're not exactly overstaffed right now."

"I'm aware of that."

Thomas had no logical reason behind his decision, but Marcus Nielsen deserved more before his death was rubber-stamped as a suicide and set aside.

"I'm happy to go on my own; you don't need to come with me if you're busy."

"OK."

Margit raised a hand and turned to her computer.

The expression on Maria Nielsen's face came into Thomas's mind, and once more he remembered the body hanging from the ceiling in the bright sunlight.

His little toe started itching again.

CHAPTER 10

As soon as she stepped on board the Vaxholm ferry, her stress began to disappear. The familiar feeling of being on the way to Sandhamn always made Nora feel better.

"I'll go and grab some seats!" Simon shouted, dashing past all the passengers alighting from the bus that connected with the ferry. He liked to sit upstairs near the cafeteria for the panoramic view of the rocks and skerries.

Nora stowed their luggage and bags of groceries and followed her younger son at a more leisurely pace. Adam and Wille trailed behind, listening to their iPods.

The weather forecast was good. The meteorologists had promised something of an Indian summer; the temperature might even reach seventy degrees, and Nora was looking forward to spending a few lazy hours in the sun the next day. She really ought to take the opportunity to replace the putty around one of the windows—there was a lot that needed doing around the house—but the effort she had put in over the summer had taken its toll, and she was tired after an intense week at work.

Simon had claimed a table, and as the boys settled down, Nora joined the line in the cafeteria. It was Friday evening; she deserved a beer, and the boys could each have a soda.

She greeted the girl behind the counter and ordered their drinks. She picked up the tray and turned around to find that there was someone in her way, and the collision was unavoidable. The tray landed on the floor, and the bottles flew off in all directions.

"Watch out!" she snapped.

The glass had landed upside down, and the beer had gone everywhere. Any sense of calm she'd had disappeared in a second.

"Take it easy," said the brown-haired man she had cannoned into. "You weren't exactly looking where you were going."

Nora stared at him and realized she knew him.

She had bumped into her new tenant, Jonas Sköld. He was renting their old family home on Sandhamn, which she had inherited from her grandparents. They had only met in passing; her parents had dealt with all the practicalities, and she had been relieved to find a tenant through a personal recommendation rather than having to advertise and end up with a stranger.

She took a deep breath, feeling embarrassed more than anything. Jonas Sköld looked tanned and relaxed. Nora suddenly became aware of her tousled hair, and the fact that her face was still bright red thanks to the spurt of anger.

She knelt down and started gathering up the mess.

"It was probably my fault," she muttered. "Sorry."

Jonas gave her a disarming smile. "I should have been more careful, too."

He picked up the empty glass and gave it to her, then held out his hand.

"Jonas Sköld. I'm your tenant."

He was wearing jeans and a short-sleeved polo shirt; his expression was open and friendly.

"I know who you are," Nora said, getting to her feet. "I didn't mean to snap at you like that; it's been a difficult week."

"No problem." He pointed to the unopened soda bottles. "Those seem to have survived." He nodded to the girl behind the counter and said, "Can I get another Carlsberg, please?" He gave her a hundred-kronor note, then placed the fresh bottle on Nora's tray. "There you go, order is restored."

"Thank you."

Nora was about to turn away when she realized she didn't want to end the conversation so abruptly. She stopped in midmovement.

"I'm sorry, I'm being very rude. Is everything OK with the house?"

"Fine, thanks." He tucked his wallet in his back pocket before continuing. "To be honest, I've hardly been there, but that's all about to change. I got an overseas posting I wasn't expecting, so I haven't spent any time on the island over the summer."

Nora tried to look encouraging in order to smooth over her earlier outburst.

"You're a pilot with SAS, aren't you?"

Jonas nodded. "I had to step in for a colleague, and ended up in France for most of the summer, but at least I've managed to paint the front door as promised."

"That's great—it really needed doing!"

The rental agreement stated that the tenant was responsible for minor maintenance; Nora had enough to do with taking care of the Brand villa. She was pleased to hear that Jonas was fulfilling his side of the deal.

"By the way," he said, "I was wondering if I could put away a few things and bring in my own stuff? If I'm going to live there for the next three years, it would be nice to make the place feel like home."

"Of course—as long as you don't throw out anything I care about."

"I was just going to stow it all at the back of the wardrobe," he reassured her with a wink.

The wink made Nora feel ancient. He was probably ten years younger than her, or at least six or seven, and she suddenly wished they had met under different circumstances.

"What are you doing, Mom?"

Adam's voice cut through the hum of conversation, and Nora gestured toward their table.

"See you around," Jonas said, setting off in the opposite direction.

They were approaching Sandhamn, and Nora got out her wallet to buy their ferry tickets before they disembarked. When she had paid and was on her way back to her seat, she saw her tenant sitting at one of the small tables by the window on the port side.

He had opened up his laptop and was concentrating hard on what looked like one of Adam's games. Roman soldiers flickered on the screen in bright colors, attacking one another as he moved the mouse back and forth. He seemed oblivious to the outside world and didn't even glance up as she walked by.

Jonas Sköld obviously liked to play strategy games. Henrik would never have considered such a thing. Nora couldn't help smiling.

CHAPTER 11

Älta was one of Stockholm's smaller suburbs, redeveloped in the 1960s and close to nature. It was in the southern part of Nacka district, and it took less than fifteen minutes for Thomas to drive out there.

He parked on the street and looked up at the façade of the apartment complex where Jan-Erik Fredell lived, according to the electoral register. The building was eight stories high, and there was no entry code.

The door to the apartment was opened by a woman in her fifties. She had short, straight hair and was wearing a gray cardigan, buttoned all the way up to the top.

"Yes?" she said.

Thomas introduced himself and asked if he could come in. She took a couple of steps back and he walked into the roomy hallway.

"Janne, you have a visitor—police!" she called out, then introduced herself as Lena Fredell. She led the way into a sunny living room with a fine parquet floor. Thomas noticed that the floor plan throughout was completely flat, with no elevated thresholds, and the reason became clear when he saw the gaunt figure sitting on the sofa watching TV, with a wheeled walker beside him. The glassed-in balcony provided a view over the forest, where yellow leaves were beginning to appear among the green.

Jan-Erik Fredell held out a shaky hand to Thomas, who tried to hide his surprise—but without success.

"I have MS, multiple sclerosis," Fredell explained. The effort involved in speaking was unmistakable. "Forgive me if I don't get up."

He reached for a remote with extra large buttons and switched off the TV.

"It started ten years ago, and here I am," he said quietly. "What can I do for you?"

Thomas sat down in the armchair beside him.

"I'm investigating a death, a young man by the name of Marcus Nielsen. Do you happen to know him?"

Jan-Erik Fredell started coughing violently, and his wife hurried in. She patted his back and held up a glass containing a blue straw she'd brought in from the kitchen. After a moment, he took a sip. When the attack was over, Lena turned to Thomas. Her tone was more than a little reproachful.

"My husband is not well, as you can see. He can't cope with any kind of upset. What happened?"

There was no reason not to be honest.

"I asked about a student named Marcus Nielsen. He was found dead in his apartment on Sunday."

Lena looked horrified.

"The young man who came to see us last week? The psychology student?"

Thomas nodded. "He came to see you—what day was that?"

"Let me think . . . it was probably last Wednesday."

"Can you tell me a little more about his visit?"

Lena glanced at her husband. "You talked to him more than I did."

Jan-Erik slowly straightened up, as if he were getting ready to talk, and Lena went back to the kitchen.

"He called and asked if he could come over," Jan-Erik began, his voice hoarse. "Something to do with an assignment he was working on, and he had a lot of questions."

"About what?"

"He wanted to know about my time in the army."

Thomas was taken aback; that wasn't what he had been expecting at all.

"Why was that?"

"He said he was writing about the military in the 1970s."

Thomas thought for a moment. Back then, more or less every male was called up for compulsory military service for about a year or so, except those who were excused on medical grounds.

"He asked about what it was like, what we had to do, and how we felt," Jan-Erik went on. "He had a form with him, and he filled it in as we talked."

"Why did he contact you in particular?"

"I guess it was pure chance; he found a yearbook with my name in it."

A fresh attack of coughing interrupted the conversation, and Thomas waited for Jan-Erik to catch his breath.

"So what did you tell him?" he asked eventually.

"We talked about a few things, but it was a long time ago—over thirty years—and my memory isn't what it used to be."

"Where did you serve?"

"I was a Coastal Ranger."

A Coastal Ranger. Thomas pictured young men in their green uniforms, with berets and buzz cuts. Fighters who lived for the military and went through the very worst ordeals in order to prove their superiority.

"So you were on the island of Korsö?"

A nostalgic smile. "Yes. Do you know the island?"

"I was with the maritime police for many years, and there's an overnight billet there. Plus, I have a summer cottage on Harö, which isn't far away."

It was clear that Jan-Erik was beginning to tire, and Thomas broke off. The shaking was much worse now, and the older man's head was drooping as if it was too heavy for his neck to bear. His skin was wrinkled, gathered in folds at the base of his throat. He reminded Thomas of a turkey with its beak sagging.

Thomas checked his watch; Jan-Erik couldn't cope for much longer.

"Did any of Marcus's questions strike you as unusual?"

A shake of the head, then a weary smile.

"I don't know. I'm so tired these days. He was a very pleasant young man. I'm sorry to hear that he's dead."

"One last question: Can you tell me anything about this assignment he was working on?"

"It was about group dynamics. He called it something in English, but I don't remember what it was."

I ought to contact his supervisor at the university, Thomas thought. *Find out exactly what he was writing about.*

Jan-Erik cleared his throat, then started coughing again. Thomas reached for the glass.

"Would you like some water?"

"Please."

Thomas held the glass as Jan-Erik drank. In spite of the straw, a few drops trickled down his chin.

Thomas was filled with sympathy. It couldn't be easy, being sick and dependent on others at an age when you should still be full of strength and energy. It was terrible when the most basic elements of everyday life, like getting up, having a drink of water, or going to the toilet suddenly became an immense undertaking rather than a simple task.

Lena Fredell reappeared, as if she had been listening outside the door. Thomas wondered how often she waited in the shadows, ready to step in and help when necessary. The loving look she gave her husband bore witness to her endless patience.

She leaned forward and wiped Jan-Erik's chin. Thomas noticed a faded scar on her forehead as she came closer—probably the result of chicken pox when she was a child.

He got to his feet and thanked them both. Lena accompanied him to the door.

"Can I ask how Marcus died?" she asked as Thomas was about to leave.

He hesitated, but it was a fair question.

"He took his own life. He hanged himself in his apartment."

Lena looked horrified.

"That's terrible! I would never have suspected such a thing when he was here. His poor family!"

Her words rang in Thomas's ears as he left the building.

CHAPTER 12

There was a rattling sound as Thomas turned his key. The dead bolt wasn't locked, so he knew Pernilla was already home. Anxiety gnawed away at his gut. She had sounded so hesitant, so tense, that he had come straight home after visiting Jan-Erik Fredell. Robert Cronwall could wait.

Several times he had almost called her during the afternoon, but then she had said it was nothing special, and he knew how busy she often was at the advertising agency. Sometimes a quick text was the only way they could get ahold of each other during the workday.

Come to think of it, Pernilla hadn't been herself lately. She had been unusually quiet in the evenings, and she had started going to bed early. They were both interested in cooking, but he had been the one to suggest trying different recipes; she had seemed distracted.

Maybe the wounds from the divorce hadn't healed after all?

After Emily's death, Thomas had been devastated, unable to break free of the conviction that someone must bear the responsibility for the loss of his daughter. Pernilla was the closest—if it wasn't her fault, then whose was it?

He knew he had a debt to repay; he had behaved unforgivably when their lives came crashing down.

"Hi," he called tentatively. "I'm home."

He could see Pernilla's shoes in the hallway, but there wasn't a sound from anywhere in the apartment. Her purse and keys were on the chest of drawers.

"Hello?" he tried again, louder this time.

"In here," came the faint response.

Thomas dropped his jacket on a chair and hurried to the bedroom. Pernilla was lying on her side, and he could see she'd been crying. Her eyes were puffy, and she was clutching a handkerchief. Her strawberry-blond hair was tousled, and the freckles the summer sun had brought out emphasized the pallor of her skin.

Tears lingered on her eyelashes.

"What's happened?"

Thomas sat down on the edge of the bed and pulled her close. She smelled of soap and apple shampoo, and he buried his nose in her hair.

They stayed like that for a while, until he gently pushed her away so that he could see her face.

She tried to smile, but it was more of a quiver of the lips.

The cold feeling in his chest continued to spread.

Pernilla had been with him every step of the way since that terrible day on the ice. Was it all too much for her? He had only himself to blame; he was well aware of that. He ran his finger down her cheek; her skin was soft and warm.

All at once he realized that the expression in her eyes was not one of pain and sorrow. It was something completely different. She was happy and scared and shocked. And disbelieving, more than anything.

Her lips moved, but when she uttered the words, he couldn't believe them either.

She had to repeat them over and over again, and it wasn't until she started laughing and crying at the same time that he understood they were really true.

"I'm pregnant, Thomas. We're having another baby."

Diary:
November 1976

My arms are still shaking, everything hurts. We had to get up in the middle of the night and go and stand in the corridor with our arms outstretched. The order was to hold out different items of clothing, one at a time.

We weren't allowed to lower our arms, however tired we got. Our muscles screamed with the strain, but we weren't allowed to change position, not one fraction of an inch.

"One sock at a time, hold it out with your arm straight, soldier!" the sergeant yelled.

We stood there for an eternity, not daring to open our mouths to protest.

"You are being trained to become good soldiers. You will learn to cope with the demands of war," he bellowed in the semidarkness.

If there was the slightest murmur, we were ordered to adopt the rangers' rest position. It's agonizing. Back to the wall, knees bent at a ninety-degree angle. Your thigh muscles are shrieking with pain after just a few minutes. Sigurd and Andersson went down first; they crashed to the floor and lay there writhing.

The sergeant stared at them without saying a word, but I could see the contempt in his eyes, particularly when he contemplated Andersson's shaking body.

"Please don't let me faint," I muttered to myself as I forced my trembling thighs to remain in the same position. Please God, don't let me faint in front of the sergeant.

Before we were allowed to go back to bed at long last, we had to sing the national anthem.

Over and over again. Louder and louder. We sang like lunatics, at the tops of our voices. It was after three by the time we got to bed, and I was dizzy with exhaustion.

The last few nights, I have slept on the floor; it saves a few seconds in the morning if I don't have to make the bed.

Kaufman and Martinger sleep in their pants and boots so they can make it to roll call on time. It's against the rules, but they take the risk. The punishment for being late is even worse.

They woke us at dawn and told us to jog to the shower room. The water was already flowing at full volume.

When the whistle blew, two of us had to run into the ice-cold water; at the next signal, those two ran to the back of the line, soaping their bodies as the others moved forward until it was time to run through the freezing stream once more.

The bitter morning air poured in through the open window.

We volunteered to come here.

I have no intention of being the first one to be sent home.

CHAPTER 13

Saturday (The First Week)

Nora opened her eyes, and for a moment she couldn't quite figure out where she was. Then she realized she was in her new bedroom.

She had chosen the north room, upstairs overlooking the sea. Aunt Signe had occupied the east bedroom, which was now Adam's. A smaller west-facing room, which in the past had been mainly used for storage, had been kitted out for Simon.

Nora had been drawn to the light up here, even though it was the coldest spot in the whole house. When the wind blew from the north, the walls creaked, and the chilly air found its way in, no matter how much she built up the fire in the beautiful old tiled stove.

But the view was stunning. She loved waking up in the Brand villa and gazing out across the water. There was a faded dark-blue roller blind, but she never pulled it all the way down. She didn't want to miss that fantastic view every morning.

Through the leaded windows with their convex panes, she could see far beyond Harö, with the tower on the island of Korsö just visible to the east. The islands and skerries extended into the distance, until they were no more than dark shadows against the pale, still waters.

To be on the safe side, Nora had bought the warmest duvet she could find and had installed an extra radiator under the window. It was all a bit much in the heat of summer, but she knew winter was on its way.

She and the boys hadn't changed too much of the house. The bedrooms had been redecorated in colors the boys had chosen, and the kitchen had been freshened up a little without losing its old-fashioned charm. She had treated herself to a dishwasher, and a coat of white paint on the paneled walls had done wonders.

She hadn't touched the generously proportioned dining room, with its elegant upholstered chairs. The Mora clock was still ticking away in the corner, and the glassed-in veranda, where Aunt Signe used to sit with her beloved dog, Kajsa, looked exactly the same as it always had. Even her aunt's old checkered blanket was still there.

Nora could afford to take her time; it really didn't matter if everything wasn't done right away. Moving into the new apartment in Saltsjöbaden had been stressful enough; she couldn't face another new project just yet.

She rolled over onto her side so that she could look out the window. *It's almost a religious experience,* she thought, *experiencing the day as it is about to begin.* The sun was shining; it was going to be a beautiful day, a reminder that autumn hadn't yet completely taken over.

There wasn't a sound from the boys' rooms, but then it was only seven thirty. Adam and Wille could easily sleep until midday if she didn't wake them, but Simon was an early bird. If she was lucky, he would come padding in for a cuddle. But he was growing up, too; soon he would wriggle free when she tried to hug him.

Who would she cuddle then?

Nora pressed her lips together and shook her head. She had only herself to blame if she didn't make the most of this glorious Saturday. She threw back the covers; time to get up.

Nora grabbed her sailing jacket, ran down the stairs, then out the door and through the gate. She glanced at the sea and saw a pearl necklace of white boats heading for Sandhamn.

The good weather seemed to have motivated a lot of people to go for one last sail before the summer came to an end. A slender old Mälar 30 was gliding through the Sound, the wind filling her sails, the polished mahogany hull gleaming in the sunshine.

A short distance away, one of her neighbors was standing on his jetty cleaning nets. Olle Granlund was almost seventy; he had grown up on the island. Nora had known him all her life. She gave him a wave.

If the fish weren't biting or you hadn't had time to lay your own nets, you could always knock on Olle's door and beg for a couple of whitefish or, if you were lucky, some delicious perch fillets.

Olle was also happy to help out with the practicalities, something Nora greatly appreciated now that Henrik wasn't around. She knew she ought to work on her skills with a hammer and nails, not to mention recalcitrant radiators and boilers, but that was on her list of things to tackle at some point in the future.

Deep down she was ashamed of the fact that she had always taken the easy way out and let Henrik deal with that kind of thing, but that was yet another sign of the hopelessly old-fashioned division of labor that had characterized their marriage.

She walked past the old Mission House with its green bay window and continued toward the southern part of the island.

It was peaceful in the pine forest; the only sound was the soughing of the tall trees. Heather and low-growing blueberry bushes had spread in all directions, and there were still blueberries to be seen, plumped up with water. Nora stopped and picked a few, even though they had long ago lost their flavor. July was the right time to eat them, not September; they didn't taste great. But there were also plenty of lingonberries; Nora thought about bringing the boys out here in the afternoon. Even her computer-crazy son could be tempted by a bowl of bright-red lingon-berries with creamy milk.

She emerged on the other side of the forest and set off along the southern shore, where lyme grass swayed in the cool breeze. It was as though the southern and northern parts of the island each had their own microclimate. When the winds were strong and bitterly cold in the north, they were gentle and mild on the other side, and vice versa. There was always somewhere to seek shelter.

"Hey!" she heard someone call out behind her. "Wait for me!"

Nora turned and saw Jonas Sköld in shorts and black sunglasses hurrying toward her. As he came closer, she saw that he was wearing deck shoes, as if it were the middle of summer.

"Hi, out for a walk?" he asked.

She had to smile at the silly question.

"How can you tell?"

"Can I join you?" he said, ignoring the sarcasm.

He fell into step beside her, and they strolled along for a few minutes without saying anything.

"So what's it like, working as a pilot?" Nora said, to break the silence.

She was a little curious about her new neighbor. There had been no talk of a wife or partner, just a teenage daughter.

"Oh, you know . . . Unsociable hours and new colleagues all the time, but we have long breaks between shifts."

"Where do you fly to?"

"So far it's been mostly within Sweden and Europe. I've spent years shuttling between Stockholm, Gothenburg, and Malmö. I've just started doing some long hauls. My daughter stays with me every other week, so I've fitted my schedule around her. But now she's old enough for me to be away for longer."

"What's your daughter's name?"

"Wilma." Jonas couldn't help smiling. "She's thirteen." He reached into his pocket and took out his cell; soon the screen was filled with a cheerful face. A suntanned thirteen-year-old with straight blond hair and a little too much mascara.

"She's really cute."

"She is."

There was no mistaking the pride in Jonas's voice.

"She looks a lot like you," Nora said.

"The eyes, maybe, but the hair color is from her mom."

A woman with a big Labrador walked by, and Nora nodded to her. The face was familiar, but Nora couldn't quite place her. It was a beautiful dog, though.

"I love the house you've moved into," Jonas said. "How old is it?"

"The Brand villa? It dates from the end of the nineteenth century; it's one of the oldest buildings on the island. Carl Wilhelm Brand, the master pilot, had it built when the old windmill was moved."

"So that's why that spot is known as Kvarnberget—because *kvarn* means windmill?"

"Exactly. Carl Wilhelm seized the opportunity when the mill disappeared."

"It's a real landmark—the house is the first thing you see as you approach the inlet to Sandhamn."

"It was a real talking point back in the day. He really went all out; he even had a bathtub with lion's feet. You can imagine the gossip in the village."

Jonas smiled at her.

"It's a fantastic location."

"I love it, but it takes a fair amount of maintenance. I don't understand how Aunt Signe managed it on her own."

"Aunt Signe?"

"The previous owner—Carl Wilhelm's granddaughter."

Nora paused; she could cope with explaining the whole situation, the fact that Signe, who had been a kind of honorary grandmother to her ever since she was a little girl, had taken her own life and left the house to Nora in her will. Henrik had wanted to sell, but Nora had refused. They had quarreled bitterly, and in hindsight, Nora could see that that had been the beginning of the end of their marriage.

"You could say she left the house in my care," she said after a moment.

"I understand." Jonas cleared his throat. It seemed as if he had noticed the shift in her mood, because he paused, gazing out over the sparkling sea, and then changed the subject.

"It really is a lovely day."

A skein of geese formed a sharp contrast against the clear blue sky.

Nora stole a glance at her tenant. How old was he? His daughter was the same age as Adam, so he must have become a father when he was pretty young. He didn't look much more than thirty-five. He wasn't very tall, only a few inches taller than her. Henrik was almost the same height as Thomas, who measured six four in his stocking feet. It felt different walking side by side with someone who wasn't towering over her.

She couldn't help wondering if he thought she looked older. Did he know she had turned forty just a few months ago?

"And you're a lawyer?" Jonas interrupted her train of thought. "I think that's what your parents said."

"Yes—I'm a legal adviser with a bank."

"Do you enjoy it?"

She had to think about that; did she?

Two years earlier, she had been offered an exciting job as a regional adviser, based in Malmö. She had turned it down, because Henrik didn't want to leave Stockholm, so she was still in the same job with the same boss, whom she didn't particularly like. But this wasn't the right time to look for a new post, since she was still in the middle of all the chaos that comes with divorce, and she liked her colleagues and the work itself.

"It's OK. I've been there for years; it's probably time to move on, but I haven't gotten around to doing anything about it."

"I'm sure other opportunities will come along."

Instead of answering, Nora knelt down to tie her shoe, which had come undone. Tears sprang to her eyes. Other opportunities—like what? She worried that the boys would be happier living with Henrik than with her, and she hated the fact that Marie had moved into their old house. The divorce felt like a huge failure. She couldn't see any opportunities at the moment.

"Did I upset you? I'm sorry, I really didn't mean to." Jonas sounded genuine.

Nora quickly straightened up. Jonas looked so distraught that she had to smile as she blinked back the tears.

"It's fine, I'm just a little tired. Things have been difficult lately."

She dug around in her jacket pocket for something to blow her nose with; she found a crumpled napkin that would have to do.

Jonas turned away and picked up a flat stone. He raised his arm and sent it skimming across the smooth surface of the water. It bounced three times before sinking. Another stone, and this time he managed a better throw—five bounces.

"Here." He handed her a dark-gray pebble; she felt its sun-warmed surface on the palm of her hand.

Nora hesitated, then sent it flying with a flick of her wrist. Four.

"Bravo!" Jonas exclaimed. "Try again!"

He gave her another pebble, which sank right away, but the third bounced five times, and Nora started laughing.

"Wow—it's been a long time since I reached that number!"

Jonas's warm eyes met hers.

"Feeling better?"

He put his arm around her shoulders for a brief moment, and Nora nodded. She did feel better, actually.

They chatted about all kinds of things as they made their way back through the pine forest and past the Mission House. She could see her house now—no, her old house, she corrected herself.

"Would you like to go out for dinner tonight, if you're not doing anything else?" Jonas said without slowing down. "It is Saturday, after all."

Nora stopped. "Sorry?"

"I wondered if we could have dinner together? To say thank-you for renting me the house."

"I don't know . . ." Nora hesitated. "I've got the boys with me, plus a friend of Adam's."

Jonas wasn't fazed.

"I thought we could go to the Divers Bar. You look as if you could use a treat."

Nora thought about it. She hadn't eaten in a restaurant for ages; she hadn't had either the time or the energy. The boys could eat in the grill bar; they would be ecstatic at the prospect of burgers and fries.

Why not?

CHAPTER 14

The sound of the doorbell took Jan-Erik by surprise. He wasn't expecting a visitor, and Lena had gone shopping, as she usually did on Saturday mornings.

They didn't have a car, so it would be a couple of hours before she was home. She usually went to Nacka Forum and picked up whatever they needed in one of the big grocery stores. She liked the lively mall, and he thought she deserved to get out of the house for a while. Looking after him all the time was hard work, and spending time among other people now and again did her good.

The doorbell rang again, and he tried to hurry, but even with the wheeled walker, progress was slow. His coordination was poor, and he knew he was steadily getting worse. It had taken him years to accept that he had been struck down by such a serious condition. Primary progressive MS, it was called. It was the most severe form of the disease; the body was continually being broken down, with no periods of remission. By this stage, his central nervous system was irrevocably affected, and there was nothing that could be done. With each passing month, his muscles grew weaker, his balance was further compromised, and he could no longer control the shaking.

Depression and apathy had come with the disease, plus a debilitating exhaustion. He had lost weight, and he knew deep down that he looked ten years older than he was. He had once been a fit and healthy PE teacher; now he was a shadow of his former self. Everything was a painful ordeal, and sometimes he wondered if it wouldn't be easier just to fall asleep and never wake up.

According to the doctors, it was unusual to be in such a poor state at his age, but it did happen. That was no consolation, especially for Lena, who had to bear an increasingly heavy load. She had halved her working hours in order to look after him. There was no cure, just drugs to slow the progression of the disease. In his case, they were less and less effective.

A slow, painful transition from the living to the dead was a high price to pay.

But he deserved it.

When he finally managed to open the door, he stood there leaning heavily on his wheeled walker. There was something familiar about the visitor. He studied the face before him; he recognized the features, and yet he didn't. An echo of a long-buried friendship.

Instinctively he backed away, using the walker as a kind of shield.

"Is it really you?"

CHAPTER 15

The call came at 3:28. Afterward Thomas was able to give the exact time, because he was just about to switch on the TV to watch a soccer game.

He had been looking forward to a lazy afternoon on the sofa. For the first time in what seemed like an eternity, he hadn't woken at six; instead he had slept past ten, much to his surprise. He was still overwhelmed by Pernilla's news, but a warm sense of expectation had taken root within him.

Pernilla had gone over to her sister's to help out with something or other, so he had the apartment to himself. He had told her to take it easy, even though he knew he sounded like an anxious mother hen who didn't want to let her chick go. However, this time there was no room for risks. They had agreed not to tell anyone until the twelfth week; it felt better that way.

When he answered the phone, he realized within seconds that there would be no soccer today.

An old familiar feeling stirred in his chest. It took a little while for him to work out what it was; it hadn't happened for a long time.

A cop's instinct.

Jan-Erik was lying on his side, fully dressed, in the bathtub, which was filled to the brim with water. His eyes were wide open, and a small amount of froth was visible at the corners of his mouth. One hand was clenched, as if he had tried to grab ahold of something but failed to hang on to it. His face was as white as the tiles on the wall.

Thomas stood in the doorway. Staffan Nilsson, the forensic technician, was kneeling by the tub; he had already started examining the scene. Thomas heard the front door to the apartment open, and Margit joined him in the bathroom doorway. They stayed put; there was no room for three adults in the bathroom.

"What can you tell us?" Thomas asked Nilsson.

"Drowned. Hard to estimate the time of death; the water affects the body temperature."

"Any sign of force?" Margit asked, stretching her neck to get a better view.

Nilsson shook his head.

"Nothing I can make out at the moment, but we'll see what the pathologist has to say. Maybe he was taking a bath and slipped; we can't exclude that possibility."

He gestured toward the living room.

"The widow is in there."

Thomas backed out and went past Margit into the living room. Lena Fredell was sitting in the same chair he had sat in less than twenty-four hours before. She was unnaturally pale. Thomas sat down beside her.

"How are you feeling?"

"I'd been shopping," she began, her voice far from steady. "I always go shopping on Saturday. Janne didn't answer when I called out to tell him I was home. I was worried; I looked in here, but there was no sign of him, even though he usually watches TV when I'm out. And the TV wasn't on."

"What did you do then?" Margit asked; she had come in without Thomas noticing.

"I called out again, then I tried the bedroom; I thought he might have gone to lie down, but he wasn't there either." She gripped the armrest tightly. "Then I looked in the bathroom and saw him lying in the bathtub."

"Can you think of any reason why he would have run a bath while you were out?"

The expression on Lena Fredell's face answered the question before she spoke.

"How could he possibly do that?" She turned to Thomas. "You saw him yesterday; he could barely walk without help."

Thomas had to agree. It was hard to imagine the man he had met yesterday making his way to the bathroom, filling the tub, and attempting to take a bath alone. With his clothes on.

"Was there any indication that he might have had a visitor? Do you know if someone was here while you were gone?"

"No." Her expression was desolate. "We don't get many visitors. As Janne deteriorated, we lost contact with many of our friends. It was too difficult; either they gradually withdrew, or we turned down invitations when he wasn't strong enough to cope." She shook her head. "We used to have such a wide circle of friends and acquaintances."

"Was the door locked when you got home?" Thomas asked.

Lena frowned, thinking.

"Yes," she said slowly. "I'm almost sure I let myself in using my key."

"Is it a Yale lock?"

"Yes."

"So someone could simply close the door from the outside, and it would lock."

"Yes." The confusion on Lena's face was apparent. "You mean someone came here and killed him?"

"We can't exclude that possibility," Thomas said.

"But why?" Her eyes filled with tears. "You saw him; there was next to nothing left. Why would someone want to kill my husband?"

"Do you think this was a suicide, too?" Thomas said to Margit as they drove back to the station. It was almost seven o'clock.

"Is that a rhetorical question?"

He gave a wry smile, and for the first time since he returned to work, Margit saw the old Thomas.

"First Marcus Nielsen, now Jan-Erik Fredell," he said. "Both within a week. A bit too much of a coincidence, wouldn't you say?"

"But not impossible. An unhappy student who doesn't want to go on, a sick man who gets a stupid idea into his head. Fredell could easily have decided to take his own life. You said he was in a bad state; maybe he didn't want to sit around and wait for death."

Thomas increased his speed and changed lanes.

"There was no sign of forced entry," Margit pointed out.

"That doesn't mean no one was there. He might have let the perpetrator in." Thomas glanced over his shoulder and switched lanes again. "We still haven't found Marcus Nielsen's laptop."

"That doesn't necessarily mean anything. He could have left it at a friend's place on Saturday night. If he was intending to kill himself, he might even have given it away."

"He had it when he was at his parents' place."

Margit sighed audibly but was careful not to show how pleased she was at his stubbornness.

Thomas hadn't been himself since coming back to work. He had seemed apathetic and had barely opened his mouth during their morning briefings. As recently as Sunday, when he turned up almost an hour late, she had seriously doubted whether he would ever fully recover.

But now her colleague was most definitely back.

"The autopsy will tell us whether he slipped or was held down under the water," she said.

"But that will take a couple of days. We ought to speak to the other people who were listed on Marcus's phone as soon as possible. Preferably tomorrow." Thomas looked pensive. "And we need to get a clearer picture of his life."

CHAPTER 16

What to wear?

Nora blushed; she was already thinking about her outfit, even though the evening was still several hours away.

It could hardly be called a proper date; Jonas was probably just trying to be polite to his landlady, but it had been so long since she had been out for dinner that she couldn't help but feel a shiver of anticipation.

There wasn't much to choose from in the spacious closet. It was almost like a room, complete with its own little window for airing out the clothes—a relic from the days when they were worn and used in a completely different way.

She opened the bottom drawer of the bureau by the window and picked out a pretty white top from last summer; that would have to do, paired with white pants.

No, not white pants. He might think she'd gotten all dressed up. Jeans would be better.

A critical inspection of her jeans revealed that they could use a turn in the washing machine; there was a large patch of grease just above the left thigh.

Typical, she thought; it must have gotten there when she was frying pancakes for the boys' breakfast. But if she washed her jeans now, they wouldn't be dry in time. She didn't have a tumble dryer, only the washing line outside.

She pulled off the jeans and tried the white pants. They really did look far too dressy, as if she were going to a cocktail party in the middle of the summer rather than a simple dinner at the Divers Bar.

It would have to be the jeans.

She put the white pants away and headed for the bathroom. She grabbed a towel, soaked one corner in hot water, and dabbed some liquid soap onto the denim. Maybe she could scrub away the mark, she thought optimistically as she set to work.

Ten minutes later, not only was the grease still there, but the entire leg was soaking wet.

Nora gave up. She put the jeans back on and shivered when she felt the dampness on her skin. Should she run over to the little clothes store opposite the steamboat jetty and buy something on sale? *Stop it,* she said sharply to herself. *This is not a date. We're just having dinner together.*

She rubbed at the wet patch with a dry towel, then took off the jeans once more and draped them over the towel rack. Maybe the stain would be less visible when the fabric had dried. Meanwhile, she would have to make do with sweatpants.

In spite of the fact that it was September, the Divers Bar was almost full when Nora walked in.

She remembered the restaurant's opening in the nineties to cater to hungry students taking diving courses on Sandhamn. The diving school had bought the old general store to provide room and board for those attending the courses, which were run in the former shipyard on the north side of the island. The school had folded after a few years, but the restaurant was still here. At this time of year, it was open only on the weekends, and soon it would close for the season.

The bar took up one wall, with a huge mirror behind it. She could see Jonas's reflection; he was already sitting at one of the low tables by the window.

"Hi," she said, sliding into the chair opposite.

The stain was indeed less visible now that the fabric had dried, but she had carried her jacket in front of her just to be on the safe side. Jonas was also wearing jeans and a pale-blue shirt with the sleeves rolled up. Nora was glad she hadn't gone for the white pants.

"Hi," Jonas replied, half getting to his feet. "Are the boys OK?"

"Absolutely—they've gone to the grill bar, and they're very happy."

He pushed a menu across the table, and Nora suddenly realized how hungry she was, much to her surprise. She nodded to some people she knew at another table, then began to read through what was on offer. As usual, it was a tempting array; she chose whitefish roe to start and veal for her main course.

"Tell me more about your work," she said, well aware that they had already discussed this topic. But it was nice and neutral. "Do you enjoy it?"

Jonas looked up from the menu.

"It's OK, but it's a tough industry these days, especially for the big companies who have to compete with the budget airlines. But I'm happy, even though the golden years are gone."

"The golden years?"

"The good old days, when pilots were treated like gods and got whatever they wanted." He raised his eyebrows and gave a meaningful nod. "When I started, we still had an incredible expense account, and we stayed in five-star hotels. Now it's one economy package after another, but, of course, we're much better off than those who work for the budget airlines."

He pointed to Nora's menu. "Have you decided?"

Nora nodded, and Jonas waved to the waitress, who immediately came over. *How did he do that?* Nora thought. It wasn't usually so easy to attract the attention of the staff. He had charisma, there was no doubt about it.

After they'd ordered and the waitress returned with their drinks, Nora took a sip of her wine; Jonas had suggested an Australian dry white with an assurance born of knowledge. It was certainly very good.

A group of four came into the restaurant, and Nora immediately recognized them as friends of Henrik's parents. Before she could turn away, she realized they had seen her. She could only hope they wouldn't pass on this tasty bit of gossip.

She frowned, annoyed with herself. It was nobody's business that she was having dinner with someone other than her ex-husband, but Jonas looked a little too handsome and was a little too young for her to be entirely comfortable with the situation.

In her peripheral vision, she saw one of the women approaching their table. It was Siv Angern, a close friend of her ex-mother-in-law, Monica Linde. Like Monica, she was beautifully made up, not a hair out of place. She was wearing an expensive designer wool peacoat.

Nora stood up to greet her, though she was unable to muster any enthusiasm.

Siv kissed Nora on both cheeks. *An upper-class affectation,* Nora thought, but that was the standard greeting in the circles in which her in-laws moved.

Typical—why did she have to bump into Siv tonight of all nights? Within a few hours, Monica would be fully informed, and, of course, she would immediately call Henrik and tell him everything. Somehow Monica would make sure this outing came back to haunt Nora.

"Nora, how lovely to see you."

"Hi," Nora replied, keeping her tone neutral. "How are you all?"

"We're only here for the weekend." Siv gestured in her husband's direction. "With the boat."

Nora knew the Angerns owned a large motor yacht, a Princess that was over forty feet long.

"I was so sorry to hear about the divorce," Siv went on. "You were such a handsome couple, you and Henrik. I never imagined you'd split up. Monica is terribly upset, as I'm sure you know."

Nora doubted that very much. She and Monica had never gotten along. Her father-in-law, Harald, might miss her a little bit.

"How are the boys taking it?"

Siv's tone was exactly the same as Monica Linde's, and Nora wondered if the women who moved in these circles were cast in identical molds. The same emphasis on clothes and appearance, with a constant flow of name-dropping to make it clear who they knew and socialized with. Utterly superficial, with a total lack of genuine emotion.

She certainly wouldn't miss that aspect of her life with Henrik.

"Anyway, I can see you're doing fine," Siv went on, ignoring the fact that Nora hadn't answered her question about the boys. The comment was accompanied by a smile and a glance at Jonas.

"Absolutely," Nora said, refusing to engage. "Good to see you—have a lovely evening."

She sat down, making it clear that the conversation was over. At that moment, the waitress arrived to take Siv's party upstairs. Far away from Nora and Jonas's table.

"Sorry about that," Nora said. "She's a friend of my ex-in-laws."

Jonas looked amused.

"Maybe she thinks you've thrown yourself into the arms of a new man. And I'm only your tenant."

Something in the way he said "your tenant" made Nora's heart sink.

"Let's eat," she said brusquely.

Three glasses of wine later, and everything was OK again. It had been a long time since Nora had felt so relaxed with someone.

By the time they emerged from the Divers Bar, it was dark. The September night was pitch black, and the sparse streetlamps didn't provide a great deal of light. If the moon hadn't appeared, they would have had to stumble blindly along the narrow alleyways.

Nora kept both hands in her jacket pockets. The temperature had dropped significantly, and there was nothing left of the afternoon's late-summer heat.

"Thanks for a lovely evening," Jonas said beside her.

He had put on a jacket, too, and was rubbing his hands to get warm.

"Thank *you*."

They reached Nora's old house and stopped by the gate. The Brand villa lay only fifty yards away, and Nora noticed that the light was still on in Adam's room, even though it was almost eleven thirty.

"Maybe we could do this again?" Jonas suggested.

"I'd like that."

He leaned over and brushed Nora's cheek with his lips.

"I think you're the cutest landlady I've ever had."

The words made Nora smile.

"Is that supposed to be a compliment?"

"You'd better believe it."

Nora turned and set off toward her new home with an unfamiliar feeling of anticipation.

DIARY:

NOVEMBER 1976

Today there is frost on the inside of the windowpanes. The others are still snoring, but I can't sleep. My body aches too much. Yesterday we went on our first march, in full battle gear weighing thirty-five pounds. It took all day, and it was almost midnight by the time we got back. We were completely exhausted.

During the last part of the march, the officers beat our backs with canes to stop us from collapsing in the forest. We must have looked drunk, weaving from side to side. Our legs gave way, and several of us threw up, first me, then Eklund and Erneskog.

We weren't allowed to eat or drink all day, and we all had cuts and blisters on our hands and feet by the time we finished, but some of the guys came out really badly. Andersson was the worst.

When we got back, it turned out that his feet had bled right through his socks. On his left foot, the skin had been rubbed away right down to the bone, and his sock was stiff with dried blood. His big toenail was dark blue.

The other big toenail had come off. He had wrapped a tissue around the toe to try to protect it, but it turned into a blood-soaked lump and stuck to the flesh. His mouth twitched with the pain whenever he touched his big toe.

He was sitting on his bed and had just taken off his boots when the sergeant came in.

We leaped up and stood to attention. The sergeant stopped in front of Andersson, staring at his injured feet. Then he laughed out loud and looked up at Andersson's tortured face.

"Do your feet hurt, little boy?" he said loudly. "Would you like me to call your mommy so she can make them better?"

Andersson shook his head without saying a word.

The sergeant smiled with satisfaction and moved on.

"You need to go and see the nurse," I whispered when the sergeant had gone.

Andersson shook his head again.

"After the first march? Are you kidding? They send you home if you complain, you know that."

He limped over to the first-aid cupboard on the wall, leaving a trail of red behind him on the floor.

CHAPTER 17

Sunday (The Second Week)

The digital clock showed seventeen minutes past six when Thomas opened his eyes. He had fallen asleep around midnight, and it would've been nice to have another hour in bed, but he still felt rested.

Pernilla was breathing deeply beside him. She was lying on her side, with one arm wrapped protectively around her belly.

Thomas gazed at her with a mixture of joy and anxiety. The fact that she was pregnant again was amazing. The last time had required a lengthy process of hormone treatment and IVF; when Emily died unexpectedly at the age of three months, the loss had been unbearable.

There was no rational explanation as to why Pernilla had conceived naturally this time around, but Thomas felt a deep sense of gratitude for this miracle.

A framed photograph of Emily stood on the chest of drawers over by the window. She was lying on a pink towel, naked and freshly bathed, smiling one of her very first smiles. It had been taken just a few days before her death, and for a long time, Thomas hadn't even been able to look at the photo, let alone have it on display. But a few weeks ago, Pernilla had simply placed it there, and to his surprise, Thomas found it a comfort. He had gotten into the habit of looking at his daughter each night before he went to sleep, and at long last, he was able to remember the joy she had brought them.

He prayed that everything would go well this time. A miscarriage would crush them both; if that happened, it would have been better if Pernilla hadn't gotten pregnant in the first place.

He swung his legs over the edge of the bed and wobbled slightly, as usual, as he got to his feet. It took a while to get used to the strange feeling when he put his foot on the floor; he would probably never completely grasp the fact that his body was no longer whole.

Wearing a robe but no slippers, he ambled into the kitchen and switched on the coffeemaker. When the black brew was ready, he poured a cup and sat down at the kitchen table. His thoughts immediately turned to Marcus Nielsen.

There was a team meeting at the station at nine thirty, and one of his top priorities would be to find out more about the people Marcus had contacted before his death. Maybe Robert Cronwall or Bo Kaufman could answer some of the questions the investigation had brought up.

It was very pleasant outdoors, even though it was only eight thirty. Nora decided to sit in the sun with a cup of coffee for a while, before it was time to get breakfast ready for the boys.

As she emerged onto the steps, she saw Olle Granlund sitting by the jetty. He raised a hand in greeting, and she waved back.

"How's life in your big house?" he called out.

Nora went over to him and sat down on the old driftwood bench that had been there for as long as she could remember.

"We're starting to feel at home, but Aunt Signe is still there, in every room. Every time I hear the Mora clock strike, I expect her to come walking out of the kitchen."

Olle inclined his head.

"Signe loved that house; it was her favorite place in the whole world. I'm glad you haven't made too many changes; you've kept its character."

Nora turned her cup around in her hands.

"It wouldn't feel right to get rid of Signe's furniture. It still feels like her house, even though I know that sounds dumb."

"Not at all. You must miss her."

"Very much; I really loved her."

"A lot of us did."

Olle gave her such a sly look that Nora was taken aback.

"And what do you mean by that?" she said, giving him a little nudge. "You never mentioned this before!"

Olle squinted up at the sun and said, with his eyes half-shut, "She was ten years older than me, but I have to admit that I had a bit of a crush on her when I was about twenty."

Nora leaned back against the boathouse wall behind the bench.

"This is news to me—tell me more!"

Olle looked pleased, as if he were once again a young man going courting.

"I made a pass at her one midsummer, when I was on leave from the army. It must have been 1958. I came over from Korsö in my smart green uniform, trying to make a good impression."

"Did you succeed?"

"Not exactly." Olle grinned. "I invited her out for coffee, but she brushed me off right away. 'What would a stylish young man like you want with an old woman like me?' she said. I couldn't persuade her."

"Typical Signe."

"Absolutely. I slunk away with my tail between my legs, but we always got along well."

Nora could see Signe in her mind's eye: the clear gaze, the firm manner that quickly softened when Adam and Simon came running, begging for a special treat.

"Do you happen to know why she never married? I've always wondered, but I never dared ask her," Nora said.

Olle's callused hand pulled a tin of snuff from his pocket, which he opened with a practiced movement.

"They say she fell in love with someone who abandoned her without a word of explanation."

"That's tragic."

"Yes, but it's just old gossip, so I can't swear to it. It was supposed to have happened a few years after the end of the Second World War; I was only a kid back then."

"So she lived all alone in that big house." Nora glanced up at the Brand villa behind them. "For all those years."

"And now you live there." Olle slipped the snuff tin back in his pocket. "It's high time a new family took over; a house like that shouldn't stand empty. I'm glad you and your boys have moved in."

Nora looked at her watch and stood up.

"Speaking of the boys, it's time for their breakfast."

"Let me know if you need help with anything—you know where to find me."

"Thank you." Nora smiled warmly at him. "That might happen sooner than you think!"

CHAPTER 18

"So what do we know about these two deaths?"

As usual, the Old Man had taken his seat at the head of the table. It was nine thirty, and the whole team was assembled.

Kalle Lidwall looked wide awake, but Erik Blom seemed half-asleep. He had swept his hair back with gel and was drinking a large coffee from 7-Eleven.

"Late night?" The query came from Karin Ek, who was sitting opposite Erik.

"You could say that."

"I assume you've got a new girlfriend," she said, an amused expression on her face. "Typical!"

Before Erik could speak, the Old Man broke in.

"Let's get down to business. Thomas, Margit."

Thomas had already put up pictures of Jan-Erik Fredell and Marcus Nielsen on the whiteboard.

"We're dealing with two people who have no obvious links, except that, within a week of their first and only meeting, both of them are dead. Nielsen was a psychology student who grew up in Täby; Fredell was a former PE teacher who retired due to ill health, and who lived to the south of Stockholm. The first death appears to be a suicide; it's possible that the second could also be suicide, but we don't know that for sure. There's no clear evidence that a crime has been committed, but the situation is far from straightforward."

The Old Man cleared his throat.

"Can you fill us in on the details of Fredell's death?"

Margit took over. "The autopsy is tomorrow, and it should tell us whether he was murdered or if he drowned himself. He was seriously ill, and his wife swears that he had no enemies."

"If we speculate that Marcus Nielsen didn't take his own life," the Old Man said slowly, "what does the pathologist have to say about him? For example, do we know that he died at the scene?"

Thomas leafed through his notes. "He definitely died as a result of the hanging; there were subconjunctival hemorrhages in the eyes, which wouldn't have been there if he'd been dead before the noose was placed around his neck."

"Postmortem lividity or hypostasis was also visible on the legs; if the hanging had been staged to hide the fact that he was killed elsewhere, the pattern would have been different," Margit added.

"Yes, yes, I know all about hypostasis," the Old Man said impatiently. "But have we found any actual evidence to suggest that he *didn't* kill himself?"

"The suicide note wasn't signed," Thomas said, "and we can't find his laptop. His parents are certain that he had it with him the day before he died. The missing laptop bothers me more than anything."

"So in other words, no clear evidence." The Old Man leaned back and took a deep breath. "What about other leads? Enemies, debts, problems in his past?"

"I can look into that," Erik offered right away. "Maybe Karin could help?" He gave her an inquiring look, and she responded with a nod and a warm smile. There was no doubt that their assistant had a soft spot for Erik Blom.

"Good," Margit said. "See what you can come up with; there could be a link between Fredell and Nielsen that we're not aware of. Thomas and I will talk to the people Marcus Nielsen saw in the last few days before his death."

"I also think we ought to request a more detailed autopsy on both Fredell and Nielsen," Thomas said. "Fredell was fully dressed when he was found, which is weird. Forensics might find something on his clothing."

The Old Man nodded; he had been paying closer attention than Thomas had thought.

"Anything else?"

"Just one more thing that might count against the theory that Nielsen took his own life. He had no history of illness."

"No history of illness?" Karin echoed.

Thomas turned to her. "Most people who kill themselves have had some kind of medical issue. Psychiatric care, anxiety attacks, frequent visits to the doctor—but Nielsen is completely clean. There's nothing."

Erik finished his coffee and tossed the paper cup in the direction of the bin. It hit the edge and landed on the floor; he got to his feet and picked it up.

"Thomas is right," he said, dropping the cup in the bin. "Marcus should have been on the radar of health services if he had suicidal tendencies."

Thomas added, "His mother swears he had never even mentioned the word *suicide*."

The Vaxholm ferry was due to leave in fifteen minutes, and Nora was trying to hurry the boys along. They didn't have much to carry, just one bag each, but still it would take a few minutes to get down to the jetty.

She locked the front door, checked that the kitchen windows were closed and locked, and looped the strap of her bag over her shoulder.

On the way, they passed their old home, and she glanced over to see if there was any sign of Jonas. The house looked deserted; maybe he had already left. He was probably working the next day.

As they approached the quayside, she saw small groups of people waiting for the ferry. The autumn schedule meant fewer boats on the weekends, and the next one wouldn't be until the evening. Out of the corner of her eye, she noticed the white ferry plowing through the Sound.

"Keep it moving, guys," she said to the boys, who were just ahead of her. "We mustn't miss the boat."

As they made their way up the gangplank a little while later, she couldn't help turning her head one last time to look for Jonas. A man was walking away from the kiosk with a newspaper in his hand; for a moment she thought it was him, and then she realized it was a stranger.

She rolled her eyes at her foolishness and went on board.

CHAPTER 19

Robert Cronwall had a single-story home in the northwestern part of the island of Lidingö, which was connected to Stockholm only by an arch bridge.

There were very few cars on the road, and Thomas admired in passing the houses clinging to the steep slopes on either side of the bridge. To the right was Millesgården, the open-air studio and museum founded by the famous artist and sculptor Carl Milles.

"The view from up there must be fantastic," Margit said, as if she had read his thoughts.

"Yes, but not cheap."

"Nothing in Stockholm is cheap."

Thomas took a right; the road continued under the bridge, and before long a sign informed them that they had reached Islinge.

"What was the address again?"

"Constantiavägen—it's the next right."

Margit pointed. The house was made of red brick, and looked as if it dated from the 1930s. The garden contained several gnarled apple trees, their branches weighed down with fruit. The number of windfalls suggested that the owner couldn't be bothered to pick the crop. Steps from a walled terrace the same color as the house led up to the front door.

Thomas rang the doorbell, and a woman in her fifties opened the door. She was wearing a pink knit sweater and pearl earrings.

"Can I help you?"

Thomas explained why they were there.

"Come in; my husband is in the living room."

They followed her into a large room with a wide brick fireplace. Through an archway, they could see a beautiful dining room with an impressive chandelier hanging above the table. A cabinet embellished with gilt stood against the far wall, with a collection of family photographs on top. One of them showed a young man in his student cap, another a young man and an older man both in uniform. In a third, a couple in 1950s clothes had been captured by the camera.

A man in reading glasses was sitting in an armchair. Classical music was playing softly in the background. Thomas vaguely recognized the piece but couldn't quite place it: a piano sonata, but which one?

The man looked up.

"Police—Thomas Andreasson." Thomas held up his ID. "We'd like to ask you one or two questions about a young man we believe you met a few days ago."

Robert Cronwall took off his glasses and stood up. His hair was turning silver, but he seemed to be in pretty good shape. Thomas thought the bag of golf clubs in the hallway might have something to do with that.

"Please take a seat."

He gestured toward the sofa, and Thomas and Margit sat down on the soft, deep cushions. Margit leaned forward.

"We were wondering if you've met a student named Marcus Nielsen."

Robert looked puzzled. "Marcus Nielsen? I don't know anyone by that name."

Thomas produced a photograph from his inside pocket.

"He was twenty-two years old and lived in Jarlaberg."

"What's this about?" Robert said as he stared at the picture.

"I'm afraid he's dead," Margit said. "We're investigating his death."

"Oh dear." The response was spontaneous. "What happened?"

"He took his own life a week ago," Thomas explained.

Robert looked from Thomas to Margit, clearly at a loss.

"We found your name in his phone, so we were wondering if you'd met, and if so, what you talked about," Thomas went on. "He was studying psychology at Stockholm University."

Robert's face relaxed. "Oh, I see. Someone called me a while ago and said he was a psychology student—could that be him?"

"More than likely."

"In that case, you're right, we have spoken."

"When did you meet up with him?" Margit asked.

"We only spoke on the phone. That's why I didn't recognize him. Let me think, when was it? It must have been around a week ago—I can't remember exactly."

"Why did he call you?"

"He wanted to interview me."

"What about?" Thomas said.

"About my time at the Royal Swedish Naval Academy—I was a cadet there." Robert nodded in the direction of the framed photographs. "He said he was working on an assignment and wanted to know about my experiences, but I suggested he call the navy instead."

"Why?"

"I didn't think there was a great deal I could tell him. I'm pretty busy; I don't really have time to sit through an interview for some university student's assignment."

There was a hint of regret in Robert's eyes.

"How long was the conversation with Marcus Nielsen?" Thomas asked.

"Very brief—he introduced himself, said he'd like to ask me some questions. I turned him down, and that was the end of that. A couple of minutes, no more."

Robert Cronwall glanced at his watch.

"If you'll excuse me, we have a Rotary dinner this evening, and there's a lot to be done. I'm the chair of the Lidingö Rotary Club, which comes with a number of obligations."

The way he spoke made Thomas wonder if he was expected to stand to attention. The silver-haired man rose to indicate that the conversation was over.

"I'm sorry the young man is dead, but there's really nothing more to say."

"One final question—do you know a Jan-Erik Fredell?"

Robert stroked his chin.

"I don't think so; it doesn't ring any bells. Unfortunately I'm better with faces than names." He shrugged apologetically. "Who is he?"

"He was a PE teacher, but he'd retired several years ago due to ill health," Thomas said. "He's dead, too. We think there could be a link between him and Marcus Nielsen."

"I'm afraid I don't know him."

Margit handed Robert her card.

"Please contact us if you think of anything."

"Just out of curiosity," Thomas said, "what was the name of the piece of music that was playing when we arrived?"

"Franz Liszt, Liebestraum no. 3. It's said that he wrote one for each mistress; it's well known that he had several."

From the hallway, Thomas could see Birgitta Cronwall in the kitchen. He raised his hand, but she didn't come to say good-bye. The last thing he saw before he left the house was her back, bent over something that looked like a leg of lamb.

DIARY:

NOVEMBER 1976

This morning we were out in the southern field. Suddenly the sergeant told us to line up. He held a rope in front of us and told us to skip over it, one by one. When we had all clumsily lumbered over, he laughed in our faces.

"You just skipped lunch!" he said.

We were given nothing to eat until dinner.

That evening, we sat playing cards.

"Come on, Andersson," Eklund said as he was dealing. "You're the only one who's never talked about girls." Eklund loves giving Andersson a hard time. "But maybe you've never been with a girl?"

Eklund has a dirty mouth. His father is a butcher, and Eklund has helped out in the slaughterhouse ever since he was a teenager. He boasts that he already knows how to survive in the wilderness: just catch a rabbit, hold it by the ears, and club it to death. When the eyes drop out, it's dead. Then all you have to do is skin it and chop it up. Don't forget to remove the intestines, otherwise it tastes like crap.

He enjoys making comments like that.

Andersson's ears went dark red. I pictured my brother, who is five years younger than me, when I tease him about something or other. The same inability to deal with it, the same frustration when he can't come up with a response quickly enough.

I have never heard Andersson mention a girl. The only photograph he's brought with him is of his mother; she is sitting on the grass hugging his little sister. I saw it inside his locker once when he'd forgotten to close it properly.

"Have you never done it?" Eklund went on, with a filthy laugh. "Come on, tell us!"

Suddenly the sergeant was standing in the doorway. The laughter stopped immediately, but he had heard enough.

"Do we have a little virgin among us?" he said, seeming to relish every word.

Nobody spoke. Andersson desperately tried to think of something to say; his ears were positively glowing.

"Maybe he hasn't reached puberty yet."

That was all the sergeant said, but Andersson turned his head away, his face flushed. I felt so sorry for him, but just as I was about to speak up, Kihlberg came rushing in.

"Captain Westerberg is on his way!" he gasped.

In a second, we were all standing to attention, including the sergeant. There is no ambiguity when it comes to rank, and the sergeant was with the rest of us when the renowned captain walked in.

"At ease, men. Tomorrow we will be receiving a visitor. The company commander is coming here, and I am assuming that you will all do your best."

"Yes, Captain," we answered with one voice.

Andersson had edged backward toward the wall, and he was now standing beside Martinger, who is a head taller than him. I saw Martinger take a step forward, as if to shield Andersson from any further comments from the sergeant. Kihlberg moved beside Martinger, hiding their fellow cadet completely.

Andersson was staring down at the floor.

Chapter 20

Monday (The Second Week)

"Sachsen here."

He didn't really need to introduce himself. Thomas was familiar with the forensic pathologist's voice; plus, they had worked together often enough for him to recognize the number.

Sachsen had become something of a celebrity lately. He had taken the stand at a trial that had attracted a huge amount of attention: a rapist had attacked a series of young girls. The pathologist had established that the perpetrator had caused strikingly similar injuries to his victims because of the weapon he had used; this, in turn, provided links to a further series of brutal rapes. Sachsen had been interviewed by just about every media outlet.

"It's a bit early for you—shouldn't you be on a daytime TV talk show somewhere?"

It was only seven thirty, and Thomas had just arrived at the station and sat down at his desk.

"Ha-ha." Sachsen was not amused. "I worked late last night so you wouldn't have to wait. You and Margit need to get over here."

"We'll be there before lunch."

"I wonder what he's found?" Margit mused as they walked from the parking lot to the low building at Karolinska University Hospital that housed the forensic pathology unit.

Fallen leaves were strewn across the lawn, and the air was noticeably chillier.

"We'll soon see."

Thomas didn't have much to say for himself; he was thinking about the conversation he had had with Marcus Nielsen's mother just before they left the station.

Maria had called to ask how things were going, and as they talked, he began to realize how badly affected the family had been. David, Marcus's younger brother, was refusing to go to school, and Maria was signed off work. Her husband was also devastated.

She had begged Thomas to find her son's killer, but he had been unable to offer any words of consolation. The truth was that they still didn't know whether they were dealing with a suicide or not.

Thomas pushed open the door of the autopsy suite where Oscar-Henrik Sachsen held court. He came to greet them, and behind him they could see a body laid out on a metal table.

The unmistakable smell of human organs reached Thomas's nostrils. It was quite different from the stench of a corpse; it was more like a meat counter, where trays of liver, kidneys, and heart had been set out without sufficient refrigeration. The odor was kind of sweet and not particularly pleasant.

"Welcome," Sachsen said without offering either of his gloved hands.

Margit didn't waste time on pleasantries.

"What have you found?"

Sachsen turned and drew back the sheet covering Jan-Erik Fredell's emaciated body, then picked up a pair of forceps and pointed.

"The cause of death is drowning, there's no doubt about that. There's water in his lungs, but"—he paused to let the words sink in—"it looks as though someone gripped him firmly by the shoulders just before he died."

He put down the forceps and moved to stand behind Margit; they were almost the same height.

"Bend your knees."

She gave him an inscrutable glance but did as she was told and crouched so that she was around six inches shorter than the doctor.

He placed both hands on her shoulders, with his fingers over the collarbone and his thumbs at the back. Then he squeezed.

"Ouch—what the hell are you doing?"

The sudden pressure almost made Margit collapse.

"Showing you what happened."

Sachsen released his grip and went on: "The skin covering the collarbone shows a clear imprint of outspread fingers that have squeezed hard. On the back are marks that could only have been made by thumbnails. If someone applies a grip like that from above, it's relatively easy to force the victim under the water until he stops breathing."

Margit rubbed her collarbone and rotated her shoulders as she tried to restore her circulation.

"Oh, come on," Sachsen said. "It wasn't that bad."

Margit's expression left him in no doubt that she would punch him if he tried any more demonstrations.

"So someone drowned him?" Thomas said.

"It looks that way, unless Fredell was made of rubber and could reach all the way around his body with his arms. There's no other way he could have made those marks himself."

"He could hardly move. He suffered from MS; I met him the day before he died," Thomas said.

"In that case, someone else pushed him down and held him there until he died."

"So we're looking at murder," Margit said quietly. "Where does that leave us in relation to Marcus Nielsen's death?"

"Hard to say." Sachsen rubbed his chin. "I didn't do that autopsy, but I've read the report, and there's nothing wrong with my colleague's examination. There was no evidence of anything other than suicide—no unexplained contusions, no biological traces from another person on the body. The death occurred at the scene."

Thomas moved closer to study the marks on Fredell's skin; he could picture those fingers mercilessly applying pressure. He tried in vain to work out what kind of individual was behind the attack; who would murder a sick, helpless man?

Sachsen glanced over at a computer on the desk; the screen was covered in small print.

"By the way, Fredell was intoxicated," he added.

Thomas turned around. "Sorry?"

"He was under the influence of alcohol at the time of death. He'd consumed a large amount of whisky. Do you know if he had a drinking problem?"

Thomas remembered the shelf above the sink in the bathroom: boxes and boxes of tablets, white boxes with red warning triangles.

"He was on a lot of medication because of his illness. It seems unlikely that he'd be drinking under the circumstances; we need to check it out with his wife."

"I don't remember seeing any bottles of booze," Margit said.

"You're sure about this?" Thomas said to Sachsen, who nodded.

"Could the killer have forced the whisky down his throat so he'd be easier to handle?"

"In that case, you'd think he would have had some kind of weapon—a gun, maybe," Margit speculated.

"Good call," Thomas said. "The killer could have forced him into the bathtub at gunpoint."

"Which would explain why I didn't find any other marks on the body," Sachsen added.

"We need to go back to the apartment, see if we can find any bottles," Margit said. "If so, it might be possible to secure fingerprints."

"One last thing," Sachsen said. "The water in the lungs. At first, I thought it was ordinary soapy water, but when I checked again, it wasn't soap—it was detergent. It looks as if that's what had been added to the bathwater."

"But why?" Thomas said.

"How should I know?"

Thomas sighed at Sachsen's reaction; sometimes the pathologist was unnecessarily quick to take offense.

"That's not what I meant," he said. "Was it poisonous? Would it have made the victim's condition worse in any way?"

"No. It's just an observation—I don't know what the significance is."

Detergent, Thomas repeated to himself. What did that mean?

A neat pile of printouts was waiting on Thomas's desk when he got back. He and Margit had grabbed a late lunch of sausages with mashed potatoes and a prawn salad; now it was almost three o'clock.

He slipped the sheets of paper out of the plastic folder. The first page consisted of a photograph of Bo Kaufman accompanied by a brief biography, put together by Karin. Thomas read through the material several times, then went along to see Margit, who was sitting at her computer. The cursor moved across the screen as she clicked away with the mouse, concentrating hard.

She glanced up when he sat down opposite her and stretched out his legs.

"I've gone through everything Erik and Karin came up with on Fredell and Nielsen," she said. "There are no points of contact at all. Nada. Nothing."

She sighed to underline her frustration and took a bite out of a half-eaten apple that was already turning brown around the edges.

"Bo Kaufman," Thomas said.

"What about him?" Margit kept on munching.

Thomas held up the printout.

"The last name in Marcus's phone."

Margit quickly read through the information.

"He lives in Brandbergen, he's single, and he's on welfare."

"Exactly."

"So no obvious link there either."

"Not really, unless you count the fact that Fredell lived in Älta, which is also a suburb to the south of Stockholm."

Thomas's attempt at humor went straight over Margit's head, and she gave him a quizzical look. Then she glanced at her watch and switched off the computer.

"I tried to contact Marcus Nielsen's supervisor at the university," Thomas went on.

"How did that go?"

"I couldn't get ahold of her. I left a message on her voice mail asking her to call me."

"OK."

Margit gathered up all her papers into an untidy heap and stuffed them in the cabinet behind her. "In that case, let's hope she gets in touch very soon. I have to go—it's my sister's birthday. Can we leave Bo Kaufman until tomorrow? I don't think another twenty-four hours will make much difference."

Thomas knew she was thinking of the visit to Robert Cronwall, which had been more or less pointless. He couldn't really argue; it was more important to spend the time on Fredell, who had definitely been murdered.

He studied the photograph of Bo Kaufman again. *Is this a fool's errand,* he thought, *or do you have some answers for us? Can you tell us why Marcus Nielsen was found hanging in his room, and why Jan-Erik Fredell was drowned in his own bathtub?*

The man in the black-and-white photograph gazed back; apparently he had nothing to say.

CHAPTER 21

The apartment was in darkness when Nora unlocked and opened the door. Henrik had picked up the boys after school, and they would be with him all week; she wouldn't see Adam and Simon for seven whole days. She knew they needed both their parents, but that didn't mean she missed them any less.

Suddenly the tears came, and she could do nothing to stop them.

A little voice in her head whispered that the whole thing was unnatural. A seven-year-old and a twelve-year-old needed to see their mom every day, not every other week. If nothing else, *she* still needed to see them each morning and night.

She went into their room without taking off her coat and lay down on Simon's bed among his stuffed animals. She groped under the pillow for his pajamas and buried her face in them. The smell of her son filled her nostrils, making her cry even harder. She lay there curled up for a long time, clutching the pajama top.

Eventually she looked at her watch; it was almost seven thirty. She ought to cook dinner, but she wasn't hungry. And setting out one single plate when there should have been three was so painful.

But she had to eat, because of her diabetes, if nothing else.

Well-meaning friends had tried to cheer her up by saying that she would have some time to herself now, that she would be able to do whatever she wanted. More than one married girlfriend had sighed over how wonderful it would be to get a chance to do her own thing, with the chaotic sounds of family life clearly audible in the background.

Anyone who said that didn't know what they were talking about.

Nora buried her face in the pajama top again and wondered what Simon was doing right now. He was probably having his bath before bedtime. She pictured her old house, saw him sitting in the bathtub with his plastic toys. Another sob fought its way through.

With a huge effort she sat up and dried her eyes. She had to take her insulin and eat something. Maybe that would make her feel better.

Nora placed a bowl of tomato soup and a couple of sandwiches on a tray and took it into the living room. She sat down in front of the TV and switched on the news, which had just started. She listened to the familiar headlines with half an ear; as usual, there was economic uncertainty all over the world, and there was no shortage of depressing stories.

Suddenly she saw a face she recognized and sat up a little straighter. She'd met the man on the screen, hadn't she? Something about him seemed familiar.

"The public are asked to be extra vigilant since a disabled man was murdered in his home over the weekend," the reporter said. "Jan-Erik Fredell was drowned in his bathtub while his wife was out shopping."

The camera showed a picture of a suburban apartment block with several police cars parked outside. Nora thought she caught a glimpse of Thomas's face; was he working on this case?

Jan-Erik Fredell.

She thought hard; she had a good memory for people and rarely forgot someone she had met.

The reporter moved on to a news item about the financial sector while Nora tried to remember why she recognized the dead man. She went and got her laptop out of her briefcase and did a search on Fredell. Most of the links she found had to do with the news story she had just seen, but there it was, farther down the page: *Enskede School, teaching staff 1981.*

Suddenly it clicked.

Twenty-six years ago, Jan-Erik Fredell had been her PE teacher; he had come straight from training college, as she recalled. All the girls in her class had been in love with him. Jan-Erik had been broad shouldered, muscular, and ridiculously good-looking, with cropped ash-blond hair and a charming smile. Nora and her friends had come up with all kinds of ways to get his attention. It was like having an American movie star in school.

Their previous teacher had been very strict, a woman who took her subject very seriously. She had sucked every ounce of joy out of the lessons by forcing the students to practice a series of gymnastic exercises that everyone hated.

Jan-Erik Fredell had shown them a completely different side of sport. Suddenly they were allowed to play baseball and football in teams that he chose, so that no one felt excluded. Even orienteering became fun.

His commitment was evident in every aspect of his work, and when Nora eventually graduated from high school, she realized he was one of the best teachers she had ever had, a man who really cared about his students.

And now he was dead, attacked in his own home, unable to defend himself. What a tragic end—and what a sad metamorphosis from the man he had been. She could hardly believe that the frail old man on TV had been the teacher she'd idolized. She decided she would send a card to his widow to express her condolences and tell her about the impression he had made all those years ago.

The telephone rang.

"Hi, Mom."

It was Simon.

"Hi, honey."

She pictured him in his favorite pale-blue flannel pajamas with the faded hippos on them. Adam had started sleeping in his underpants, but Simon still wore pajamas.

"I just wanted to say good night."

"It's so great to hear your voice, honey. I was thinking about you a few minutes ago."

"Good night, Mom."

"Good night, and sleep well. See you Monday."

"How long is it until Monday?"

"Seven days, sweetheart."

"That's such a long time."

"It'll go real fast, you'll see."

Simon sounded upset, and Nora felt a stab of pain in her heart.

"Have you got Teddy with you?"

Simon loved his gray bear, whose fur was worn away in several places. It went everywhere with him, and it was the first thing he put in his bag when he was going to stay with Henrik.

"Yes."

"Give him a good-night kiss from me."

"OK."

There was a brief silence; Nora had the feeling Simon didn't want to hang up, and she didn't have the heart to end the call.

"Did you have a nice dinner?"

"No."

Now he sounded sulky.

"Why not?"

"Marie made a salad with some weird stuff in it. Disgusting fried cheese and disgusting brown seeds."

"Don't call food disgusting," Nora said gently.

"It was disgusting, it was horrible," Simon insisted.

"I expect it was bulgur wheat, or maybe couscous."

"I don't know what it was, but it didn't taste good. I hardly ate anything."

"You have to eat, honey, otherwise you'll be hungry before bedtime," Nora said, against her better judgment.

"Yes, Mom."

She understood her sons very well. Bulgur wheat and halloumi weren't the right things to serve to boys of their age. Henrik should have known that, even if Marie didn't.

"You can call me tomorrow to say good night if you like, but now you have to go to sleep."

She heard a noise in the background, then Henrik's voice.

"Simon, you shouldn't be on the phone at this time of night—you've got school tomorrow."

"Yes, Dad."

"Good night, sweetheart," Nora said, and hung up.

She stared at the TV, not taking anything in as tears scalded her eyes.

CHAPTER 22

It was almost ten o'clock. Pernilla was in bed, and through the closed door she could hear Thomas moving around in the kitchen. He had gotten home very late.

Under normal circumstances, she was a real night owl, but these days she was unbelievably tired in the evening, her eyelids starting to droop by nine. It had been exactly the same last time; she had wanted to do nothing but sleep for the first three months of her pregnancy.

She already had a little bump. It had happened much sooner than when she was expecting Emily; she could hardly button up her jeans. Her breasts were growing, too—that was why she had begun to suspect that something was going on. Her bras cut into her flesh and seemed too small, but it had still taken several weeks for her to summon up the courage to take a pregnancy test.

She had done three, one after the other, terrified of the result— whatever it might be.

The possibility that they would get another chance to be parents had been so remote that she hadn't even considered it. When they first got together, it had been years before they gave up and joined the waiting list for IVF treatment. When she finally got pregnant after several rounds, it had felt like a miracle. She wasn't a believer, but that day she had thanked God.

When Emily died, joy had turned into a grief deeper than anything Pernilla had ever known. Every step hurt; every movement was an effort. Sorrow took over her life; it was like looking at the world through a filter that colored everything gray. Tears couldn't ease the pain, but still she wept until her eyes ached and her head throbbed.

Thinking back brought a lump to her throat; she adjusted the pillow, trying to chase away those terrible memories.

It was so easy to fall back into anxiety and despair. Over the past twelve months, she had started to believe that she was getting over the loss of her daughter, but those feelings were still very close to the surface.

Hormones, she told herself. She had been tearful when she was carrying Emily, too. All pregnant women cried easily, and many felt like they were on an emotional roller coaster. It was nothing unusual.

She turned her head to look at Emily's photograph. It still hurt, but it was easier now.

She stroked her belly with her fingertips and tried to imagine the life that had begun to grow in there. They were scheduled to go for an ultrasound next week, and she would see her child for the first time.

She hadn't gotten much done at work today; instead she had sat around surfing the net. Her jaw muscles tightened as she remembered searching for information about sudden infant death syndrome, and, in particular, the chances of it affecting two children in the same family. She had used every search term she could think of in an effort to find reassuring statistics, research that showed it was highly unusual for parents to experience the same tragedy twice.

Her joy at being pregnant was constantly tinged with the fear of something going wrong. She couldn't stop herself from brooding, even though she knew it didn't help. Quite the reverse, in fact: it put her in a dark, gloomy state of mind, when she ought to be thinking positive thoughts, to be wrapping her baby in a sense of security.

Happy thoughts, she said to herself, remembering the story of Peter Pan; you had to think happy thoughts in order to fly.

Thomas had brightened up since she'd told him she was pregnant. He had regained the lust for life that had been missing during the summer, when he battled with nightmares and struggled to get used to the new way of walking.

Once again, she stroked her belly. When had she gotten pregnant?

Since she didn't think she could conceive naturally, they hadn't used any protection or taken particular note of her menstrual cycle.

Pernilla rolled over onto her back and tried to think.

It was now September 24, and she was in her eighth week—so it must have happened in the second half of July, when they were still on Harö.

Suddenly the memory came to her.

It had been a beautiful morning, and she had woken early. The weather had been glorious, and the forecasters had promised that the heat would last for the rest of the week. She had padded down to the jetty and taken a morning dip—without a stitch on, because it was so early and there was no one around.

Their house, a converted barn which they had renovated a few years earlier, occupied its own inlet, and their closest neighbors were Thomas's parents and his brother, Stefan, and his family. Trees, at that moment in full leaf, grew between the properties, and the green wall created a sense of peace and privacy.

The water had been warm. When she swam to the surface, a family of eider ducks were paddling by at a stately pace. The smell of seaweed lingered in her nostrils, and she pushed her wet hair back from her forehead. She got out and sat on the jetty for a while, allowing the sun to dry her skin.

When she got back to the house, Thomas was still asleep. He was lying on his side, and he looked almost the same as when they had first met, on a mild summer's evening in Stockholm ten years earlier.

The pale stubble made him appear younger, and Pernilla smiled as she thought about its roughness against her cheek. His hair was slightly damp at his temples, and the thin summer sheet was in a crumpled heap at the foot of the bed.

She had lain down beside him, feeling the contrast between her own cool skin and the warmth of his back. The tan line at his waist was very distinct.

She lay there motionless for a little while, enjoying the closeness.

Then she had gently nuzzled the back of his neck and softly kissed him. He had moved a fraction nearer, and she pushed her leg between his thighs. To begin with, he hardly moved, as if he were still asleep, but she knew he was awake; a faint, almost imperceptible smile played around the corners of his mouth.

Then he turned and raised himself on one elbow, looking down at her with his eyes half-closed. Their faces were inches apart, and he lowered his head and kissed her.

Afterward, he had held her tight, and she had dozed in his arms for a long time.

DIARY:
NOVEMBER 1976

"Today you're going to learn to freeze."

The sergeant uttered the words with a smile, as if he had said something very amusing. It was five o'clock in the morning, and we had been woken early, with no warning. It was still dark outside as we silently dressed and grabbed our packs.

I have begun to get used to these sudden awakenings, to being dragged from my bed at all hours. The unexpected has become part of my expectations.

We were ordered to line up on the hill; the temperature was below freezing, and a fine layer of snow covered the ground.

"Now you're going to learn to freeze," the sergeant repeated.

I looked around, but no one seemed to understand what he meant. However, the unmistakable glee in his voice didn't bode well.

The sergeant led the way, and we marched along behind him. There was very little light in the forest, and visibility was poor. I had to be very careful where I put my feet in order to avoid tripping. Eventually we reached an area to the west of the barracks. It looked like a field that might once have been used for agriculture; it had been plowed at some point, and the muddy furrows were full of water with a thin film of ice on top. The dark earth was edged with rime frost.

The sergeant held up his hand, and we stopped. We obeyed without a sound. As usual, we stood to attention and waited for the next order.

"Take off your packs and coats!" he barked.

I glanced uncertainly at the others, but when everyone started to comply, I did the same.

"Fold up your coats and put them on top of your packs!"

"Yes, Sergeant!" we answered with one voice.

"Take off your caps, scarves, and gloves."

"Yes, Sergeant!"

He gives the orders and we obey—it's that simple.

The cold was immediate. It bit into our cheeks and spread through our bodies in minutes. Our attention was focused on the sergeant, but he made us wait, almost as if he were enjoying the unspoken question: What next?

As the seconds ticked by in the dim morning light, he kept his eyes fixed straight ahead. He was in no hurry.

"Lie down on your backs!" he said at long last.

We did as we were told.

The ground was ice-cold, and my left leg ended up in the water. In no time at all, I was so cold that I was shivering.

I turned my head so that I could see the others out of the corner of my eye. They were all lying there motionless, gazing up at the sky. No one complained, but those closest to me were shivering, too, and their lips were blue.

Andersson was to my left, shaking violently.

Time passed: fifteen minutes, half an hour. I tried to empty my mind; that made it easier to bear. Time lost all meaning and I lay there half-awake, half in a trance.

At some point, the sergeant would decide that we had had enough; until then, all we could do was try to stick it out.

After an eternity, maybe an hour, maybe more, I heard a strange noise from the side where Andersson lay. It took a little while before I figured out what it was.

His teeth were chattering so hard it sounded like gunshots across the open field. The sergeant heard it, too. He came over and stared down at Andersson.

"Permission to stand up, Sergeant." Andersson somehow managed to force out the words.

"Permission denied."

It was brave to ask the question. I would never have had the nerve. I lay there silently admiring Andersson. He doesn't say much, but he has a strong sense of what's right and wrong.

Eventually we were allowed to stand up. Except for Andersson—he had to stay down for another fifteen minutes.

As I scrambled to my feet, I stole a glance at him, but he didn't meet my eyes. Instead he gazed up at the gray, overcast sky, his expression grim.

When he was permitted to get up, his legs refused to cooperate. We had to help him back to the barracks. Martinger, who is the strongest of us all, carried him on his back for the final stretch.

We were looking forward to a hot shower, but no such luck. The hot water had been turned off for "repairs." We had to cover Andersson with thick blankets to try to raise his body temperature.

We certainly did learn to freeze today.

CHAPTER 23

Tuesday (The Second Week)

The tower block in Brandbergen was like a monument to the building frenzy of the 1960s, when Stockholm had to be expanded by adding suburbs to house those who'd come to the city from rural areas and from other countries in order to find work.

The walls on both sides of the door were covered in graffiti, and the window in a door that probably led to the basement was cracked.

"Do you think it's safe to leave the car here?" Margit muttered, tilting her head in the direction of a bicycle with broken spokes, next to something that might have been an attempt at a flower bed. There was garbage everywhere—candy wrappers, empty beer cans, torn plastic bags. The only greenery was the odd clump of grass, interspersed with dandelions. Any flowers that had been planted had given up long ago.

"The question is whether it's better or worse to show that we're police," Thomas said. A short distance away, a group of boys was standing around smoking. They all wore hoodies, and they should have been in a classroom at this time of day. He wondered if they were waiting for Margit and him to leave so that they could strip the car, or if they just had nothing better to do.

"Maybe one of us should stay here?" Margit suggested.

Thomas locked the car. "It'll be fine. Let's go."

The unmarked police vehicle was equipped with a powerful alarm; if anyone touched it, he and Margit should be able to hear the racket and get back before too much damage was done. If it had been his Volvo, he might have made a different decision.

He slipped the keys in his pocket and headed for the main door. A board inside informed them that Bo Kaufman lived on the fourth floor; there were thirteen floors in total.

The elevator was working, although it, too, had graffiti scrawled all over its walls. Thomas wondered how the families who lived at the top of the building coped when the elevator broke down.

They reached the fourth floor, walked down the hall, and rang Kaufman's doorbell. According to Karin's notes, he lived alone. There were no details about his former profession or any permanent employment; apparently he was able to survive on state handouts.

When no one answered, Thomas rang again, keeping his finger on the bell for longer this time.

Eventually they heard shuffling footsteps, then the door opened a crack.

"Yes?"

"Bo Kaufman? Police—we'd like to speak to you."

Thomas was aware of a slight movement as Kaufman tried to close the door. He grabbed the frame with one hand and stared straight into a pair of bloodshot eyes. Kaufman let go of the handle and stepped back. The door opened to reveal a man in a grubby white T-shirt straining over his gut.

"What the fuck, I ain't done nothing," he muttered.

"Nobody says you have," Margit said firmly, "but we need to talk to you. Can we come in?"

They stepped inside the sparsely furnished apartment and followed Kaufman into the tiny kitchen. He sat down on one of the two chairs by the table. Over by the wall, there was an old refrigerator that seemed to be held together with gaffer tape, and the battered sink was piled high with dirty dishes.

Judging by the number of glasses and full ashtrays on the draining board, Bo Kaufman had done his fair share of partying recently.

The shaking hands, the open pores, and the empty bottles all pointed to serious long-term alcohol abuse. *He probably makes ends meet by taking the odd job whenever his benefits run out,* Thomas thought. Cash only, of course. He had seen similar cases before.

Margit removed a pile of junk mail from the other chair, but left one leaflet for protection before she sat down opposite Kaufman. Thomas looked around and found a stool pushed under the worktop.

"Have you had visitors recently?" Margit asked.

Kaufman ran a hand over his hair, which was slightly too long at the back. His face looked puffy, and Thomas wondered if he was sober. Probably not. In his state, the alcohol rarely left the body completely. Before the level of booze in his bloodstream dropped too much, he probably made sure he topped it off again.

"I had a couple of pals over last night."

"Do you live alone?"

"Mmm." A shrug. "I had a girl for a while, but she took off."

"Any kids?"

"A boy, but I don't see him too often."

Thomas took out the photograph of Marcus Nielsen and placed it on the table.

"Do you know this guy?"

A cursory glance. "No."

"Take a closer look," Margit insisted. "Are you sure you've never met him?"

Kaufman picked up the photo with a trembling hand, the dirty nails standing out against the white border.

"Never seen him before."

"Are you absolutely certain?"

"That's what I said!"

"His name is Marcus Nielsen, and he was a student of psychology at Stockholm University," Thomas explained. "Unfortunately he's dead, and we found your name in his cell phone."

An uncertain expression came over Kaufman's face.

"Why?"

"That's what we're trying to find out," Thomas said patiently.

"You've no idea why Marcus would have had your name?" Margit asked.

"Nope."

Kaufman rummaged in the pocket of his filthy jeans and produced a crumpled pack of cigarettes. He lit up and took a deep drag.

Margit leaned forward. Thomas could see that she had had enough.

"What were you doing the weekend before last, and this past Saturday?"

"What?"

"What were you doing last Saturday, and the weekend before that?"

"I don't know—I guess I was with my pals."

Kaufman seemed taken aback; he looked at Thomas for some kind of explanation, or possibly sympathy, but Thomas was finding it hard to summon up any compassion, partly due to Kaufman's lack of interest in answering their questions. The guy didn't give a shit about the rest of the world, as long as he could get a drink.

"Is there anyone who can confirm that?" Margit folded her arms and waited for a response, never taking her eyes off him.

Anger flared in Kaufman's eyes.

"What the fuck? What are you accusing me of? Like I said, I ain't done nothing!"

"We just want you to tell us where you were last Saturday and the weekend before. That's all."

Margit was still staring at him.

Kaufman sucked on his cigarette. When he had exhaled a cloud of smoke, his face brightened.

"Tobbe was here all day Saturday, you can talk to him." His tone became conciliatory. "I don't remember exactly what I was doing the previous weekend. You can't accuse me of something just because I have a bad memory. I told you, I've never seen that guy before."

Thomas tried a new angle.

"Do you know a man by the name of Robert Cronwall?"

Another deep drag, then Kaufman shook his head without saying a word.

"What about this man—do you recognize him?"

Thomas placed a picture of Jan-Erik Fredell on the table next to the photograph of Marcus Nielsen. There could easily have been fifty years between the two men, although, in fact, it was roughly half that.

"I've never seen him either, I swear. Does he live around here?"

"His name was Jan-Erik Fredell," Margit said. "Ring any bells?"

Kaufman began coughing violently. He got to his feet and bent over the sink, still coughing.

Margit stood up and tried thumping him on the back, but he waved her away. When the attack was over, he filled a glass with water and drank it straight down. Then he lit another cigarette and inhaled deeply.

"Are you OK?" Margit said.

"Chronic chest problems," he mumbled hoarsely, wiping tears from his eyes.

"So should you really be smoking?"

"That's what the doctor said, too. He told me I have to stop drinking and smoking." Kaufman grinned. "Fucking know-it-all. If I give up booze and cigarettes, I might as well lay down and die right now."

He exhaled slowly. The nicotine seemed to be having a calming effect; he sat down and picked up the picture of Fredell again, this time with genuine interest in his eyes.

"His name was Jan-Erik Fredell," Thomas said. "He died on Saturday, at the age of fifty."

Something seemed to spark in Kaufman's addled brain. He blinked and dropped the photograph as if it were red hot.

"What did you say his name was?"

"Fredell. Jan-Erik Fredell."

"That's Jan-Erik Fredell?"

"Yes."

"Janne Fredell . . . He looks like an old man, for fuck's sake!"

You don't look so good yourself, Thomas thought. "He was suffering from multiple sclerosis," he said out loud. "He could hardly get around anymore."

"And he's dead?"

"Murdered," Margit said. "Last Saturday."

"Jeez."

"Someone drowned him in his own bathtub."

A sudden intake of breath as Margit's words sank in.

"Are you sure?" he croaked.

"Absolutely. We're trying to find out why—can you help us?"

Kaufman used his cigarette to light a fresh one before stubbing it out on a saucer.

"Jeez," he said again. He got up, went over to the counter, and started shaking the beer bottles that were lined up. After several attempts, he found one with a few drops left; he raised it to his lips and emptied it, then stood there, cigarette in hand, rocking back and forth on his heels.

"Fredell . . . murdered. Why, for fuck's sake?"

Thomas was getting tired of repeating everything over and over again.

"We don't know, but we're wondering if you have any information that could help move our investigation forward. How well did you know him?"

Bo Kaufman leaned back to rest his head on a shabby cupboard door and closed his eyes. The roar of a motorbike starting up outside shattered the silence.

Thomas thought about their car, but so far the alarm hadn't gone off.

After a few seconds, Kaufman opened his eyes; they were filled with sadness.

"We did our national service together."

"And where was that?"

"We were Coastal Rangers—artillery." There was a touch of nostalgia in his voice.

Another Coastal Ranger. Thomas's attention was now fully focused on Kaufman.

"When was this?"

"In the seventies. First in Vaxholm, then on Korsö just off Sandhamn. Wait a minute."

Kaufman disappeared into the living room, leaving Thomas and Margit alone in the stuffy kitchen. They could hear drawers being opened and closed. Margit wrinkled her nose.

"Jesus, it stinks in here; I can hardly breathe."

She was about to open the window when Kaufman returned, clutching an old photograph album with a red cover.

"Look."

He pointed to a photo of himself in full uniform with the familiar green beret on his head. In the background, Thomas could just see something that he thought he recognized as Vaxholm Fortress.

"That's me—Cadet Kaufman at your service."

He gave a clumsy salute, and now Thomas did feel a surge of compassion for the young man in the picture who had gotten lost somewhere along the way. He must have dreamed of a different life once upon a time; what had gone wrong?

Kaufman sat down and turned the pages until he reached a photograph somewhere near the middle of the album. It showed a group of bare-chested soldiers on a sandy shore. The sun was shining, and several kayaks were drawn up beside them. It looked as if it had been taken in the afternoon; the shadows were long. Pine trees and wooden barracks could be seen behind the men, who were all smiling broadly at the camera.

They look as if they haven't got a care in the world, Thomas thought. "That's me."

Kaufman pointed to a young man in the center. He was handsome and muscular, with an impressive tan—the very epitome of good health. The contrast with the shambling wreck sitting opposite was terrifying. It was almost impossible to believe he was the same person.

How could someone change so much?

"Is Jan-Erik Fredell in the picture, too?" Margit asked.

"Yes." Kaufman pointed to another smiling figure. "There."

They could have been brothers. The same cropped hair, the same suntan, the same ripped upper body. Fredell was squinting at the camera, one hand on his hip.

He, too, looked utterly carefree.

He, too, had changed beyond recognition.

"So is this your national service troop?" Margit asked. "Did you serve together?"

"Yes, we were in the same group, the first platoon."

Thomas tried to remember the structure of the Coastal Rangers. He thought the soldiers were divided into smaller groups, small enough to operate efficiently and to allow the men to bond and communicate effectively. Four or five groups formed a platoon, and they stayed together throughout their training.

He had done his own military service onboard a minesweeper in the Baltic. The navy had been an obvious choice after all the time he had spent at the family's summer cottage in the archipelago. However, he had never been tempted by the Coastal Rangers, even though their base was just a stone's throw from Harö. There was something unpleasant about a specially chosen team whose members thought they were superior to everyone else. That kind of elitism was completely alien to him.

"Who else is in the picture?" Margit wanted to know.

Kaufman scratched his head.

"Let me think. This is Kihlberg, he was our team leader, and he was a hell of a nice guy."

"What was his first name?"

"I don't . . . Back then we never used first names, just number and surnames." He took a deep breath and let it out through his mouth with a slight hissing sound.

"I was 108. 108 Kaufman."

Thomas realized that his tone had changed. He was calmer, less like a man on a downward trajectory. It was as if an echo of the military life had crept into his voice, evoking the disciplined young man he must once have been.

Margit pointed to a soldier on the right. "And who's this?"

"That's Erneskog," Kaufman said slowly. "We shared a room on Korsö."

"Any idea what his first name is?"

Kaufman stubbed out his cigarette and lit yet another. The air in the kitchen was so thick with smoke that Thomas's throat hurt. He stood up.

"Mind if I open the window?"

Kaufman ignored him. He was frowning with the effort of trying to recall the events of thirty years ago.

"His name is . . . Sven, that's it. Sven Erneskog, and the guy next to him is . . . Eklund. Stefan Eklund."

He seemed delighted with this achievement; he looked up at the two officers with triumph in his eyes.

"My brain's still working!" he said. "I'm not finished yet!"

Thomas jotted down the names.

"What about the last two?" Margit said, nodding in the direction of the soldiers who had yet to be identified.

"Now, what were their names . . ."

A look of despair passed across Kaufman's unshaven face. His upper lip trembled, and for a second, Thomas thought he might burst into tears. Had he been so deeply affected by talking about old memories? Or had he been struck by the sudden realization of how far he had fallen?

"I don't remember anymore. They're gone, just like Kihlberg's first name. I never thought I'd forget that."

"Could we borrow this photograph?" Thomas asked. "I promise you'll get it back, but I'd really like to make a copy."

Kaufman nodded, and Thomas gently removed it from the album and held it in the palm of his hand. He looked at it again. The late-afternoon sun shone on those muscular bodies. One of the men was holding a beret, the Coastal Ranger's emblem glinting in the light.

Thirty years ago, Kaufman had been a member of an elite group of soldiers. Now all that remained was a piece of wreckage.

CHAPTER 24

"What a mess," Thomas said as he turned the key in the ignition.

In spite of their fears, the car had been left untouched. The boys who had been standing around smoking outside the apartment building had disappeared.

"I have a feeling it won't be long before he drinks himself to death," he went on as he signaled left.

A light drizzle was falling, and he switched on the windshield wipers. It was almost three o'clock.

"That was upsetting," Margit said. They had both come across all kinds of human degradation during their years as police officers: addicts who had committed the very worst crimes in their desperate quests for drugs, and victims of abuse who were barely recognizable. They had seen apartments that had been totally trashed, and human remains that had made their stomachs turn.

"You never get used to it," she went on.

"No, but maybe that's good," Thomas said as he changed gears. "You don't want to lose the ability to feel."

"I just hope my kids never end up like that."

It sounded as if Margit had taken the encounter with Kaufman more personally than she usually did; she was very experienced, she rarely lost her cool, and she could handle most situations. However, her two teenage daughters, Anna and Linda, were a constant source of anxiety, and she often talked to Thomas about her fears.

Her job made her all too familiar with what could happen to young girls if they weren't careful, and as a result she went too far in the opposite direction. Margit was an overprotective mother, which led to frequent arguments about boundaries. The fact that her husband refused to take sides, and simply withdrew when all hell broke loose, merely increased her frustration.

"Linda was drunk when she got home on Saturday," she said after a while. "She threw up in the flower bed before she came in, then tried to tell me she had an upset stomach." Margit let out a bark of laughter. "An upset stomach, did she really think I'd buy that?"

"What happened?"

"Eventually she came clean. She and her friends had been competing to see who could take the most tequila shots. Tequila shots! She's old enough to know better."

"She's only seventeen. At that age, you don't think about consequences; you want to see what you're capable of. Weren't you like that at seventeen?"

"I mean, we've talked about this kind of thing," Margit went on as if she hadn't heard Thomas's comment. "She knows how dangerous it is for a girl to get so drunk that she can't take care of herself, for God's sake!"

She pushed back her hair with an angry gesture.

Thomas reached out and adjusted the fan. The car they were using was an older model, and it was always either too warm or too cold.

"Maybe she learned her lesson, if she was as wasted as you say," he ventured. "She must have felt like crap the next day. I'm sure it'll work out; I don't think Linda would do anything dumb."

"Let's hope not."

Margit stared out of the window. "I just get so worried when she goes out," she went on. "She's so small; she wouldn't be able to fight back if anyone attacked her."

Linda took after Margit, who was slim and wiry, without an ounce of extra fat on her bones. Both daughters were very pretty, with long blond hair.

Thomas and Margit knew that all it took was for one man to get out of line. Every summer, the police received one complaint after another from girls who'd had too much to drink and had been attacked; these events had the potential to haunt the victims for the rest of their lives. Thomas understood why Margit was so anxious, but there was no point in making her feel worse.

"I'm sure Linda will be a little more careful, at least for a while," he said, patting her reassuringly on the arm. "If she had a real humdinger of a hangover after too much tequila, she probably won't want to touch alcohol for quite some time."

"She definitely won't be doing that," Margit said grimly. "She's grounded for a month."

CHAPTER 25

Thomas was at his desk, trying to gain an overview of the investigation. He had piles of papers in front of him—interview transcripts, witness statements, and notes—and was starting to go through them.

Erik Blom and Kalle Lidwall had spoken to various people connected to Marcus Nielsen—relatives, former school friends, and other students who lived in the same building. The picture that had emerged was of a young man very similar to most others who were studying at the university.

He had consistently gotten good grades and had been a committed student. "Kind of nerdy," as one of his classmates had put it. Nielsen often stayed up late playing computer games or surfing the net, and he enjoyed chatting online with people from all over the world.

Nothing out of the ordinary.

Someone had said that Marcus was considering working with young people when he finished his course; he had asked about an additional minor in youth psychology. His mother had mentioned that Marcus's kid brother had been bullied at school; maybe that had sparked his interest.

When asked directly whether Marcus would have given away his laptop or possibly lost it, every single person had said no. The general consensus was that he never went anywhere without it.

Thomas was convinced that part of the answer lay in that missing laptop.

He took a sip of lukewarm tea and flicked through the next pile, which consisted of interviews with Jan-Erik Fredell's relatives, friends, and neighbors.

According to Lena Fredell, it was unthinkable that anyone could have wished her husband harm. He had been a PE teacher throughout his adult life, and a very popular one. He had won the "teacher of the year" award at his school several times.

Lena refused to believe that he could have had any enemies, insisting that a random burglar must have attacked her husband. Admittedly, there had been a spate of organized gangs ringing the doorbells of elderly people and trying to rob them in their own homes, but Thomas wasn't convinced. This homicide seemed too well planned; plus, no money had been taken from the Fredells' apartment.

If Fredell had been killed because the perp was disappointed at the lack of cash or valuables, then the MO should have been completely different. A fatal blow delivered in a moment of rage, a shot fired in anger—Thomas could have accepted either of those, but drowning a fully dressed man in his own bathtub was something else, and it suggested another motive altogether.

Door-to-door inquiries among the neighbors had produced nothing. Few had been at home on that sunny Saturday; nobody had noticed anything unusual in the stairwell.

As Thomas studied the report, he wondered how long it would have taken the killer to dispatch Jan-Erik Fredell. He picked up the phone and called Sachsen.

"Hi, it's Thomas Andreasson," he said when the forensic pathologist answered. "I have a question regarding Jan-Erik Fredell. Have you any idea how long it might have taken?"

"To drown him, you mean?"

"The whole thing."

Sachsen thought for a moment. "From the moment the killer entered the apartment until Fredell's lungs filled with water . . ."

Another pause; Thomas waited.

"How long does it take to fill a bathtub?" Sachsen said.

Thomas wasn't sure; he usually took showers. "I don't know—fifteen minutes, maybe? No more than twenty."

"There you go, then. Let's assume it took fifteen minutes at the most to gain access to the apartment and force Fredell into the bathroom. Add twenty to fill the bath. Push Fredell down; maybe another six or seven minutes, to be on the safe side. Where does that leave us?"

"Thirty-five to forty-five minutes."

"There were no unidentified fingerprints, so presumably the killer wore gloves; that means he wouldn't have to waste time wiping anything he'd touched."

"Carefully planned, in other words."

"In every way. You're dealing with a highly efficient killer."

Thomas thanked him and hung up, then reflected on what he had just heard. So it had taken three-quarters of an hour at the most. A calculating killer had gotten into the apartment, forced Fredell to get into a bathtub full of water with his clothes on, then held him beneath the surface.

Why choose that particular method? There were many easier ways to kill someone.

Thomas got up and began to pace to get his circulation going. In the building opposite, a woman was standing by the open window, sneaking a cigarette instead of going outside, in spite of the fact that smoking was now banned inside offices. Thomas had colleagues who had switched to nicotine gum, muttering crossly that it was inhuman to force people out into the cold when they wanted a smoke. But the woman by the window didn't seem to care about the ban.

Thomas looked away and continued to ponder.

The killer must have had a gun in order to force Fredell to get into the bath. Therefore, it was also possible that he could have compelled

Marcus Nielsen to stage his suicide. He could have made Marcus climb up onto the desk, place the noose around his neck, and take that fatal step into thin air.

The rope had been sent off for analysis; with a bit of luck, there would be fibers or something else to prove that another person had been in the room. Nothing new had emerged from the more detailed autopsy.

Then again, if the perpetrator had been carrying a gun, why hadn't he simply shot Fredell? He had made no effort to make the death look accidental, so it should have been easy to pull the trigger. If he had used a silencer, no one would have heard a thing.

Once again, Thomas felt he was going around in circles.

He sat down with a clean sheet of paper in front of him, hoping to arrange the facts into some kind of order, but he just sat there, pen in hand.

It was possible that the two deaths were unrelated; there was no clear proof of a link. However, if they were related, another question came to mind: Why did someone want to hide the fact that Nielsen had been murdered, when Fredell's murder was so obvious?

It didn't make sense.

Thomas jotted down his thoughts, then went back to Nielsen's cell phone and checked through the list of contacts one last time, just to make sure they hadn't missed anything. When he had ticked them all off, he brought up the calendar. Once again, he noted Nielsen's visit to a pharmacy, Apotek Beckasinen in Farsta, on the Thursday before he died.

He flicked through one of the piles of documents and quickly found what he was looking for.

Marcus Nielsen had been in good health before his death and hadn't been on any medication. Nor did he suffer from any allergies.

So why had he made an appointment to visit a pharmacy in Farsta, far from both his apartment and his parents' house? If he needed something, surely he would have gone to the nearest place, for example in the Nacka Forum shopping mall, which was five minutes from where he lived.

Time to head over to Farsta.

Diary:

December 1976

We are not "punished." What happens must never be referred to as punishment. Our commanding officers issue "rewards."

Rewards.

We are rewarded with nonstop push-ups and endless repetitions of the rangers' rest position. We run around the yard when the temperature is below freezing or do frog jumps in the pouring rain.

I didn't know my body could hurt so much. My feet are the worst. Sometimes I don't even want to acknowledge my feet. The pain transforms them into enemies; when they refuse to obey me, they become symbols of the fact that my own body is working against me.

Every morning they are swollen, reminding me of what awaits me during the course of the day.

"You're worth no more than dogs," the sergeant says to us. "You must be trained to obey orders."

But dogs are treated better than we are. Dogs are given praise and encouragement to help them learn a certain pattern of behavior, not unrelenting physical punishment.

Kaufman lost his gas mask yesterday. He knew what to expect.

A reward, a special reward.

He searched all over the place, in ever-increasing circles, until he ended up standing at his locker, close to tears as he went through the contents for at least the tenth time. He was like a terrified child who has misplaced a new toy. He was so scared he didn't know what to do with himself.

The only thing he knew for sure was that the sergeant would come up with something particularly unpleasant as his reward.

The sergeant smiled when Kaufman eventually stammered out what had happened. It was almost as if he felt sorry for him. Then he pointed to the yard.

"Two circuits of frog jumps, on your knuckles."

The color drained from Kaufman's face.

His knuckles and the backs of his hands were already red-raw from countless push-ups on the gravel.

Every time the sores began to heal, it happened again.

"Can't I do something else? Anything at all—please, Sergeant!"

He was on the verge of tears.

The sergeant rocked back and forth on his heels as he considered Kaufman's request. He seemed bewildered.

"So . . . you're refusing to obey a direct order? Have I got that right?"

Kaufman shook his head.

He is one of the fittest members of the group, a former elite swimmer who usually holds out longer than most of us during the exercises. Not one of the smartest guys, but a good comrade. He does as he is told, without question.

Despite his broad back and muscular shoulders, at that moment he looked like a child afraid of being beaten as he begged for a little understanding.

"In that case, you'd better get started."

Kaufman did as he was told.

We stood there motionless, watching him frog jump around the yard as the sweat poured down his face. Toward the end, he was making small whimpering noises; he just couldn't help it.

When he completed the last circuit, he collapsed.

We had to carry him to the sick bay, where he was given a tetanus shot. The doctor said his hands would probably become infected, and the aftereffects could be with him for life.

Right now he is lying two beds away from me, and I can hear him moaning softly in his sleep.

He got his reward.

CHAPTER 26

Wednesday (The Second Week)

The Farsta Centrum really had a face-lift, Thomas thought as he parked the car. The sleepy shopping mall to the south of the city had grown and now offered a wider range of stores.

He slammed the door and waited for Margit to get out on the passenger side. It was twenty to eleven.

Apotek Beckasinen was located at the far end of the mall. There were plenty of people at the counter when they walked in, and Thomas noted that anyone who'd come in to fill their prescription would be fifteenth in line. Several elderly customers were sitting patiently waiting for their turn, while a man in a trench coat was staring angrily at the ticket he had just taken, as if he could speed things up by the sheer force of his irritation.

Thomas went over to a tall woman in a white coat at the information desk. According to her name badge, she was Annika Melin.

She favored him with an impersonal smile, no doubt expecting him to ask about a particular type of medication or where the fluoride tablets could be found. Something in her posture told him that she was used to dozens of questions like that every single day.

Thomas flashed his ID.

"Thomas Andreasson, Nacka police. We'd like to ask the manager a few questions."

The smile was replaced by a wary expression. Thomas always tried to sound reassuring in order to counteract the effect of his police ID; Annika's reaction was far from unusual.

"What's it about?" she said.

"I'd rather speak to the manager."

"That's me."

Margit stepped forward.

"We just want to ask you a couple of questions; it won't take long." Annika still looked dubious.

"Could we go somewhere a little more private for a few minutes?" Thomas suggested.

Annika Melin waved her hand. "We can talk in the break room."

Thomas noticed that she was wearing a loose maternity top under her white coat, which was unbuttoned. *She must be around five or six months along,* he thought.

Last night he had lain in bed with his hand on Pernilla's belly for a long time, trying to imagine the little life that was growing inside her. It was a miracle; there was no other word for it.

"When are you due?" he asked.

"Not for a while—after Christmas."

Annika let them in through a locked door and led the way to the break room. A coffeemaker was on, and there was an inviting sofa with green upholstery, the same color as the pharmacy's logo. A pile of medical magazines lay on the table.

"Coffee?"

Thomas shook his head, but Margit nodded. "Please."

As Annika poured two cups, Thomas sat down on the sofa. He waited until she had joined him.

"We're investigating a death, and we'd like to know whether a man named Marcus Nielsen has visited this pharmacy over the past couple of weeks."

"Marcus Nielsen?"

"This is a photograph of him," Margit said, handing over a picture. "He was twenty-two years old, and he was a psychology student. He'd made a note of an appointment here before he died."

"I don't . . . I mean, dozens and dozens of people come in here every day." Annika sipped her coffee, then put down the cup.

"I realize it's very busy, but he did look a little bit different from the norm, with his dyed black hair," Margit said encouragingly.

Annika pushed back her bangs and gently touched a bandage on her forehead.

"I'm sorry, I don't know how I can help you."

"We're trying to work out why the name of this pharmacy was in his phone," Thomas persisted.

Annika took another sip of her coffee.

"When I was pregnant, I couldn't even stand the smell of coffee," Margit said. "It's the only time in my life I've ever given it up."

Thomas, who had witnessed the countless cups of coffee Margit usually knocked back, could only agree. She was the epitome of all those clichéd cops who consumed undrinkable swill night and day.

"I haven't had any problems so far."

"Lucky you," Margit said with a smile.

Annika glanced at her watch. "Is this going to take long?"

Thomas shook his head. "We'd just like to show you some more photographs."

Margit spread out the pictures of Jan-Erik Fredell, Robert Cronwall, and Bo Kaufman.

"Do you know if any of these men have been here? They were also in contact with Marcus Nielsen shortly before he died."

Thomas noticed how different the three men looked when their photographs were placed side by side.

Fredell was marked by his illness, white-haired and gaunt. Bo Kaufman looked haggard, his face puffy. He was staring straight into the camera, and his expression reminded Thomas of an American "Wanted" poster.

Robert Cronwall, however, looked fit and well.

Margit pointed to Fredell.

"This man died last Saturday, not long after he'd spoken to Marcus Nielsen, and we're trying to find out if there's any connection between them."

Annika studied the photographs; she seemed confused more than anything.

"So you think this Marcus Nielsen came here?" she said eventually. "But why?"

"That's what we're trying to find out," Margit said.

"I realize it's not easy to recall one specific person," Thomas broke in. "But maybe you could show your colleagues these pictures, ask them to contact us if anyone remembers anything?"

Annika looked at her watch again. She sounded slightly irritated as she picked up the photograph of Marcus Nielsen.

"I'll ask around. I'm sorry, but I really have to get back to work now."

"OK," Margit said. "We won't keep you any longer, but please get in touch if anyone recognizes Nielsen."

Annika got to her feet. She ran a hand over her belly, then nodded.

DIARY:
DECEMBER 1976

Early tomorrow morning, we will be catching the ferry across Oxdjupet Sound and on to the island of Värmdö.

It is time for the Rangers' March, the fourth and final test before we are given the much-longed-for beret. Our training has just one purpose: to separate the wheat from the chaff. Those recruits who are not up to scratch will be dismissed.

It will be five days of hell, with insufficient food and sleep. The beret with its golden trident shimmers before us, along with those magic words: "Cap off—beret on!"

We are due to set off in a little while. It is pouring; the heavy rain started during the night. It has been hammering on the windows for hours.

I have checked my equipment three times to make sure I have everything I need.

Andersson has bound his feet in the hope that he will be able to cope. His soles are red and swollen after all these months of marching, but if he is to become a ranger, they will have to hold up.

We marched in nonstop rain. Fifty minutes' marching, ten minutes' rest. Every six hours, we took a food break, but more than once we didn't manage to eat anything, because the whistle blew to signal an ambush or something else, and we had to pack up immediately and move on.

Kaufman was in front of me, and I clung on to a strap on his pack, while behind me Andersson clutched the strap on my pack. Kihlberg led the way, with Sigurd bringing up the rear.

We kind of dragged one another along.

When we reached an embankment, the sergeant was waiting for us, legs apart.

"Listen to me, you pissheads. The quickest way to get across is to put one foot right in the middle."

Those who followed his advice got their feet soaking wet, then had to continue the march with sodden socks and boots.

He was just messing with us.

Day turned to night, night turned to day, and we carried on marching.

We all had blisters; the ones on the soles of our feet were the worst. When they burst, the skin became shredded; with every step I took, I was walking in my own blood and pus.

A sudden jerk on the strap stopped me in my tracks.

Andersson wasn't moving. He was standing there with his mouth open, staring straight ahead. Then he started babbling.

"Would you like some manure? That will be seventy-five kronor," he mumbled politely.

Utter nonsense was coming out of his mouth.

"Horse manure or cow dung?" he went on, looking past me to someone who wasn't there. "It's very good for the flower beds, particularly if you grow roses. Which would you prefer?"

He had fallen victim to what is known as a "field coma"; it happens to a lot of men, due to a combination of too little food and sleep, low blood sugar, and dehydration.

Andersson carried on talking about manure, and I looked around, wondering what to do.

Kihlberg came to the rescue. He produced a bar of chocolate that he had hidden in his pack and pushed a couple of squares into Andersson's mouth. That brought him back to us; his eyes were still wide open, but at least he was able to focus.

"Come on, we need to keep going," Kihlberg said. He placed the strap of my pack in Andersson's hand and wrapped his fingers around it, then gave him a push to get him moving.

After a while, it happened again. This time, it was Erneskog who lost the plot. He lay down on the ground and curled up, howling like a small child.

The sergeant came over and gave him a kick. "Are you a man or a mouse?" he yelled as Erneskog groaned. Eventually he whispered, "Mouse. Mouse, mouse."

Martinger managed to get him to his feet and half dragged, half carried him until we reached Myttingeviken.

Using a rope, we had to cross the inlet from the south to the north side where we were to pitch our tents and rest.

When we arrived, no one dared take off their boots; we knew it would be impossible to get them back on.

That's when I started to hallucinate.

I could smell food, and I saw a roast chicken right there in front of me. I reached out, convinced I was holding a leg and chewing on it. My jaws moved rhythmically as I devoured the food that wasn't there.

We are back in the barracks now, but I am still frozen. By the glow of a bonfire last night, we received our berets. All of us.

I have been awake for over ninety hours.

But we made it.

CHAPTER 27

Thursday (The Second Week)

Thomas had just gotten back to his office after the morning briefing when his phone rang. He didn't recognize the number on the display.

"Andreasson."

"Hi—my name is Susanna Albäck. I'm Marcus Nielsen's supervisor."

She doesn't sound very old—thirty at the most, Thomas thought.

"Thanks for calling."

"I'm sorry I didn't get in touch earlier; I was at a conference in Paris, and I had problems with my voice mail. I wasn't able to access my messages until today. What's this about?"

Thomas explained the situation, and the sharp intake of breath on the other end of the line made it clear that Susanna Albäck had had no idea that one of her students was dead.

"Oh my God," she said, unable to suppress a sob. "Excuse me a minute."

Thomas heard the sound of a tissue being pulled from a box; he waited for her to blow her nose and compose herself.

"How can I help you?" she said eventually.

"We're trying to get a picture of the last few days of Marcus's life, but we can't find his laptop. I'm wondering if there's anything you might know about his studies that could help us move forward."

"That's odd—Marcus always had his laptop with him."

Susanna's comment strengthened Thomas's suspicions that someone had stolen Marcus's computer.

"We've searched everywhere—in and around his apartment and at his parents' house—but there's no sign of it, so we were hoping you might be able to help us instead. What was Marcus working on before his death? Are there any e-mails from him or any assignments he handed in that we could take a look at?"

There was a brief silence, and Susanna's voice was thick with tears when she spoke.

"I'm at home right now, but I can go over to the university and pick up everything I have from Marcus."

"That would be great. I'd appreciate it if you'd call me back as soon as you can," Thomas said.

Susanna Albäck called back within the hour. Thomas was talking to Margit when her number appeared on the display screen.

"I've gathered together all of Marcus's work," she said.

"Excellent—can you scan it and e-mail it to me?"

Susanna sounded hesitant.

"Unfortunately we don't have the technology to do that; is it OK if I photocopy everything and mail it to you instead? It should get to you by tomorrow."

"That's fine."

Margit nudged him. "Ask her what she's found," she whispered.

"What kind of material will you be sending over?"

There was a rustling sound, as if Susanna was leafing through a pile of papers.

"I've got the outline of the assignment he was working on, plus a list of his sources. The title of the assignment is 'Group Dynamics in a Closed Environment.'"

"What does that mean?" Thomas switched to speakerphone so that Margit could hear.

"Marcus was in his third semester of the psychology program, and this fall he was taking an elective on the structures and processes that affect the interplay between individuals in a variety of group situations."

"Hmm." That was the best response Thomas could come up with; high-flown academic language wasn't exactly his thing.

"The emphasis is on norms, leadership, decision-making, and conflict within and between groups."

Susanna Albäck had adopted a slightly pedagogical tone, as if she were in a lecture room, and Thomas wondered if all university tutors were equally long-winded. Maybe she had fallen back on a familiar pattern in order to handle her own insecurity.

"The course also deals with verbal and nonverbal communication, together with relevant research methods."

"Sorry to interrupt, but could you maybe explain what Marcus was working on in more concrete terms?"

"Of course—forgive me. Students in that class have to describe and analyze the structures and processes within a particular group. They were given the assignment at the beginning of the semester, four weeks ago."

"OK."

"They have to write an essay of around thirty pages, analyzing a real situation within a theoretical and historical context. They're studying the theory of group dynamics, and that's their starting point."

"Which group did Marcus choose?"

"He wanted to look at how groups in a military environment function under extreme pressure."

Thomas and Margit exchanged a look.

"The way external pressures affect group dynamics and group loyalties," Susanna went on. "What happens to internal norms as a consequence of external factors."

"Could you translate that into layman's terms?" Margit asked.

"My colleague Margit Grankvist is listening in," Thomas explained.

"Marcus had decided to write about a military unit," Susanna went on. "He did some research and interviewed several people, then opted for a corps that makes a point of exposing its recruits to difficult ordeals."

"What do you mean by that?" Thomas asked.

"Certain military organizations carry out exercises that could be regarded as both cruel and inhumane; their aim is to weed out those who aren't up to the mark." Susanna paused. "The theory is that those who succeed form an unbreakable bond, while at the same time building up a strong self-image, both individually and collectively, which, in turn, is reinforced by the group. Their loyalty is unquestionable, and gradually a so-called elite force is created."

"And this was Marcus's focus?" Margit asked.

"Yes. The idea was that he would study how such a group functioned in difficult physical and mental circumstances, and how this affected the internal dynamics. He also wanted to investigate whether there was any long-term effect on the members of the group many years later."

"Do you know which branch of the military he went for?" Thomas asked.

A telephone rang in the background, and Susanna excused herself. They heard her telling someone she would call them back in ten minutes.

"Sorry, can you repeat the question?

"Which branch of the military did Marcus choose?"

There was a pause as Susanna flicked through the papers again.

"The Coastal Artillery," she said. "He was going to write about a unit from 1976."

"Why so long ago?" Margit wanted to know.

"Apparently things were really tough back then. I think several incidents were recorded in the seventies, which would make the case study more interesting."

"Which unit was he looking at?"

"The Coastal Rangers."

CHAPTER 28

Karin Ek came into Thomas's office carrying a blue plastic envelope.

"This is the copy of that photograph you wanted. Shall I send back the original?"

"Please. Thanks for your help."

Karin placed the copy of Bo Kaufman's photograph on the desk and left the room. Thomas heard her cell phone ring in the corridor, then her voice telling someone, presumably her youngest son, not to forget his kit before he went to judo.

He slid the picture out of the envelope to take a closer look. It must have been taken on a summer's day; there were wildflowers in the grass in front of the young men on the shore. There were six of them apart from Kaufman, and they knew the names of four: Jan-Erik Fredell, Sven Erneskog, Stefan Eklund, and the guy whose surname was Kihlberg. The other two were still unidentified.

A group of Coastal Rangers who had served together well over thirty years ago. One of them was dead. Marcus Nielsen, who had been interested in this unit, was also dead.

What had happened to the rest of them?

Thomas logged on to his computer and decided to start with the men whose first and last names he knew. He typed in "Sven Erneskog."

The search results showed only one person in the whole country by that name. He lived in Västerås, and his address was Graningevägen 7. No one else was registered with the same phone number.

He tried Stefan Eklund and found thirteen people by that name, in several different locations throughout the country. It was impossible to work out which of them had done his military service on Korsö in the midseventies.

Next he typed in Kihlberg. There were over fifteen hundred people with that surname in Sweden; without a first name, it would be impossible to find him. He would have to ask Karin Ek to look into Kihlberg and Stefan Eklund, but, meanwhile, he could try to dig up more information on Erneskog.

He found the relevant ID number and checked for both criminal records and those suspected of crime.

Nothing.

Thomas thought for a moment. If Erneskog had featured in any kind of investigation, the details would be recorded in the systems linked to the relevant local police authorities. Right now, the nationwide database they had been wanting for so long would have been invaluable; he could simply have looked up Sven Erneskog, and all available information would have appeared on his screen. As it was, he was going to have to speak to someone in the district where Erneskog was a resident.

He reached for the phone and called the police authority in Västermanland.

"Hasse Rollén," came the response after a few rings.

Thomas introduced himself and outlined the situation. He asked Rollén to check if there was anything more on Erneskog in their database.

"No problem."

Thomas waited, and after a few minutes Rollén was back.

"The guy is dead."

"Are you sure?"

"Yes."

"When did he die?"

"A week and a half ago."

"Could you be more specific?"

"He died on September 16."

Thomas realized he was breathing more rapidly.

"How did he die?"

"Let me see . . . He was found dead in his own home."

"Can you give me any details?"

"You'll have to speak to the officer in charge of the case—Detective Maria Mörk."

"Do you have a number where I can reach her?"

Rollén gave him the number, and Thomas thanked him for his help and ended the call. He sat there holding the phone; another person in the photograph was dead, and he'd died the same weekend as Marcus Nielsen.

There was no way that could be a coincidence.

He tried Maria Mörk, but there was no reply. It was almost eight o'clock in the evening; she had probably gone home.

He stood up, yawning. He had been working for over twelve hours; no wonder he felt exhausted. Mörk could wait until tomorrow.

He left a note for Karin, asking her to check out the thirteen men named Stefan Eklund. All of a sudden, he felt it was urgent to track down everyone from that old photograph.

CHAPTER 29

It was seventeen minutes past eight by the time Thomas got in the car to drive home. He couldn't get the photograph of the Coastal Rangers on the shore out of his mind. He had been on the island of Korsö many times, because the maritime police had an overnight cabin there, but he knew nothing about its history.

Impulsively he pressed Nora's number on speed dial before pulling out of the parking lot.

"Hi, it's Thomas."

"Hi—you're very crackly!"

"I'm in the car. I wanted to ask you something, since you have such a strong connection to Sandhamn. What do you know about the Coastal Rangers' operations on Korsö?"

"Korsö? Why?"

"We're involved in an investigation that might have links to the island."

"I've just walked through the door. Give me a few minutes, and I'll call you back."

Nora went into the living room and sat down on the sofa with the phone in her hand. She kicked off her shoes and tucked her legs beneath her.

What did she know about Korsö?

She pictured the tower, the dark, brooding structure by Sandhamn's eastern inlet. Korsö was a fortified island that had always been a no-go area when she was growing up. As a child, she sometimes saw soldiers in camouflage gear paddling by with serious expressions on their faces.

She had never been ashore.

She called Thomas back.

"Hi. I don't know much, but I think most of the military activity was wound down in the nineties. What's this about? You sound so mysterious!"

"You haven't heard any stories?" Thomas asked. "Any strange rumors?"

"I remember some TV reporters trying to get ashore in the nineties; there was a hell of a fight."

A TV news program had decided to try and prove that the military surveillance on the island was lax. They had anchored a sailboat offshore with the aim of filming some activity; before they knew what was happening, the boat had been boarded by the Coastal Rangers.

Instead of pictures of top-secret military facilities, the press coverage featured the journalists themselves, lying on the beach with their hands bound behind them, guarded by grim-faced soldiers holding automatic weapons. Needless to say, the rival TV stations were only too happy to carry the story.

"I remember that, but I'm looking for old injustices or scandals—does that ring any bells?"

"What do you mean?" Nora asked.

Thomas sounded hesitant, as if he wasn't sure what he wanted.

"I can't be any more precise, but sometimes there's old gossip, something that stands out."

Nora discovered a small run in her tights, and she couldn't help picking at it. Needless to say, it immediately ripped up her leg, becoming at least twice as long as it had been when she'd found it. She sighed; she was going to have to throw the tights away.

"Actually, forget it," Thomas went on. "I don't really know what I'm looking for. I just thought I'd ask, since your family has lived on Sandhamn for such a long time."

Nora recalled the conversation with Olle Granlund down by the jetty.

"I'm afraid I don't know much, but I have a neighbor on Sandhamn who did his military service on Korsö many years ago. I could ask him if you like."

"OK. Don't go to any trouble, but if you're going over there this weekend, maybe you could speak to him."

Nora pictured the inlet: the eighteenth-century customs house behind the Falu-red homes, white buoys bobbing off the jetties. Jonas, smiling as he raised his glass in the Divers Bar.

Should she go over on Friday? Why not?

"I think I will," she said. "The boys are with Henrik this week, so I'm on my own. I'll talk to Olle."

"Call me if you find out anything interesting."

"Absolutely, or maybe we can meet there? Aren't you and Pernilla going to Harö?"

"Probably, unless I have to work."

"In that case, why don't you come over for dinner?"

"That would be good. I'll call you on Saturday."

Nora remembered the news report from the other evening.

"By the way, I saw you on TV—there was a story about the murder of one of my old teachers, Jan-Erik Fredell. Are you involved in the case?"

"Something like that." All of a sudden, Thomas didn't have much to say.

Nora had once bumped into her teacher on the subway. He had been in uniform, with a green beret on his head. He had told her he was on his way to a refresher course.

"He was a Coastal Ranger, wasn't he?" she said. "Is that why you're asking questions about Korsö?"

Nora remained sitting in the dark when the conversation was over.

Thomas had completely clammed up when she'd asked about Fredell and Korsö. She was a little irritated, to be honest—first of all, he was the one who'd called her. And he had asked the questions, then refused to explain when she wondered why. She hadn't managed to get anything out of him.

It was almost as dark inside as outside, but she couldn't be bothered to switch on the lights. Instead she sank back against the cushions.

Tomorrow it would be Friday, the end of the week. The weekends were always hard when she didn't have the boys with her. She could fill the weekdays with work, and occasionally she would go to the gym or meet up with a friend for a glass of wine or to see a chick flick.

But weekends were family time; no one was interested in getting together with a lone divorcée. Perhaps it was just as well; Nora had been invited over for dinner by her married friends a few times, and the experience had proved less than pleasant.

People didn't know how to react to the divorce, which meant the atmosphere around the table was pretty strained. Some assured her that they didn't want to take sides, then launched into long explanations about how difficult it was to invite Henrik and Nora to the same party. Others wanted her to open up and were quite persistent with their questions about Henrik's new partner. What did Nora think of Marie? How did she feel about the fact that Marie had moved into Nora's former home? How were the boys coping?

The questions kept on coming, in spite of Nora's efforts to change the subject. Afterward, she'd tell herself that she wasn't prepared to go through that again.

So she had stopped seeing some of their mutual friends. She had completely lost contact with the sailing gang, whom Henrik had known since he was a child. Not that she was losing any sleep over them . . .

Wearily, she got to her feet and switched on the light, then she picked up the remote control; it was time for the news.

She really ought to make herself something to eat, but she didn't feel like anything in particular. She had also forgotten to go shopping, so all she had in the house was cereal and yogurt. However, signs of a dip in her blood sugar levels meant that she had to eat very soon.

All at once, she felt a deep longing for Sandhamn and the calm she always found on the island. If she packed a bag tonight, she could go straight from work tomorrow. She might even leave an hour or so earlier than usual to avoid the traffic.

The loneliness was easier to bear on Sandhamn, despite the fact that the Brand villa was more than twice as big as her apartment. If she felt lonely, she could always pop over to see her parents or acquaintances she had known all her life, or simply exchange a few words with a neighbor over the fence.

On Sandhamn it didn't matter whether she was married or single. No one cared about her recent separation. When she was there, she was simply herself, simply Nora.

Diary:
January 1977

It's time for ice training. We are going to march all day, with a full pack, of course, then we have to get ourselves across the channel to Vaxholm in the pitch dark. The temperature has been around minus ten for several weeks, so they have to open the shipping lane with an icebreaker every other day.

The channel looks like a black gash in the ice, a wide, gaping mouth filled with gray ice floes aimlessly drifting along.

The ice is slippery, even though it is rough, and the floes tip over if you put your foot in the wrong place. You have to keep moving, otherwise you'll fall in.

The sergeant has explained how to get across to the other side by jumping from one floe to the next.

Last year, a guy fell in. According to the sergeant, he developed pneumonia and had to be sent home. He smiled, and the scorn in his eyes was unmistakable.

Then he fixed his gaze on Andersson. He stared at him for a long time without saying another word, as if he already knew that Andersson was doomed to fail.

The message was clear: "Tomorrow is going to be hell, and I will be watching."

"Are you asleep?"

I had almost dropped off when Andersson's voice reached me through the darkness. Everything was quiet, apart from the sound of someone snoring over by the door. A strip of white light from the full moon shone in through the nearest window.

"Are you asleep?" he said again.

"Almost," I mumbled.

"I don't know if I've got the nerve to jump on the ice floes tomorrow."

His voice was muffled, strained, as if he were on the verge of tears. I pushed the thought aside; Coastal Rangers don't cry.

"I nearly drowned in a hole in the ice when I was little. My dad managed to pull me out at the last minute."

I turned over; it was hard to make out his features in the gloom, but I could tell he was facing me.

"It'll be fine."

"What if it isn't?" The words were little more than a whisper.

I could hear faint noises now, sighs and exhalations from the others in the room. The silhouettes of sleeping bodies under gray blankets were just visible. Kaufman was lying on his back, snuffling like a big baby.

"They're not trying to kill us," I attempted to reassure Andersson, "even if it sometimes feels that way. It's all part of the game, you know that."

I was hoping for a casual tone, but all I achieved was clumsiness. "They will only let us out onto the ice if everything is OK. It'll be fine."

I heard something like a cross between a cough and a sob.

"Are you sure?" His voice a little steadier now. "Is that what you really think?"

"Absolutely."

I injected a confidence I didn't feel into my voice.

"If you do fall in, we'll pull you out. That's all there is to it; you won't be the first. They probably intend for some of us to fall in so we can use our ice claws and practice our rescue technique."

I turned over.

"We need to get some sleep; they'll be waking us up very early. You heard what the sergeant said."

Andersson didn't say anything. Sigurd coughed and tugged at his blanket in his sleep.

Once again, I was struck by how much Andersson reminds me of my kid brother. The same puppyish movements, the same eagerness to belong. What are you doing here if you're scared of a channel in the ice? I thought. What the hell are you doing here?

By the time we reached the channel, we were already exhausted from the march. I could see my breath in front of my face, and the ice-cold air seared my lungs. I sank to my knees panting, desperate for a few seconds' rest before it was my turn.

Somehow, I got across. Andersson was behind me. He was the last man in our group; everyone else had already made it. When I looked around, he was out there among the floes.

He was bobbing up and down, trying to jump from floe to floe. The beam of the lighthouse swept across the ice, illuminating his face. It was as gray as the ice. He was terrified, scared of going on, even more scared of staying put. His eyes were wide open, total panic just seconds away.

The ice was creaking all around us.

Suddenly he seemed to lose his balance. He wobbled, and I inhaled sharply. I moved forward; if he fell, I had to try and pull him out, even though I knew I wouldn't get there in time.

Out of the corner of my eye, I could see the sergeant. He was standing perfectly still, his face expressionless.

Andersson's arms flailed as he tried to regain his balance; I didn't think he was going to do it. But then, suddenly, he somehow managed to leap onto another floe and then another, and all at once he was by my side.

He sank to the ground, utterly spent. The only sound was his deep, labored breathing. I saw that his brow shone with sweat as the beam of the lighthouse swept by once more. I reached out to help him up.

"Come on, we need to get going—we don't want to lose the others."

The sergeant had already given the rest of the group the signal to move on. Kihlberg was lingering at the edge of the forest, waiting for us.

"I'm coming," Andersson mumbled. "I'm coming."

Then he bent forward and threw up all over his boots.

CHAPTER 30

Friday (The Second Week)

The morning briefing had already begun when Thomas arrived, bringing with him the report from the National Forensics Laboratory.

"Sorry," he said, holding up the bundle of papers. "The printer was acting up."

"What have you got there?" the Old Man wanted to know.

"The analysis of the rope Marcus Nielsen used to hang himself. They must have a night owl working at the lab—the e-mail arrived at midnight."

He had everyone's attention.

"So?" Margit said impatiently, leaning back and folding her arms.

"They've found fibers on the rope that don't match anything Marcus Nielsen was wearing," Thomas said, looking around at his colleagues. "And someone else's DNA."

"What does that mean?" Erik Blom said, clicking his pen.

"It means we can match the DNA to a possible perpetrator."

"Or we can identify a store assistant who sells rope," the Old Man said dryly.

Of course he is right, Thomas thought. DNA in itself wasn't particularly useful at this stage, but it could eventually provide evidence linking the killer to Marcus's death and might be a key factor when the prosecutor had to decide whether or not to charge someone with the crime.

If it was a crime, and not a suicide.

"Better than nothing," Margit said. "And it came through more quickly than usual. How long will it take to run the results against the DNA register?"

"A while, I should think," Erik said.

Thomas nodded.

"Unless we have a suspect and we're looking for a match," Margit added.

"It's the same as with fingerprints," the Old Man muttered. "These results can only help us if we're dealing with a perp who's already in the database." He scratched the back of his neck. "But at least it's a start," he conceded.

He turned to Kalle Lidwall, who hadn't said a word so far. He seemed to be in a world of his own, but he straightened up when he realized the Old Man was looking at him. Kalle was the youngest member of the team, but he was a wizard when it came to computers.

"Kalle, can you monitor this development?"

"Sure."

Kalle picked up his pen and opened his notebook. Thomas was interested to see that it wasn't standard issue; instead it looked like an old-fashioned hardback book with a gilded leather cover. Thomas knew they were being sold in trendy bookstores; Pernilla had bought one. He found it amusing that his quiet colleague was suddenly showing signs of good taste.

"What about their phones?" the Old Man asked. "Any luck there?"

Kalle found the relevant page in his expensive notebook.

"Jan-Erik Fredell didn't have a cell phone, but we've gone through his landline records. We also checked out Marcus Nielsen's cell."

"Did you find anything interesting?"

"Marcus called both Cronwall and Fredell; the dates match the information they gave us, and Fredell's incoming calls. However, we didn't find any attempt to contact the last person on his list."

"You mean Bo Kaufman," Margit supplied.

"That's right."

"Kaufman said he hadn't been in touch."

"Which is probably true," Kalle said. "But he did call another person of interest."

"Who?" Thomas asked.

"Sven Erneskog—the name you gave us after you'd spoken to Kaufman."

Thomas sat up a little straighter.

"Sven Erneskog," Margit repeated slowly. "One of the soldiers in the photograph Kaufman showed us."

"He's dead," Thomas informed them quietly.

"What did you say?" the Old Man snapped.

"Sven Erneskog is dead. I spoke to the Västerås police late last night. He died less than two weeks ago."

Kalle let out a low whistle, and Margit gave Thomas a reproachful look. He realized it had been a mistake not to mention this right away, but he had wanted to wait until he had gotten ahold of Maria Mörk and found out the details.

"How did he die?"

"I'm afraid I don't know; I was only told that he's dead."

He glanced at his watch to see how long it had been since he'd tried to contact Maria Mörk.

"I left a message for the officer in charge of the case, but she hasn't gotten back to me yet. I'll try her again if she doesn't call soon."

The Old Man leaned back, and his chair creaked alarmingly. He weighed at least forty pounds too much, and there was no doubt that he was on the verge of obesity. He ignored every well-meaning attempt to get him to lose weight; in fact, he was the first one to reach for the buns and cookies that sometimes appeared at their morning briefings. His wedding ring was so deeply embedded in his swollen finger that it was barely visible.

Regardless, his ability to lead an investigation was impressive, and he was very good at handling prosecutors and his superiors, leaving his team to work in peace, even though he found the budget constraints that rained down from above more than a little wearing.

He turned to Thomas.

"There's something strange about this whole thing. You were right all along; it can't possibly be a series of suicides."

Thomas hadn't expected a pat on the back; it wasn't the Old Man's style.

Margit got up and went over to the whiteboard and the photos of Marcus Nielsen and Jan-Erik Fredell. She picked up a marker and added Sven Erneskog's name in big letters.

"Kalle, I want you to find out as much as you can about this guy," the Old Man said. Kalle nodded.

"We also need to find the other men who were in Bo Kaufman's photograph," Thomas said. "Karin, did you get my message? Could you get on that as quickly as possible?"

"Absolutely—as soon as we're done here."

"Margit, how about a trip to Berga?"

"Berga?"

"Good idea," said the Old Man, who knew what Thomas was getting at. "That's where the Coastal Rangers headquarters is based these days. It's time you spoke to someone about their activities on Korsö in the seventies."

CHAPTER 31

As if someone had been eavesdropping on the morning briefing, there was a note on Thomas's desk when he got back to his office.

Maria Mörk from the Västerås police called, it said. He didn't recognize the handwriting, but they had a temporary receptionist at the moment, so presumably it had come from her.

He sat down and returned the call. When his colleague answered, Thomas briefly introduced himself.

"I tried to get ahold of you this morning, but you were in a meeting," Maria said.

Thomas opened the drawer and took out the relevant folder, then reached for his notepad and pen.

"I have some questions about a man named Sven Erneskog, who died just over a week ago. I believe you're handling the case."

"That's right."

"Can you tell me what happened?"

"Let me check my notes . . . The message just asked me to call you; it didn't say why."

She put down the phone, and while Thomas was waiting, he studied the photograph Bo Kaufman had lent him. He was even more certain now that tracking down Stefan Eklund and the others was a matter of urgency.

Maria was back. "OK, let's see . . . It was the neighbor who found Erneskog. They always used to take a walk on Sunday mornings, but on this particular day, Erneskog didn't show up."

Marcus Nielsen had also been found dead on Sunday morning, and the pathologist had established that he must have died between ten on Saturday night, and two a.m. the following day.

It was hard to believe that this could be a coincidence.

"The neighbor waited a while, then went and rang the doorbell. He also tried phoning, and when no one answered, he got worried. According to him, Erneskog was always on time."

Old military habits, Thomas thought. Military precision that had never left him, even though over thirty years had passed?

"The neighbor had a spare key, so he let himself in. He discovered Erneskog's body inside."

"How did he die?"

"He drowned."

Thomas stiffened.

"Can you repeat that?"

"He drowned. He was found in his bathtub."

So two men who had been Coastal Rangers in the same platoon had died in exactly the same way.

"Was there an autopsy?"

"Of course; it's standard practice when someone dies at home, but I don't know if we've received the results yet. Hold on." She put down the phone again. After a minute, she picked it up again. "No, we haven't had the report yet, but it wasn't prioritized."

"Could you give me the name of the person who's doing the autopsy?"

"Sure, but I'll have to get back to you—I'll find out the details and e-mail you later."

"Did CSI check out the apartment?"

"Do you think we're just plain old country folk here in Västerås?" Maria said. She still sounded pleasant, but her tone was a little sharper.

"I'm sorry." Thomas backed off right away. "It wasn't a criticism, I was just wondering."

"Of course CSI was involved, even if we have no reason to suspect that a crime has been committed at this stage."

"So what are you thinking?"

"It seems to have been an accident. We found an empty whisky bottle in the bathroom. Getting in the bathtub when you've had too much to drink really isn't a good idea."

So Erneskog had been drunk when he died, just like Fredell.

"I understand."

"Presumably he fell asleep because of the booze and slipped under the surface without waking up."

"What did the apartment look like?"

"There was no indication that anyone else had been there, no signs of forced entry, no damage, and nothing was missing. Erneskog's wallet was in his pocket, and neither the TV nor the computer had been touched."

"Did he live alone?"

"Yes. He had a partner who had her own place, but she was away with a friend when he died."

"So she has an alibi."

"Yes. We've spoken to her, and she also confirmed that everything looks just the same as usual, and that nothing is missing." Maria paused. "As I said, there's absolutely no indication that a crime has been committed."

Thomas thought for a moment. Should he tell her about Fredell? He decided to leave it for the time being, at least until he had spoken to the pathologist.

"By the way, was there a smell of soap in the bathroom?"

"I don't remember, but if so, it would hardly be unexpected."

"This might sound strange, but I have to ask you one last question. Was Erneskog dressed when he was found in the bathtub?"

Maria laughed.

"No, of course not. Do you know anyone who takes a bath with their clothes on? He was naked, of course."

CHAPTER 32

There wasn't much traffic when they set off for Berga. Thomas took the freeway to Slussen, then stayed to the left so that he could take the exit onto the E73 to Nynäshamn.

Several ships were waiting patiently to pass through the lock from Lake Mälaren and out into the Baltic Sea. It still worked, but only just; the other day, the local newspaper had carried an article about the urgent need for repairs.

Thomas glanced at the dashboard clock. They had an appointment at thirteen hundred hours with a Captain Harning, who was apparently the information officer at the base.

Thomas had spent his naval training at the Muskö base not far away, so he knew the way to Berga. They passed the Globe Arena on the right, and, as always, he was amazed at the sheer size of the place. It looked like a close-up of an enormous white golf ball.

A tall woman greeted them with a firm handshake. Her blond hair was tied back in a sleek ponytail, and she was wearing a dark-blue uniform with gold epaulettes. In spite of the severity of her attire, Thomas thought she looked surprisingly feminine. Maybe it was partly due to her sheer tights.

"Captain Elsa Harning," she said before showing them where to sign in. She led them down a long corridor to a conference room with a wonderful view of the harbor. In the foreground, gray vessels lay moored at a pontoon, with white letters and numbers painted on their hulls, while red brick buildings were just visible on the right.

"This is the best view we can offer," she said. "There's coffee, too."

She pointed to the table, where coffee cups and a thermos awaited them. The chairs made Thomas think of old-fashioned English furniture.

"So how can I help you?" Elsa Harning asked.

"We'd like to ask you about a group of Coastal Rangers who trained back in the seventies," Margit began.

"The seventies? I'm afraid that's long before my time."

"We realize that," Thomas said. "I'm sure a great deal has changed since then."

"The Rangers are our elite force. They've existed in Sweden for over fifty years. As you may know, they used to be based outside Vaxholm; they moved to Berga relatively recently."

Thomas met her gaze.

"I have a summer cottage on Harö, not far from Korsö," he said.

"In that case, you know that operations on Korsö have been reduced."

"So I heard—why is that?"

"Why is that?" Elsa Harning repeated. "I guess you'd have to ask the government. They're the ones who make decisions about cuts in the defense budget. Fewer resources inevitably bring changes, not all of which are popular. One result of the latest review was the decision that it was necessary to relocate all activity to Berga."

"Can you tell us something about the Coastal Rangers?" Margit asked.

"What do you already know? Do you know how they operate?"

"It's probably better if you explain."

"The Coastal Rangers' role is primarily to gather intelligence for the other amphibious units. Their secondary function is combat, either in groups or in platoons. These are elite soldiers who undergo a demanding training program."

Margit listened with interest.

"Anyone who applies to become a ranger must be extremely fit," Captain Harning went on. "The selection process is rigorous and requires physical stability, a good physique, a wide range of abilities, and, of course, excellent eyesight, hearing, and general health."

Thomas thought back to when he had signed up for his own military service: young men standing in line, the embarrassment over the medical examination.

"Before they're accepted, they are subjected to a series of both physically and mentally taxing exercises; the aim is to test their willpower, strength, and attitude."

"Could you give us some examples?" Margit asked.

"They have to run six miles; they have to complete a route march carrying a full pack. They are also assessed by psychologists, doctors, and physiotherapists."

"Then what?" Thomas said.

"Those who are accepted follow an eleven-month training course based in the archipelago. The program is divided into blocks that include reconnaissance, nocturnal combat, interrogation techniques, weapons training, and specialist modules."

"Sounds tough," Margit commented, her narrowed eyes fixed on Elsa Harning.

"It's meant to test their boundaries, but within strict guidelines for peacetime versus critical combat situations. That training happens later, for when we're involved in peacekeeping operations overseas."

Margit frowned.

"You send Coastal Rangers overseas?"

"It has been known to happen."

"Do you ever make a mistake, take in someone who shouldn't be there?"

"You mean gun-crazy kids who just want to kill something?"

Margit was taken aback by Elsa's choice of words. Thomas noted how skillfully the captain had turned the question around. She was utterly professional in every way.

"Kind of," Margit said feebly.

"It does happen, but it's very rare. We use highly sophisticated evaluation models in order to avoid such an occurrence."

"Has that always been the case?"

"I'd like to think so, but of course everything improves over time."

"What was it like in the seventies?" Thomas asked.

"I can't answer that, but it wasn't so very long ago. There were more applicants back then, and they all went through the selection process."

Thomas took out the copy of Bo Kaufman's photograph and placed it on the table.

"We're trying to find out as much as we can about the recruits in this photograph. They were all in the same group as the man who gave it to us. This is him, in the middle of the picture. Bo Kaufman."

Elsa Harning picked it up and spent some considerable time examining it.

"When was it taken?"

"July 1977."

"Are they on Korsö?"

"Yes."

She gave him a sharp look.

"May I ask why you're looking for these men? We're happy to help the police in any way we can, of course, but it would be helpful to know what this is about."

"We're investigating a series of deaths over the past couple of weeks." Thomas leaned forward. "This is Jan-Erik Fredell," he said, pointing to the picture. "He was drowned in his own home last Saturday, even though he was already terminally ill with MS. Then we have Sven Erneskog, who died just under two weeks ago. Like Fredell, he drowned in his bathtub, although at the moment we can't say for sure whether he died from natural causes or not. Another person linked to Fredell and Erneskog has also died under suspicious circumstances."

A change in Elsa Harning's expression told him that she understood the gravity of their request.

Thomas went on: "Next to Erneskog is Stefan Eklund, then we have a man called Kihlberg—we don't know his first name, and it's a fairly common surname. He was the group leader." He paused to take a sip of his coffee. "We know nothing about the other two—we don't have their names or any information about where they live."

"We need details about the members of this group so that we can access their ID numbers and track them down," Margit clarified, gazing steadily at Elsa Harning.

Thomas took over once more.

"Just to summarize: We are dealing with a number of deaths, of which at least one was definitely homicide. The only link we have been able to establish so far is that two of the three victims did their military service together in the seventies, and the third victim had shown an interest in their military background. That's all we have, I'm afraid."

If Elsa Harning was worried about the information Thomas had just passed on, she showed little sign of it. However, her expression was alert, and she was listening carefully. She started to twist her elegant ladies' watch back and forth around her wrist—maybe she wasn't quite so calm after all.

"So that's why we need to get ahold of everyone in the group," Thomas concluded. "We'd like to speak to them all."

"I understand. I'll do my best to find the details you need, but that means asking someone to go through archive material that's thirty years old. Unfortunately not everything is computerized yet, so we may have to go through the documentation on microfiche, which takes time."

She glanced at her watch.

"It's already Friday afternoon, so I can't promise anything until after the weekend."

"The sooner the better," Margit said.

"I'll do what I can, but this kind of thing is dealt with by civilian staff, and they have fixed hours. Plus, they don't answer directly to me," Elsa said as she got up to show the visitors out. She stopped in the doorway and turned to Margit.

"Do you have a hypothesis about what's going on?"

"Not that we can discuss at this stage, I'm afraid."

The truth is that we don't have a hypothesis at all, Thomas thought. Every new development brought new questions.

Like a mirror that had been shattered in the middle, with the cracks shooting off in all directions.

CHAPTER 33

Thomas's cell phone rang as they were passing Skarpnäck on the way back to Nacke.

"Grönstedt here."

It took a couple of seconds for Thomas to realize that it was the forensic pathologist from Västerås. He must have picked up the message Thomas had left before they set off for Berga.

"I believe you have some questions about the autopsy on Sven Erneskog?"

The voice was deep, with a marked Skåne accent. Thomas wondered what a native of Skåne was doing in Västerås, but of course there could be any number of explanations.

"That's right. Have you carried out the autopsy?"

"No. We're behind. Staff shortage. It'll probably have to be Monday; I don't think we'll get around to him today."

"So you haven't looked at him?"

"Just a quick visual examination, that's all."

Thomas hesitated, then said, "We think Erneskog's death could be linked to one or more deaths in the Stockholm area."

Grönstedt inhaled sharply; the sound grated in Thomas's ear.

"That changes the situation. We'll prioritize the case."

"Could you do me a favor?" Thomas asked.

"Sure."

"Could you check to see if there are any finger marks, any traces of bruising, or anything else that could suggest the use of force?"

Grönstedt immediately understood what Thomas was getting at.

"You mean someone might have held him under the water?"

"Exactly."

"No problem." A brief pause. "So you don't think his death was an accident, in other words."

"You could say that. We had a very similar case in Stockholm a few days ago."

Thomas told him what Sachsen had found during the autopsy on Fredell.

"OK, thanks for that; I'll e-mail you a copy of the report as soon as we're done."

Thomas cleared his throat, and Grönstedt took the hint.

"Was there anything else?"

"Yes . . . Could you check for any traces of detergent on the body or in the lungs?"

"You mean like the detergent you'd use to clean the floor?"

"Exactly."

Lena Fredell looked around the bedroom. She had been cleaning for days, with a feverish intensity that drove her from room to room, and now there wasn't a speck of dust left anywhere. Every surface had been wiped down, every floor had been vacuumed or swept and mopped. She had defrosted the freezer and cleaned out the refrigerator.

Tiredness overwhelmed her; she sank down on a chair and let the tears come. She still hadn't slept at home since they had found Janne, and she had no intention of ever doing so again.

As soon as she had cleared away all traces of the strangers who had invaded her life with their loud voices and insensitive questions, she would hand the keys over to a realtor.

She could only think about what had happened for short periods; if she allowed her mind to dwell on it, she began to feel a heavy weight on her chest and she had difficulty breathing. What kind of person would attack a sick man who could barely move? They had been visited by a monster; that was the only possible explanation.

He had been inside their home; he'd walked around, forced Janne into the bathtub, then held him under the water until he drowned.

Lena shuddered. She could hardly bring herself to go into the bathroom. She kept seeing her terrified husband's face, the fear he must have felt when he couldn't get any air into his lungs as the water closed in above him.

Over the past few years, she had gradually come to terms with the knowledge that Janne was going to die. As his health deteriorated, the idea that she was going to be alone had solidified, until one day she understood that she had accepted it. It had become a part of their lives, as ordinary as waking up in the morning and going to sleep at night. He was going to die, and she would be widowed far too soon. Nothing could change that, however much she raged or wept.

That knowledge had taught her to make the most of the time they had together. Instead of getting upset about the challenges of his decline, she had appreciated the opportunity to make his life easier. She had experienced a new sense of happiness, even though the reality of their life together was a million miles from what they had planned.

Twenty-four years ago, she had made a solemn vow before the priest—in sickness and in health—and to her surprise, she discovered that there was joy to be found in adversity, too. The gratitude in her husband's eyes when she intuitively knew what he needed, without his having to say a word. The love expressed in a caress from a trembling hand.

It became her mission to make sure he could still find pleasure in life despite his failing body, and she was filled with an energy she hadn't known she possessed.

But she could never have imagined that he would leave her like this.

The funeral was due to take place next Friday at Nacka Church. She had gone through the details with the priest, chosen the hymns and the flowers. Afterward there would be refreshments in the community center. She couldn't bring herself to invite people back to the apartment. Not after what had happened.

Many of Janne's old friends had been in touch—friends who had disappeared during his illness but now wanted to say a last good-bye.

About time.

Where had they been during those hard years as he got sicker and sicker? She ought to tell them to go to hell, but she couldn't summon up the strength to make a proud gesture. As soon as all the practicalities were resolved, she was going to move. Annelie was a student in Gothenburg and liked the city. Lena had decided to settle there, close to her daughter.

She hauled herself to her feet with the help of the bedpost and opened the door of the closet. There were no more rooms to clean, but there was still plenty to sort out. She had to go through Janne's clothes; most of them would probably have to be thrown out, but some could be given away.

It took her an hour to finish the first closet. When she was done, she was left with two black plastic bags, one for the trash and one for the Red Cross. She opened the second closet, which also contained their photo albums and old papers.

She took out one of the albums; a smiling four-year-old with curly hair and rosy cheeks met her gaze, and Lena's eyes filled with tears once more.

Annelie had always been as bright as a button, a real daddy's girl. She had wound Janne around her little finger with no effort whatsoever.

Lena had asked the police to call Annelie and tell her what had happened; she just couldn't do it.

There were only the two of them left now.

She climbed up on a stool to reach the top shelf and noticed a space between the neatly labeled boxes. One was missing; where could it be?

Then she remembered. Janne had had it out when Marcus Nielsen came to visit. Had he allowed the young student to take it away with him? He was normally so meticulous when it came to documents and paperwork.

Why would he do such a thing?

CHAPTER 34

The wind had picked up by the time Nora boarded the ferry to Sandhamn. It was just after six, and dusk was falling. The sky was a little cloudy, but the forecast had promised fine weather. She was hoping for at least one good day over the weekend. Soon the autumn darkness would set in, with many months to wait for the light-filled evenings of the summer.

Nora shuddered. She liked being on the island in the fall, while at the same time she always felt melancholy when the summer came to an end, and she knew that cold and snow weren't far away.

She adjusted the sports bag hanging over her shoulder and nodded to the crewmember who was standing at the top of the gangplank, ready to haul in the ropes. As usual, she made her way to the stairs leading to the upper deck; like Simon, she enjoyed sitting by the cafeteria with its view of the rocks and skerries.

She looked around for a seat; there were usually plenty at this time of year, when hordes of tourists were no longer invading the boats. During the high season, it was hard to even find room to breathe on board, let alone choose where you wanted to sit.

Suddenly she spotted a familiar profile at a corner table, and her stomach flipped.

Jonas Sköld glanced up, and a big smile spread across his face.

"Hi—are you going over to Sandhamn for the weekend?"

Nora nodded. "Looks that way."

He stood up and moved his things.

"There's room here."

She sat down opposite him.

"Are you on your own?" Jonas asked. "No young men keeping you company this time?"

She shook her head. "Adam and Simon are with their father." With an enormous amount of effort, she managed to keep the bitterness out of her voice.

"So we both have a child-free weekend," Jonas said.

Nora tried to remember his daughter's name; he hadn't said much about her over dinner. They had been too busy talking about other things.

"Wilma's with her mom," he went on. "She's getting so grown up that soon I won't have any say in what she does; I suppose I should be grateful that she even turns up from time to time."

"So what does she think of Sandhamn?"

"She's hardly been over this year; as I said before, we had to change our plans because of my work schedule. I'm hoping she'll spend a few weeks with me next summer."

"The island is perfect for kids," Nora exclaimed. "There's so much to do—tennis, surfboarding, and plenty of other activities."

Jonas started to laugh. "Are you working for the tourist board? You're really selling the place!"

Nora couldn't help feeling embarrassed. "Sorry, I didn't mean to sound like a commercial." She ran a hand through her hair. "It's just that I've been there every summer since I was born, so I can't help sing its praises."

It was getting warm; Nora took off her jacket and hung it on the back of her chair, then unzipped her fleece top a couple of inches. "Anyway, I get the message—I won't keep on about it."

"No problem—I like Sandhamn, too." Jonas stood up. "Can I get you a drink?"

"A beer would be great."

She watched him as he headed for the counter. He was wearing a dark-blue wool sweater and jeans. Once again, she was struck by how good he looked. He wasn't conventionally handsome like Henrik, who had an almost Grecian profile. Jonas's features were somehow softer, more open. Henrik had dark hair and brown eyes, but Jonas's hair was more medium brown, as were his eyes.

She decided Jonas had lovely eyes. Shame he was so young . . .

He returned with two bottles of beer in one hand and two glasses in the other. He put them on the table and poured the foaming golden-brown liquid. It smelled wonderful.

"Cheers," Jonas said. "Thank God it's Friday."

Nora took a sip of the cold beer and felt her muscles begin to relax. She reached up and removed the clip holding her hair in place, allowing it to fall loose around her shoulders.

"Are you staying through Sunday?" Jonas asked.

"Yes. We swap after each weekend, so Adam and Simon won't be back until Monday afternoon. How about you?"

"I'm only staying until Sunday morning; I'm flying to Bangkok in the evening."

"Sounds amazing—you really do live a life of luxury."

"Not really." He put down his glass. "The new EU regulations mean we can work eleven hours straight. When we arrive at whatever destination we go straight to the hotel, then it's the same again on the return trip."

Nora must have looked surprised, because Jonas raised an eyebrow.

"There are advantages, of course. Sometimes we have free time between shifts when we can relax by the pool or do some shopping; you should see all the orders we get from friends and family. Some of the flight attendants take the opportunity to make a little extra on the side."

"Compared with writing credit agreements, it doesn't sound too bad."

Nora pictured her office at the bank, the piles of documents, the blue law book on her desk, the bookshelves packed with legal tomes and files.

A top hotel in Thailand seemed like a pretty appealing alternative.

The engines throbbed away in the background, and outside the wide windows, Nora could just make out the skerries as colorless silhouettes in the gathering dusk. The loudspeaker crackled behind them: "As we have no passengers disembarking on Idholmen this evening, we will be going straight to Sandhamn. Next stop Sandhamn."

Nora contemplated her tenant from beneath her lowered eyelids. It was easy to enjoy his company. He had taken off his sweater to reveal a short-sleeved shirt. He looked toned; no doubt he took care of his body.

What was she thinking? How embarrassing . . .

Jonas had draped one arm over the back of the booth and was holding his glass in the other hand. There was a hint of dark stubble on his cheeks, like a faint shadow. Nora had to stop herself from reaching out and touching him. Instead she closed her eyes and leaned back. The silence was relaxing. It was Friday, and she was on her way out into the archipelago. For the first time in what seemed like an eternity, a childless weekend didn't feel like an endless countdown of the hours until the boys were back with her.

She opened her eyes to find that Jonas was watching her.

DIARY:

FEBRUARY 1977

I'm worried about Andersson. The sergeant loves sending someone home. He's like a predator stalking his prey, and he seems to have decided that Andersson is the one he wants to break.

And I think Andersson can feel it. His face twitches, and he mumbles and twists and turns in his sleep.

It ought to be a relief for him to leave and never have to see the sergeant again, but every time I try to bring it up, he changes the subject.

Kihlberg does his best to cover for Andersson. He has been designated our group leader, and he takes care of us, just like Martinger.

The other day, we had to remake our beds eight times. In the evening, we were all cursing the sergeant.

Andersson more loudly than anyone else.

A little too loudly.

The sergeant had been standing in the corridor, and he heard every word. He came into the room grinning from ear to ear, delighted by the opportunity that had just presented itself.

Shit, *I thought.* What's he going to do now?

He ignored the rest of us and went straight over to Andersson.

"Chinese bow!" he roared. "Forehead on the floor!"

That is the worst punishment of all. The color drained from Andersson's face, then he bent down. He placed his hands on his back and adopted the position, so that his body resembled an upside-down V with only his forehead and toes touching the hard floor.

I saw the sweat break out on his face right away.

The Chinese bow is agony. After fifteen seconds, it feels as if your skull is in a vice; after thirty seconds, it is sheer torture.

Few men can manage more than a minute.

Andersson didn't last very long. He collapsed, writhing around with his eyes closed.

The sergeant looked at him in disgust.

"Fetch a spade!" he bellowed. He ordered the boy to dig a latrine with a depth of at least three feet. "Right now, Andersson!"

Andersson somehow dragged himself to his feet.

The temperature outside was minus thirteen, and it was snowing heavily. The snow filled the trench as fast as Andersson dug. He struggled for over an hour, but the ground was frozen solid. The only way to get through was to hack away, inch by inch.

He couldn't do it, of course.

I watched him through the window, a lone figure that looked like a shadow through the whirling snow. We should have been out there, but the sergeant had chosen to pick on him.

Eventually Andersson gave up and came in. There was a thin layer of ice and snow on his cap. He went over to the sergeant, who was sitting at a table playing cards with two fellow officers.

He stood to attention, shivering.

"Permission to stop digging, Sergeant," he said.

His lips were blue, and he was shaking so much he could hardly get the words out.

The sergeant raised his head, a quizzical expression on his face. He took a drag of his cigarette, then slowly stubbed it out. With his blond hair and his high forehead, he reminded me of an officer in an old war movie.

"Is the trench three feet deep?" he drawled.

Andersson shook his head. His hands were trembling, and the tips of his ears were white.

The sergeant laughed, but his eyes were cold, narrow slits in a face without a trace of compassion.

At that moment, I hated him.

"Pain is a higher form of pleasure, Andersson."

He returned to his game, selecting a card and tossing it onto the table.

"Come on, that's enough," said one of the other officers. His name was Lieutenant Kolsum, and he had a good reputation. He gestured toward Andersson.

"The kid's like a block of ice—let him come in and get warm."

The sergeant hesitated, then shrugged and took a card from the pile in front of him.

"Fill in the trench," he said without even glancing at Andersson.

CHAPTER 35

Saturday (The Second Week)

The hand unscrewing the bottle was far from steady.

Bo Kaufman swore. Why did it have to be so hard to open the god-damn bottle? He wiped his sweaty palm on the leg of his pants and tried again. A firm twist, and it was open. He took a long swig.

He had been drinking nonstop ever since the police had left the apartment. He knew he was in bad shape, worse than he'd been for a long time. He found it difficult to concentrate, and his whole body felt shaky.

It had been quite a while since he had eaten properly, but there was nothing in the refrigerator. He had run out of cigarettes, and this was his last bottle of booze. He would have to go down to the mall before the state-run liquor store closed for the weekend; otherwise, he would have to buy on the black market, which was the last thing he wanted to do. It was too expensive, and you could never be sure what kind of crap you were getting.

He went into the tiny bathroom for a piss. He tried to avoid look-ing at his reflection but unfortunately caught a glimpse as he stood over the toilet fumbling with his pants.

Jeez.

Why the fuck had the cops come snooping around?

When he was done, he splashed a little water on his face and under his arms. Then he brushed his teeth for the first time in days and went to find a clean T-shirt. He had to make a bit of an effort if he was going to buy booze; if he looked like shit, they might refuse to serve him. It had happened to him before.

When he walked into the bedroom, his legs gave way, and he sank down on the unmade bed.

He had tried to keep the memories at bay for over thirty years. It had cost him his wife, a decent life, a relationship with his son.

He was still terrified.

When the cops had started asking questions, he hadn't dared say anything. He had pretended that he didn't know what they were talking about, as if he didn't remember.

He was just as cowed today as he had been back then. The booze was the only thing that made the fear loosen its grip, kept the blackness that scratched and tore at him at bay.

For many years, he had managed to hold down his job as an electrician. He pulled himself together during the day and drank only in the evenings and on weekends. He needed his car to get around, so he didn't take any risks; he didn't want to get caught out in a police check.

Things had been pretty good when the boy was little. He had put his son first, tried not to give in. They had been happy for a while.

But gradually the nightmares came back, and the only thing that made life bearable was the vodka trickling down his throat.

How many times had he told himself that he would stop? Before everything went to rack and ruin.

Empty promises.

When the boy became a teenager, that was the end of it. He was ashamed of his father and went off with his friends instead of doing his schoolwork. Eva got sick of nagging. For years, she had begged him to seek help. She'd threatened to leave him if he didn't quit drinking, and in the end that was exactly what she did.

Deep down, he had always known that he would end up like this. He had expected to be abandoned; he didn't deserve any better.

Not after what he had done.

There was no help out there. It was too late.

The shrill sound of the telephone sliced through the silence, and Bo Kaufman gave a start. He rarely got a call, so rarely that he almost appreciated it when some young telemarketer tried to sell him something he didn't need. At least it was a human voice; he particularly liked the young girls who wanted him to sign some kind of contract.

He got up and went to the phone in the hallway. Just as he was about to pick up, it stopped ringing. He stood there staring foolishly at the receiver, which was covered in grubby fingerprints.

It rang again.

"Kaufman," he said hoarsely.

He didn't recognize the voice but answered the question anyway.

"Yes, I'm home."

DIARY:
MARCH 1977

I panicked when we were doing our gas mask test this morning. Worse than that—I collapsed completely.

They lined us up and pushed us into a gas-filled room, two at a time. There was so much smoke that we couldn't see a thing; the officers had to use flashlights to show the way to the exit, otherwise we would never have found our way out.

Our instructions were crystal clear. We were to enter the room, take off the mask, and take a deep breath before putting it back on again. Then we had to ask permission to leave the room, using the correct form of address, in order to be let out.

During the briefing, we learned that mustard gas smells of garlic, while nitrogen mustard has a distinct fishy odor. Nerve gas kills in minutes.

I grew more and more anxious as we stood in line. My fellow recruits returned one after the other, sounding as if they were coughing up their lungs.

Kaufman came hurtling out; he fell to his knees and threw up, retching until there was nothing left but bile. He stayed there for quite some time, his whole body shaking.

By the time it was my turn, I was already having difficulty breathing, and my head was pounding. I put on my mask but remained standing in the doorway. A hard shove from the sergeant, and I stumbled into the dark room.

"Go!" he mumbled behind his mask.

I took a few more steps. Beside me, I saw two members of our group gasping for air, a glassy look in their eyes.

With trembling hands, I took off the mask and inhaled.

The effect was instantaneous.

I wanted to throw up, I wanted to spit, I wanted to cough. My neck and hands, which were unprotected, felt as if they were on fire, and I immediately put the mask back on. It didn't help. I thought I was going to die right there.

Martinger grabbed ahold of me. He seemed to be immune to the gas in some strange way. Afterward, I found out that some people don't have a reaction; the gas doesn't affect them.

He dragged me out of the room and held on to me when I tried to pull off the mask to get some fresh air.

"Calm down!" he yelled. "Breathe into the mask, you have to breathe into the mask."

I spewed phlegm and mucus everywhere as I screamed uncontrollably. I struck out at him, desperate to free myself and rip off the black rubber mask.

Martinger held on tight.

Later, he explained that the gas remains on the clothes. If I had removed the mask, the fumes in my clothing would have gotten into my eyes and nose, making everything much worse.

My eyes are still sore. I will never forget the panic I felt.

CHAPTER 36

It was after one, and Nora was feeling restless. She had slept well and hadn't woken until nine—almost a personal record.

After a leisurely breakfast, she had decided to take things easy. She had brought some paperwork from the bank, but that could be her Sunday evening reading. She had no desire to think about her job this weekend; instead she had settled on the veranda with a book.

She went into the kitchen to make a hot drink—equal parts coffee and milk. She had drunk it that way ever since she was a teenager.

Nora still hadn't quite gotten used to the idea that Aunt Signe's kitchen was now hers, even though she had brought in a lot of her own possessions. Signe's net curtains were still there, freshly washed but unchanged.

She sat down at the old folding table. The white wooden chairs were battered and worn, but Nora liked them. Not everything had to be shiny and new.

Through the window, she could see the rowan tree, laden with berries. According to folklore, that meant a hard winter to come. The leaves had begun to change color, turning red and gold.

Olle Granlund was busy down by the boathouses, and Nora remembered her promise to Thomas; she was supposed to ask her neighbor about Korsö. She pulled on her jacket and stuck her feet in a pair of deck shoes that had seen better days. She closed the door behind her and went down to the jetty.

"Hi, there," she called out. "How are you?"

Olle turned around.

"Hi, Nora—are you coming over here every weekend?"

"It looks that way at the moment."

She sat down on the bench, which was set on the rocks. Pale-brown seaweed had washed up and was floating at the water's edge in front of her. The air was fresh and clear.

"It's a lovely place to be this time of year," she added.

"And no tourists."

"True, but it's nearly always quiet at the north end of the island, even in July when most of the visitors come."

"I remember when there was hardly anyone around," Olle said wistfully.

The influx of tourists was a frequent topic of conversation on the island, almost as reliable as the weather. If there was nothing else to talk about, you could always complain about the summer invasion, when the harbor was crammed with people, and you had to push your bicycle through the village because that was the only way to get through.

"But we do need the tourists in order for the island to survive," Nora said, as she had so many times in the past. "How would the local traders make a living otherwise? On what you and I spend?"

Olle snorted, but it was a good-natured snort. He was wearing blue dungarees, and Nora could see a well-used folding ruler sticking out of his pocket. She ran her hand along the smooth wood of the rustic bench. It was warm from the sun, and she wondered how many times she had sat here watching the sun set over the sea.

She thought about how to broach the subject of Korsö. If she mentioned that the police were involved, Olle might clam up. She opted for a half-truth.

"I wanted to ask you something. Last weekend you told me you did your military service over on Korsö. I have a friend who's interested in the island's history; do you remember anything else about your time there?"

Olle nodded. "Indeed I do. Was there anything in particular you wanted to know?"

There was a brief silence; Thomas hadn't been very specific.

"Did you know that Russian prisoners of war built the lighthouse in 1747?" Olle asked.

Nora shook her head. "When did the Coastal Rangers arrive there?"

"Let me see." Olle sat back. "It was between the wars, when Europe was still very unstable. They wanted to be able to block the shipping lanes so they could defend the route into Stockholm if there was an invasion. I think they started building the heavy battery in the midthirties, and power cables were installed in the tower."

Nora knew that Korsö lighthouse had been replaced by the Sandhamn lighthouse in 1869; Korsö had been decommissioned and designated a watchtower instead.

"So the whole island was fortified?"

"It happened over time, as they added new defenses. By the time I was there, many of the tunnels had already been dug. They continued to build until the midnineties. That was when the bell tolled for Korsö. The battery was emptied of ammunition; most of the buildings were torn down, and the tunnels were filled in. It's still used in the summer, but to nowhere near the same extent."

As Olle was talking, he sat up a little straighter and gestured with his hands. Nora could see the young ranger he had once been.

"How do you know all this? You're like a living encyclopedia!"

"Once a Coastal Ranger, always a Coastal Ranger."

There was a new tone in Olle's voice. "There's an organization for old soldiers like me, so I get to hear what's going on. We meet up on the island from time to time, and the new recruits enjoy showing off their skills to the old guys."

"It's so close," Nora said, turning her head in the direction of Korsö, which was just visible across the Sound. "And yet I know very little about it."

"Have you never been ashore?"

"Of course not—it's not allowed."

Olle gave her a long look.

"I promise," Nora said quickly. "I'm a lawyer, I do as I'm told."

"Shall we take a little trip?"

He pointed to his old motorboat, moored by the jetty.

"But surely it's still forbidden?"

The smile on Olle's weather-beaten face was cunning, to say the least.

"Do you think anyone is going to come along and arrest us if we step ashore?"

Nora shook her head.

"There you go, then."

Olle stood up and headed for the jetty without waiting for a response.

CHAPTER 37

It was almost two o'clock, and Thomas knew he ought to go home. He had spent all morning at the station going over the material he hadn't managed to get around to during the week, but he was still none the wiser. His back ached, and he was sick of piles of paper.

He called Pernilla.

"I'm leaving shortly; shall I pick up something for dinner?"

"I don't know, I'm not that hungry." Pernilla laughed. "You know why . . ."

"I'll stop off at the grocery store, see what I can find."

"So we're not going to Harö? Is it too late?"

Thomas had been longing to get out to the archipelago; even when he only had twenty-four hours or so, he preferred it to staying in the city. But Pernilla was tired, and there were fewer ferries at this time of year; had the last one of the day already gone?

"I guess it is. Listen, Nora asked if we wanted to come over for dinner if we were at the cottage; could you call her and tell her that we're not going to make it?"

"Won't she be disappointed?"

"It's fine, it wasn't a definite plan."

"OK, see you later. Drive carefully."

Less than a minute later, the phone rang again. Thomas assumed that Pernilla had decided she did want him to pick up something special for dinner, after all, but instead an unmistakable Skåne accent filled his ear.

"Thomas Andreasson?"

"Yes."

"Grönstedt from Västerås. I'm pleased to find that the Stockholm police are working over the weekend."

"So are you, I gather."

"You roused my curiosity, Andreasson, so we took a look at Sven Erneskog this morning."

Thomas's grip on the receiver tightened.

"And what did you find?"

"The cause of death was drowning. He had water in his lungs and had been drinking heavily when he died. His blood alcohol level was one and a half percent. He must have knocked back the entire contents of that whisky bottle you found."

Thomas grabbed a notepad.

"Anything else?"

"You were right to mention the possibility of finger marks. I didn't find any, but there was a round mark on his chest, a distinct contusion beneath the skin that must have been made immediately before death."

"Could there be a natural cause?"

"Hardly. It must have been made by an object that someone else was holding. It looks as if it was pressed into the flesh, from above and at an angle."

"Any idea what it might be?"

"Definitely not a finger or part of a hand."

"Can you describe it to me?"

"It's perfectly round, two inches in diameter. Think of the tip of a baseball bat."

Thomas pictured Sven Erneskog lying in the bathtub, very drunk, his face just above the surface of the water. It wouldn't have taken a great deal of strength to push him down with a long, solid object. Three to four minutes; presumably he would have struggled only at first.

"Could he have slipped?" Thomas asked, even though he knew the answer.

"The body would have looked completely different; there would have been other marks; plus, the bruise would have had ragged edges."

"I understand."

"I would say that Sven Erneskog was probably murdered," the pathologist said. "I'm assuming that's what you thought?"

"Yes."

So they were dealing with a serial killer. The situation was as bad as Thomas had feared.

"Oh, and by the way," Grönstedt went on, "you were right about something else. There was detergent in both the bathwater and the lungs."

CHAPTER 38

As they traveled across the water, Nora saw several yachts moored by the jetty, even though it was so late in the year. However, the area in front of the Royal Swedish Yacht Club was deserted, and the tables outside were unoccupied.

The air was fresh, and the wind blew back her hair as they sped along. The sun was low, and she shaded her eyes to see better. They passed Lökholmen and the shallow waters the sailing school used in the summer, although all the skiffs and dinghies had long since been transported to Saltsjöbaden, where the yacht club had a new clubhouse.

The sea was a little choppy when they reached the mouth of the inlet. Olle made a wide turn, and they headed into Korsö Sound, bordered to the west by Krokö. Nora could see the wide concrete quayside now, running parallel with the wooden jetty on the shoreline. She had often seen fast combat craft around the island when she was out with the family in their own launch.

Olle cut the engine and hove to with a practiced hand. Nora made fast the forward rope and jumped ashore. She stood there, feeling a little nervous. However, no soldiers materialized, just a few gulls hovering high above the water as they searched for food.

"Come on, it's fine," Olle said with a wave of his hand.

Nora followed him. A well-maintained asphalt road that couldn't be seen from the sea led to an open square, surrounded by Falu-red two-story buildings with black doors and dormer windows.

"These are the barracks," Olle explained.

"I didn't realize the place was so big."

"There's plenty more to it—there's another road with identical blocks up to the left."

Nora stopped in front of an impressive building with barred windows. The façade was dark brown, and steps led up to imposing double doors.

"This was the store, where you could buy cigarettes and other bits and pieces."

Nora looked around. It was like a ghost town. Everything was here—except the people.

"Let's go to the tower," Olle said.

It was taller and steeper than Nora had imagined. She was out of breath by the time they reached the tower, but the view was worth every painful step.

The Baltic was spread before them in a seemingly endless panorama. The Almagrundet lighthouse was just visible where sea and sky melted together in a blue haze, the rocks and skerries standing out against the water like small gray and brown flowers.

The sea was so flat that Nora could understand why people in medieval times had been absolutely convinced that the earth couldn't possibly be round.

"I didn't know Korsö was so hilly," she said.

"That's why it's the perfect location for both surveillance and defense. It has strategic military importance, that's what they used to say."

Olle pointed to a modest white house a short distance away.

"That was the old lighthouse keeper's home. Have you heard of Avén?"

"I don't think so."

"He was the lighthouse keeper, and a legendary rose grower. The poet Elias Sehlstedt wrote a poem dedicated to him one Midsummer's Eve."

"Wow."

Nora gazed up at the tower. There were narrow openings in the stone façade, and at the top, she could see an octagonal lantern room with windows all around. It reminded her of an air-traffic-control tower with a 365-degree view.

"Have you been up there?" she asked.

"Many times. There's a kitchen and a bedroom about halfway up; they're pretty small but adequate."

Olle patted the rough wall as if it were a dear old friend. "The tower was also used by the military for various exercises."

"Like what?"

"Like climbing down the outside with a rope, all the way from the top."

Nora blinked. "You're kidding me."

She looked up at the tall tower once more. The thought of climbing down from the top was terrifying. There was nothing to hold on to, nothing to break your fall except the unforgiving rock below.

"But you could kill yourself," she said.

"True." Olle laughed. "But if you're going to turn boys into men . . ."

"That's crazy. Surely recruits aren't placed in mortal danger? At least not in the Swedish military."

"You can't begin to imagine what the Coastal Rangers were made to do. There were worse things than this—much worse."

Nora shuddered. "Like what?" she said again.

Olle Granlund turned away, as if he regretted having said anything. He set off down the slope without another word.

The shadow of the tower suddenly felt threatening.

DIARY:

MARCH 1977

A group of visiting journalists was shown around today. We stood in a huddle as they passed by, and I heard them asking about what went on.

Were the rumors true, did some of the officers have sadistic tendencies?

"There's a lot of talk about the training regime," said a guy wearing tinted aviator shades and a beige polo shirt. He seemed excited, as if he was expecting a revelation.

Captain Westerberg shook his head. He was at least six inches taller than the skinny reporter. He leaned forward and explained that one or two officers could be a little "overconscientious" occasionally, nothing more. Then he smiled disarmingly, underlining the absurdity of the suggestion. Strangely enough, the reporter dropped the subject, and they moved on.

They ought to meet the sergeant, *I thought.* Then they'd see what goes on.

The other day, I read about his father in the evening paper. There he was with some other representatives of the top brass, in full admiral's uniform, adorned with gold braid and sporting his medals. Apparently there had been some kind of state visit from foreign naval vessels, and he had been invited to dinner at the palace following the ceremony.

I couldn't help wondering if the sergeant had read the article about his father. Were they alike, father and son? Were they both bastards?

The other officers can be vile sometimes, too, but none of them goes as far as the sergeant when it comes to punishments. Sometimes I wonder if he's in his right mind.

But everyone lets him carry on, no one intervenes.

I'm sure it's because his father knows our company commander. They all socialize together, all those big shots, and they watch each other's backs.

CHAPTER 39

Margit answered almost right away when Thomas called her from his office.

"The pathologist from Västerås has been in touch. Erneskog was murdered."

"First Fredell, then Erneskog."

"And maybe Marcus Nielsen."

"I guess you're right." Margit suddenly sounded weary, as if the implications of what she had just said were sinking in.

"It looks like we're dealing with a serial killer," Thomas said.

"Yes. And the question is not only who, but why."

There was a brief silence.

"We need those names from the military," Thomas said. "As soon as possible."

"I'll try to hurry Elsa Harning along."

"Good—there could be more . . ."

Thomas didn't need to go on; Margit knew exactly what he meant.

"Kaufman?" she said.

Thomas glanced at his watch. He had told Pernilla he was on his way home, but he had a bad feeling about Bo Kaufman.

"I'll call him; if he doesn't answer, I'll go over there."

"On your own?"

"I promise I'll be careful."

Olle Granlund led Nora eastward past the tower. The pine trees were sparser here, and only the odd bush or tangle of juniper grew in the crevices. Nora picked her way cautiously over piles of rubble and sharp rocks.

After a while, they reached a concrete bunker with a flat roof, built into the steep hillside. Small square openings faced the sea.

"This is called an eagle's nest," Olle explained. "There were platforms under the holes for machine guns and ammunition."

Nora studied the strange structure; it had become part of nature, and yet it hadn't. It was a weird mixture of ancient gray stone and modern construction material.

"How many of these are there on the island?"

"Quite a few, but most are more effectively camouflaged, or have been demolished." He pointed. "The entrance to a firing site for anti-aircraft guns used to be over there."

Olle turned away and spat a plug of chewing tobacco into the undergrowth. A swarm of blackflies rose up like a cloud of dust and dispersed in all directions.

"The Subway Hill is down that way," he went on.

"That's a funny name."

"The command center was in there. It was built in the eighties, and the entrance was a tunnel made of corrugated iron that looked like a subway."

Nora gazed around. There was something melancholy about this place that had been left to its fate after so many years of intensive use.

"It must have cost a fortune to build all this," she said. "It's hard to understand why it was abandoned."

"There are installations all over the place deep inside the hill: emergency rooms, corridors, engine rooms, ammunition stores. Gas-proof doors, of course, in case the enemy used poison gas."

Gas. The word gave Nora the creeps.

"Is it possible to go inside?" she asked.

Olle shook his head.

"Everything that's left has been filled in, but this bunker is in good condition. Come and have a look."

Nora moved closer. Almost seventy years had passed; weeds were growing in the cracks in the concrete, and the cement was slowly crumbling away. She went down a couple of steps and found herself on a level with the lookout point.

She noticed something in a corner; she bent down and picked up a torn-off yellow label. The words on it looked as if they had been typed on an old-fashioned typewriter a very long time ago.

TAG, to be attached to the equipment belonging to injured (sick, dead), it said in faded letters.

A body tag.

There wasn't much traffic; Thomas took the freeway and stuck to the speed limit. With one hand on the wheel, he tried Bo Kaufman's number. There was no answer this time either; he had called just before he left the station. He let it ring, and eventually a robotic voice informed him that the person he was calling was not available at the moment but that he was welcome to try again later.

"Answer the goddamn phone," he muttered. His anxiety was growing by the minute.

He was about to try one more time when he heard a loud bang, not unlike a gunshot, somewhere up ahead of the car. It was totally unexpected, and he dropped his cell phone. Suddenly he saw a truck heading toward him around the bend, the driver frantically sounding his horn. It was swaying alarmingly, and it was on Thomas's side of the road. The heavy load was lurching uncontrollably, leaning at an angle that suggested it was dangerously close to tipping over.

Thomas saw a chalk-white, terrified face behind the wheel and acted instinctively. He slammed on the brakes while at the same time trying to swerve out of the way of the load.

He had to get away; nothing else mattered.

His Volvo was tiny in comparison with the huge truck looming above. If it went over, he wouldn't stand a chance. He fought to stay in control of the car, hoping that the brakes wouldn't lock; if that happened, he would crash into the truck. Head-on.

The road was damp. Was that good or bad? He couldn't remember.

The distance from the truck was diminishing fast.

Thomas gritted his teeth.

CHAPTER 40

They had walked in a semicircle and were now approaching the quay-side once more. On the way back, Olle had shown Nora a number of sealed-up entrances and openings, many of which she wouldn't have noticed. They were cunningly concealed and blended perfectly with their surroundings.

A few hundred yards from the quay, they came to a hill where the entrance to a bunker was surrounded by a network of barbed wire. Weeds and grass had become intertwined with the metal over the years, making it almost impossible to see the door.

"I spent many a night in there," Olle said. "It brings back a lot of memories, wandering around like this."

His words reminded Nora of Thomas's question about old rumors. Tentatively she asked, "Have you ever heard about anything strange going on out here?"

"What do you mean 'strange'?"

Nora shrugged.

"Oh, you know, stories, gossip, that kind of thing. I'm sure there were plenty of tales about what the recruits had to go through."

An icy gust of wind blew against her cheek.

"I'm not sure . . . Yes, there were plenty of stories, but . . ." A shadow seemed to pass across his face. "Nothing I'd care to pass on."

He took a few steps, then stopped.

"You have to understand that the men who came here were training to become members of an elite force. Their ability to deal with stress had to be tested to the limit. It was a matter of bringing out a controlled aggression, creating soldiers who would never, ever allow themselves to be prevented from achieving their goal."

The words came out of Nora's mouth before she could stop them.

"It sounds like pure fascism to me."

Olle blinked. "I've never thought of it that way."

They heard rustling in the undergrowth and the sound of an old motorboat in the distance. Nora closed her eyes and tried to imagine the island as it must have been when hundreds of soldiers were billeted here. Young boys with buzz cuts, so well drilled that they immediately obeyed orders without question. Ruthless and without boundaries, if she understood the implications of what her neighbor had said.

She pictured her sons with their smooth cheeks and slim bodies. Could they be pushed to breaking point in an environment like this?

Nora went over and touched the barbed wire. A feeling of claustrophobia overwhelmed her. She couldn't imagine what it must be like to sit in a tiny, damp room inside the bunker, surrounded by guns and silent, grim-faced soldiers.

All with a single goal: to stop the enemy at all costs.

How did you move on when you had undergone such harsh training? Surely it must mark a man for the rest of his life—what kind of person would he become?

CHAPTER 41

The truck was no more than three feet away when Thomas managed to swerve. The Volvo plowed on for several yards before stopping. The back of the truck clipped the hood of the car, pushing it sideways and forward so that it ended up with the front end halfway down into the ditch.

The impact threw Thomas to one side, but his seat belt held him in place. At least the car didn't flip; it shuddered one last time, then everything went quiet. Strangely enough, the airbag hadn't gone off.

After some time, Thomas noticed he was still clutching the wheel with both hands. His pulse was racing, and sweat was pouring down his back. He forced himself to breathe slowly and evenly. He looked in the rearview mirror and saw his own chalk-white face. The truck had stopped about twenty yards behind him, with the load partially across the roadway.

He gradually realized that the truck driver was standing by the car. He made a huge effort and managed to let go of the wheel and open the window. The acrid smell of burned rubber came pouring in.

"Are you OK?"

The truck driver spoke with a Finnish accent. He looked terrified and was sweating profusely. Thomas nodded.

"I think so. What happened?"

"Something punctured my tires." He pointed to the back of the truck, and Thomas could see that two tires were completely flat. "There was a bang, and I lost control. Then you appeared. Jesus."

Thomas became aware that the seat belt was cutting into his chest. He slowly released it and opened the door. He felt very shaky, and he put down his feet very carefully. He was overcome by dizziness and had to hang on to the car roof.

"I'm going to need a tow truck," the driver said, looking worried as he fiddled with his cell phone. "My boss won't be too pleased; I was already running late. I'm supposed to be going to Södertälje."

Thomas tried to think. He took out his ID; opening his wallet seemed kind of complicated.

"I'm a police officer."

The driver looked even more worried, and beads of sweat started dripping from his nose and onto his shirt.

"I haven't been drinking," he almost whimpered. "It was an accident, you can see that for yourself. The tires just exploded. It wasn't my fault."

Thomas slowly put his wallet back in his pocket with a trembling hand.

"You'll probably be Breathalyzed anyway."

"I swear I haven't touched a drop."

"Good," Thomas said wearily.

He looked around; he was going to have to stay until the police and a tow truck arrived. The area would have to be cordoned off as soon as possible to stop anyone from crashing into the truck. He could probably reverse his car onto the road, but it was going to take a while to sort all this out. He needed to call Pernilla and let her know.

Gradually his brain began to function once more.

Kaufman.

He reached into the car for his cell phone and tried the number again.

Still no reply.

CHAPTER 42

It was past three o'clock by the time Nora and Olle got back to Sandhamn. Nora thanked her neighbor for the trip, then went home.

Going ashore on the island of Korsö had been an interesting experience, but it had left an unpleasant taste in her mouth. She found it difficult to come to terms with Olle's tales of what the soldiers had been put through.

She stretched out on the old wicker sofa on the veranda. The sun was shining, and before she knew it, she had dropped off. The sound of the telephone woke her.

"Hi, Nora, it's Pernilla."

"Hi!" Nora was a little dazed, but she was always happy to hear from Pernilla. Thomas had been a different person since she'd come back. The old Thomas, her best friend since childhood, had returned after those terrible years.

Nora had always been very fond of Pernilla. Unlike Henrik, she had never had a problem with the long-standing friendship between Thomas and Nora, which dated back to the time when they found themselves in the same confirmation class.

"Are you coming over for dinner tonight?" Nora asked.

"I'm afraid not. Thomas called a while ago; he's still at work. We're not going to make it over to the island today."

Another lonely evening. Nora was reluctant to admit even to herself how much she had been looking forward to having some company.

"What a shame," she said, doing her best to keep her voice neutral and to hide her disappointment.

"I know, but Thomas is working incredibly long hours right now. Will you be OK?"

"Of course. I can go over to the restaurant, or I might just have something in front of the TV."

She could hear how pathetic that sounded.

"Now I feel guilty," Pernilla said.

Nora made an effort to sound more cheerful. "Really, it's fine. Anyway, I'll see you both on Tuesday for Simon's birthday, won't I? I mentioned it to Thomas a while ago."

"Yes, absolutely, we'll be there to celebrate Simon's birthday." Nora could have sworn that Pernilla didn't have a clue they'd been invited over; she suspected Thomas had forgotten to pass on the message.

"What would he like as a present—anything in particular?"

Nora pictured her son on the floor, surrounded by LEGOs.

"Anything to do with LEGOs—he can sit for hours making different things."

"Perfect."

Through the window, Nora could see two Japanese tourists photographing her house. It happened from time to time; people would stop and admire the beautiful building.

Pernilla said tentatively, "Will Henrik be there on Tuesday?"

"I'm afraid so. I mean, I can't exactly ban him from his own son's birthday party."

"And Marie?" Pernilla sounded as if she hardly dared ask.

"Absolutely not. It's nothing to do with her. He's not her son."

Nora realized she couldn't even mention Marie without sounding truculent.

"We'll be having a princess cake, of course," she went on, once again forcing herself to sound cheerful. "It's Simon's favorite."

Pernilla gratefully seized on the change of subject. "Great—Thomas loves princess cake, too. See you Tuesday."

There was a click as Pernilla hung up. Nora sat there holding her phone; what was she going to do this evening? She didn't want to be alone with her thoughts. It was too easy to sit around feeling sorry for herself, going over everything that had happened between her and Henrik.

If they had at least divorced because they had both agreed that they were no longer in love, it would have been easier. It wouldn't hurt so much. But no, they had split up because she had found out he was being unfaithful; she had felt doubly betrayed.

On top of all that, the object of his love had moved into their house. Nora hated the thought that his new woman was eating breakfast exactly where she used to sit with her first cup of coffee of the day, and falling asleep in the same double bed Nora and Henrik used to share.

If Simon woke up in the middle of the night and went padding into the bedroom to seek comfort, another woman would be lying next to his daddy.

That hurt most of all.

In a moment of clarity, Nora knew this wasn't about turning back the clock. She didn't want to be married to Henrik any longer, and, after all, she was the one who had insisted on the divorce.

But it would all have been so much easier if he hadn't brought Marie into their home right away. How could he move on so quickly? After fourteen years of marriage and two children, surely he ought to be mourning the fact that it had ended like this? They hadn't fulfilled their greatest obligation: to raise their boys in a happy and loving family.

The familiar feeling of failure came over her, and tears sprang to her eyes. She got up and went into the kitchen to make a cup of coffee. Maybe that would help.

She looked out and saw her old house. Jonas had said he was alone this weekend, too; perhaps she could return the invitation? Having dinner with him was a lot more appealing than an evening in front of the TV.

As if he had read her mind, the front door opened, and Jonas appeared. Nora waved through the window; before she had the chance to change her mind, she went outside and across to his gate. Jonas came to meet her.

Nora hesitated; now that she was here, she didn't quite know how to ask him to dinner.

"Hi—lovely day," she said instead.

Not very original, but Jonas didn't seem to mind.

"It sure is."

"We often have good weather out here, even when it's raining in town. Sometimes you can actually see the clouds above the mainland, but the sun is shining here."

Now she was babbling. Nervously she pushed her hands in her pockets and wondered how to broach the subject.

Jonas's hair was damp, as if he had just had a shower, and there was a small patch of shaving foam under one ear.

"I was thinking of going out for something to eat," he said.

Nora couldn't make up her mind. Could she bring herself to suggest they go together? Her courage failed.

"Sounds like a good idea. Enjoy."

She turned to go back to the house, silently berating herself. Why hadn't she said something? Now she would definitely be spending the evening alone.

She heard his voice behind her.

"Would you like to come with me? I was just on my way over to knock on your door."

She stopped and turned back. Suddenly everything felt so much better.

"Yes. Absolutely. Yes, please." A deep breath. "Actually, I was going to ask if I could invite you to dinner, to say thank-you for last weekend."

Jonas smiled; he didn't seem to have any objection to her suggestion.

"I'll just go fetch my purse," Nora said.

"No need—I've got my wallet."

Nora moved so that she was standing directly in front of him. She was equally surprised each time she looked into his eyes.

"I wanted to invite you."

"It's fine."

"No, this time it's my turn. I won't be a minute."

She ran back to the house before he could say anything. She raced upstairs, changed into a nicer top, and dragged a comb through her hair. The trip to Korsö had put some color in her cheeks; a slick of lip gloss, and she was done.

She decided the result wasn't too bad; she smiled at her reflection in the mirror.

CHAPTER 43

It had taken hours to clear the road. Long traffic jams had built up in both directions, and when Thomas was finally able to leave, it took him an eternity to get away.

He looked at his watch.

He had called Pernilla around two and now it was almost six o'clock. He had considered asking Margit to take over, but he hadn't expected the salvage operation to go on for quite so long, and it seemed unnecessary to ask her to drive all the way through the city when he was already halfway there.

However, as he reached the area where Bo Kaufman's apartment block was located, he was beginning to regret his decision. He was exhausted; all he wanted to do was go home and sleep. He was still in shock from the accident, and no doubt there would be some kind of delayed reaction in due course. His chest hurt where the seat belt had dug into it.

Anyway, he was here now.

Kaufman still hadn't answered his phone.

A woman with a stroller was passing as Thomas got out of the car. He smiled at her, but she simply averted her eyes. He was surprised, but then what did he know about the atmosphere around here?

He made his way over to the main door of the building. Hopefully there was a simple explanation for Kaufman's failure to pick up; he was probably out cold after a drinking session and hadn't even heard the phone. If Thomas kept his finger on the doorbell for long enough, maybe Kaufman would come around.

Then he could go home and rest.

This time the elevator wasn't working, and Thomas had to take the stairs to the fourth floor. When he reached the landing, he paused and looked around. He could hear the theme song of a popular TV program through a neighbor's door; not a sound from the other apartments. The faint smell of fried food reached his nostrils.

He rang the bell, but nothing happened. He tried the handle; the door wasn't locked. His tiredness was swept away by the sudden rush of adrenaline that surged through his body.

He drew his gun and pushed the door wide open. There was no sign of anyone, just a pile of junk mail spread across the brown rug and a jacket hanging on a hook.

Thomas edged forward. He could see straight into the dirty kitchen, which actually looked worse than before. The air was thick with stale cigarette smoke and the smell of rancid beer. The sink was piled high with empty cans.

Slowly he made his way into the small living room. There was very little furniture—just a stained sofa and a coffee table covered in rings left by beer cans, plus a large old-style TV in the corner.

Kaufman wasn't there.

Thomas turned his attention to the bathroom door; could he hear something from inside? Silently he grasped the dark-gray handle and pushed it down.

There was nothing to see apart from a filthy toilet. The sudden draft made the shower curtain flutter, and the stench of urine came toward him. Instinctively he took a step back; the smell was revolting. How could Kaufman live like this?

And where the hell was he?

There wasn't a sound to be heard in the apartment, and Thomas paused to take stock. There was only one place he hadn't been.

The bedroom.

The door was closed. Thomas flung it open and saw Bo Kaufman lying on his back on the grubby sheets, his mouth open.

There was no doubt that he was dead.

DIARY:

APRIL 1977

Tomorrow we are being transferred to Korsö, the Coastal Rangers' very own island just off Sandhamn.

We will be there until the end of August, almost five months, staying in what is known as Korsö base, a collection of barracks to the east of the main quay.

We will be sleeping in two- or four-bed rooms, narrow cabins with bunk beds and barely enough space to turn around. But it will be good to escape from the dormitory with all that mumbling and snoring during the night; I'm so sick of it.

Not far from the quayside where the boats are moored, there's a big rock with the Coastal Rangers' oath of allegiance carved into the surface:

"I [ranger's name] swear before our patron Torleif to be a role model for other soldiers by always doing my best in every situation, being a good comrade, and never giving up.

I will bear the Coastal Rangers' symbols, the beret and the trident, with honor and respect."

It is that oath that drives us on.

CHAPTER 44

Several hours had passed without Nora even noticing. She and Jonas had ordered a beer, and then another and another . . . She was a little giggly by this point.

The sadness of the afternoon was long gone. Jonas was easy to talk to, there was no shortage of topics of conversation, and his tales of crazy passengers made her laugh. He was a born storyteller.

Quite a lot of people had arrived during the course of the evening, and a pleasant hum of conversation filled the room. Some of the locals were chatting at the bar, and the beer taps were being kept busy.

Nora and Jonas had some privacy, because they were sitting slightly to one side at a table for two.

"Are you ready to eat?" Nora asked. Her stomach had started rumbling. "Do you want to stay down here, or shall we go upstairs?"

"Which would you prefer?"

"I think we should try the à la carte restaurant on the second floor," she said with a smile. "It's still early; we should be able to get a table on the veranda overlooking the harbor."

She got to her feet and picked up her jacket. Jonas followed; he seemed amused at her decisiveness. The heavy oak door of the restaurant creaked as Jonas opened it. Nora pointed to a wood-paneled room with old-fashioned decor straight ahead.

"This is the oldest part of the building, one of the island's original schnapps bars from the eighteenth century. It was the only consolation for agricultural workers from Eknö when they were conscripted to Sandhamn to pilot sailing ships into Stockholm, over three hundred years ago."

Jonas took a quick look as Nora kept walking up the stairs to the restaurant.

Only half the tables were occupied, so they had no problem securing a view of the water. Dusk was falling, and the lights of the Sailors Restaurant on the other side of the harbor shone brightly against the deep-blue sky. The silhouette with the little red tower on the top was a classic symbol of Sandhamn.

Nora ordered the fish stew, which was always delicious, and a glass of white wine, while Jonas opted for steak with a glass of red. The waitress brought their drinks right away.

"Tell me more about your daughter," Nora said.

"Wilma, the most stubborn teenager in the world." Jonas leaned back and continued in a gentler tone. "She's thirteen, and she can't live without her computer and her cell phone."

"Sounds familiar."

Nora pictured Adam, her proud, precocious son who took after his father. He was just as talented, just as stubborn. A warm feeling filled her heart.

"She scatters her clothes all over the floor and has a complete breakdown if she's left her favorite top at Margot's—her mother's—place." Jonas ran his fingers over the tablecloth, his expression a little melancholy. "Now and again, she curls up beside me on the sofa to watch TV, but that's happening less and less often these days. She's growing up."

"Does she find it difficult, spending one week with you and the next with your ex?" Nora had to ask. She worried about the situation every time she had to pack the boys' bags.

Jonas thought for a moment. "I don't know," he said eventually. "She was only little when we split up, so it's kind of always been this way. We live pretty close to one another, and so far it's worked well."

"She's never mentioned it?"

"No."

Nora felt a great sense of relief. Maybe she was fretting unnecessarily.

"Has Margot remarried?"

"Yes, many years ago. Our relationship broke down soon after Wilma was born."

Nora realized the conversation was turning into an interrogation, but she couldn't stop herself.

"And did she have more children?"

"A son, plus her husband has a boy from a previous relationship. It takes a bit of juggling at Midsummer and Christmas and so on, but we've always managed to sort things out."

Jonas raised his glass as if to celebrate the success of the arrangement.

"Do you get on OK?"

"You could say that. It's been well over ten years since we separated, and we both thought it was the best solution. We were far too young and immature to make it work. Wilma wasn't exactly planned; we were completely taken by surprise. Now we help each other out; if I have a flight, she steps in, if something comes up on her side, I do the same."

"Sounds perfect."

"So far, so good. What do you and your ex do?"

"What do we do?" Nora hesitated. Sometimes she couldn't imagine getting along with Henrik ever again. Every conversation seemed to end up in a heated argument.

"I guess we haven't really gotten into a pattern yet. It's only been six months since we separated."

She spread her hands in a weary gesture.

"Are you finding it difficult?" Jonas asked.

Nora looked away. She had to swallow hard before she could speak.

"Yes."

"It does get better, I promise. After a while, you build up a life of your own, which gives you some distance. The early days are the worst, but then things settle down. Believe me."

Jonas gave her an encouraging smile, and Nora relaxed. To her surprise, she noticed that her glass was empty. She stole a glance at Jonas's glass, which was virtually untouched.

"The wine was delicious," she said, as if to excuse herself. Jonas waved the waitress over and ordered another glass. The chivalrous gesture appealed to Nora. She buttered a piece of bread and took a bite, enjoying the sourdough taste on her tongue.

"What grade is Wilma in?"

"She's just started seventh grade, but she looks older. It happened over the summer; she suddenly shot up and started wearing makeup. She used to talk to me about her friends and boyfriends, but now she doesn't say much at all. I'm not even allowed to go into her room without knocking. The door is always closed."

Nora knew exactly how he was feeling. It was good to hear that other kids were hard to understand, not just her son.

"These are the trickiest years," she said.

"So they say. In my innocence, I thought it would get easier as she grew up. I guess it's a phase that will pass." He pulled a face. "Is it just as tricky with boys?"

"What can I say?" Nora smiled. "I have no experience with raising girls, but Adam is well on the way into puberty, and he has mood swings like you wouldn't believe.

"We have quite a bit of trouble with Adam," she went on. "Simon is still a little boy, thank goodness. You know what they say: small children, small problems."

The waitress arrived with their food. The aroma of the fish stew was seductive, and Nora could hardly wait. Jonas was served an enormous portion of fries and Béarnaise sauce with his steak; Nora's fish looked like a healthy meal in comparison.

As Jonas bent over his plate, his necklace glinted in the light. Nora saw that his daughter's name was engraved on it, which she found touching.

"Have you never wanted more children?" she asked.

Jonas put down his knife and fork and picked up his glass. He turned it slowly around and around, the red liquid shimmering with the movement.

"I've thought about it, of course. But it's never worked out . . ."

He sipped the wine, an unreadable expression on his face.

CHAPTER 45

"Go home and get some rest, Thomas. You look like a ghost," Margit said.

It was as if a swarm of insects had invaded the small apartment. The unnatural silence in Bo Kaufman's home had been replaced by the voices of those investigating the scene of the crime.

Staffan Nilsson, the forensic technician who had dealt with Fredell's body, had been called in and was busy in the bedroom.

A colleague walked into the kitchen and made a face.

"This place is disgusting."

It's as if she finds the mess in the sink worse than the dead body in the bedroom, Thomas thought. Then again, the body probably constituted a normal day's work for her, while the kitchen offended her views on personal hygiene. What did he know?

He was rapidly running out of energy. He was slumped on a chair, elbow on the table, his cheek resting on his hand.

"When did you last eat?" Margit asked.

Thomas had to think about it. It was quite some time; he had bought a hot dog before he got in the car. That was all he'd had since breakfast.

"Here." Without waiting for an answer, she produced a Toblerone from her purse. "Eat."

He gratefully broke off a large chunk and put it in his mouth. It definitely helped.

"I heard about the accident. You're taking on a lot at the moment." Margit's tone was concerned rather than reproachful. "You ought to stay home and take it easy, at least for tomorrow."

Thomas shook his head, but Margit wasn't giving up.

"You've only just come back to work after your sick leave. You have to take care of yourself; you don't want to relapse."

She was right; he knew that. But there was too much going on right now. He would rest some other time. He waved a dismissive hand, then got up and joined Nilsson in the bedroom.

"How's it going?"

Nilsson straightened up. He moved with surprising suppleness, given his corpulent frame. He was wearing latex gloves on his plump hands and holding a pair of tweezers.

"As I'm sure you've already noticed, there is no obvious cause of death. He hasn't been shot or stabbed—no sign whatsoever of external force."

Kaufman's body was exactly as it had been when Thomas had found him—on his back, with his eyes closed. He was wearing jeans and a surprisingly clean T-shirt; had he been planning to go somewhere?

"Are we looking at natural causes? Are you telling me Kaufman wasn't murdered?"

It was possible but seemed unlikely: three members of the same Coastal Rangers' platoon who just happened to die within a couple of weeks?

Not a chance.

Nilsson shook his head, then gestured toward the bed. "There's your murder weapon."

Thomas saw a pillow in a faded-red pillowcase next to the body. Nilsson carefully picked it up by one corner with the tweezers. Thomas leaned forward and examined the fabric; he could just make out a faint round impression in the center, with several paler marks beside it.

"The perpetrator smothered him," he said, half talking to himself, "while he was sleeping. He might not even have woken up if he'd been drinking. A couple of minutes of pressing the pillow down on his face, and it was all over."

"The pathologist will find out for certain whether he was drunk, but you're probably right."

Thomas sniffed the air: whisky. The other victims had consumed whisky before they were killed, but when he had visited Kaufman a few days ago, there had been only empty beer bottles on the kitchen counter.

Whisky was expensive for someone who needed to drink themselves into oblivion every day.

"Any sign of a whisky bottle?" he asked.

"Yes, there was an empty one under the bed."

"Be especially careful with it, please."

The next question was difficult, but he had to ask.

"When do you think he died?"

"He hasn't been dead very long." Nilsson looked at his watch. "A few hours, maybe. Rigor mortis has barely set in."

A few hours.

Thomas gritted his teeth.

Could he have saved Kaufman's life, if a few square inches of galvanized rubber had held for just another half mile?

"Thomas."

Margit was standing by the front door.

"I think I know why the door was unlocked. Look."

She pointed to the lock; it was the kind that needed a key to lock it.

"If the killer didn't have the key, he wouldn't have been able to lock up from the outside."

"So it must have been someone who didn't have a key to the apartment. An unknown individual . . ."

"Yes and no. Kaufman knew him well enough to let him in; there's no sign of forced entry. But he wasn't close enough to have his own key."

Thomas nodded.

"The question is whether we're dealing with the same perpetrator," Margit went on, running a hand over her short hair with its startling red highlights. Her cell phone buzzed, and she glanced at the screen.

"Bertil's wondering if I'm going to be late. His cousin is coming over for dinner."

She entered three letters, then pressed "Send." It wasn't difficult to work out the answer.

"Two drowned, one suffocated, and possibly one hanged," she said pensively.

"Different methods," Thomas said. "And we still don't know for sure whether Marcus Nielsen died by his own hand."

He turned around.

"Wait—I just want to check something."

He went back to the bedroom, with Margit close behind. Nilsson looked up inquiringly as they appeared in the doorway.

"I bet he has detergent in his lungs," Thomas said.

"I'm sorry?" Nilsson looked bewildered.

"The others had soapy water in their lungs—detergent. Can you see any traces?"

Nilsson picked up a sealed evidence bag.

"I can't tell you right now, but this glass was next to the whisky bottle. I'll check it out when I get back."

Margit leaned against the wall and folded her arms.

"So what's the significance of the soapy water? What do you think?"

226

"Good question—I just wish I had the answer." Thomas turned back to Nilsson. "Let me know as soon as you find anything."

"Of course."

They left him to work in peace and went back to the living room. Margit picked up a pile of newspapers and sat down on the grubby sofa, while Thomas took the armchair.

"Why do the murders always take place right before the weekend?" Margit said. "There has to be a reason."

"The same thought crossed my mind." Thomas was starting to have trouble concentrating; his head felt heavy, and there was a tightening band of tension across his temples. He sat back and closed his eyes.

"It's as if our perp is following some kind of weekly schedule, however weird that sounds," Margit mused. "But why?"

Thomas forced himself to open his eyes. Margit was leafing through her diary.

"Maybe he has very strict working hours," she suggested. "Someone who's tied to their workplace, like a teacher, for example. They can't just sneak off any old time to commit a crime."

An ironic smile.

Thomas made a huge effort to stay focused. His rib cage was aching.

"What about a person who commutes?" he said.

"Good call! Someone who's only in Stockholm on Saturdays and Sundays. That would explain it; our perp isn't in town during the week. So what kind of job might he have?"

Thomas couldn't suppress an enormous yawn. It was no longer possible to hide his exhaustion.

Margit put away her diary.

"Enough," she said. "Go home and sleep; I'll find someone to drive you. You're in no state to get behind the wheel. I'll stay awhile."

Thomas didn't have the strength to argue.

"I'll call the Old Man, bring him up to speed," Margit said.

Thomas hauled himself to his feet. He was starting to feel slightly nauseated, and he swallowed hard a couple of times.

He stopped in the doorway as a thought took shape in his weary brain. They were looking for someone who either lived or worked outside Stockholm and therefore could only get here in his free time.

"What about a soldier serving in a different town?"

As soon as he uttered the words, Thomas realized their significance. Another Coastal Ranger. Still on active duty.

CHAPTER 46

Darkness had fallen, but a pale half-moon hovered over the horizon.

Nora stirred her coffee, even though the cup was almost empty. She wondered where the time had gone. The wine was all gone, too, but she didn't feel drunk—just happy and relaxed.

Jonas hadn't objected to her interrogation, but he had asked a few questions of his own. He hadn't mentioned a girlfriend, and she hadn't asked. He didn't seem that much younger than her now; in fact, he could easily have been a contemporary. After all, Adam and Wilma were the same age—surely there couldn't be too many years between them?

His hair curled slightly at the nape of his neck; he would need a haircut in a few days, otherwise it would look too long. Now it was just tousled.

Nora carried on moving her spoon around.

"I don't think there can be much left in there," Jonas said, brushing his hand against hers.

Nora dropped the spoon. Had he done that by accident, or was it deliberate? It was so long since anyone had touched her as a woman, and even longer since she had wanted them to. She pushed back a strand of hair, trying to hide her confusion.

"You're probably right," she said with a smile.

The other tables were empty. The waitress had passed by several times, probably trying to hurry them along without making it too obvious. And now she was back.

"I'm sorry, but the kitchen is about to close. Would you like to order anything else?"

"No, we're fine," Jonas assured her. "Unless you'd like something?" he said to Nora.

"I'm good—that was delicious. Could we have the check, please?" She reached for her wallet, ignoring Jonas's protests.

"My turn to pay—that's what we agreed."

Thomas had gone to bed as soon as he got home. His body ached with exhaustion, and the foot with the missing toe was throbbing.

He woke around eleven with a raging thirst. His tongue was stuck to the roof of his mouth, and he could hardly swallow. It was as if every drop of saliva had dried up.

The bedroom was in darkness, and the only sound he could hear was Pernilla's steady breathing. He hadn't told her what had happened; he had simply said it had been a hard day. There was no point in burdening her with the knowledge that he had been close to death once again. It might be part of the territory for a cop, but he knew how badly she would take it. That was the last thing she needed in her condition.

Without switching on the bedside lamp, he got up and went into the bathroom. He drank two big glasses of water to quench his thirst. He leaned on the sink and contemplated his reflection. His eyes were swollen, and he felt worn out, as if all his energy had drained away. He had no idea how he was going to get up, get dressed, and go to work in the morning. Right now that seemed like an impossible task.

He could see the truck swerving across the highway, feel the panic as the car refused to obey him. He clutched the edge of the sink so hard that his fingers ached. His heart was pounding, and he realized he was breathing in short, shallow gasps.

With a huge effort, he forced himself to let go. He bent down and sluiced his face with cold water until his pulse slowed. Clumsily, he refilled the glass; this time he drank slowly.

As he put down the glass, he bumped into the side of the bathtub. He remembered the sight of Jan-Erik Fredell lying in his bathtub, his lifeless face beneath the surface of the water.

Grönstedt had sent over photographs of Sven Erneskog lying in almost exactly the same position: on his back in a bathtub filled to the brim, with his head underwater.

Suddenly Thomas knew why Bo Kaufman had been smothered with a pillow.

He thought back to the tiny bathroom in Kaufman's apartment: toilet, sink, and a cramped shower.

The killer had been forced to use a different method.

Kaufman didn't have a bathtub.

CHAPTER 47

Sunday (The Third Week)

Nora and Jonas strolled back from the restaurant, arm in arm. It was well after midnight. They passed the hill that the kids liked to slide down until the backsides of their pants were completely ruined, and the old marina, its windbreaks at the end of the jetties providing a reminder of bygone days.

Most houses were dark, and they didn't meet anyone along the way. All too soon, they reached the gate of the Brand villa.

Nora turned to Jonas. He was standing very close to her, their faces just inches apart. She felt her body respond to his proximity. The collar of his sailing jacket brushed against Nora's chin, and she didn't pull away.

It would be OK if she gave him a little hug just to say good night. That wouldn't send any kind of weird signal. She raised her hands, slowly, so that he wouldn't get the wrong idea. He smelled so good.

And instead of stepping back, he put his arms around her as if it was the most natural thing in the world, making Nora's heart race. They stood there for a long time without moving.

The warmth of Jonas's body enveloped her. She had forgotten what it was like to be so close to another person. Her face burned as if she were sitting in front of an open fire. The wine was also making its presence felt. Her skin tingled, but she made an effort to keep still, afraid the moment would be lost if she moved.

Then she raised her head and looked straight into Jonas's eyes. She couldn't read his expression, but it didn't matter. Their lips brushed against one another, and suddenly nothing was more important than his mouth, his tongue, his body against hers.

It was wonderful to give in, to let go; she was always so calm and in control. She was taking a risk, and it filled her with joy.

After a little while, she started to become aware of the cold. The temperature had plummeted, her toes were numb, and she couldn't suppress a shiver.

"Come inside," she said. "We can't stand out here all night."

She took his hand and led him indoors. Without switching on the light, they continued up the stairs and into the bedroom.

My bedroom, she thought just before he slid his hands under her sweater. *It's my bedroom, and I can bring home whomever I like.*

Impatiently, she tried to pull off both her clothes and his. She fumbled with the waistband of his jeans as she unzipped her own. His fingers met hers with the same aim, and she shivered as he touched her bare skin.

She turned back the covers and drew him onto the bed. Jonas gently shifted her onto her back. She wrapped her legs around his, once again feeling the heat of his body. She ran her thumb and forefinger down his spine and over the curve of his bottom.

Tenderly, he cupped her face in his hand, his palm warm and dry against her cheek, and once again she looked straight into his eyes.

The only light in the room came from the half-moon in the dark autumn sky casting long shadows over the bed where they lay.

"Come to me," she whispered, her voice thick with emotion.

"You're so lovely," he whispered in her ear. "You're so beautiful, Nora."

DIARY:
MAY 1977

Jesus, what a fucking day. What a horrific day.

They woke us early in the morning. We were to undertake the Tarzan Run, an obstacle course that involves crawling and wriggling over virtually the whole island.

We were given no breakfast, we were simply ordered to put on our overalls and line up.

I gobbled a chocolate cookie that was in my pocket, and I could see that several others had had something hidden away. Sigurd and Kaufman were munching furiously as we got ready.

It was drizzling when I opened the door, and the sky was gray and overcast. The fog had lifted, but I could still see it lingering on the horizon.

After an hour's running and climbing, we reached a long underground tunnel. The entrance was pitch black, and we eyed it with suspicion.

The sergeant produced a knife and a flashlight in order to scare away any snakes that might be lying curled up just inside.

"In you go!" he yelled.

Kihlberg went in first, and I was second in line. I got down and crawled a few yards, using my elbows to wriggle forward. It was so dark and narrow that I could hardly get through. Before long it was impossible to crawl, and I was just dragging myself along. Suddenly I felt something scuttle over my back, and I let out a gasp.

"What's wrong?" Kihlberg hissed.

"Nothing," I mumbled and kept going.

Soon I bumped into a pair of boots and realized that Kihlberg had stopped. A second later, Andersson collided with the soles of my boots.

It felt as if we were stuck there for an eternity. If they blocked the entrance, we would never get out, we would be caught like rats in a trap.

I wondered if this was yet another task designed to test our resilience.

Probably. So how long were they going to leave us in here?

In order to try to stay in control, I forced myself to breathe evenly, and I also scratched my hand. The physical pain made it easier not to think about the fact that we were trapped.

Eventually I would have done anything to get back to the daylight.

After what seemed like an eternity, Kihlberg managed to move forward. I felt a surge of relief as I followed him out onto the rocks and into the open air.

Where the shit trench was waiting for us.

An old tradition on Korsö.

The final part of the exercise is to get through a water-filled trench, a filthy ditch that is only three feet wide but thirty feet long. It is full of rotting vegetation and shit.

Literally.

Rumor has it that, before the exercise, the latrines are emptied into the trench. The officers grinned as they told us about it over dinner yesterday.

"You've got the shit trench to look forward to tomorrow," they said, gleefully studying the looks on our faces.

"It stinks to high heaven," the sergeant said. "Guess where every intake goes for their last shit before they leave the island?"

There was a wooden grille three inches over the water, which left very little room for the swimmer to keep his nose and mouth above the surface. At the end of the trench, the grille was underwater, so there would be no choice but to dive down beneath it then through a narrow opening before emerging on the other side.

"Try to avoid swallowing the water," the sergeant warned us. "It's not good for your health."

I stared at the filthy ditch and couldn't help retching. The stench was indescribable. Then I took a deep breath, closed my eyes, and got in. It was harder than I had expected; I sank to my shoulders, but I still had to lower myself further to get under the grille.

The disgusting slop was touching my chin, and I forced myself to keep going. When it reached my ears, I wanted to throw up. The feeling of powerlessness was even worse than the smell.

I kept my eyes fixed on the sky, breathed through my nose, and pulled myself along with the help of the grille until it came to an end, and I realized I was going to have to dive.

I took another deep breath and went under, desperately searching for the gap that would enable me to escape. I was concentrating so hard I was no longer thinking about what was all around me.

When I came out on the other side, I lay down flat on my belly so that as much of the foul liquid as possible could run back into the trench.

Martinger emerged next, then Andersson. As his head popped up above the brown sludge, the sergeant was waiting, legs apart, uniform perfectly pressed as if he were about to set off for an afternoon stroll around the gardens of a royal palace.

"I'm not impressed, Andersson," he said with a cold smile. "I'm afraid you're going to have to do it again. Be a good boy and swim back, so we can be sure you know how it works."

I almost thought Andersson was going to lose it. His jaw stiffened, and his eyes narrowed. For a moment, I was convinced he was going to leap out and punch the sergeant.

Kihlberg made a movement as if he wanted to come to Andersson's rescue, but Andersson sank down once more.

What a fucking day.

CHAPTER 48

The room was light when Nora woke. She tried to look at the clock, but her left arm was trapped under Jonas's back, and she didn't want to disturb him. Around five, five thirty, she guessed. She felt as if she hadn't had much sleep, so it must've been pretty early.

She remembered drinking quite a lot of wine with dinner, but she didn't have a hangover. Maybe it would catch up with her later.

Neither of them had thought of drawing the blinds, so she could see Jonas clearly in the soft dawn. He was lying on his back, his steady breathing occasionally interrupted by a faint hissing sound. Not a snore, more like a little snuffle. She decided it suited him.

She studied his face for a long time. Dark stubble, just like his hair, but flecked with white. Good—maybe he wasn't so young after all. She still hadn't dared to ask him his age.

He had an irregular birthmark by his hairline; it was usually covered by his fringe, but now it was clearly visible. She reached out to touch it but stopped herself.

She was excited and terrified at the same time.

If she woke him, the magic might disappear. At the same time, she wanted him again; it had been many months since she'd experienced pure lust like this.

What if yesterday had been a huge mistake, something she would regret every time she bumped into him by the gate? The thought made her stomach contract. Jonas was a pilot and a single father; maybe he wasn't interested in anything other than a one-night stand. No point in thinking about a relationship.

But she wanted him so much.

She gently brushed his shoulder with her lips, still watching his sleeping face. His eyelids flickered, as if he were dreaming. About something nice, hopefully.

No, Nora thought, *I will never regret this night with Jonas, no matter what happens.*

CHAPTER 49

Thomas plodded wearily into the conference room. He could easily have slept for many more hours. He hadn't woken Pernilla; he had just left her a note telling her he had gone to work. On the way, he had stopped and bought a large coffee in the hope that it would revive him.

Margit looked up as he walked in, then pushed a plate of cinnamon buns in his direction.

"How are you feeling?"

A yawn was his only response.

The Old Man arrived, with Kalle Lidwall, Erik Blom, and Karin Ek close behind. Karin closed the door, and they all settled down around the table.

Margit summarized what had gone down in Kaufman's apartment the previous day. She had already put up a photo on the whiteboard so that everyone could see how he had been lying when he was found.

Thomas turned his stiff neck; he could hear the vertebrae complaining.

"We have to be looking at the same killer," he stated firmly.

"Even though he wasn't in the bath?" the Old Man said.

"Where do you drown someone if you don't have access to a bathtub?" Thomas asked.

A flash of comprehension passed over Margit's face.

"Kaufman only had a shower, no bathtub," she said slowly. "The perp couldn't kill him in the same way as Fredell and Erneskog."

"So he had to improvise." The Old Man's dry comment sounded unintentionally comical.

"Unless he knew the layout of Kaufman's apartment in advance," Thomas countered. He could picture the course of events.

The doorbell rang, and Kaufman let his visitor in. A glance into the bathroom, which turned out to have only a shower stall. The instant realization that a different approach would be required this time. Was there anything in the apartment that he could use instead?

Presumably it didn't take long for the killer to come up with a solution. All he had to do was shuffle the drunken man in the direction of the bedroom.

Had Kaufman realized what was waiting for him in there? Hopefully not.

Thomas got up and went over to the whiteboard. He picked up a pen and sketched the rooms in Kaufman's apartment.

"Kaufman lets the perpetrator in," he said, drawing a red arrow by the door.

Margit took over. "Somehow, probably by threatening him with a gun, he forces Kaufman to lie down on the bed and knock back whisky until he's too drunk to offer any resistance."

"Which probably wasn't that difficult," Thomas interjected.

"Then he used the pillow," the Old Man concluded.

"Fredell also let his killer in," Erik Blom noted, clicking his ballpoint pen.

"For some reason, they're not scared of their visitor," Thomas said.

"Which means they must have some kind of relationship with him," Margit cut in right away. "They know one another."

Karin looked up from her notepad.

"If he has a gun, why doesn't he just shoot them?"

Thomas went back to his seat. It was a question he had already asked himself.

"There could be a simple explanation," Erik Blom said. "He doesn't have a silencer. So it would make a hell of a noise to shoot someone inside their apartment. The risk of being caught would be significantly higher."

"It's also very messy, particularly at close range," Kalle pointed out. "You're going to get blood and God knows what else all over your clothes, and the forensic evidence would be virtually impossible to get rid of."

Margit agreed.

"So far, everything has been very neat and tidy. We've found no trace of the perpetrator. Everything has been meticulously planned, from start to finish."

"Apart from the pillow," Karin said.

"But that wasn't part of the plan," Thomas said. "With a bit of luck, we'll find the killer's DNA on the pillowcase; he must have used his weight to press down on Kaufman's face."

"So everything suggests that we're dealing with an intelligent individual," the Old Man mused. "Sufficiently cold-blooded to handle a setback and smart enough to find a way around it."

"It seems like he's upping the level of difficulty," Karin remarked.

All eyes turned to her.

"What do you mean?" Thomas asked.

"He started with the easiest—Fredell. Then he went for the alcoholic."

"But what about Erneskog? How do you know he was 'easy' to kill?" Margit asked, drawing quotation marks in the air.

Karin didn't have an answer, but Thomas thought for a moment, then spoke up.

"In a way, I think you're right. The killer has a plan. He is choosing the order in which he dispatches his victims. And he's getting more confident, hence the alternative method in Kaufman's case."

"Do you think he's practicing?"

Once again, Karin had said something unexpected.

"Practicing?" Margit repeated.

"Each time it's a little more tricky, a little more challenging. I'm thinking about my son's judo classes." Karin moistened her lips with her tongue. "It might sound crazy, but I couldn't help thinking of his training, where the level of difficulty gradually increases."

Thomas closed his eyes. If Karin was right, which was highly likely, that meant more people were in danger. The killer was getting ready for the tasks that lay ahead.

Who was his next victim?

There was a knock on the door, and the temporary receptionist appeared with a newspaper in her hand.

"This just arrived—I thought you ought to see it."

The Old Man took the paper and held it up so that everyone could read the headline. THE WEEKEND KILLER, it said in big black letters. The Old Man quickly scanned the report.

"OK, so now the public has a well-informed account of our investigation," he said crossly. "Most of the details are here."

"How did they get ahold of this?" Karin exclaimed.

"A homicide on Saturday or Sunday, three weeks in a row. That's bound to rouse interest," Margit said. "There was a lot in the papers about Fredell last week; a disabled guy attacked in his own home makes a good story. It was only a matter of time before they put two and two together."

The Old Man tossed the paper aside. "We'll deal with the press when we're done here. Any volunteers?"

His question was met by absolute silence. He snorted, but without much conviction. Thomas stood up and went back to the whiteboard. He picked up a blue marker and wrote *DETERGENT* in capital letters.

"What's going on with the detergent? The autopsy showed traces in two of the victims, and I'm betting the same will be true in Kaufman's case."

"What do you use detergent for?" Margit said, thinking aloud. "You clean, you wash, you get rid of dirt and stains."

"Maybe the killer has some kind of hang-up," Erik Blom speculated, running his fingers through his slicked-back hair. "Something to do with water and cleanliness?"

He looked as if he hadn't shaved this morning, but then again, the faint stubble was probably intentional rather than the result of a hurried departure from home. He reminded Thomas of a trendy advertising executive, not a down-to-earth cop.

"Perhaps he's washing his hands," Erik went on.

"I'm not sure what you mean."

"I'm just wondering if our perp is trying to say he's not guilty, that he's somehow not to blame?"

Thomas was doubtful. If Erik was right, the killer should have been the one undergoing the cleansing process, not the victims.

"I don't agree," he said. "I think the detergent is connected with the men who were killed."

"Any traces of detergent on Marcus Nielsen's body?" the Old Man wondered.

"Not as far as I know."

"He was much younger than the others," the Old Man went on. "Could the age difference be a factor?"

"You mean he was 'cleaner' in some way?" Once again, Margit drew quotation marks in the air. "Less guilty than the rest?"

"Something like that."

"It's possible." Margit leaned back in her seat. "But it's weird. I don't get it, anyhow."

She wriggled out of her thick cardigan and dropped it on the empty chair beside her.

"Where does this guilt come from?" Thomas said. "Why would the killer be trying to cleanse his victims?"

They all looked at one another. Nobody had an answer.

After the meeting, Margit followed Thomas into his office and sat down. He had picked up the newspaper on his way out of the conference room, and he'd glanced through the rest of the article. The journalist had a good overview of the course of events, but he didn't know all the details.

"At least they haven't made the link with the military," Thomas said when he'd finished reading.

"I can't get ahold of Elsa Harning," Margit said. "I've left several messages, but she hasn't gotten back to me."

"We need the names of the rest of that group." Thomas stood up and went out into the corridor. "Karin!" he called.

Karin emerged from her office; her cheeks were slightly flushed, but she looked pleased with herself, as if she knew what he wanted. She was carrying two plastic folders.

"Any luck with Eklund and Kihlberg?"

"I was just coming to see you. I got in at seven this morning to start searching."

"Thank you."

Thomas took the folders and went back to Margit. One was marked *Stefan Eklund*, the other *Leif Kihlberg*. Eklund's contained only a single sheet of paper.

"Eklund is no longer in Sweden," he said. "He emigrated to Australia in the eighties. Karin hasn't managed to find a current address."

"What about Kihlberg?"

Thomas skimmed the closely written text.

"He lives in Gothenburg."

"Not Stockholm," Margit said pensively. "I wonder if he's visited the city over the past few weekends?"

Thomas knew exactly what she meant.

"I suggest we go to Gothenburg tomorrow and ask him in person."

Thomas remembered the words attributed to the famous jazz pianist Count Basie: It's not the music that's important, it's the notes you don't hear that count.

Which notes should they be listening for?

Chapter 50

Nora was alone in the bed when she woke up again. It was past ten o'clock; she had slept much later than she'd intended.

At first, she was disappointed that Jonas was gone. Then she remembered: he had mentioned on Friday evening that he would be flying to Bangkok on Sunday. No doubt he had caught the early morning ferry to Stavsnäs. She sank back against the pillow and lay there for a while half-dozing, half-awake as her mind wandered.

She kept on seeing Jonas in the moonlight. The silhouette of his body as he slept, her naked stomach against his back when she opened her eyes at dawn. His soft smile when she kissed him awake.

Eventually she got up and pulled on her robe. She decided not to shower and get dressed just yet; she didn't want to wash away last night. Instead she would treat herself to a cup of coffee on the veranda. It still felt strange, doing as she pleased without having to think about making breakfast for the rest of the family, but for the first time since she could remember, it was good to be alone.

There was a little note on the kitchen table.

Hugs and kisses, Jonas, it said in pencil. Beside it stood a glass containing a rosebud that was just about to flower. He must have picked one of the last red roses from the climber scrambling up the side of the house. The romantic gesture warmed her heart, and she bent down to sniff the bud. The faint scent reminded her of summer. *Even if it was only one night, it wasn't a mistake,* she told herself again.

Nora was locking the front door behind her when she heard someone calling her name. She turned and saw Olle Granlund.

"Are you heading home?"

"I'm afraid so—I have work to do, and the boys will be back from Henrik's tomorrow."

Saying it out loud intensified her longing to see them. She checked her watch; the last ferry of the day would be leaving in fifteen minutes. She mustn't miss it. Last night's lack of sleep was making itself felt now; she had tried to have a nap in the afternoon but couldn't settle. She slipped the keys in her pocket and walked to the gate.

Olle was holding a sheet of paper that looked as if it had been torn from an old block of file paper; there were four round holes in the margin on one side, and a faint thumbprint was visible in one corner.

"I found the poem by Elias Sehlstedt, the one I mentioned yesterday on Korsö. I wrote it down for you."

Nora was touched.

"That's really kind—thank you."

She took the paper and read the poem out loud.

> *"Three cheers for Avén! Salute his name!*
> *May happiness pick her flowers for you!*
> *Here you have your own commission,*
> *You will never be disturbed by the Skeppsholm bell.*
> *At the top of this tower, high in the sky,*
> *You will sit like the sun itself,*
> *Shining your light out across the sea*
> *So that the sons of the sea will not founder.*

"It's wonderful. Thank you so much."

Nora could have sworn she saw a faint blush on the old man's cheeks.

"I thought you might like it," he said.

Nora glanced at her watch again; she really couldn't afford to miss the ferry.

Olle was shuffling as if he had decided to tell her something but didn't know how.

"I've been thinking about what you asked me yesterday," he began. "Old rumors about the Coastal Rangers."

"Yes?" Nora opened the gate.

Olle looked around as if he were afraid someone might overhear.

"You remember I told you that the Rangers were trained to be hard on themselves and on others?"

Nora nodded. Olle shifted from one foot to the other, looking anything but happy.

"Sometimes things went wrong; sometimes the officers got out of control."

Nora felt as if she was prying into matters that didn't concern her, but she shook off her concerns and listened anyway.

"Training for the Rangers was always tough, but there were some pretty unpleasant characters back then, the kind who went too far because they liked it, not because it was necessary."

Nora put down her bag.

"Complete sadists, to tell the truth. One sergeant in particular had a terrible reputation. I heard about a recruit who was willing to do anything to be sent home; he was on the point of collapse. The pressure got too much for the poor guy."

"What happened to him?"

"He stabbed himself with a knife. He made a deep gash in one leg; there was blood everywhere, and, of course, he couldn't march anymore. I guess he thought they'd have to send him home then."

"And did they?"

"No. The sergeant was a complete bastard. He just stood there when he saw what the kid had done. Told him to slash the other leg as well."

The words made Nora recoil. "You're kidding me!"

Olle bowed his head. "That's not the worst of it."

Nora could see the sorrow in his face. And something else. Shame over a brother-in-arms.

"How could it get any worse?"

"Eventually the soldier managed to get away, but he died in a car accident shortly afterward. They say that this particular sergeant proposed a toast in the mess, because the recruit hadn't been up to the mark as a Coastal Ranger, and he was glad to be rid of him."

"That sounds crazy."

"Yes, but like I said, these were bad apples, the exception to the rule."

Olle ran a hand over his gray hair, still thick despite his age.

"You have to remember that the majority of them were fine soldiers. The purpose of the Coastal Rangers has always been to defend Sweden from attack, which means the stamina and resilience of those men has to be tested to the limit."

Nora was torn between her desire to hear more and her need to catch the ferry. One last question, then she would have to run.

"Do you remember the name of this sergeant?"

Olle scratched the back of his neck. His blue overalls had brown patches on the knees, presumably because he spent so much time kneeling on the jetty repairing things.

"It's such a long time ago . . ." He rubbed behind his ear, looking disappointed. "But I can try to find out."

Nora picked up her bag.

"When did all this happen?"

"In the seventies."

DIARY:
MAY 1977

"My father," Andersson said tersely.

We were on the northern side of Sandhamn, on a hill just before the inlet to the harbor. Behind us lay a large villa with a fantastic view out across the sea.

For once, we had been given evening leave and permission to go over to Sandhamn. The villagers don't like our visits; they think we make too much noise. Therefore, there is a tacit agreement that we stay on Korsö and avoid Sandhamn as much as possible. But it's not possible to keep us cooped up there all the time, so occasionally we're allowed to come over. It only takes ten minutes to row across, and we had been looking forward to this visit for a long time.

We had moored our camouflage-painted boat by the pilot's jetty last night. There were twenty of us, and we went and had something to eat at the inn. After dinner, the others went off to the Sailors Bar where there was a dance, but Andersson and I went up to Kvarnberget with a couple of beers to watch the sun go down. Admittedly, we'd had a few drinks, but we weren't drunk, just a little subdued.

I'd had a letter from my mother; she and my father were getting divorced. And Andersson—well, I guess he just didn't feel like painting the town red.

It was almost eleven, but the endless early-summer sky had only just begun to grow dark. In the distance, a cargo ship made its way toward the Baltic, its red superstructure rising above the tops of the pine trees, making the forest look like a shrunken backdrop in an animated film.

I had to ask the question that had been occupying my mind for a long time. I took a drag on my cigarette as I wondered exactly how to put it.

Why didn't he tell the army to go to hell?

Why did he let the sergeant pick on him, day after day? Nobody should have to suffer as much as Andersson did.

"Why do you take so much crap from the sergeant?" I said at last.

He made a funny little noise. At first, I thought he wasn't going to answer, then his mouth moved, barely visible in the twilight, and the pale, downy hairs on his chin quivered.

"My father."

"Your father?" I repeated. I could hear how stupid I sounded.

I took a last drag and stubbed out my cigarette on the damp ground. The bare branches of the birch trees sprawled below us; their leaves had only just started to appear, and the lilac hedges surrounding the houses in the village were covered in pale-green buds.

Andersson shrugged.

"My father was stationed here after the war. He's a captain in the reserves, and he's always talking about his old comrades in the Coastal Rangers."

He took a swig of his beer, then wiped his mouth with the back of his hand.

"He was part of one of the first cohorts of Rangers, and he never stops telling me about those days—how they spent that year out here, everything they went through, the cold and the hunger. But they put up with it all for the sake of our country. The war was still fresh in their minds, of course."

He almost seemed to be talking to himself now; he was speaking quietly.

"Every year he goes off on military exercises for at least a week at a time. Then he comes home and boasts about it—'The old man isn't finished yet!' Sometimes he and his pals from the Rangers meet at our place; they toast the old days while my mother runs around serving them food and drink. They get totally wasted and stay up half the night, laughing and talking."

A heartfelt sigh, deep in his chest.

"The following day, he's hungover, and my mother and sister have to clean up as usual."

Far away, I could see the Getholmen lighthouse flashing. The sky had turned deep blue, and the beam of light sliced through the gathering darkness. A motor launch chugged by, its red port light glowing on our side.

"What do you think he would have said if I'd applied to a different regiment? Or opted for community service instead?" Andersson gazed out at the horizon as he went on: "'I'm so pleased you're making your own choices, son.' Or maybe he would have wished me luck . . ." The bitterness in his voice was unmistakable. He was squeezing the beer can so hard his knuckles were white. "I have no intention of getting kicked out and slinking home with my tail between my legs. I can do this."

He looked down at the can, crushed almost beyond recognition.

"Then I'll tell my father to go to hell."

CHAPTER 51

"Thomas. Thomas, you need to wake up."

The sound of Pernilla's voice slowly penetrated Thomas's consciousness. Exhaustion had gotten the better of him that afternoon; he had gone home and crashed out on top of the bedclothes.

"How long have I been asleep?" he mumbled.

"A long time." She sounded worried. "It's almost six."

Pernilla stroked his cheek; the palm of her hand felt cool against his warm skin.

"How are you feeling?"

He rolled over onto his back and looked up at the ceiling.

"Worn out."

"You mustn't overdo it. Don't forget that this is your first major case since going back to work."

He pulled her close and buried his face in her hair. As always, it smelled fresh and newly washed, and he lay there for a few seconds without moving. Then he raised his head, and their eyes met.

"Don't worry about me. The most important thing right now is in there."

He patted her slightly rounded belly. Had it gotten bigger over the past week, or was he just imagining things?

"Snuffkin," she said. "Our little snuffkin."

"Snuffkin?"

"Well, we have to call it something." Thomas was struck by the happiness in her eyes. "We need a working title for the newest member of the family. Maybe you have a better suggestion?"

She lay down beside him, and Thomas was on the point of falling asleep again when she spoke.

"By the way, you had a phone call."

He propped himself up on one elbow. "Why didn't you wake me?"

"You were completely out of it. I came in and tried, but I got nowhere."

Thomas swung his legs over the side of the bed.

"OK. I'll go and check who it was, just to be on the safe side."

He went into the hallway and took his cell phone out of his jacket pocket. *Missed call.* It was a Stockholm number, but he didn't recognize it. He pressed redial and waited.

"Fredell."

Was it Jan-Erik Fredell's widow, Lena? Thomas wasn't sure.

"This is Thomas Andreasson. I think you tried to reach me earlier—is that Lena?"

"My name is Annelie Fredell—I'm her daughter."

Thomas went into the kitchen and sat down.

"I have a missed call from this number, a couple of hours ago."

"That must have been my mom. Hold on, and I'll get her."

After a few seconds, another voice came on the line, sounding weary and listless.

"Hello."

Finding her husband murdered must have been horrific, Thomas thought. It was Lena who had been the backbone of the family during Jan-Erik's illness; had his dependence been the fuel that kept her going? Had she now simply run out of strength?

"Hi, Lena, it's Thomas Andreasson. I think you tried to get ahold of me; how can I help?"

"I hope I'm not disturbing you."

"Of course not."

Thomas could hear her breathing, but she didn't say anything.

"What can I do for you?" he said.

A sharp intake of breath, then Lena seemed to make up her mind.

"I . . . There's something I need to tell you." Her voice was far from steady.

"Tell me."

"It might not be important, but I thought I'd mention it all the same." She coughed. "When I was clearing out the closets yesterday, I found Janne's old diaries."

"He kept a diary?"

"Yes, all his life, until his illness made it too difficult for him. He used to write for a while before he went to sleep. I sometimes wondered if he secretly dreamed of becoming an author; he had such a way with words."

"I understand."

Thomas pulled out the top drawer, searching for something to write with. The first pen didn't work, but he had better luck with the second. He transferred the phone to his left hand.

Lena Fredell swallowed hard.

"When Marcus Nielsen came to see us, he asked questions about Janne's military service."

"Yes, your husband mentioned that."

"As you know, Janne was finding it harder and harder to remember because of his illness. Marcus brought up all kinds of things, and in the end, Janne asked me to fetch the diaries."

She fell silent for a moment. "He wanted to be able to leaf through them during the conversation," she went on. "As a memory prop."

These diaries could help us track down the rest of the group, Thomas thought, *which would save waiting for the military to dig through their archives.* And maybe Jan-Erik Fredell's notes would provide other vital information.

"Janne went through them, and Marcus was very interested in what he had to say. They spent quite a while together."

"Could I take a look at these diaries?"

"I can't find them. I think Janne must have let Marcus take them. He got tired; maybe he lent Marcus the diaries when he couldn't talk anymore."

"Do you know what was in them?"

Lena's voice was stronger, less afraid and uncertain, as if she was now confident that contacting Thomas had been the right thing to do.

"No, I was never allowed to read them. Janne always kept them tucked away."

But why did he show them to a stranger if the contents were a secret? Thomas wondered. It didn't make sense.

"Janne was very careful with his diaries; he actually kept them locked away in boxes," Lena explained. "It wasn't like him to act that way. In fact, he didn't really enjoy talking about his military service like a lot of men do."

"Why not?"

"I don't know, but I was surprised that he was willing to speak to Marcus."

"He didn't give you an explanation?"

"No. Did Janne tell you that Marcus came across his name in a yearbook? Perhaps that was why he got involved. I'll never know . . . He might have told me eventually, but . . ."

A barely audible sob.

"I forgot all about it after Janne died; I was in such a state when I saw you. It wasn't until I started going through the closets that I realized they were gone."

"Don't worry," Thomas reassured her. "One last question: What do these boxes look like?"

"They're black, with a small lock, and they're all marked with the year. The one Marcus must have taken is 1977. There's a whole shelf filled with boxes, all in order. But I haven't read a single word. I haven't opened any of them."

Thomas wondered why she was so keen to convince him; was she suffering from a guilty conscience? He was sure he hadn't seen a box like that in Marcus Nielsen's apartment. He would need to check the records to make sure, but he should have noticed it if it had been there. Could it be at Marcus's parents' house?

"Thanks for your help, Lena. I'm so glad you called and told me all this."

He hung up, then went through the notes he had made during the conversation. So now both Marcus's laptop and Jan-Erik Fredell's diaries were missing.

That couldn't possibly be a coincidence.

Thomas was in the bathroom, toothbrush in hand, when his cell phone rang. The display informed him that it was Nora; what did she want at this hour?

She got straight to the point as usual.

"You asked me to speak to my neighbor, Olle Granlund. He told me quite a lot about what the military got up to on Korsö."

Thomas went into the living room and sank down onto the sofa. Pernilla had gone to bed shortly after nine, and he didn't want to disturb her. He leaned back, fighting off the tiredness. It just wouldn't go away, even though he had slept all afternoon.

"What did he say?"

"He described it as an unusual place, to say the least. He said the aim was to push the soldiers to the breaking point; only then could they be built up again into real Coastal Rangers. An elite force with particular combat skills, he called them. It sounds pretty sick, if you ask me."

Thomas could hear clinking and clattering in the background, as if Nora was unloading the dishwasher, putting away glasses and china.

She continued. "Apparently there were some officers who crossed the line." She told him about the recruit who had stabbed himself in the leg. "So what do you think of that?"

"It sounds appalling. Any names?"

"Olle mentioned a sergeant who was especially sadistic, but he couldn't remember his name."

When the call was over, Thomas remained sitting on the sofa with Nora's words ringing in his ears. *The aim was to create an elite force by pushing the soldiers to the breaking point.*

Was there someone out there who had been pushed too far thirty years ago?

CHAPTER 52

Monday (The Third Week)

The long corridor with its white-painted walls seemed endless. Thomas and Pernilla went the wrong way several times before they finally reached the small reception desk. A sign above said "Ultrasound Reception" in blue letters.

Pernilla had had to remind Thomas about the appointment that morning. With a sigh, she had waited while he called Margit from the car to tell her he wouldn't be in before ten; they would have to catch a later train to Gothenburg.

A friendly nurse showed them into a room with the blinds drawn. There were various machines, one of them with a flashing green light. Pernilla was told to lie on the bed and pull up her top. The nurse smeared a clear gel on her stomach.

"I'd forgotten how cold it is!" Pernilla said.

Thomas stayed in the background. He hadn't said anything for quite some time, and his expression was grim. Pernilla could see that the situation was making him uncomfortable. She tried to catch his eye but without success.

If something was wrong, it was better to find out now, before their little snuffkin was born and became a real person, a child she could hold in her arms and hug and kiss. *It's better to lose a fetus than a full-term baby*, she thought, although she had to steel herself at the idea.

"You can sit down," the nurse said to Thomas, pointing to a stool beside the bed. Thomas did as he was told. Pernilla took his hand and gave it a reassuring squeeze, but the tension was still there in every line of his face, and he was sitting up as straight as a poker.

They had been together exactly like this when they saw Emily for the first time. Pernilla swallowed to get rid of the lump in her throat.

This time everything would be fine; it just had to be.

The door opened, and the doctor came in. His hair was drawn back in a neat ponytail. He seemed far too young to be doing this—he looked as if he'd just graduated from college. Then Pernilla realized it wasn't the doctor who was too young, it was she and Thomas who had grown older. He was forty-one, and she would be forty in November.

Mature parents, whichever way you looked at it.

But not first-time parents.

The doctor held out his hand.

"Peder Backlund. Welcome."

Pernilla managed a wan smile.

"OK, let's see what we've got here," he said, switching on the ultrasound machine. With a practiced hand, he moved the metal probe over Pernilla's stomach; it felt cold and sterile against her skin.

The little screen next to the bed flickered, and a gray-green, extremely grainy image appeared.

"You're in the ninth week, is that correct?"

Pernilla nodded.

"And how are you feeling?"

"I'm very tired, but otherwise OK."

"Any nausea?"

The doctor was glancing from her stomach to the screen and back as he asked questions.

"Quite a lot, especially in the mornings. But it should pass soon—at least I hope so."

Pernilla stared at the screen. A curled-up figure was clearly visible; she knew it was actually only about an inch long at this stage.

There really was a life in there, a tiny heart beating away. From time to time, the arms twitched, small movements caused by primeval instincts and reflexes. The minute head moved a fraction, as if it was wondering who was out there. Who was peeping in.

The eyelids, just discernible on the diffuse image, were no more than black dots, and the hands, or what would become hands in a few months, were sticking out.

A little fish, swimming in the sea Pernilla's womb had created.

A wave of relief flooded her body.

"There it is. Look, Thomas." She turned to him. "Can you see it? That's our baby."

Thomas didn't speak or move, but he seemed marginally less tense. Pernilla could see that his eyes were suspiciously shiny.

Peder Backlund calmly described what the probe was picking up behind the layers of skin and muscle. *It's remarkable,* Pernilla thought. Remarkable and incomprehensible that the instrument being passed across her stomach could produce these images, that it was possible to see her child many months before the birth, enabling a doctor to establish that everything was as it should be, even though the fetus was only a couple of months old.

"So these are the legs, and here you can see both arms," Dr. Backlund explained.

The gentle pressure of the probe wasn't unpleasant, just a little chilly.

"And this is the spine."

He repeated the circular movement and leaned forward, closer to the screen.

"Now, let's see . . ." he murmured.

Pernilla froze.

"Is something wrong?"

The air grew thick; she could hardly breathe. Dr. Backlund shook his head.

"Nothing to worry about, I just want to check something. One second."

He reached for the tube of gel and spread another layer over Pernilla's stomach. This time, she didn't make a sound when she felt the coldness against her skin. Anxiously, she studied the doctor's face, trying to work out what he wasn't saying. *Please don't let anything go wrong.*

Not again.

She was terrified and squeezed Thomas's hand so hard that he gently released her grip. He still didn't say anything, but as he stroked her hair, she knew that he was equally worried.

The only sound in the small room was the hum of the fan cooling the mechanism.

The doctor picked up his stethoscope and listened carefully for a minute or so, then he turned up the volume on the ultrasound machine.

Was that her baby's heartbeat? It sounded irregular—was that a bad sign?

"Is this your first?"

Thomas shook his head.

"We had a daughter a few years ago," Pernilla whispered, "but she died when she was a baby."

On the screen, shadows drifted in and out of one another like a kaleidoscope in black and white, forming patterns that dissolved a second later.

"There we go, all done." Dr. Backlund was smiling. "I can tell you the sex, if you'd like to know?"

Pernilla looked at Thomas, then nodded. She was still so frightened. "OK, so . . ."

Dr. Backlund put down his stethoscope and pointed to the screen where the little head had just been swaying like a reed in the wind.

Pernilla sat up so that she could see better. The shadow had turned slightly; she couldn't help touching the screen with her fingertips.

"Congratulations," the doctor said. "You're having a little girl."

Chapter 53

Pernilla couldn't stop crying, but she kept assuring Thomas that he didn't need to worry about her.

"I'm just happy," she said. "Honestly." The words came spilling out so fast that he couldn't keep up. "It's crazy, Thomas, we're going to be a family again, I can't believe it."

"Just calm down, honey," Thomas said, blinking away something damp in the corner of his eye. "We've still got a long way to go."

He dropped her off at the office, wondering how she was going to avoid giving her secret away as soon as she walked in. The ultrasound had made the pregnancy real for both of them; suddenly they dared to believe in a miracle.

He was still processing what the doctor had told them when he arrived at work. He was due to meet Margit, but when he stepped out of the elevator on the third floor, she was waiting in the corridor.

"I managed to get ahold of Leif Kihlberg—he's in Stockholm. Well, not exactly, but he's arriving late tonight for a conference tomorrow, so I've arranged to meet him at his hotel at eight thirty in the morning."

"That's good—so we don't have to go to Gothenburg."

She gave him a searching look.

"Are you OK?"

"Sure."

Thomas did his best to appear normal.

"Absolutely sure?"

Suspicion was written all over Margit's face. She took a step closer, keeping her eyes fixed on him.

Thomas gave in. She knew him too well.

"I've been to the hospital with Pernilla for an ultrasound. We're having a baby." He couldn't help grinning. "A little girl."

"Oh, Thomas!"

For once, Margit seemed deeply affected.

"Come into my office." She turned on her heel, and Thomas followed her. He sank down in the visitor's armchair and realized he couldn't stop smiling. Yesterday's tiredness was completely gone.

Margit closed the door.

"Congratulations—that's fantastic!"

"We didn't think we could have another baby, at least not without IVF or something. I never imagined we'd get another chance," he said quietly.

Margit's sharp features softened, and Thomas saw genuine warmth in her deep-set eyes. Her normally furrowed brow smoothed out, and she got up to give him a big hug.

"I'm so happy for you both. You really deserve this, especially after everything you've been through."

She seemed embarrassed by her outburst of emotion, and she quickly returned to her seat.

"We're keeping it quiet for a while," Thomas said. "Pernilla's only in her ninth week."

"I understand. I won't say a word."

Margit took a deep breath and clapped her hands.

"So it's back to the sleepless nights!"

"I know. Or at least I think I know. I probably have no idea what it's going to be like this time around. I still feel as if I'm dreaming."

There was a knock on the door, and Karin Ek came in.

"Good morning—have you recovered?" she said to Thomas, who had no idea what she was talking about.

Margit came to his rescue.

"I explained that you were taking things easy after the accident on Saturday."

Thomas gave her a grateful look.

"I'm feeling much better, thanks."

"The military have been in touch." Karin held out a bundle of papers with an official stamp at the top of the first page.

"Is that from Elsa Harning?" Margit asked.

"Yes."

"Let's see," Thomas said. He quickly glanced through the contents and got to his feet.

"Karin, can you gather everyone together right away please," he said decisively.

CHAPTER 54

Thomas had pinned up the pages on the whiteboard. Each one consisted of a biography of an individual, complete with personal data and a photograph from the seventies. The young men were eerily alike, with their cropped hair and grim expressions. They were all staring straight into the camera as if they were hypnotized by the lens.

Thomas read aloud: "Leif Kihlberg, team leader; Anders Martinger; Björn Sigurd; Jan-Erik Fredell; Bo Kaufman; Sven Erneskog; Stefan Eklund.

"So now we know who was in Kaufman's group. We must thank Captain Harning and the military for their assistance." His tone was ironic. He marked the names of the three victims with a black X: Fredell, Kaufman, and Erneskog.

"Margit and I are meeting Kihlberg tomorrow morning," he went on. "He works as a deputy fire chief in a suburb of Gothenburg. He's married for the second time and has two boys aged twenty-one and twenty-three from his first marriage."

He paused and took a step back.

"Björn Sigurd made a career with the military and completed several overseas tours of duty, including a spell with the peacekeeping forces in Bosnia."

"So he was a real soldier," Kalle Lidwall said.

Thomas could have sworn he saw a glimmer of admiration in his younger colleague's eyes.

"Hang on . . . Sigurd is dead."

"What happened?" Margit immediately wanted to know.

"Let's see . . . He was killed in the line of duty in Bosnia. He was traveling in a truck that hit a land mine. Everyone on board died instantaneously."

Kalle Lidwall looked suitably chastened.

"Any relatives?" Erik Blom wondered, clicking his pen.

"A widow," Thomas read. "Anne-Marie Sigurd—she's a nurse. No mention of any kids."

"So who does that leave?" Kalle said.

"Martinger and Eklund," Margit replied. "But Stefan Eklund emigrated to Australia in the nineties, and we don't have his address."

"I've started searching for him," Karin said apologetically, "but it's not that easy to find a Swedish immigrant in Australia. They're not too quick getting back to me from the other side of the world. Thank goodness for the Swedish ID number system; we can locate anyone with the click of a button."

Thomas moved on to the final biography.

"Anders Martinger joined the air force. He flew combat aircraft, mainly the Viggen, then moved over to the commercial sector at the end of the eighties and started working for SAS. He lives in Sigtuna, and he's also on his second marriage. Three children, a son of nineteen and two daughters aged fifteen and five. His current wife, Siri, is a flight attendant."

"Does shaving off their hair make them emotionally stunted?" Margit snorted. "Or are they just too macho to stick with one woman?"

"Sweden has the highest divorce rate in the world, if you include those who live together but don't marry," Karin informed her. "It's not just the Coastal Rangers' relationships."

The Old Man interjected. "So the former rangers haven't done too badly, with the exception of Bo Kaufman."

Margit snorted again.

Erik continued clicking his ballpoint pen as he stared at the board, until Karin couldn't stand it any longer.

"Could you stop doing that!" she snapped.

"Seven men," Margit said pensively. "They did their military service together over thirty years ago. One died in Bosnia, three have been murdered, and a young man who tried to get information from them is also dead."

Erik Blom suddenly stood up and went over to the board. He took down the sheets of paper, reorganized them, then pinned them back up again.

- *Stefan Eklund*
- *Sven Erneskog*
- *Jan-Erik Fredell*
- *Bo Kaufman*
- *Leif Kihlberg*
- *Anders Martinger*
- *Björn Sigurd*

He returned to his seat without saying a word. There was no need.

"Alphabetical order," Margit exclaimed. "The bastard is killing them in alphabetical order!"

"One by one," Erik agreed.

"With military precision, you mean," Karin said. She blushed. "Sorry, that just slipped out."

"So Leif Kihlberg could be next," Margit said slowly. "Then Martinger."

The silence in the room was palpable.

"There is another possibility," Thomas said after a moment. "Yes, Kihlberg or Martinger could be the perpetrator's next victim . . ." He ran a hand through his blond hair as he considered his words. "Or one of them could be the perpetrator . . ."

"A ranger killing other rangers?" Kalle said.

Thomas gave him an appreciative look.

"Let's assume that there's an old grudge within this group, a perceived injustice that happened many years ago. For some reason that we don't understand, it's come to the surface now."

He pointed to Kihlberg's and Martinger's biographies.

"A pilot and a firefighter. Two men in highly qualified professions that require the ability to keep a clear head in critical situations. Everything about the MO suggests that our perpetrator is both intelligent and has the capacity to improvise."

He could see Kaufman's bedroom in his mind's eye. All the killer had needed was a gun, a bottle of whisky, and a pillow. Less than half an hour, and the deed was done.

"Two of the group are still alive and living in Sweden," he went on. "Kihlberg and Martinger. Plus, they both have jobs that could explain why the murders took place on the weekends. Kihlberg lives in Gothenburg, and Martinger is a pilot."

Margit looked dubious. "I thought Elsa Harning said there was a strong bond between the Coastal Rangers. Would they really be prepared to kill one another?"

Thomas considered her question.

"They're soldiers who've been trained to cut themselves off emotionally," he said. "Nothing must stop them from carrying out their task."

"The end justifies the means," Erik said.

"Exactly. With that kind of attitude, I would imagine that they could definitely turn on their own—if the situation requires them to do so."

"But why is this happening here and now?" Kalle said.

Thomas shrugged. "I've no idea, but it must be something deeply personal to make someone go overboard like this."

"It might not necessarily be an injustice," Margit said. "Maybe he wants to keep something under wraps—information that mustn't come out?"

"It's a bit extreme, murdering three, or possibly four, people to prevent a secret from being revealed," the Old Man remarked.

"Yes, but these elite soldiers *are* extreme," Thomas countered.

"I still don't understand how Marcus Nielsen fits in," Karin said.

Thomas thought back to Lena Fredell's phone call.

"Fredell's wife contacted me; she thinks her husband might have lent Marcus Nielsen some of his diaries."

"And what was in them?"

"She didn't know, she's never been allowed to read them. I checked the list of Nielsen's belongings, and there's no mention of any diaries, so it looks as if they're missing."

Something suddenly occurred to Thomas. Had Jan-Erik Fredell felt the need to talk about an incident in the past? He knew he didn't have long left; maybe he saw the diaries as a way of passing on a secret he had carried for many years. When Nielsen called him out of the blue, he might have thought this was his last chance to put things right. The student would be his messenger.

Fredell couldn't have predicted the catastrophe he was about to unleash.

"Maybe Marcus found something in the diaries," Thomas speculated.

"In which case, it must have been pure dynamite," Erik said.

The killer's actions certainly indicate that he is consumed by a deep anger, Thomas thought.

"So how did the perp know what Marcus had found?" Kalle demanded, folding his arms. His cropped hair reminded Thomas of the young men in Kaufman's photographs.

"We know who Nielsen contacted, and that doesn't help us," he said. "Plus, several of them are dead; they can hardly have murdered themselves."

"In which case, Nielsen must have gotten ahold of our killer by some other means," Erik said.

"Just a minute." Kalle's hand went to his forehead. "We checked Marcus's calls from his cell phone, but didn't he spend a lot of time at his parents' place?"

"He did," Margit confirmed.

"We haven't checked the calls from their landline. Marcus could have used their phone to contact the killer."

"Get on it right away," the Old Man said.

Margit sat up straight, the look in her eyes even more intense than usual.

"Don't forget Stefan Eklund," she reminded them. "We haven't managed to track him down; he could be the joker in the pack."

The same thing had occurred to Thomas.

"We need to find out where he is as soon as possible. Meanwhile, let's deal with the two who are still in Sweden."

"We're seeing Kihlberg tomorrow," Margit said.

"And Martinger?" Thomas said, then answered his own question. "We need to find him right away, too."

Margit turned to Karin.

"Do what you can to get ahold of a current address for Eklund. Ask the Foreign Office to help you if necessary, and call Elsa Harning."

Karin made a note on her pad. "I'm on it."

"We need to check whether Kihlberg and Martinger have alibis for the relevant times," Margit said, turning to the Old Man.

Thomas was already on his way out of the room.

CHAPTER 55

Nora had left work early to pick up the boys. The sun was shining, but it was nowhere near as warm as it had been the previous week. She parked outside Simon's school and got out of the car with her purse over her shoulder. Laughter and cheerful shouts filled the yard. She recognized one of Adam's former teachers standing by the door.

Both boys had attended the Igelboda school from first grade, but Adam had moved over to the hundred-year-old coeducational school at the end of fifth grade. Simon would be following in his footsteps in a few years.

Nora spotted her youngest son with a group of boys scrambling like monkeys over a jungle gym in the middle of the yard.

"Simon!" she shouted as she got closer. "Simon!"

He stopped and turned his head. As soon as he saw her, he clambered down and came running. Nora dropped on one knee and held out her arms.

"Hi, sweetheart."

She hugged him and rubbed her nose against his hair until he wriggled free.

"Everything OK?" she asked.

"Yes," he said, then frowned.

"What's wrong?"

"You know I have to bring ice cream tomorrow?"

Whenever someone had a birthday, they took in ice cream for the whole class.

"It's already in the freezer, so you don't need to worry."

Nora tried to take his hand, but he wouldn't let her. Too many friends around, she realized. By the time he moved up to the next class, he would no longer be her baby boy.

"Can we go home? I'm hungry."

"Didn't you have a snack at recess?"

"Yes, but I'm still hungry."

He patted his tummy; the gesture made Nora think of a little old man, and she couldn't help smiling.

"OK, but we have to pick up Adam first. Can you hold out a while longer?"

"Mmm."

Adam usually made his own way home, but Nora picked him up on Mondays because he had his bag with him after staying at Henrik's. To tell the truth, she didn't mind at all; she rarely went anywhere near his school these days, and she was glad for the excuse.

"OK, let's go."

Just as she got behind the wheel, her cell phone beeped. She gave a start; was it a message from Jonas?

She rummaged around in her purse and grabbed her phone, feeling ridiculously excited. She had been hoping to hear from him all day.

However, the message was from Henrik, and much less welcome.

Simon left his English book here. Can you pick it up?

Any trace of happiness disappeared in a second.

Every time the phone rang over the past twenty-four hours, she had hoped it would be Jonas. She was like a coiled spring as she waited for him to contact her. It reminded her of being a teenager, when the key was to play hard to get rather than being too keen. She hadn't been comfortable behaving that way back then, but it was hard not to fall into old habits.

It was sixteen years since she'd last been single, and she didn't know how to play the game anymore. She had no idea how dating worked these days, and she certainly didn't know what the rules were when you'd slept with someone.

She stuffed the phone back into her purse.

They had spent a night together, that was all. She had to stop thinking about him and get on with her life. Anyway, he was in Thailand, on the other side of the world.

Nora noticed Simon glancing sideways at her, and she pushed all thoughts of Jonas aside. She dug her phone out again and called Henrik; he answered almost right away.

"It's Nora. I got your message. You can drop by and leave the book in the mailbox."

"I won't have time today. I'll be at the hospital until late."

"You're the one who forgot to put it in his bag."

Why should she have to go and pick up the book, when it was Henrik's fault that it had been left behind? She had no desire to go anywhere near their old house; she certainly didn't want to catch a glimpse of Marie through the kitchen window.

"I didn't do it on purpose."

"I realize that, but I've got a lot going on this week. I work full-time as well, just like you."

"I have patients I can't leave."

And there it was, that patronizing tone.

As a doctor, Henrik was used to being obeyed. He was a respected radiologist, and it was rare for anyone to question his decisions.

"Oh, come on," he continued. "Surely you can drag yourself away from your credit agreements for a while? Simon's schoolwork is the most important thing, after all."

Typical. His job had always come before hers, but for once, Nora wasn't upset or angry. Instead she felt unexpectedly calm.

"In that case, I suggest you drop the book off first thing in the morning, before you go to work. Perhaps you could get up a few minutes earlier than usual. Good-bye."

Nora ended the call before he could protest. She stuck out her tongue at her reflection in the rearview mirror with a childish surge of triumph. She hadn't lost her temper, and she hadn't allowed him to get his way. She had simply told him what she wanted, like a grown woman.

It was a new experience.

Things were a lot quieter outside Adam's school. There were small groups of children sitting around, and there was nowhere near as much activity as in the Igelboda school yard.

Nora checked her watch; Adam should have finished ten minutes ago. He usually met her outside the gate, but there was no sign of him. She asked Simon to wait in the car, then got out to look for his brother.

Adam was standing under a large oak tree in the middle of the yard with a group of his peers. There was a girl with long dark hair by his side; she was wearing a short cutoff denim skirt with pink embroidery, and something about the way she was leaning toward Adam stopped Nora in her tracks.

Were they holding hands? She moved forward, trying to see, but just then Adam glanced up and saw her. He picked up his backpack and said something to the girl, who whispered in his ear. Then he set off toward Nora.

She tried to give him a hug, but he jerked away. She had to make do with ruffling his hair.

"Don't, Mom!"

He opened the car door and threw his bag on the backseat, then climbed in the front beside her. Nora tried to find the right words.

"I'm just glad to see you—you've been away for a whole week." She kept her tone light. "I've missed you so much—moms are allowed to do that, you know."

He softened slightly.

"I've missed you, too."

He allowed her to pat his cheek.

"So who was that?" Nora said, trying to seem only vaguely interested.

"Who was who?"

"That girl you were talking to."

"Lisa."

"Is she in your class?"

Adam shrugged, which Nora interpreted as a yes.

"What's her last name?"

Another shrug. He turned away and stared out the window. Nora said nothing but wondered if Lisa might be his first girlfriend. He was definitely growing up.

She started the car, made sure there was nothing behind her, then reversed out of the parking space.

She always felt better when the boys were back with her.

CHAPTER 56

It didn't take Karin Ek long to track down Anders Martinger. When she walked into Thomas's office, her short hair was slightly ruffled, as if she had gotten a little stressed and run her hands through it.

"I've spoken to human resources at SAS," she began.

"How did it go?"

"OK. Anders Martinger is on his way to New York; he won't be back until Wednesday morning. He's due into Arlanda at ten thirty."

"Well, at least he's safe until then," Thomas said.

"Or the other way around."

"Exactly."

Thomas knew what Karin meant. If Martinger was the killer, then Leif Kihlberg was out of his reach for the next two days. That gave them some breathing room.

"I asked them to send over his flight schedule for September." She came farther into the room, waving a piece of paper. "Martinger has been in Sweden over the last three weekends."

Thomas nodded toward the visitor's chair.

"Tell me more."

Karin sat down and crossed her legs.

"On the Sunday when Marcus Nielsen and Sven Erneskog were found, Anders Martinger wasn't on duty until the evening. He then flew to"—she paused and checked the schedule—"Copenhagen, because he was flying from Copenhagen to Chicago the following day. The next weekend was almost the same: he was on the Copenhagen to New York route; he started work on the Sunday evening when he traveled down to Kastrup."

"And last weekend?"

There was a hint of satisfaction in Karin's voice: "He was free—four days in a row. Pilots work on a rolling schedule, so that was his long weekend."

So Martinger had been home when the three men were murdered. Thomas considered the information.

"Well done," he said. "By the way, did you get a phone number for him?"

Karin handed over a piece of paper. "That's his cell, but you probably won't be able to contact him before eight o'clock this evening, Swedish time. I've written down the address of his hotel as well."

"Great—thanks for your help, Karin."

It had taken over an hour to shop for groceries and unpack the boys' things when they got home, and now the washing machine was humming away.

Nora took out her cell phone and checked her messages again, even though she had promised herself earlier in the afternoon that she wouldn't.

Nothing.

It must've been at least the fifteenth time she had looked to see if there might be a text message, but she just couldn't help it.

She knew perfectly well that Jonas was in Bangkok, and that he would be there for most of the week. Still, he could have shown some sign of life . . .

Had their night together been a distraction, an opportunity he had taken because it was offered? She just hoped she hadn't come across as a desperate divorcée who would jump into bed with anybody. The very thought was upsetting.

She slipped her cell back in her purse and went to get a start on dinner.

One thing she knew for sure: if he didn't get in touch, that was that. No way was she going to risk rejection. It was bad enough that Henrik had moved another woman into their home so quickly, as if all those years together had meant nothing.

Did she even want to see Jonas again?

The more she thought about it, the more uncertain she felt. One minute she was longing to see him; they had had a wonderful evening and night. After the lengthy torpor of the spring, those hours with Jonas had seemed like a gift.

But she refused to be hurt and abandoned all over again. And she would never, ever put up with a relationship like the one she had had with Henrik.

That's the last time I give in to another person, she thought bitterly.

Her ears burned as she remembered how she had meekly gone along with Henrik's routines and wishes. While he worked or went off sailing, she had taken care of the family and run the household. Time after time, she had done exactly what he wanted.

Never again.

She pulled herself together and took out a saucepan for the tortellini Simon had requested. She filled it with cold water, added a spoonful of salt, slammed on the lid, and put the pan on to boil.

One night, and he was already occupying her every waking thought.

It had cost her so much to regain control over her own life. She had no intention of relinquishing it now.

Time to stop thinking about Jonas Sköld.

Diary:
June 1977

I'm the only one who's awake. It's past midnight. The images keep passing through my mind, the feeling when it was my turn up there, the line slipping through my sweaty fingers.

My ankle is throbbing like crazy.

We had to climb down the outside of Korsö Tower, with a lifeline attached to our waist. The decommissioned lighthouse is around eighty-four feet high, and there are no natural footholds on its stone surface. The exercise was supposed to improve our coordination and muscle control, and the goal was to bounce off the façade as few times as possible.

"The record is zero," the sergeant bellowed. "Something to think about!"

The view from the top of the tower is astonishing. That's what most people say, anyhow. I just felt terrible when I looked down. It's a long, long way to the ground, and there is nothing at the bottom but solid rock and granite. Nothing to break a fall, no soft landing if you lose your grip.

I have never liked heights, I never wanted to go on roller-coaster rides when I was a kid. My stomach turns over at the mere thought of going up there.

We were to do the climb one at a time, and we waited in line on the narrow stone staircase inside. The atmosphere was tense; nobody said a word. The silence was broken only by rapid, nervous drags as some of us smoked, and the only thing we could see in the semidarkness was the glow of those cigarettes. Whenever a match was struck, I saw rigid, introspective faces.

I was fourth.

The sergeant was at the top with Captain Westerberg. They checked that the lines were secure. Safety was important. It was one thing if we fell because of our own clumsiness or incompetence, but they were responsible for ensuring that we had the right equipment and that it was correctly fastened.

When it was my turn, my mouth was filled with the taste of bile. I watched as Kihlberg let go and disappeared from view, and I knew it was time to step out onto the platform.

I wanted to throw up.

The sergeant clipped the lines to my body and took a step back. Cold sweat was trickling down the back of my neck.

There hadn't been much wind at ground level, but up here, the gusts made the cable swish around as if it had a life of its own. It hurled itself at the tower like an unruly puppy tugging at the leash.

I felt myself wobble; my legs didn't want to carry me. The sergeant yelled, "Get a move on!"

It was only sheer terror in the face of his rage that made me take a step forward to the very edge of the platform. I looked down and saw a blurred image of rock and heather. A second passed, then another. With hands that were slippery with sweat, I grabbed the rope and parted company with the tower.

I was convinced I was going to plunge to my death, but somehow I managed to work my way down. The whole time, a voice in my head was screaming that I could fall at any second.

I heard voices at the foot of the tower.

"Well done, Erneskog."

"*Nice work, Kihlberg.*"

"*Jeez, Andersson—you only bounced off the tower three times. Good work.*"

Those who had already succeeded were buzzing with a sense of achievement, and they shouted encouraging words to the rest of us.

You can do this, *I whispered to myself.* You can do this.

I was only yards from the ground when my sweaty fingers slipped, and I fell. A second later, I could feel nothing but an agonizing pain in my calf. When Andersson rushed over to ask if I was OK, I could do nothing but groan.

He dropped to his knees and gently felt my foot, at which point I let out a scream. The foot had already started to swell, and Andersson undid my boot so that it wouldn't have to be cut off.

"*What an idiot,*" *I managed to say as Andersson fumbled with my laces.*

"*You need to see a medic,*" *he said, helping me to stand.*

The sergeant was still at the top of the tower, but Kihlberg came over to help. Together they managed to get me down the hill and into the sick bay, which is in one of the smaller barracks beyond the mess. It's a Falu-red building like all the rest, equipped with a number of beds.

The medical provision on Korsö is a joke. The doctor, whose name is Tallén, is notorious. He does exactly as he's told, and his orders are to keep the men going. Whatever's wrong, his solution is cortisone—an injection instead of rest. Unless you're dying, all you can do is grit your teeth and carry on.

Tallén's favorite prescription is butazolidin; I'd never heard of it until I joined up. It eases the pain, but it makes you tired and nauseous, and the body is never given a chance to recover.

It took Tallén only fifteen minutes to "cure" me.

Andersson was waiting outside; the sun was shining, and he was sweating in his thick uniform by the time I emerged.

"*How are you feeling?*" *he asked, getting to his feet.*

I gave him a wry smile. "OK at the moment, but the pain will come back when the injection wears off. I've got some pills for tonight."

I held out my hand and showed him the clear bottle containing pink pills.

"Do you want a cigarette?" he said. He reached into his pocket for a packet of Princes and lit one for me. I took it and sank down on a flat rock by the side of the building. I was exhausted. After a few deep drags, I tried to stand up but quickly sat back down, grimacing with the pain.

"Jeez, that hurts!" I said.

"Take it easy. You can't use your foot. Didn't Tallén give you sick leave for a few days?"

I shook my head. "He told me to come back tomorrow for another injection so I don't miss any training."

He had bandaged my foot, and it looked twice as big as the other one. It looked grotesque, to be honest.

"How the hell are you going to get your boot on?"

I shrugged. "It doesn't matter. The sergeant isn't going to let me rest anyway."

There was no point in complaining. Andersson knew I was right.

He carried my pack for the rest of that week.

CHAPTER 57

Tuesday (The Third Week)

Leif Kihlberg's hotel was on Nybrogatan, just north of Östermalmstorg in central Stockholm. When Thomas and Margit walked into the foyer, they were met by a sign informing them that the fire service was holding their conference in the Saturn suite on the third floor.

The reception desk was next to a dining room styled to look like a library. Shelves packed with a wide variety of books ran from floor to ceiling, and there were yet more books, magazines, and newspapers on round tables.

It's like walking into someone's living room, Thomas thought.

Margit went over and asked the receptionist to call Leif Kihlberg, but before she had time to pick up the phone, Thomas saw a tall, broad-shouldered man get to his feet and come toward them.

"Margit Grankvist?" the man said.

"That's right."

"Leif Kihlberg."

Margit held out her hand. "How did you recognize us?" she asked with a frown.

Kihlberg shrugged. "A cop isn't that hard to spot, even without a uniform."

"So I've heard," Thomas said, then introduced himself.

"We can sit down over here," Kihlberg said, pointing to the table where he had been sitting. "Would you like coffee from the buffet?"

"We're fine, thanks," Thomas said.

He studied the firefighter as they got settled. Leif Kihlberg looked good; his hair wasn't thinning, and he hadn't put on weight. He was wearing a dark tweed jacket with an open-necked shirt and dark-gray pants. His eyes were surrounded by fine lines, suggesting that he was a man who liked to spend a lot of time outdoors.

It wasn't hard to imagine the young Coastal Ranger Kihlberg had once been. *Are you an honest man, or just someone who's used to getting along by making a positive impression?* Thomas wondered. He decided to reserve judgment.

"How can I help you?" Kihlberg asked.

Margit quickly summarized the events of the past few weeks. Thomas said nothing; they had spent an hour the previous afternoon planning their strategy. If Kihlberg was the killer, they mustn't reveal any hint of suspicion; they had to lull him into a false sense of security until they had sufficient proof. However, if he was the next potential victim, they had to find out as much as possible in order to protect him.

It was a delicate balancing act, to say the least.

"So that's the situation," Margit concluded. "Three of your former comrades have been murdered, and we're still looking for a motive and a killer."

A chill passed through the room.

Kihlberg's neck muscles had grown increasingly taut during Margit's account, and by the end, both hands were clenched into fists, resting on his knees.

If he was pretending to be surprised, he was doing it very well.

"You had no idea about any of this?" Thomas asked.

Kihlberg shook his head. "I haven't had any contact with the old gang for a long time."

He opened his hands so slowly that it looked as if he was having to force himself to do it. When he picked up his coffee, it was shaking so much that he had to put the cup down again without taking a sip.

"I live in Gothenburg, and most of them stayed in Stockholm or the surrounding area. You know how it is—you get together now and then during the first few years, then the meetings grow less and less frequent. Everyone gets on with their own life, has a family, and suddenly there are other things to think about."

His face was a little paler than it had been when they'd met him a few minutes earlier.

"I knew Björn Sigurd died in Bosnia," he went on, "and I'd heard that Kaufman was in a bad way with the booze. But I had no idea Fredell was so sick . . ." He shuddered. "Poor guy. I'd like to go to the funeral."

He reached for his coffee once more and managed to drink it this time. Then he looked up, as if he had reached a decision.

"Not all my memories of that time are entirely positive; I guess I kind of withdrew."

"You didn't keep in touch with anyone?" Margit asked.

"There was one guy." Kihlberg's expression was serious. "Anders Martinger. We were on a combat placement together. He stayed in the military for a while, but now he works as a pilot for SAS. We meet up from time to time."

Is that a coincidence, Thomas thought, *or a key piece of information?* He made a mental note.

"When did you last see Martinger?" Margit wanted to know.

"In the middle of September. I was in Stockholm with my wife, and we had a night out with Anders and Siri."

"What was the date?"

"I guess it was about three weeks ago. Let's see . . ."

Kihlberg got out his planner and flicked through it until he found the relevant page.

"It was the weekend of the fifteenth/sixteenth—we had theater tickets."

"Did you stay with the Martingers?"

"No, we booked a hotel. They live in Sigtuna, so it's quite a ways from the city center. But the four of us went for a meal after the play."

Thomas decided to get straight to the point.

"Have you any idea why someone would want to kill the members of your group?"

"I haven't a clue. It doesn't make any sense at all."

The answer was immediate and decisive.

Margit followed it up with another direct question.

"You can't think of anything that you or your colleagues were involved in that might explain this?"

Kihlberg leaned back and closed his eyes. Then he opened them and finished off his coffee. He seemed more composed now.

"I can't imagine what that would be."

"Are you absolutely certain? We've heard the training for the Coastal Rangers could be brutal. Could someone have been nurturing a grudge all this time?"

Kihlberg's response was sharp.

"It was over thirty years ago. How could something that happened back then have any relevance in this situation?"

His words provoked a reaction in Thomas. He wasn't sure why, but for a brief moment, he thought he'd picked up something in his tone that shouldn't have been there.

"Do you know of any other connection between these men?" he asked. "For example, did any of them do business together?"

"Not that I know of, but as I said—we lost touch a long time ago."

Margit took over once more. "Has anything unusual or suspicious happened to you lately—anything that made you feel uncomfortable, for example?"

Leif Kihlberg seemed taken aback rather than afraid.

"You mean, I could be in danger, too?"

"We're seeing a pattern, and you're a part of that pattern," Thomas explained. "We believe there's cause for concern, because right now we don't know what's driving the killer."

"I'm perfectly capable of defending myself."

The firefighter sat up a little straighter and pushed back his shoulders; Thomas had no doubt that he believed what he had just said. However, things would be very different if Kihlberg was naked and drunk, and someone was pointing a gun at him.

"I'm sure you can," he said in a placatory tone, "but at this stage, we believe that we're dealing with a skilled and meticulous perpetrator. It wouldn't do any harm to be on your guard."

"If that bastard tries anything with me, he'll get a nasty surprise."

The authority in Kihlberg's voice was unmistakable; Thomas could see why he had been nominated group leader at the age of twenty.

"We would still advise you to be careful for the immediate future, and please contact us if anything occurs to you."

Thomas handed over his card. "Call me anytime."

Kihlberg slipped the card into his pocket. By the light pouring in through the tall windows, Thomas could see how tired he suddenly looked.

When they were in the car about to set off back to Nacka, Thomas turned to Margit.

"So what do you think?"

She put on her seat belt, then said, "To be perfectly honest, I don't know."

"Kihlberg is in good shape. He's strong enough to attack Kaufman and the other victims."

"According to him, he has an alibi for two of the three weekends. We need to check with his wife to see if she or someone else can confirm that he was in Gothenburg when Nielsen, Erneskog, and Fredell died."

Thomas turned the key in the ignition and pulled out into the street. There was heavy traffic in the city center, and progress was slow in spite of the fact that the morning rush hour was long past.

He remembered the moment during the conversation when a faint alarm bell had gone off in his head. It was when they were discussing something that might have happened thirty years ago. Kihlberg had firmly dismissed any suggestion that events in the past could have any relevance for the current investigation.

Thomas had picked up some kind of deviation from the pattern, and now he realized what it was. Kihlberg's answer had come too quickly, almost as if he had been expecting the question.

CHAPTER 58

The call from the National Forensics Laboratory came after lunch.

Thomas listened with growing interest, then went straight to Margit's office. She was on the phone, with three empty plastic coffee cups on the desk in front of her and a fourth, barely half-full, in her hand.

She ended the conversation and looked up at him.

"I've just spoken to forensics," he said.

"And?"

"They've found foreign DNA in Fredell's home. It doesn't match the DNA found on the rope at Marcus Nielsen's."

"Are they sure?"

"Ninety-nine-point-eight-three percent, as they always say."

Margit smiled.

In the world of forensic science, 100 percent simply didn't exist; they were always a few decimal points away. However, a score above 99 percent went a long way.

"In that case, it's probably true," she said.

"Unfortunately it doesn't match anything in our database."

"That's a shame," Margit said laconically, finishing off her coffee as she considered the information. "They didn't say anything about DNA from the crime scene at Kaufman's or Erneskog's?"

"It's too early. The Västerås police didn't send over anything from Erneskog until we asked them to, and that was less than a week ago. The samples from the pillow at Kaufman's went on Sunday; they've probably only just reached the lab in Linköping."

Margit drummed her fingers on the desk, which was cluttered with piles of papers.

"The problem is still that we don't know who the various DNA samples belong to," she said. "If it's the person who sold the rope to Marcus, or someone who'd just stopped in to see the Fredells, they're useless."

Thomas knew she was right, but it was still a step forward.

What had Karin said about Martinger's schedule? He had been free during the first two weekends when Nielsen, Erneskog, and Fredell were murdered. He hadn't been on duty until Sunday evening. In other words, it was theoretically possible that he could have killed the three men before starting his shift.

If he was the perpetrator.

Kihlberg claimed to have been in Gothenburg during the relevant period, but he didn't have an alibi for the time of Kaufman's death.

Kihlberg and Martinger were the only remaining members of a tight, close-knit group. But how close were they?

"What if they've identified DNA from two different killers?" he blurted out.

"What do you mean?"

"Could Kihlberg and Martinger be working together?"

He adjusted his position on the chair and felt a stab of pain in his rib cage, which was still sore from the accident. He suspected that he had cracked one of his ribs when his body was thrown forward into the seat belt; he found it difficult to lie comfortably on his right side. He also had a huge bruise, which he couldn't hide from Pernilla.

He had played the incident down as much as possible, but she had still been upset because he hadn't told her about it at the time.

"Working together?"

"What if they're colluding? Kihlberg has an alibi for the first three murders, Martinger for the fourth. By taking turns, they can reinforce each other's alibis. Genius."

Margit raised her coffee cup to her lips and seemed surprised when she found that it was empty.

"Two killers?" she said.

"It's a long shot, but it's not impossible. Don't forget they met up during the weekend when the first body was discovered; Kihlberg told us that himself just a few hours ago. They went to the theater. What did they do then? Maybe they went their separate ways, one to Västerås and one to Marcus Nielsen's apartment in Jarlaberg."

Thomas opened his notebook to check that he had remembered the details correctly.

"Martinger's the only member of the old gang that Kihlberg has kept in touch with. They've been friends for over thirty years, and their families hang out together."

"But we still don't know why the murders were committed," Margit pointed out. "There must be an incredibly strong motive, if that's the case."

"If only we could track down those diaries . . . I'm sure we'd find the answer there."

Margit twirled her empty cup around several times, then balled it up and threw it away. The other three could stay where they were.

"They're taking a hell of a risk," she said. "If two people are involved, it takes a whole different level of planning—and a huge amount of trust."

"That's what their time in the Rangers was all about. Those two are trained to kill, remember."

"We need to check their phones," Margit decided. "See if they've been in touch recently. Get a detailed picture of their lives."

"I'll ask Karin and Kalle to take a look, if you'll speak to the prosecutor," Thomas said. "We have to assume that Martinger knows we'll be waiting for him at the airport in the morning; Kihlberg is bound to have warned him."

He left Margit and headed back to his office, passing the meeting room where the biographies supplied by the military were still on the whiteboard.

The old pictures of Kihlberg and Martinger showed two comrades whose appearance was almost identical. They had once been willing to die for one another. Were they also prepared to kill for one another?

CHAPTER 59

Nora took a step back and admired her handiwork. In the middle of the kitchen table was a splendid princess cake with eight candles. She had gotten up extra early to bake and make all the preparations for Simon's birthday celebration.

She really wanted his first birthday since the separation to be perfect. The divorce mustn't be allowed to spoil his big day.

It was almost seven o'clock, and the guests would soon be arriving. She looked around the spacious kitchen, which had been the main reason she had fallen for the apartment. Everything was ready.

Her stomach flipped when she thought about the fact that both Henrik and his parents would be here. She had never gotten along too well with Monica and Harald Linde, but for Simon's sake, they'd been invited.

To tell the truth, it was mainly her mother-in-law who was the problem; Harald was a kind and considerate man. He had just retired after a long career as a diplomat, and now he had to put up with Monica all day, unable to seek refuge in the Foreign Office. Nora almost felt sorry for him.

The doorbell rang, and Nora took off her apron and ran a hand through her hair. She had changed out of her sober work clothes into black pants and a pretty top. Her hair was freshly washed, and she had even managed to redo her makeup. She had no intention of letting either Henrik or his mother know how much the divorce had affected her—not under any circumstances.

"Simon!" she shouted. "Go and answer the door—they're your guests."

He came racing in from the living room.

"Is it Daddy?"

Nora's heart sank. It was still painful, even though they hadn't lived together for six months. When would it stop? When would Henrik become a person who could be mentioned in conversation without her feeling so uncomfortable?

"Go and see," she said, trying to smile. "I'll just finish up in here."

Simon ran to the front door, and she heard him turn the latch. He was so proud of his Spiderman T-shirt; if he had his way, he would never take it off.

"Adam," she called out. "Turn off the TV, please—our guests are arriving."

No reaction.

"Adam! We have visitors."

"Hi, Daddy!" she heard Simon say in the hallway. Henrik had arrived; time to take the bull by the horns. Nora took a deep breath and adopted a suitable expression before leaving the kitchen.

Her smile froze in a second. Henrik was standing in the doorway holding Simon, and behind him Nora could see an all-too-familiar face.

Marie.

At least she had the decency to look nervous.

Henrik came in and put Simon down.

"Marie came along, too, I hope that's OK," he said. "She really wanted to wish Simon a happy birthday."

Nora closed her eyes.

She couldn't explode in front of her son, however much she wanted to. Running into Marie occasionally in her old home was bad enough;

the last thing she needed was to socialize with the woman in her new home.

She didn't want to see her at all, in fact.

Breathe, she thought. *Just breathe. You can do this.*

Fortunately, she heard footsteps on the stairs at that moment, followed by Thomas's familiar voice. Nora felt the tension ease slightly.

"Anybody in here celebrating a birthday?"

Thomas walked in; as usual, he was taller than everyone else. He held out his arms, and Simon hurled himself at his godfather.

"And how's my godson today? All grown up?"

Simon looked thrilled, and Nora was grateful for the breathing room Thomas's arrival had given her.

Pernilla was right behind Thomas, and Nora could see that she immediately understood the situation. She rolled her eyes and tilted her head in the direction of Henrik and Marie, who were busy taking off their coats.

And the icing on the cake was the sound of Monica Linde's strident tones in the elevator.

Nora had to smile in spite of herself. She was so sick of Henrik and his parents. She realized this was a new sensation, the feeling that it was good to be rid of him. She remembered the previous day, when she had stood her ground over Simon's English book, and the memory warmed her heart.

She greeted her ex-in-laws with the obligatory kiss on the cheek and took their coats.

"Dear Nora," Monica said. She was wearing an elegant skirt suit with bound edges, and a double row of pearls around her neck; she smelled of French perfume. Monica examined Nora with a critical eye.

"How are you?" She took a step back and frowned. "You've lost weight. You need to take better care of yourself. You know Harald and I are happy to look after the boys at any time. Just because you and

Henrik have split up, that doesn't mean we have to lose touch. You know how much we love Simon and Adam."

The look on her face was challenging, and Nora shuddered. She hadn't forgotten how Monica had treated her six months ago, threatening that Henrik would seek sole custody of the children unless Nora came to her senses and gave up any idea of leaving him. That was Monica's way of handling the bad news; divorce was unthinkable in the Linde family.

Nora had been at her wit's end, but for once, Henrik hadn't given in to his mother. He had never mentioned it, and they had applied for joint custody with very little bad feeling.

"Where are your mom and dad?" Pernilla asked when she had taken off her coat and stuck her head around the living room door, where Adam was still sitting on the sofa. He got up and gave her a hug.

"I should think they'll be here soon," Nora said. "Dad likes to be punctual."

Sure enough, the doorbell rang a couple of minutes later. Simon did his duty once again, and found Lasse and Susanne Hallén standing outside. Lasse was clutching a large, beautifully wrapped present.

"Is that for me?" Simon said reverently. "It's huge!"

"A big present for a little man," his grandfather said, shaking his hand. "Shall we go inside and open it?"

Nora gave her father a look of warm appreciation. Her parents had given her invaluable support over the past few months, once they had come to terms with her decision. As usual, her mother had focused on all the problems that might arise; Susanne liked to deal with trials and tribulations in advance and was always convinced that the worst would happen.

However, for once, Nora's father had spoken up and told Susanne to cut it out. The situation was what it was; Nora had chosen not to live with Henrik any longer, and they must respect that choice.

From then on, Susanne had stopped moaning, and Nora's parents had taken care of a lot of the practicalities. They had driven the boys to various activities and picked up Simon in the afternoons when Nora couldn't. They had helped her find a new apartment and dealt with every aspect of the move. Their unfailing support had made her feel a little better during that long, difficult spring as she gradually dismantled her married life.

Lasse Hallén caught sight of Henrik and Marie, and his lips narrowed to a thin line. Nora was surprised that her parents would show their disapproval so openly; though, like her, they couldn't forgive Henrik for what he had done. They had always liked their son-in-law—Susanne had been particularly fond of him—and that made his betrayal of their daughter so much harder to bear.

Now they simply held out their hands politely as if Henrik were a distant acquaintance, not someone they had known for sixteen years and regarded as a member of the family.

Fortunately, both boys had gone off with Thomas. Nora didn't want them to pick up on the frosty atmosphere between their father and their beloved maternal grandparents.

Pernilla, quick thinking as always, rescued the situation.

"Come on, let's go and watch Simon unwrapping his presents."

She drew Nora's parents into the kitchen, where Monica and Harald were already ensconced.

Nora turned her back on Henrik and joined them.

CHAPTER 60

Simon was sitting at the head of the table, his cheeks glowing with excitement after opening his presents. His maternal grandparents had bought him a complete train set with a classic wooden track, and Adam had already started putting it together.

Henrik had brought various LEGO sets, which had evoked squeaks of excitement from the birthday boy, while Thomas and Pernilla had luckily ignored Nora's advice and had given him a police uniform, accurate down to the smallest detail.

Simon had been so thrilled that he had immediately taken off his Spiderman T-shirt and put on his new outfit. Now he was watching Nora as she lit the brightly colored candles on his cake. He took a deep breath and blew them all out.

"Well done—make a wish!" Nora said, stroking his hair.

She cut him a big slice, then pushed the cake over to Pernilla, who cut herself a small piece before passing it on to Susanne.

"Don't you like princess cake?" Nora asked her friend. "I thought you had a sweet tooth!"

"I just don't feel like it this evening," Pernilla replied, getting to her feet. "Is it OK if I make myself a cup of tea instead of coffee?"

"Sure."

Nora was surprised; Pernilla usually preferred coffee. "The tea bags are in the cupboard on the right. Just help yourself."

Pernilla reached for the kettle, and Nora's eyes lingered on her loose-fitting top. She glanced at Thomas, who was absorbed in a discussion on speed limits with her father. Thomas had been in a fantastic mood ever since he'd arrived.

"Delicious cupcakes," Monica exclaimed, turning to Nora. "Did you make them yourself?"

Nora shook her head, dismissing thoughts of Thomas and Pernilla. It was perfectly obvious that the identical, beautifully decorated cupcakes were store bought.

"No, I got them from a bakery."

"Of course. You wouldn't have time, what with your job and everything else you do. It was foolish of me to think such a thing. I know you're a real career woman."

Monica picked up a chocolate cookie.

"The cinnamon buns are homemade," Nora said, regretting the words as soon as they left her mouth. She didn't need to justify herself to her ex-mother-in-law. Pernilla came to her rescue once more.

"I'm surprised you don't help Nora with that kind of thing, Monica," she said, smiling sweetly. "My mother-in-law is an absolute angel. She always turns up with a big box of goodies when we celebrate Thomas's birthday; she knows I'm too busy to bake. Wouldn't it be nice if you took care of things next time?"

Nora suppressed a smile. Monica wouldn't dream of touching a bowl of sticky dough with her well-manicured fingers.

At that moment, her father cleared his throat. He got to his feet and put down his glass. Simon gazed up at him expectantly. He had already spilled cream on his new police uniform, and his mouth was full of green marzipan. He looked so happy, sitting there surrounded by his whole family, and Nora allowed herself to relax a little. Inviting

Henrik and his parents had been the right thing to do. And she had even managed to cope with Marie's presence.

"Time to toast the birthday boy," Lasse said. "Three cheers for Simon! Hip, hip, hurrah!"

"Did you enjoy your birthday?"

Nora tucked Simon in and smoothed down the covers. She stroked his warm cheek, which was still rosy with the excitement of the day. The guests had left around half-past nine, and it was definitely bedtime. The boys had school tomorrow, as usual, which meant she would have to wake them at twenty to seven.

"Mmm."

He yawned and turned over, Winnie the Pooh firmly clutched under his arm. Sleepily he snuffled his favorite cuddly toy.

That bear needs a wash, Nora thought, wondering how on earth she was going to get Simon to agree. There was a battle every time she suggested giving Winnie a bath in a bowl of water with gentle detergent, but his fur must've been crawling with bacteria by now.

"Did you like the cake?"

"It was really good."

"Do you remember making a wish when you blew out the candles?"

Simon nodded.

"Do you want to tell me what you wished for, or is it a secret?"

He hesitated, then his blue eyes cleared as he made his decision.

"I wished that you and Daddy would be friends again so that we can all move back home."

Chapter 61

"I think Nora suspects something," Pernilla said, then followed it up with a big yawn. She was lying on her side in bed, her head resting on Thomas's shoulder. It was almost eleven o'clock.

"What makes you say that?"

Thomas put down his book.

"She was looking at me strangely. At my stomach."

Thomas bent down and kissed Pernilla's forehead.

"Are you sure you're not imagining things? There's nothing to see yet."

"Are you kidding me?" Pernilla pulled up her nightdress and poked at her tummy; her navel was protruding slightly. "Can't you see how round it is already? It's like a ball. I'm going to be enormous!" A big smile spread across her face. "She's going to be a big, strong baby!"

Thomas shook his head. "You're not showing at all."

"I can hardly fasten my jeans, and I've still got seven months to go. I'll be walking around wearing a tent by the end."

Pernilla sank back against the pillow with an exaggerated groan. Thomas picked up his book, and she ran her forefinger down his back.

"Simon was cute tonight, wasn't he?"

"Mmm."

Thomas was absorbed in his novel.

"He blew out all the candles at once, and he's so little."

"Mmm."

Pernilla propped herself up on one elbow and contemplated her husband.

"Have you heard a word I've said?"

Thomas gave a start. "Sorry?"

"I was impressed when Simon blew out all his candles. He's only eight."

Something stirred in Thomas's subconscious.

"What did you say?"

"Simon was cute tonight."

"No, the other thing."

Pernilla frowned. "I said I was impressed when he blew out all his candles. He's only eight."

Eight. Where had he heard the number eight before? He pictured Bo Kaufman, the wrinkled face lighting up as he leafed through the old photo album.

I was 108. 108 Kaufman.

There had been eight Coastal Rangers in the group, but they had been given only seven names by the military. Or was he mistaken?

"I just need to check something," he said, getting out of bed. "Go to sleep—I won't be long."

He went into the kitchen and got a pen and a notepad out of the top drawer. By the light shining in from the hallway, he quickly scribbled down the names: *Kihlberg, Fredell, Kaufman, Martinger, Erneskog, Eklund.*

Six . . . was that everyone? He chewed his pen, trying to remember the biographies Elsa Harning had sent over.

He had missed Björn Sigurd, the soldier who had died in Bosnia. He added *Sigurd* to the list.

There were only seven names.

There must have been another Coastal Ranger.

DIARY:
JUNE 1977

It's almost ten thirty at night, but it's still light outside. We've been paddling all day, and my body certainly knows it. The base of my spine hurts, and my muscles are aching, even though it's several hours since we got back.

I ate quickly so that I could have a bit of peace in the room before the others came to bed. Sometimes it's nice to be alone. I had just stretched out on my bunk when I heard them.

Two officers were standing outside the window, chatting. At first, it was just an indistinct murmur, but I thought I picked up his name, and I made an effort to tune in.

They must have been standing right by the wall—two men talking about a third. They were talking about the sergeant.

"Nobody else pushes the recruits as hard as he does," one of them said. "He won't accept anything less than perfection. He's brutal."

The smell of cigarette smoke drifted in through the open window. Silently I slid out of bed and crouched down by the sill.

"I guess he just wants to show off, like everyone else."

"To make up for the fact that he failed to get into the Royal Swedish Naval Academy?"

The scorn in the laughter that followed was unmistakable.

"He probably thought he could walk straight in, his daddy's an admiral."

One of them struck a match and lit another cigarette. I pressed my body closer to the wall; I didn't want to miss a word.

"Wouldn't you think the same? Fucking embarrassing, not being accepted as a reserve officer in the navy when you've got a father like that."

I couldn't make out the next few words.

"He can still apply to be a reserve officer with the Coastal Artillery in the September intake. It's not as impressive, but otherwise he'll just end up as a regular."

"And what would Daddy say then?"

Another burst of laughter.

"If he messes up in the final exercise in August, that's it. He'll be fucked, just like all the recruits he's booted out."

Someone spat on the ground.

"I guess that's why he drives his boys. He's desperate for them to perform well, the poor bastards."

I could hardly contain myself.

"As far as he's concerned, it's deadly serious."

"That's what I'm saying. He needs to prove himself to Daddy. You know there's talk of him being promoted to commander in chief?"

The voices grew fainter, and I could hear footsteps moving away. In the distance, the gulls were screaming as they squabbled over the day's kitchen scraps.

I had a bad feeling, and I couldn't shake it off.

CHAPTER 62

Wednesday (The Third Week)

Simon's words before he went to sleep had hit Nora hard. She had struggled to hold back the tears as she cleared away the dishes and got ready for bed.

Move back home, he had said. To the house where they used to live.

The new apartment counted for nothing; it was just a temporary solution until he could go back to his real home.

When the alarm went off at five past six, Nora didn't want to wake up; her body was slow and heavy from lack of sleep. She dragged herself into the bathroom and got in the shower, wishing she could just stay there in the stream of hot water. She had no idea how she was going to face the day, but eventually she turned the shower off and reached for a towel.

It was still dark when she walked into the kitchen, and she lit some candles to chase away the gloom.

That was when the tears came.

She slumped down at the table, her shoulders shaking as she wept over what Simon had said, the fact that Henrik had brought Marie along, and Jonas's failure to get in touch.

It felt like an eternity since she had sat in the restaurant on Sandhamn with him, feeling so happy and full of anticipation.

When she finally pulled herself together, her nose was red, and her mascara was ruined. She took a shaky deep breath and tore off a piece of paper towel to blow her nose. She splashed her face with cold water, filled the kettle and switched it on, then went into the bathroom to repair the damage. She needed to wake the boys up; there wasn't time for any more crying.

She fixed her makeup, then went into Adam's room. His alarm clock had rung, but he often went back to sleep. She sat down on the edge of the bed and gently touched his shoulder.

"I'm awake," he mumbled.

"I just wanted to check."

Nora hesitated, then she leaned forward and gave him a little hug. He pulled away so often these days; it wasn't easy to know if he would accept a gesture of affection from his mom. To her surprise, he hugged her back, almost as if he realized she was a little fragile this morning.

Holding her eldest son close for a few seconds made her feel much better.

"I thought Dad was dumb yesterday," he murmured into her shoulder.

Nora moved a fraction so that she could see his face.

"What do you mean?"

"He shouldn't have brought Marie."

"Don't you like her?"

"It's not that." He shook his head. "But we live here, not her. I didn't like her being here."

"Oh, honey . . ." Nora stroked his hair. "I don't think Dad meant any harm."

Adam nodded. "By the way, is it OK if Lisa comes home with me this afternoon, before I go over to Wille's?" he said quietly.

Nora carried on stroking his hair, and he didn't protest. She smiled and patted his arm.

"Of course. There are cinnamon buns and cake left over from yesterday—just help yourselves."

"Thanks, Mom—you're the best."

Nora's eyes filled with tears once more.

Thomas had picked Margit up earlier than usual in order to avoid the morning rush hour. He didn't take much notice of the speed limits on the way to Berga. He'd only had six hours' sleep, but he felt well rested. As soon as she'd gotten in the car, Margit had nodded off with her head resting against the side window, and Thomas concentrated on the traffic.

They whizzed past Gullmarsplan and Årsta, and Thomas noticed that the worst of the congestion seemed to be in the opposite direction. Hopefully it would be cleared by the time they headed back. Martinger's plane was due to land in a few hours.

He didn't speak until they were approaching the exit for Berga. It was five past eight.

"Nearly there," he said, gently touching Margit's arm.

"I'm awake. I was just resting my eyes."

The faint snores that had been coming from the passenger seat for the past twenty minutes suggested that this wasn't entirely true, but Thomas didn't contradict her.

"I'm wondering if we should ask Martinger and Kihlberg to give us a voluntary DNA sample," Margit said as she stretched her arms. "If they don't have anything to hide, it shouldn't be a problem."

"Now there's an argument nobody has ever used before," Thomas said.

Margit ignored the sarcasm.

"It usually works—at least until they've spoken to a lawyer."

"It's certainly worth a try. By the way, what about their phones—what did the prosecutor say?"

"We got permission. I've asked Kalle to check out their cell phones and landlines. He's also contacted the provider with regard to Marcus Nielsen's parents' phone records."

"When does he think he'll get the results?"

"Today or tomorrow; it shouldn't take long."

Thomas took the turn for the military base. Soon they would be meeting Elsa Harning again. He remembered her aura of professionalism, but he had his doubts about her honesty and openness.

"Do you think the military is deliberately trying to hide something?"

Margit took a moment before answering.

"I don't know," she said at last. "But it's odd that the number of recruits doesn't match up."

Chapter 63

The guard at the gate was unimpressed when it turned out that Thomas and Margit had arrived unannounced. He refused to let them in until Thomas produced his police ID and demanded to speak to his superior officer; he made a point of noting down their car registration plate and personal ID numbers.

He must have phoned as soon as they had gone through, because Elsa Harning was waiting for them just inside the main door. As before, her uniform was perfectly pressed, but this time her blond hair was pulled back into a simple bun, secured by a barrette.

"I believe you want to speak to me again?" she said in a civil tone of voice. "It might have been easier if you'd called in advance to make an appointment; I can't spare you much time, I'm afraid."

"It's not the only thing that might have made life easier," Thomas couldn't help saying.

They followed her along the same corridor as before, but on this occasion, she led them into her office, a large, light-filled room overlooking the sea. There was nothing on her desk apart from a leather mat, two files, and a pen holder. Thomas couldn't see any personal items in the room—no photographs of children or dogs, nothing to give a clue as to who the woman in front of them actually was.

The only unusual item was a particularly large plant standing in one corner; it had wound its way all around the window frame. If nothing else, Captain Harning had a green thumb.

"How can I be of assistance this time?" she said, gesturing toward the visitors' sofa. "Would you like coffee, by the way?"

"Please," Margit said.

Elsa Harning picked up the phone, and after only a couple of minutes, the door opened and a young woman came in carrying a tray with three mugs and a jug of milk. No sugar.

"We've gone through the material you sent us on Monday—thank you for that," Thomas began. "However, we have reason to believe it's incomplete."

Elsa frowned. "Incomplete?"

"We received names and further details about seven men who belonged to the group we're interested in. But we know that one of our homicide victims had the designated number 108."

Thomas said each number slowly to make sure it sank in, keeping his eyes fixed on Elsa.

"We're a little confused, and we'd like an explanation."

Elsa looked taken aback, then a furrow appeared between her well-shaped eyebrows.

"You think we've deliberately withheld information?" she snapped.

"We don't think anything, but we have four homicide victims, and we don't want any more. We need your help, and we don't want you to hold back information that could be important." Thomas lowered his voice. "Above all, we don't want to waste time asking questions about something we should have been told in the first place."

"I understand."

Elsa's eyes were still cold, but she got up and went over to the desk. She picked up the phone once more and asked someone to come along to her office.

A minute later, there was a knock on the door, and a gray-haired woman of about sixty came in with a thick file under her arm. She wasn't in uniform, and Thomas assumed she was one of the civilian employees Captain Harning had mentioned on their previous visit— one of those who didn't like working overtime on a Friday.

"This is Birgit Hagelius; she deals with archive inquiries," Elsa said. "She retrieved the information we sent over to you."

She introduced the two police officers and quickly explained what had happened.

"They're wondering if someone is missing, and if so, why."

The older woman sat down. She was wearing a navy cardigan with a pleated skirt of the same color. She reminded Thomas of a character in a British detective series. She seemed anxious; she plucked at a loose thread on her skirt as she spoke.

"I do hope I haven't caused you any problems. I did try to find the information you requested."

"Nobody's saying you've made a mistake, Birgit," Elsa said reassuringly. "But maybe you could clarify the situation."

"Absolutely."

Birgit Hagelius took a deep breath and stopped fiddling with the thread.

"It's perfectly simple. A certain percentage of the recruits are sent home during the course of the year, and that is allowed for within the intake system."

"Why are they sent home?" Margit asked.

"Because not all of them achieve the required standard," Elsa said, as if it were the most natural thing in the world.

"In what way?"

"Sometimes they fail at the physical challenges, sometimes they don't have the necessary mental strength. Some are sent home right away; others stick it out for a while but fall by the wayside during the journey. The men can't be sure that they will complete their training, and there's a psychological purpose behind that approach. It creates a competitive atmosphere that intensifies everything on both the physical and mental level."

"What's that got to do with the matter in question?" Thomas asked, turning directly to Birgit.

She coughed. "To begin with, this group consisted of eight aspiring Coastal Rangers, but only seven completed their training." An invisible fleck of dust was brushed off the dark-blue skirt. "When you requested details of the group members, I assumed you only wanted to know about those who actually qualified as rangers."

"I see." Margit's tone suggested that she wasn't satisfied with the explanation.

"So that's why I put together seven biographies." Birgit glanced nervously at Elsa Harning. "It really wasn't my intention to cause any trouble."

"What was the name of the eighth recruit?" Margit said.

Birgit pointed to the file she had brought with her and placed on the table. It was dark blue, with *1976* written in black on the spine.

"Pär Andersson."

"And why was he sent home?" Thomas wondered.

Birgit picked up the file but answered without opening it.

"He wasn't sent home. He died."

CHAPTER 64

"He died?" Thomas said. "How?"

Birgit Hagelius looked far from happy. She smoothed down her skirt.

"He killed himself."

"I'm sorry?" Margit said.

"He took his own life. It was a very sad story."

"Highly unusual," Elsa Harning chimed in. "It's very rare for someone to commit suicide in the military. That's one of the reasons why we carry out such rigorous tests at the earliest possible stage; those with suicidal tendencies should be picked up before they even sign on."

"But that clearly didn't work this time."

Elsa shook her head. "I'm afraid not."

Thomas turned his attention to Birgit once more. "What happened?"

She opened the file and turned to the section marked *A*.

"OK, let's see. Pär Andersson was found early one morning in the shower room of the block where his group was billeted. He'd hanged himself. By the time his body was discovered, he'd been dead for several hours, and it was too late to do anything."

"That must have been a real shock for everyone," Margit said.

Birgit nodded. "Now maybe you can see why I left him out."

"Do we know why he killed himself?" Thomas asked.

"Yes, he left a note in his room saying that he couldn't take it anymore."

"Couldn't take what anymore?" Margit shot back.

Elsa stepped in.

"The Coastal Rangers' training was particularly tough in those days, as I mentioned when you were here before. Presumably he couldn't cope with the pressure. It's extremely unfortunate, but these things can happen. The odd soldier lacks the necessary killer instinct, and that realization can be difficult to bear on an individual level. In this case, it was clearly too much for Andersson."

"When did the death occur?" Margit asked icily. Thomas recognized the signs of irritation. Elsa Harning's attempt to blame Andersson meant that Margit would automatically take the side of the dead soldier.

"Let me just check . . ." Birgit skimmed the text. "It was late summer 1977—August 31, to be exact."

"Almost exactly thirty years ago . . ."

"Yes."

"And where did he die?" Thomas asked, although he could have made an educated guess at the answer.

"On Korsö."

Thomas nodded. Yet another indication that Korsö was the key.

"Could we have a copy of Pär Andersson's information?" Margit said.

Elsa looked uneasy but quickly hid her discomfort behind a neutral question.

"May I ask why?"

Thomas responded in kind.

"Is there any procedural reason why we shouldn't be given access to this material?"

Elsa shook her head, as if she had instantly analyzed the pros and cons of refusing to cooperate.

"Just remember it's sensitive, and for your eyes only," she said. "This man took his own life while undergoing military training. It would be"—she searched for the right words—"unfortunate if it came out that a Coastal Ranger committed suicide on Korsö. Even if it was many years ago."

Without looking Thomas or Margit in the eye, she picked up her coffee and took a sip. For the first time, Thomas saw a crack in her cool, impeccable façade.

She was worried.

He wasn't convinced that Pär Andersson had been omitted as a matter of routine. He assumed the military wanted to prevent any possible speculation about the cause of the young man's death, despite the fact that it had occurred so long ago.

Even if it hampered an ongoing police investigation.

"There's been a certain amount of press over the past few years about the Coastal Rangers," Elsa went on. "About the forms of . . ." She broke off once again. "About the training the recruits underwent. That's why we're keen to deal with this discreetly."

"I don't understand," Margit said, so innocently that Thomas knew the tone was intentional. "Did nobody know Pär Andersson had killed himself? Was the whole thing hushed up?"

A faint flush began to spread up Elsa Harning's throat.

"No, of course not."

"So . . . ?" Margit's tone was even more innocent now, if that were possible.

That troubled furrow appeared once again between Elsa's brows.

"It was a challenging situation. Everything was handled with the utmost discretion, out of consideration for Andersson's family. There is nothing to be gained from unnecessary publicity when something like this occurs."

"Of course not," Margit agreed. "The press always try to twist things, don't they? And that's no fun for anybody involved."

Elsa looked confused, as if she wasn't sure whether Margit was being genuinely sympathetic or sarcastic.

"As I said, we'd like copies of everything," Thomas reminded her. "As soon as possible."

A barely perceptible intake of breath told him Elsa wasn't going to refuse his request.

"By the way, who found the body?" Margit asked. "Was it another member of Andersson's group?"

"Er . . ." As Birgit leafed through the folder, the image of Bo Kaufman came into Thomas's mind: the man destroyed by booze, as far from the image of a successful elite soldier as it was possible to get. He remembered the pride that had briefly shone in Kaufman's eyes as he turned the pages of his old photo album, the way he had straightened his back as he recounted his memories of his days in the military.

Bo Kaufman had enjoyed being a Coastal Ranger. Had he turned to alcohol in an attempt to wipe out the past? The image of a dead comrade hanging from a noose?

"No, it was an officer who found him," Birgit said.

"What was his name?"

"Cronwall. Robert Cronwall."

Diary:
July 1977

We have to paddle just over one hundred nautical miles in the outer archipelago. They're going to transport us to Forsmark in 200-boats, then we have to make our way back.

It's called distance paddling, and it will take forty-eight hours, virtually without a break. We've been warned that our wrists will swell, and that our backs will take the most punishment. We'll be paddling in twos, in Klepper canoes that weigh around seventy pounds. In the prow, there'll be a small bucket to piss in.

According to the rules, we paddle for fifty-five minutes, then rest for five, with a break every six hours. However, there's a rumor going around that we paddle a thousand strokes, then rest for one.

When we're done paddling, we have to survive for several days on what nature has to offer. We're not allowed to take any supplies, or a change of clothes, or toilet paper. We have to prove that we can survive whatever happens, under any circumstances.

They say that, last summer, a group ate raw herring. They were so hungry, they couldn't wait to start a fire and cook them; instead they simply stuffed the fish in their mouths as they caught them.

Another group ate snakes that they found out in the archipelago on their last day. They cut off the heads, removed the spine, and fried the meat in a billycan over an open fire. While they were eating, they reeled off all the delicious food they could think of—chocolate pudding, spaghetti, meat pie, fried eggs. Anything to make them forget what they were actually putting in their mouths.

I've tried to read up in advance so that I will be prepared. I know that the leaves of the Sedum telephium *are juicy and keep your guts working so that you can digest your own body fat. You can survive for almost a month as long as there's water—two and a half liters a day, but no more than one liter of the Baltic's brackish brew, which must be boiled for at least forty minutes.*

Andersson interrupted me last night as I was lying reading on the top bunk. He came and stood beside me and looked at my book.

"What's that?"

"Survival tips."

I showed him the page and read aloud: "Burdock contains carbohydrates, and it is possible to eat cow parsley, but the stomach will pay the price before too long. Lichen is not harmful, and the roots of reeds can be consumed if cooked for a long time."

Andersson laughed. His face was tanned, his hair almost white at the temples. He pulled off his sweater and sat down on the bottom bunk.

"An unfiltered Chesterfield in the morning takes away hunger. That'll do me."

He laughed again, cheerful and carefree.

CHAPTER 65

Fortunately, Martinger's flight was slightly delayed, so Thomas and Margit got to Arlanda in time. Now they were sitting in an interview room that had been put at their disposal by the airport police. A colleague would meet the captain at the gate and bring him along.

"Robert Cronwall," Thomas said. "He's involved in all this somehow."

Cronwall had been sitting in his living room listening to classical music when they went to see him ten days ago. His expression had given nothing away when they asked about Fredell and Nielsen, and he hadn't even mentioned his time in the Coastal Rangers.

He ought to have recognized Fredell's name at least. Could he really have forgotten which men had been under his command when Pär Andersson was found dead?

Why hadn't he said anything about Fredell?

The door opened and a tall, broad-shouldered man in a dark-blue uniform with gold epaulettes walked into the room. *He looks like the archetypal airline captain,* Thomas thought, *reassuring and trustworthy.* Exactly the kind of guy who should be at the controls of your plane, according to the commercials.

Martinger was pulling a wheeled suitcase and carrying a plastic bag with the words "Duty Free, New York" on one side. He put aside his luggage and looked at them, eyebrows raised.

"Please sit down," Margit said, pointing to the chair. She and Thomas introduced themselves, and she contemplated the penultimate member of the group that had been brought together all those years ago.

"I was informed that the police wanted to speak to me," Martinger said. "I believe it's about my time with the Coastal Rangers."

Thomas nodded but said nothing.

"Leif Kihlberg called me last night," Martinger went on. "He told me you'd met and what you discussed."

Thomas wasn't surprised.

"A lot of old friends have died lately. Is it our turn now, Leffe and me?"

"Why do you say that?" Thomas asked.

"Why do I say that? Well, what am I supposed to think? Someone is murdering our former comrades, one by one, if I understood Leffe correctly."

Anders Martinger's voice was steady and bore no trace of fear—rather a hint of sorrow, perhaps.

A kind of resignation.

"We're trying to find out what's going on," Thomas said. "We think the motive behind these homicides lies in the past. We'd like you to tell us about your training with the Rangers."

A dark shadow passed across Martinger's face, then he lifted his chin with an air of determination.

"Eight of us joined up together, all dreaming of becoming elite soldiers in Sweden's finest fighting force. We were in good shape, fit and healthy, all athletes, and we had applied to the Rangers because that was where we wanted to be. We knew the training was hard, and only a handful would make it through. I still remember how happy I was when I found out I'd gotten in. I felt . . . special. Chosen."

"But that soon passed?" Margit said.

"It was hell on earth. The normal rules didn't apply. The way they treated us . . ."

Martinger leaned back in his chair and loosened his tie. Thomas saw a man who had been trying to close the door on these memories for a long time.

"Things are very different now," Martinger went on. "The approach has changed radically. The principles of modern leadership have gained a footing, even in those circles."

He managed a weary smile.

"Highly trained soldiers are a valuable resource, and the military can't afford to let some power-crazed lunatic loose on its recruits, but in the seventies, they had free range. The officers had total control, and extreme punishments—sorry, rewards, that's what they were called back then—were the norm. It's hard to explain, but it felt normal then. Today it just seems ridiculous."

"Was that why you didn't stay in the Coastal Artillery?"

Martinger nodded. "I applied to the air force, where they encourage the kind of attributes that are important in the rest of society: humility, the ability to think as an individual, flexibility. Everything that was missing on Korsö during our training."

Thomas could see conflicting emotions in Martinger's face; loyalty toward the comradeship he had known in the Rangers and a desire to be honest.

"The more I think about it, the more I have to distance myself from the values that were promoted at that time. When I look back today, I find it hard to understand how it could have been allowed to continue, or why I didn't speak up in certain situations. It haunts me sometimes."

A faint flush stained his cheeks.

"I don't know how to explain it to you. We kept our mouths shut and obeyed orders, and we felt relieved if someone else was the focus of an outburst of rage. I mean, we stuck together, of course, but sometimes . . ."

He didn't finish the sentence.

"And yet you stayed in the military for many years," Margit said.

Martinger ran a hand over his hair.

"The military has given me an enormous amount, I have to stress that. I received the very best training, both as a pilot and a leader, and I got to know men who will be friends for life. I was very happy in the military, just not with the ethos of the Coastal Rangers at that point in time. If I hadn't had a very attractive offer from SAS, I would still be in the air force."

Thomas changed tack.

"You had a sergeant named Robert Cronwall when you were on Korsö; what was he like?"

Martinger sat up straight.

"He was a total bastard. He was a staff sergeant who wasn't much older than we were. He had joined up a few years earlier, and he wanted to carry on as a reserve. The reserve officer training started just a few days after we finished."

"Can you tell us about him?" Margit said.

A heavy exhalation.

"He was something else. Most officers knew where the boundaries were, even if they did push us too hard sometimes. But you could never be sure with Cronwall."

Margit leaned forward. "What do you mean by that?"

Martinger let out a joyless bark of laughter.

"Let me give you an example. One day, a guy in our group fell asleep—Bo Kaufman, in fact. Who is no longer with us."

"We met him before he died," Margit interjected.

Martinger nodded.

"We'd been on a tough training exercise in the snow, and then we had a strategy session indoors. It was hard to stay awake in the warm classroom, and Kaufman nodded off. Bam! Cronwall woke him up by punching him right in the face."

Margit inhaled sharply. Martinger noticed her reaction but continued without changing his tone of voice.

"Blood poured from his nose. Surprise, surprise—we had no problem staying awake after that."

"Did no one report Cronwall?"

Martinger shook his head and looked at Margit with a sympathetic expression, as if she hadn't a clue what she was talking about.

"You have to understand that things were different in those days. There were no limits to the officers' power; we feared them more than we feared the enemy. No one would have dared to report anyone or anything. Kaufman was a big guy, but he was terrified of Cronwall. We all were. No one would have dreamed of standing up to him," he said, sounding utterly resigned. "Good God, we didn't even have the nerve to report ourselves sick. To do that, we had to fill in a special form and hand it to Cronwall. What do you think he did with those forms?"

Margit and Thomas exchanged glances.

"He tore them up, of course. Weakness was met with contempt; toughness was the only thing that mattered."

Thomas felt very strongly that Martinger was no killer, and neither was Kihlberg. He trusted his first impression of the firefighter.

"Can you tell us what happened to Pär Andersson?" Margit said.

The response was a heartfelt sigh. "Poor bastard. He killed himself out on Korsö; it was the last night before we left the island."

"Do you know why he did it?"

Martinger slowly stroked his chin. Eventually he said, "Andersson messed up in the final exercise—I mean, really messed up, so that it affected the whole group. Cronwall bawled us out; I've never experienced anything like it. He was furious. When we got back, we were all tired and pissed off; we turned our backs on Andersson that night. I can't describe it any other way."

His voice grew quieter, and he looked down at the table as he continued. "On top of everything else, he was sick and felt like crap . . . But I could never have imagined that he would take it so hard; no one could. It was such a shock. I felt terrible—we all did."

"Were there any signs that he had suicidal tendencies?" Margit asked. "Had he ever talked about taking his own life, or showed any signs of having mental health issues?"

Martinger licked his lips.

"Andersson was a bit of a whipping boy. Cronwall often picked on him. He was given the worst tasks, the most extreme punishments. Sometimes it was sheer hell, but I never heard him talk about killing himself."

He was slumped in the chair now, his shoulders sagging.

"It never crossed my mind that he might do that, but I've been haunted by his death ever since. It's still hard to talk about it."

The expression on Martinger's face was painful to see; Thomas could feel his pain, even though so many years had passed.

"I believe it was Cronwall who found him that morning," Thomas said. "Were you with him?"

"No, we were due to go back to Rindö that day. As I said, we'd just come back from the final exercise—fourteen intensive days out in the archipelago, with the whole unit taking part. We were completely exhausted, and I fell asleep as soon as we'd eaten; I think most people did. I was woken early in the morning by Kihlberg, who told me Andersson had been found dead in the shower."

Martinger closed his eyes, as if he were reliving the moment.

"So you have no idea what happened that night?"

"No. We'd had so little sleep; I had nothing left." Martinger's face was gray. "Could I have some water? I've been flying all night, and I'm pretty tired."

Thomas went out into the corridor and found a small staff room containing a water dispenser. He filled a cup and took it back to the office.

"Thanks," Martinger said. He drank the water in one go and put down the cup.

"We've been trying to track down your former comrades," Thomas explained. "There's one person we can't locate: Stefan Eklund. Do you have any idea where he might be?"

"I'm sorry, I've mainly kept in touch with Leif Kihlberg over the years. Andersson's suicide affected us deeply; we all saw one another at first, but then our get-togethers grew less and less frequent . . . I guess we all felt guilty."

"Can you think of any reason why Eklund might decide to take revenge on the rest of the group?" Thomas asked.

Martinger looked genuinely surprised.

"No."

"Are you sure?"

"Why would he want to do that?"

"I hoped you might be able to tell me. There are only three of you left alive, and he's the only one we can't get ahold of. I'm sure you can see why we're interested in him."

"Tell me something," Margit said; her tone was matter-of-fact, but the look in her eyes was intense. "Was Cronwall alone when he discovered the body that morning? Could Eklund have been with him?"

Thomas suspected he knew where she was going with this.

"No." Martinger shook his head. "He was asleep in the same room as me; Kihlberg woke both of us."

"So Eklund couldn't have seen something related to Andersson's death?" Margit persisted.

"It seems unlikely."

Margit frowned, as if she was trying to pin down a fleeting thought. She leaned forward.

"I'm just wondering if something happened on that final evening, something that might have contributed to Pär Andersson's suicide. All of a sudden, there's a danger that it might come to light—maybe Eklund was involved?"

"I understand what you're saying, but I really don't know how I can help you. As I said, I was fast asleep all night."

"So Cronwall was alone when he found Andersson," Thomas said.

Martinger shook his head again.

"No, Eklund wasn't there, but some of the others were—the ones who shared a room with Andersson."

Thomas looked up. "And who were they?"

"Kaufman, Fredell, and Erneskog. The rest of us slept in a four-bed room upstairs."

The color drained from Martinger's face. "It can't be true," he whispered.

Margit was staring at Thomas.

"Shit," she said. Thomas saw his own thoughts mirrored in her eyes. They were on the wrong track. Martinger and Kihlberg were neither killers nor victims. It was Robert Cronwall who was in danger—the sergeant they'd all hated.

Karin Ek had been right. The perpetrator had been practicing, and now he was ready for his real quarry. It was Cronwall's turn.

But who was after him?

CHAPTER 66

"We need to get ahold of Cronwall right away," Margit said as they left the airport and joined the E4 heading for Stockholm. It had started to drizzle, and Thomas switched on the windshield wipers.

"I'll give Lidingö council a call, see if he's at work," Margit went on. "Then I'll text Karin and tell her we're going straight there."

"OK."

Thomas couldn't stop thinking about what Martinger had told them. Thirty years ago, a boy had hanged himself and died alone in a shower room. Now everyone associated with his death was being picked off. One by one.

Margit ended her call. "Cronwall didn't turn up to work today. He hasn't called in sick either."

Thomas's stomach contracted. "Try him at home."

Margit contacted information, and Thomas heard her ask about a Robert Cronwall, with a postal address in Lidingö. The call was put through, but then she lowered the phone.

"The line's busy."

"Try again in a few minutes."

Thomas put his foot down on the gas and pulled into the passing lane.

"I'm still wondering where the detergent fits in," he said.

He had mentioned it to Martinger, but he'd been unable to help.

"Sorry?"

"The detergent in the victims' lungs. No one we've spoken to has any idea why they've all ingested detergent."

"Pär Andersson was found in the shower," Margit said slowly.

"But you use soap in the shower, not detergent. I'm sure it has a particular meaning; I just can't figure out what it is."

Thomas banged the wheel in frustration as Margit tried Cronwall's number again.

"Still busy."

It was impossible to tell if anyone was at home in the red house. The old apple trees that had been laden with fruit on their previous visit were now almost bare, with only the odd apple still clinging to the gnarled branches.

Thomas screeched to a halt and leaped out of the car. He glanced up at the kitchen window, but there was no sign of anyone. A black Volvo was parked in the driveway. Was it Cronwall's car? The one that should have been parked at his workplace at this time of day? He was pretty sure it had been there last time, too.

As they ran up the steps, the door opened and Birgitta Cronwall appeared, clutching the phone.

"At last," she said shakily. "I've been waiting all morning. Come in."

Margit and Thomas looked inquiringly at each other, then followed Birgitta into the kitchen. She was clearly upset. Her hair was bound in a messy bun, and there was no trace of the discreet makeup she'd had on the previous time.

"I'm sorry, but I'm not really following," Margit began. "I don't think we arranged to meet today."

Birgitta Cronwall looked as if she thought she was dealing with an idiot.

"But I spoke to the police several hours ago."

"Not to us, I'm afraid," Thomas said.

Birgitta's voice grew shrill. "I called the police this morning and reported Robert missing! He didn't sleep here last night, and he hasn't been in touch. I've contacted all our friends, but no one's seen him. I'm so worried!"

She sank down on a chair and started to cry.

"OK, let's go back to the beginning," Margit said quietly, tearing off a piece of paper towel from a roll on the counter and handing it her. "Tell us what's happened."

Birgitta blew her nose and managed a wan smile. Thomas sat down beside her.

"When I got home yesterday evening, Robert wasn't here, even though his car was in the driveway. I started making dinner, but by eight o'clock, there was still no sign of him. He wasn't answering either his direct line at work or his cell."

"So what did you do then?"

"I waited a few more hours, and then I began calling around, but no one had seen him."

She gave a little sob and swallowed hard.

"This isn't like Robert at all; he's always so punctual. Eventually I went to bed, but I couldn't sleep; I just lay there listening for the sound of the front door opening. At around seven this morning, I called the police. Over the past few hours, I've spoken to everyone we know."

"So he hasn't been home for something like twenty-four hours," Thomas said. "When did you last see him?"

"Yesterday morning."

"And was everything normal then? You hadn't quarreled?" Margit asked.

Birgitta shook her head. "No—I can't think of anything different, except I was home a little late; I have a Spanish class on Tuesdays, so I don't get back until seven."

"What time does Robert usually arrive home?"

"Around six."

Thomas thought about the other victims. Two had been drowned in their own bathtub, and now Cronwall had disappeared, according to his wife.

Or had he?

"Birgitta," he said gently, "have you searched the house?"

She looked horrified. "What do you mean?"

"You're sure he's not here?"

That didn't go down well.

"Of course I'm sure!"

"Do you mind if I take a look around?" Thomas stood up and pushed his chair under the table. "How many bathrooms do you have?"

It was obvious that Robert Cronwall's wife had no idea where Thomas was going with this line of questioning, but she answered obediently. "There's one upstairs and one in the attic, next to the guest room."

"Have you checked up there?"

An uncertain expression came over her face.

"No, I just shouted his name—I didn't go up." A tear trickled down her cheek. "Should I have?"

"It's fine—I'll just take a look to be on the safe side."

Thomas left the kitchen and headed up the wide staircase that led to a spacious landing with bedrooms on either side. He caught sight of a neatly made double bed in one of them.

Behind a closed door, he found the bathroom, tiled in beige with a gold border halfway up the walls. A large corner bath dominated the space, and a shelf above the sink was crowded with toiletries and a half-full bottle of perfume.

He left the bathroom and quickly searched the rest of the second floor, but nothing caught his attention.

Which left the top floor.

He made his way slowly up the narrow dark pine staircase, the wood creaking beneath his feet. There was a slightly musty smell, as if it had been a long time since anyone had ventured up there.

He took the last two steps in one stride and found himself in a corridor with two doors. The first was ajar, and when he pushed it open, he saw two beds with a bedside table between them. This must be the guest room. There was a folded green towel at the foot of each bed.

He backed out of the room; the next door was just a few feet away.

It was unnervingly quiet. The only sound was the rain hammering on the roof and water gushing through the drainpipes. Despite the fact that it was cooler on this floor, Thomas could feel sweat trickling down the back of his neck.

A faint grayish light seeped in through a square skylight overhead.

He moved toward the bathroom.

CHAPTER 67

"How could you? How could you bring Marie with you?"

Nora was finding it difficult to keep her voice steady. Once again, all the bitterness she felt at Henrik's betrayal was coming to the surface: those long months when she had struggled to keep the family together while he was deceiving her, all the times he had lied about having to work an extra shift when in fact he was with Marie.

How he must have laughed at how easy it was to fool his gullible wife.

"What were you expecting? Did you think we were going to fall into each other's arms and become one great big happy family? It's bad enough that she's living in the house we used to share—am I supposed to let her take over my new home as well?"

Nora had to pause to catch her breath. It was fortunate that her office door was closed, she thought, otherwise her colleagues would have seen a very different side to her; under normal circumstances, she was totally in control. She couldn't remember ever having lost it at work, but right now her upper lip was beaded with sweat.

She had intended to broach the subject calmly and matter-of-factly, but when she realized how much it had upset Adam, she just couldn't do it. The more she thought about Marie standing in the hallway, the more furious she became.

Her ex-husband's voice was subdued when he finally managed to get a word in.

"Maybe it wasn't such a good idea."

"Maybe it wasn't such a good idea? Really? Couldn't she see the problem, by the way?"

"She noticed—neither you nor your parents were exactly welcoming."

Henrik sounded stiff and formal, but he wasn't biting back, as he had done so many times in the past.

"I thought I'd made it perfectly clear that she isn't welcome in my home."

"Nora, I'm sorry things turned out as they did." His tone was surprisingly conciliatory, Nora noticed, but it didn't make her any less angry. "I should have realized it wasn't going to work," he went on.

"Plus, you forgot Simon's book," Nora snapped. "He needs it for English tomorrow."

"I'll drop by with it tonight."

"You do that."

"Nora . . . I don't want us to keep on arguing, especially in front of the children."

"You should have thought of that before."

She had no sympathy for him; he had made his bed, and now he could lie in it.

Henrik cleared his throat.

"The reflection period for the divorce is up in a week."

"I'm well aware of that."

Nora knew to the day when their marriage could be dissolved. She had submitted all the documentation on April 10, just over a month after she had found out about Henrik and Marie. She had rarely been more sure of anything when she sent off that big brown envelope to the court.

She sank down on her chair. Six months earlier, they had met to discuss the situation. She had still been living in the house in Saltsjöbaden at that point, while Henrik had temporarily moved in with his parents. He had come over at ten o'clock one night, when the boys were asleep. Nora had already laid out all the relevant paperwork on the kitchen table, everything that was necessary to put an end to their marriage. The color had left Henrik's face when he realized she had made up her mind. Nora refused to budge; she had simply pointed to the table.

"You need to sign there," she had said firmly. "But if you don't, I'm going to file for divorce anyway."

All she had wanted was for him to sign and leave, but Henrik had made one final attempt. His eyes had been suspiciously shiny. He had opened his mouth, presumably to say something that would make her reconsider.

"It was a mistake," he had said eventually. "Marie means nothing, you and the kids are the most important thing in my life. I know I have no right to ask, but can't you forgive me—for Adam and Simon's sake?"

The pleading expression in his eyes had almost done her in. They'd sat down at the table, and he had reached out his hand and covered hers. His gentle touch, the warmth of his fingers, had brought back a thousand memories.

"Please, Nora. I love you, I really do. I can't live without you and the boys."

His voice had broken. He had turned away, his head drooping. And then he had begun to cry.

Like Adam, Nora had thought. *Just like Adam when he's upset. They're alike, those two. My husband and my son.*

The doubts had come flooding back; was she really doing the right thing?

At that moment, his cell phone had rung.

Henrik had ignored it, but after thirty seconds, it had rung again. He'd let go of Nora's hand, taken the phone out of his pocket, and rejected the call.

But by then it was too late. Nora had already seen the name on the display.

Marie.

That had been enough to bring her back to her senses. The rage that had carried her through the previous month had returned with full force. She had pulled her hand away and leaped to her feet.

"Just sign it. You can cry all over Marie when we're done. We have nothing more to say to each other."

A few weeks later, Nora had moved to the new apartment, and just seven days after that, Marie had taken up residence in the house. Nora had happened to come by to pick up a toy Simon had left behind, and she had seen the boxes being carried in.

Every time she mourned the collapse of her marriage, she conjured up the image of Marie's boxes.

"Six months will have passed on October 10," Nora said now. "The court should make its decision next Thursday. It's no more than a formality."

Henrik didn't say a word.

"We'll be divorced in a week," Nora said.

"Do you have to rush things like this?" Henrik said plaintively. "Is divorcing me really so important that you're counting down the days?"

Nora went over to the window. It was raining. She could hear the dull roar of traffic from the street below. A few yellowing leaves drifted by outside.

She rested her forehead on the cool glass.

"Yes," she said. "It is."

CHAPTER 68

Thomas yanked open the bathroom door, all his senses on full alert. He stared at the bathtub for several seconds before he grasped the fact that there was no one there; he had been so sure he would find Robert Cronwall lying under the water.

His chest hurt; he was still holding his breath. With a huge effort, he exhaled and looked around.

The unprepossessing bathroom was pretty old-fashioned, the walls covered in square white tiles. The enamel bathtub was chipped and stained. Thomas took a step closer and ran his hand over the surface. It was completely dry—not a hint of dampness. Just to be sure, he checked the drain, but there were no traces of water there either. In fact, the room carried a faint smell of drains, as if the trap had dried up. No one had used the bath or shower for a long time.

Thomas sat down on the toilet seat and put his head in his hands. If Robert Cronwall wasn't in the house, then where the hell was he?

When Thomas came downstairs, Birgitta and Margit were still in the kitchen. He caught Margit's eye and shook his head.

"Nothing," he said quietly as he sat down.

Birgitta shuffled uncomfortably on her chair.

"Robert lied to you," she said.

"About what?"

"He said he hadn't met that student, Marcus Nielsen, but he was lying."

Thomas swore silently. He should have pushed Cronwall harder.

"Oh?" he said.

"He came here one evening and talked to Robert. They spent quite a long time together in the library."

"When was this?"

Instead of replying, Birgitta got up and went over to a calendar hanging on the wall next to the refrigerator. She ran her forefinger down the page until she found the date she was looking for. Without turning around, she said, "It was September 14—a Friday evening."

Two days before Marcus Nielsen died, Thomas thought.

"Are you sure?" Margit said.

"Yes. We usually watch a quiz show on Fridays, and Marcus rang the doorbell just before it started," Birgitta said as she came back to the table. "To be honest, I was quite annoyed. I thought it was rude of him to disturb us on a Friday, but apparently Robert had arranged to see him then."

"You're absolutely sure of the date?"

Birgitta nodded. "Yes, it was the season premiere. The following weekend we were in Gävle visiting friends, so we missed the next episode. It was definitely September 14."

"Do you know what they talked about?" Margit asked.

"I'm afraid not."

"You didn't overhear any of their conversation?"

Birgitta looked troubled, as if she didn't want to be accused of eavesdropping. "I knocked on the door to let Robert know that the show had started, and he told me to leave them in peace. He was quite sharp with me, actually. When I opened the door, I heard Marcus asking about something that seemed to be related to Robert's time with the Coastal Rangers."

"What was it exactly? Please try to remember—this could be very important," Margit said.

"I think he mentioned someone called Pär or Peter."

Pär Andersson, Thomas thought. *He asked about Pär Andersson, who was under your husband's command in the military. The same Pär Andersson who took his own life on the island of Korsö after your husband had punished him.*

"Have you any idea why Robert didn't tell us this?" Margit asked.

Birgitta bit her lip and didn't answer.

"You do know that Marcus Nielsen was found dead in his apartment two days later?" Margit went on.

"We think he died on Saturday night/Sunday morning," Thomas added.

Birgitta started crying again, but this time she made no attempt to dry her tears.

"Robert was away that Saturday night," she said, her voice trembling.

Thomas exchanged a glance with Margit.

"He left at around eleven and didn't get back until two in the morning. He probably thought I was asleep; I often take a pill because I sleep badly, but I hadn't taken one that night. So I heard him start up the car and drive off."

Red blotches had appeared on Birgitta's throat, and she was nervously wringing her hands.

"I heard him come home, too; he sat in the library for quite some time, drinking whisky. I must have nodded off eventually, but I woke up when he came to bed. The clock was showing quarter past four."

"How do you know he'd been drinking whisky?" Thomas asked; he couldn't quite keep the tension out of his voice.

"Because he snored; he only does that when he's been at the single malt. Plus, there was a glass and an empty bottle on the table when I got up in the morning."

Margit looked Birgitta in the eye until the other woman lowered her gaze.

"Do you realize how serious it is that we weren't told this earlier? You have deliberately withheld important information from the police."

"I know," Birgitta whispered, her eyes again filling with tears. "But Robert told me to stay out of it. He said we'd get dragged into the police investigation for no reason if we mentioned Marcus Nielsen's visit. He said it was irrelevant."

Her voice gave way; her expression begged the two detectives for understanding.

"I'm so sorry, I didn't know . . . I'm so worried about Robert. Where can he be?"

Thomas was just about to say something reassuring when Birgitta's hand flew to her mouth.

"What if he's dead?" she exclaimed. "What if he's been murdered, too?"

DIARY:
JULY 1977

We had been paddling for several hours when huge storm clouds loomed up in the west. We had passed Kapellskär and were about to cross Svartlöga Bay when the rain started and the wind picked up.

Without warning, a wave struck us from the side, pushing our canoe off course. I was sitting in the prow, with Andersson behind. My paddle got stuck under the hull, and we lurched over.

"Drop the paddle!" Andersson yelled. "Drop the fucking paddle before we capsize!"

As if in slow motion, the canoe began to tip. I could almost feel the waters closing in over my head. I was already half-blinded by the pouring rain, and my clothes were soaked through. I tore at the paddle, trying to free it.

Just as the canoe was about to capsize, Andersson hurled his upper body over to the side to balance the weight. Miraculously, I managed to free the paddle, and the boat righted itself. We tipped in the opposite direction, then settled.

"Fucking hell!" Andersson bellowed in my ear. "Fucking hell, that was close!"

Up ahead, I could see other canoes that had turned over; one was being smashed against the rocks by the waves, just outside the inlet we were heading for. Kihlberg and Martinger were in the water, their heads bobbing up and down, until they were able to grab their canoe.

The waves carried us toward the inlet, and we managed to get through without coming to any harm.

We are far out at sea, in the Nassa archipelago. The canoes have been dragged into the reeds along the shoreline, and the rocks we sat on this evening are still warm from the afternoon sun.

We didn't go hungry. We caught enough fish to get by, and on the skerry we found cloudberries that stained our fingers yellow as we ate them.

Andersson had the most success when it came to fishing; he's good at laying out his line exactly where the herring hang out, then whipping out one shimmering silver fish after another. It's as if he instinctively knows when they are nibbling at the hook. He tenses his body like a cat about to pounce and flicks his wrist at precisely the right moment.

"What would we have done without you, Andersson?" Martinger exclaimed after we'd eaten.

We had made a fire in a crevice down by the water, and we hadn't wasted a scrap of the piping-hot fish.

Andersson straightened up, and the faint flush on his cheeks showed that he valued the appreciation of his comrades. He looked happy in the fading evening light.

Thanks to him, we were all sated.

The horizon was on fire over in the northwest, the sun a burning red ball low in the sky. The sea was as smooth and shiny as if a satin cloth had been carefully spread over its surface.

Tomorrow we return to Korsö, two in each canoe. Kihlberg and Martinger, Sigurd and Eklund, Kaufman and Erneskog, me and Andersson.

We are filthy and exhausted but incredibly pleased with ourselves.

CHAPTER 69

Thomas and Margit left the parking lot and dashed toward the door of the police station through the pouring rain. When they reached the conference room, most of the team was already there. The Old Man was at the head of the table, flanked by Karin Ek and Erik Blom.

"We've put out a nationwide search for Robert Cronwall," he said as soon as they appeared in the doorway. "The search warrant for his home is on its way."

"We took some strands of hair from a jacket so that we can compare Cronwall's DNA with the DNA found on the rope in Marcus Nielsen's apartment," Thomas informed his colleagues.

"And the pillow," Margit reminded him.

"So you think you've found our killer?" the Old Man asked.

Thomas nodded as the door opened and Kalle Lidwall came in.

"I've checked all the phone records," he said, turning to Thomas and Margit. "Leif Kihlberg contacted Anders Martinger the day you spoke to him."

"We already know that."

"OK." Kalle looked exhausted.

"What about Nielsen's parents' phone?" Margit asked.

Kalle's expression brightened. "I found some calls to numbers his parents don't recognize. They were made during the day in the weeks leading up to Marcus's death."

"Which suggests it was Marcus who used their phone," Erik said. "Both parents are at work during the day."

"According to his mom, he sometimes spent time at the house between lectures," Kalle went on. "Täby isn't far from the university." He flicked through his papers, then added, "Marcus called two cell phone numbers that are of interest—one is Leif Kihlberg's, the other is registered to SAS."

"Martinger, of course," Thomas said immediately. "He tried to get ahold of him, too."

"The calls are very short, no more than twenty, twenty-five seconds," Kalle said. "Presumably he just left a message." His eyes were red-rimmed, as if he had been reading small print for many hours. "I don't think he actually spoke to either of them."

"Well, at least we know he tried," Thomas said. "Do you have the dates?"

Kalle checked his notes.

"Both September 13, Kihlberg at 15:23 and Martinger one minute later."

Thomas opened his notebook to remind himself of the date when Marcus Nielsen had met Jan-Erik Fredell. He went over to the whiteboard and drew a black horizontal line—a time line.

"OK," he began. "Marcus meets Fredell on Wednesday, September 12, and is given the diaries, which presumably contain key information about the Coastal Rangers' time on Korsö."

He marked the date with an *X*.

"On Thursday, September 13, he calls Martinger and Kihlberg. He can't get ahold of them, so he leaves a message."

Another *X*.

"One day later, on Friday evening, he goes to Cronwall's house and stays for around an hour. The following day, Saturday, he spends some time with his parents, then goes back to his apartment."

A third *X*.

"That night, he puts a noose around his neck, climbs up on the desk, steps out into thin air, and dies."

He put down the pen, folded his arms, and turned around.

"At the same time that Robert Cronwall is away from his home for about three hours with no explanation. His wife also informed us that he was away for several hours on the afternoon when Erneskog died." He leaned back against the wall. "Have I missed anything?"

Kalle cleared his throat. "Just one more thing: Marcus Nielsen made another call on that Thursday."

"Who to?"

"A guy named Urban Melin. He's forty-three years old, and he works as a dental technician at a practice in Tyresö."

"Why did he call a dental technician?" Karin wondered. "Did he have problems with his teeth?"

Margit picked up her folder and started looking for Sachsen's autopsy report.

"No. At least there's nothing to suggest that in the report, but I suppose that doesn't necessarily mean he didn't need some kind of treatment."

"Hang on," Karin said. "Kalle, didn't you say Marcus called Melin's home number?"

"Yes—he lives in Farsta, Måndagsvägen 23."

"So why call him at home rather than at work?" Karin said.

Melin, Thomas thought. Why did he recognize that name? Suddenly he pictured the woman from the pharmacy—wasn't her name Melin? Marcus had made a note on his phone about an appointment at the pharmacy in the Farsta Centrum mall.

"Is that phone line registered only to Urban Melin?" he asked.

"I don't have any further details," Kalle said.

"I can check right now," Karin offered. She left the room and was back in minutes. The look on her face said it all, and she didn't even bother to sit down before she started talking.

"Listen to this. Urban Melin lives with his wife, Annika. There's a call out for her, too—her husband reported her missing this morning."

Thomas felt his heart rate increase. Another person linked to the investigation had disappeared.

Margit spoke first.

"Do you think Cronwall has abducted her?"

CHAPTER 70

Nora was about to leave the office when her phone rang. She dug it out of her purse just before the voice mail kicked in.

"Nora Linde."

"Hi, Nora, it's Olle, Olle Granlund. Am I disturbing you?"

"Not at all—I was just finishing up for the day."

"I've been thinking about the conversation we had the other day, after our trip to Korsö."

"OK . . ."

Nora pulled on her coat and switched off the light. With her purse over her shoulder and her briefcase in hand, she closed the door behind her and set off toward the elevators.

"Do you remember I mentioned a sergeant who had a really bad reputation?"

"I do."

Nora pressed the green call button.

"If you're still interested, I've found out a bit more, including his name."

Nora froze. The button was flashing to show that the elevator had arrived, but she ignored it; the reception was better here.

"Go on."

"His name is Robert Cronwall, and he served with the Coastal Artillery for a short period. It was easier to track him down than I expected; there are still plenty of people who have very bad memories of that guy."

Nora listened carefully. On Simon's birthday, she had exchanged a few words with Thomas about the case, and he had mentioned that they were looking into links with the Coastal Rangers in the 1970s.

"Anyway, I had a chat with a couple of old friends, and they thought he'd been using anabolic steroids back then."

"Drugs?"

"In those days, steroids weren't classified as drugs. Plenty of guys took them to build muscle."

"But surely they're banned?"

"Today, yes, but in the seventies, you could take all kinds of stuff. We had no idea about the side effects. In Cronwall's case, it seems they affected both his mood and his judgment, unfortunately. As I said before, he was a complete bastard. He really made his men suffer."

"I still don't understand why he was allowed to carry on."

Nora put down her heavy briefcase. As usual, it was stuffed with documents that had to be read by the next day.

"Different times . . . But what I really want to tell you about is a terrible incident that happened just before he left Korsö. One of the men under his command took his own life."

"That's terrible."

Nora leaned against the wall and closed her eyes. Imagine sending your son off to do his military service and getting him back in a coffin.

"The young lad hanged himself."

Olle paused, as if he was reluctant to go on.

"According to the rumors, the poor kid was driven to it."

"What do you mean?"

"That's all I've managed to find out so far; it's still a sensitive subject. But there are also rumors that the death wasn't quite what it seemed."

"I don't understand."

Olle made a noise that suggested he had just spat out a plug of chewing tobacco. Nora pictured him standing on the jetty in Sandhamn.

"There was a suicide note, but it was typewritten, and it wasn't signed."

Nora thought for a moment; surely an incident like this should have triggered a formal investigation within the military?

"Wasn't there an official inquiry?"

"No. The soldier was sent home to his family in a coffin. They were told he'd been unable to handle the pressure and had chosen to end his life. Suicide was still something to be ashamed of back then; I don't think anyone wanted to look into it."

"I feel so sorry for his family."

"Yes; I believe he was the only son. They took it very hard, apparently."

"And what happened to Cronwall?"

"He started as a cadet at the Royal Swedish Naval Academy but didn't complete his reserve officer training. He left the military after a while—he might even have been asked to leave. There were plenty of rumors, but nothing ever became public."

Olle coughed.

"Anyway, now you know. I hope you find the information useful."

"Thank you so much."

"You will handle this discreetly, won't you?"

Nora wondered whether to tell him that she would have to pass it on to Thomas, but decided against it; there was no point in worrying Olle for no reason. She opted for a compromise.

"I won't pass it on unnecessarily, I promise."

Nora pressed the elevator button again. Robert Cronwall had a great deal to answer for. She needed to call Thomas right away.

CHAPTER 71

It was still raining when Thomas and Margit got in the car, and as they drove, wet leaves from the side of the road whirled up and got stuck under the windshield wipers.

Urban and Annika Melin lived in a semidetached house in Farsta Strand.

A far-from-new VW Passat with a dent in the front was parked outside. A plump man in his forties opened the door as soon as they rang the bell.

"Police?"

Margit held up her ID. "Urban Melin?"

The man nodded; he looked as if he were on the verge of tears. "I'm so worried about Annika. What if something's happened to her?"

An unpleasant feeling of déjà vu came over Thomas. This was exactly how the encounter with Birgitta Cronwall had started just a few hours earlier.

"I've been waiting by the phone all day," Melin said. "I called in sick so that I could stay home in case she called, but I've heard nothing."

He ran a hand over his forehead, disturbing the thin hair arranged in a comb-over to hide his bald spot. He didn't seem to notice that he had ruined his coiffure.

Thomas saw that his nails were bitten down to the quick.

"Tell us everything, and start from the beginning," Margit said once they were settled on a brown leather sofa that took up most of the living room. A gray cat that had been sleeping on an armchair lifted its head, then slunk off in the direction of the kitchen, wearing a martyred expression.

"Annika didn't come home last night; she hasn't been in touch, and she's not answering her cell phone," Urban Melin began.

"Could she be visiting friends or relatives?" Margit asked.

"Her father and her brother died many years ago, and her mother has dementia; she's in a nursing home."

"Did you have a fight?" Thomas asked.

Melin shook his head. "No. Everything was perfectly normal before she disappeared."

"Maybe she's with a girlfriend?" Margit suggested. "Is there any possibility that she could have slept over at a friend's place without letting you know?"

"No. I've called everyone; no one's seen her. We don't have many friends; my wife isn't easy to get along with."

It was an odd thing to say. Thomas was going to let it go for the time being, but Margit picked up on it. She gave Melin a searching look.

"Why not?"

Melin obviously wished he'd never mentioned it.

"Annika has a few . . . issues. She's a little . . . unstable."

"In what way?"

Melin appeared to be torn between the desire to protect his wife and the need to convey the gravity of the situation.

"You don't need to hold anything back," Margit said gently.

"She . . . she suffers from mood swings. Sometimes she's very down, criticizing herself for all kinds of things, then suddenly she's furious, blaming all her problems on other people. It's hard to predict how she's going to react. She can be . . . destructive." A nerve under his eye began to twitch. "I'm afraid she might come to harm in some way."

"What makes you think that?" Thomas asked.

Urban Melin produced a handkerchief and wiped his bald spot.

"Things have been difficult for us recently, that's why I'm so worried. We . . ."

He broke off yet again, and Thomas and Margit waited patiently.

"We were expecting a baby," Melin said after a long pause, "but we lost it three weeks ago, and the situation has gotten much worse since then."

Thomas frowned. "Did you say three weeks ago?"

"Yes, in the middle of September."

"I'm sorry to push you on this, but I think we met your wife a week or so ago. Doesn't she work at the pharmacy in the Farsta Centrum mall?"

"Yes, she's a pharmacist," Melin said eagerly. "She's worked there for quite some time."

Thomas glanced at Margit, who looked equally confused.

"When we saw her, she was pregnant."

Melin shook his head wearily.

"No, she wasn't. She had a miscarriage at the Southern District Hospital on Friday, September 14. Trust me, I was there."

He buried his face in his hands, and Margit leaned forward and gently touched his arm.

"Can you tell us what happened?"

At first, Melin didn't answer, as if he were debating with himself whether to tell the truth. When he finally spoke, his voice was a monotone.

"Annika had a car accident. There was no one else involved; she went out late one night and crashed into a road sign. She wasn't too badly hurt, but the impact drove the steering wheel into her belly, and the baby couldn't be saved. She was five months along." His voice broke. "We'd been trying for such a long time."

Thomas remembered his recent accident; he pictured Pernilla in the car when she was pregnant with Emily, her swollen belly almost touching the steering wheel. It wasn't hard to understand why Urban Melin was pale and hollow-eyed.

"I'm so sorry," Thomas said. "But it really did seem as if Annika was pregnant when we met her."

Surely she had been wearing a loose maternity dress? He'd asked when the child was due, and she hadn't corrected him; after Christmas, she had said.

Strange.

"How could Annika cope with being back at work so soon after the miscarriage?" Margit asked sympathetically.

"She insisted she'd go crazy if she sat at home brooding. I managed to persuade her at least to go part-time, but she's not easy to convince when she's made up her mind. I don't think she even told her colleagues that she'd lost the baby."

He made a funny noise, halfway between a cough and a sob.

"She's been worse than ever lately. One minute she's depressed and anxious, the next dramatic and furious. She changes all the time, and there's no way of predicting how she's going to react. To be honest, it was a relief when she went back to work; she seemed to pull herself together when she was with her coworkers."

"Has she behaved like this in the past?" Margit asked.

Melin rocked back and forth on his chair.

"She's always been fragile. It's hard to believe—she's so tall and elegant, and she gives an impression of being extremely capable. But inside she's like a little child, terrified of being abandoned. And yet, at the same time, she pushes people away and feels worthless."

"Has she received any counseling or psychiatric help?" Thomas asked.

"She would never agree to anything like that." The answer was instant and decisive.

"It can't be easy for you to deal with," Margit said.

"No, it isn't. I try to reassure her, of course, I tell her she's wonderful, but it's hard to reach her when she's in that mood."

"Have you been together long?"

"Nine years."

"How did you meet?"

"At the pharmacy where she works. My ex had left me for another man, and I was in a bad place. My doctor prescribed sleeping pills, and when I went to pick them up, I met Annika. We started chatting, and one thing led to another."

He straightened a pile of magazines on the coffee table in a quick, nervous movement.

"We kind of found each other right away, and we soon moved in together. She was like a whirlwind, everything had to happen *now*. The engagement, the marriage . . . she was the one who found this house." He looked at them, his eyes full of sorrow. "The only thing we had to wait for was a baby."

"That must have been a strain, if she's as temperamental as you say," Margit said.

"It was." Melin turned his wedding ring around and around. "Sometimes she'd lose it completely. She once twisted my arm so hard that she fractured it. I was in a cast for weeks."

"That's abuse," Margit said. "Did you report it?"

An embarrassed silence gave her the answer, but somehow Melin seemed relieved at being able to talk about his dysfunctional relationship with his missing wife.

"Who would have believed me? Men abuse women, not vice versa. Annika broke down in tears afterward, and she kept apologizing. She said she'd kill herself if I left her. I forgave her, of course. I always do." He looked utterly lost.

"Always? Has she hurt you more than once?"

Melin lowered his eyes. "Yes." He pointed to a scar on his forearm. "She cut me once when she was really mad."

"With a knife?"

"Yes, she grabbed a carving knife from the kitchen drawer. She was unrecognizable. I'd worked late several evenings in a row, and she claimed I was having an affair with a female colleague. There was no truth in it, of course. I've never been unfaithful to my wife."

"So what did you do that time?" Thomas asked gently.

Melin adjusted the perfectly tidy pile of magazines once more and kept his eyes fixed on the table as he spoke. "I forgave her. She promised she'd never do it again."

"And you believed her?"

"Yes. When she's on an even keel, she's sweet and kind. She looks after me. She loves me very much; I know she does."

Domestic violence, Thomas thought. *You're not the only man who's suffered. Female abusers are more common than people think, but men are reluctant to admit it, let alone report it to the police. If you can't be with the one you love, you have to love the one you're with. Is that why you stayed with her? Or were you afraid to leave in case she carried out her threat and took her own life? Or was there something else?*

Thomas got to his feet.

"Do you mind if we take a look around?"

"No problem—where do you want to start?"

"What's upstairs?"

"Our bedroom, a guest room, and Annika's study."

"Shall we start with her study?" Margit suggested. "It would also be helpful if you could find us a recent photo. You'll get it back, of course."

"There's one in my study." Melin opened a door, and Thomas saw a desk covered in pictures of dentures and rows of teeth. There was also a framed photograph, which Melin picked up and brought over to them.

"There you go. This was taken last summer, in June."

Thomas studied the picture of Annika Melin. She had well-defined features, and although her eyes were serious, she was smiling into the camera. She was slimmer than when he had seen her at the pharmacy, but presumably she had put on weight during the pregnancy. She looked strong and fit; she was wearing blue-and-white running gear, and there was a square cloth with a number on it pinned to her chest.

Melin looked proud.

"That was at the Stockholm marathon. Annika's run it several times, and she's pretty good. She trains in all weather; sometimes she keeps going until she throws up. She has incredible stamina, my wife."

"Shall we go upstairs?" Margit said.

Melin led the way. When they reached the landing, Margit pointed to a closed door. Melin seemed embarrassed.

"That's Annika's study. She doesn't like me going in there, so the door is always shut."

"Is it locked?"

"I don't think so; it's just that I never go in there." He tried the handle. "No, it's open."

The room was comparatively small and contained a desk made of dark wood and several well-filled bookshelves. An old-fashioned leather office chair was pushed under the desk. The only window, which was streaked with rain, looked out onto a silver fir; it was so close that the branches were practically brushing against the house.

There were a number of framed photographs dotted among the books, and Thomas's attention was immediately caught by a portrait of a young man in his late teens or early twenties. He had cropped hair and was leaning against a fence.

He was wearing a green uniform, and on his head was a beret with a golden trident on the front.

Thomas pointed to the picture.

"Who's this?"

Urban Melin came closer and picked it up.

"That's Pär—Annika's brother."

Chapter 72

Thomas took a step toward Urban Melin so that they were face-to-face.

"Pär? What's his last name?"

"Andersson, but he's no longer with us."

"Pär Andersson was Annika's brother?" Margit exclaimed behind them.

"Yes." Melin took a step back. "But I never met him."

"How come?"

"He died a long time ago, back in the seventies. Annika was only a little girl; there was a big age difference between them."

"What happened to him?"

"I think he killed himself, but she didn't want to talk about it."

"Why not?"

Melin fingered his wedding ring again.

"It was a terrible shock for the family; her father started drinking, and her mother suffered from depression. It wasn't easy for Annika, growing up in an environment like that. From what I can gather, her mood swings and panic attacks started when she lost her brother."

"Do you know how old he was at the time? Was it during his military service?" With a huge effort, Thomas managed to keep his voice calm—much calmer than he actually felt.

The pieces of the puzzle were falling into place.

"Thomas!" Margit called out before Melin had time to answer. She was gazing down at the papers strewn across the desk. "Look at this."

Thomas joined her. "They're maritime charts showing the shipping lanes around Sandhamn," he said. He pointed to one chart. "That circle is Korsö."

Margit moved the pile to one side. "There's more."

Thomas saw a list of addresses and telephone numbers, and he immediately recognized the names: Fredell, Kaufman, Erneskog.

Robert Cronwall.

There was an open book with the title *Fifty Years of the Coastal Rangers*.

Was this the book Marcus Nielsen had used when he chose the group of rangers he wanted to study? He couldn't have known what a deadly choice that would turn out to be.

Everything pointed in one direction: Annika Melin had been gathering evidence against her brother's killers.

Was that why Cronwall had gone after her, too?

Nora had called Thomas when he was in the car on his way to Farsta. She had told him about the rumors, the suggestion that Cronwall had driven Pär Andersson to take his own life.

Thomas wondered if the truth was even worse.

Both Andersson and Marcus Nielsen appeared to have hanged themselves, but in both cases there was a question mark over the suicide notes they had left behind. Neither had been signed.

Thomas was beginning to see a pattern.

Had Annika confronted Cronwall and accused him of having caused her brother's death? He remembered Cronwall sitting in the living room of his fine house in Lidingö, dismissing them with a few polite phrases when he had had enough of the conversation.

Cronwall was a man with power, a good citizen with a prominent position on the council and the high social status that came with it.

Maybe Annika had threatened to tell the truth about the respected councillor and chair of the Rotary Club.

Was that why he had murdered everyone who could bear witness to what had really happened on that night when Pär Andersson died in a shower room on Korsö? Right on cue, Margit let out a low whistle. She had taken a pile of black-bound notebooks out of one of the desk drawers and had opened one of them. The first page was filled with closely written text, with the date at the top. Inside the cover was a name: *Jan-Erik Fredell.*

"She must have gotten them from Marcus Nielsen," Margit said slowly. "That's the only possible explanation."

Thomas turned to Urban Melin, who was standing by the window.

"Do you know if Annika met someone named Marcus Nielsen? Twenty-two years old, black hair—he was a student at the university."

The words came spilling out; this was urgent. Robert Cronwall and Annika Melin had been missing for almost twenty-four hours. God knows what he could have done with her during all that time . . .

The top of Urban Melin's head, where the hair follicles had given up long ago, was shining, and his forehead was beaded with sweat.

"He was here. The day she crashed the car. He was leaving just as I got home from work; we met by the garden gate."

"Do you know why he came here?"

"No, but Annika was terribly upset afterward—she was in pieces. She shut herself in her study and refused to eat any dinner. At about ten o'clock that night, she came downstairs and grabbed the car keys without telling me where she was going."

Melin looked as if he was about to burst into tears.

"At midnight, I got a call from the Southern District Hospital to say she'd been in an accident." He turned to Margit. "What the hell is going on?"

Margit walked over to him. "I wish I knew, but we'll do everything we can to find out."

DIARY:
JULY 1977

When we got back to Korsö, the sergeant was waiting on the jetty—legs apart, arms folded, as if he knew exactly when we would appear, although that was impossible.

Several canoes were already lying on the shore; that meant we were the last to arrive, but so what? What did it matter if everyone else had gotten there before us? We had completed our mission: we had managed to survive for five days without food or the other necessities of life. Now we belonged to the elite.

The sergeant's glance swept over us and the canoes. His lips were pressed together; it was obvious that he wasn't happy. When he spotted Andersson, his expression changed. He kind of stiffened.

I tried to understand. Was he blaming Andersson for our late arrival? We had fulfilled the task within the allotted time, we just weren't the first to reach Korsö. He couldn't criticize anyone for that.

Or could he?

As the sunlight danced on the surface of the water, we paddled the last fifty yards to the jetty.

I have known for a long time that the sergeant has a problem with Andersson, but I interpreted it as a bully's need to take out his anger on someone. In every group, there is a pecking order, and it just so happened that Andersson was at the bottom of that pecking order.

But at close quarters, I could see malice in the sergeant's eyes that went far beyond the aim of transforming callow nineteen-year-olds into true Coastal Rangers.

I clutched the paddle so hard that it hurt, as fear flooded my body.

The sergeant is a dangerous man.

CHAPTER 73

Thomas's cell phone rang; it was Erik Blom.

"We've found Nielsen's laptop; it was hidden in Cronwall's attic. Kalle's started to go through it."

Thomas had had the feeling that Cronwall had taken it.

"But there's something else," Erik went on. "We've checked Cronwall's alibi, and several independent witnesses have confirmed that both Birgitta and Robert were in Gävle the weekend Fredell was killed."

"And the following weekend, when Kaufman died?"

"They were both in the country with close friends, at their summer cottage on an island in Roslagen."

Erik sounded exhausted, almost resigned.

"I understand," Thomas said.

This didn't make sense. He loosened his grip on the phone and switched hands. He could feel Erik's disappointment coming down the line.

Where was the missing link?

"So Cronwall can't have murdered Fredell and Kaufman," Erik said, as if to underline his own frustration. "He must have been working with someone else."

In his peripheral vision, Thomas could see Urban Melin watching him anxiously. Margit was still busy going through Fredell's diaries. Thomas had another question for Erik.

"Have you seen any record of an autopsy report on Pär Andersson?"

"I don't think so."

"Any idea why not? Is there an explanation?"

"Do you think an autopsy was necessary? I mean, he left a suicide note, so there was no doubt about the cause of death."

"Exactly," Thomas said, mainly to himself. "A quick burial, and that was the end of the matter. I wouldn't be surprised if a military medic discreetly supplied the death certificate." He was becoming increasingly convinced that Andersson's death had been staged to look like suicide. Just like Nielsen's.

"Thanks for the information," he said. "Talk to you later."

Thomas ended the call and shook himself to try and get his brain working. It had been an intense day. He asked to use the bathroom, and he splashed his face with cold water to chase away the tiredness. It would be hours before he could go home to Pernilla. He longed to hold her, feel the slight bulge of her belly.

He reached for a towel and saw his reflection in the mirror. His face was gray, his eyes bloodshot. As he hung up the towel, he felt a stab of pain in his bruised chest.

Meanwhile, his mind was racing.

Robert Cronwall was a murderer, but he had an alibi for the deaths of Fredell and Kaufman. Therefore, he must have had an associate.

But who?

Who had killed those men, if not Cronwall?

The maritime charts on Annika Melin's desk came back to him. Suddenly he saw the full picture. They had been right all along—but wrong at the same time.

The realization made him sink down onto the toilet seat.

It wasn't Robert Cronwall who had taken the lives of the former Coastal Rangers.

CHAPTER 74

Thomas slowly made his way back to the study. He had to tell Margit everything without alarming Urban Melin, who was already starting to lose his grip.

He found her with one of the diaries in her hand. Before he could speak, she burst out, "You have to read this! It was Cronwall who murdered Andersson. He decided to punish him by pushing his face into a mop bucket full of water, but somehow it went too far, and Andersson died."

Margit broke off to catch her breath.

"This explains everything, including the detergent. It was in the water." Margit's face reflected the disgust she was feeling. "It was pure torture."

Thomas glanced in Melin's direction.

"Could you give us a few minutes? We need to have a word in private." Melin left them without saying anything.

Thomas tried to gather his thoughts; where to begin?

Birgitta Cronwall had pointed them in Marcus Nielsen's direction. She was afraid that her husband had murdered the young student, and Cronwall had indeed silenced him in the same way he had dealt with

Pär Andersson: by making it look as if he had killed himself, and leaving a fake suicide note.

Jan-Erik Fredell must have revealed the secret to Nielsen through his diaries, and before Nielsen died, he had passed them on to Andersson's sister.

The team had discussed various possible perpetrators, and their main suspects had been Kihlberg and Martinger. Now Thomas knew they should have been looking at two completely different individuals.

Robert Cronwall. And Annika Melin.

She must have decided to avenge her brother's death.

"It's not Cronwall who's abducted Annika," he said. "It's the other way around."

"What?" Margit's eyes narrowed. "Read this."

She held out the diary.

"Fredell was there; he saw what happened the night Andersson died. He describes it in detail. It's Cronwall we should be looking for; Annika is his next victim."

Thomas clenched his fists. Time was of the essence.

"No, we got it all wrong, Margit. Annika Melin is our killer."

He forced himself to speak quietly; he didn't want Urban Melin to overhear. Margit put down the diary.

"Annika Melin is both strong and aggressive," Thomas went on. "We know she's capable of violence—you heard what her husband said. She's the one who killed the Coastal Rangers, not Cronwall. Erik just called—Cronwall has an alibi for all the murders except Nielsen's."

Margit folded her arms, but Thomas knew her well enough to see that she was no longer quite so convinced of Cronwall's guilt.

"Why would she do that?" she said dubiously.

"For the sake of her brother. And her ruined childhood. Don't forget that she lost her baby when she found out the truth. At some point, it all became too much for her."

Thomas placed a hand on Margit's shoulder to add emphasis to his words.

"Annika Melin is a killer. We have to find her before Cronwall dies, too."

He gave her a moment to allow the truth to sink in. He could see it all so clearly now. They had been thinking along traditional lines: a male suspect abducting an innocent woman.

But Annika Melin was neither traditional nor innocent. She was a raging fury, hell-bent on revenge. For many different reasons.

They were dealing with two separate perpetrators, and now one had abducted the other.

Robert Cronwall had switched from hunter to prey.

"How would she have gotten him to go with her? Could she really do that?"

Margit sounded less skeptical; her doubts were fading.

"With a gun. And some kind of sedative. She's physically strong, and, as a pharmacist, she has access to drugs."

"What about Nielsen?"

"I think that was Cronwall trying to prevent the truth from coming out. He couldn't have known that Nielsen had already told Annika everything."

Margit sat down.

"I think you're right . . . But I don't understand why she took him, instead of killing him at home."

She linked her hands behind her head, the simple gesture expressing her frustration. "What do we do now? We have to find them as soon as possible. It might already be too late . . ."

Thomas's gaze fell on the maritime chart on the desk. The answer was right there in front of them.

"I think I know where she is," he said. "She wants to avenge her brother's death in the place where he died. She's taken him to Korsö."

"How would she do that? There are no transport links to the island."

"In our boat," Urban Melin whispered.

He had come back into the room without their noticing. He was standing in the doorway, fear and anxiety etched on his face.

"We own a Bayliner 265," he said hoarsely. "Annika often pilots it—she's very experienced."

"Are the keys missing?" Thomas asked.

"I'll go and check."

Melin went into the bedroom, and they heard the sound of a drawer being opened.

"They're gone!" he shouted, his voice shaking.

Thomas strode across the landing.

"Where's the boat moored?"

"Bullandö Marina."

Right next to Djurö and the maritime police launch. It would take no more than thirty minutes to get to Korsö from there.

"That's where she is, I'm sure of it," Thomas said. "We need to head out to Korsö right now. I'll call for the police helicopter."

CHAPTER 75

The rain was hammering on the car roof as they set off; big fat raindrops hit the windshield and were quickly swept aside by the wipers. Margit drove as Thomas scrolled through the contacts in his cell phone to find the number for Mats Larsson, the psychologist from the National Crime Unit's Perpetrator Profiling Group who had helped them the previous winter, when they had been trying to understand the mind of an embittered killer who had abducted a young girl on Sandhamn.

This time he needed help with Annika Melin.

He found the number, and a familiar voice answered almost right away.

"Mats Larsson."

"Thomas Andreasson. I want to ask you something, and we don't have much time."

Thomas was aware that his brusque tone was bordering on rudeness, but he couldn't afford the luxury of a lengthy explanation. He had to try to understand Annika Melin, so that they could find her and Cronwall.

Larsson picked up on the gravity of the situation.

"How can I help?"

"We're dealing with a perpetrator who's already killed three people and has abducted a fourth."

"I understand. Go on."

"I'm trying to understand the perp's behavior, work out what we can expect."

"Can you describe this person?"

"Her husband says she's aggressive and has violent mood swings. She's also threatened to kill herself and has assaulted her husband—on one occasion, she attacked him with a knife. A less common form of domestic abuse . . ."

"So we're dealing with a woman?"

"Yes—does that mean anything?"

"Not really; violent behavior is more common in men, but women are also capable of it. Is she unstable or suffering from anxiety?"

What else had Melin said about his wife? Thomas tried to remember.

"Her husband said he's afraid she might do herself harm. And she often blames others, or thinks the world is against her."

Larsson didn't say anything for a moment.

"We could be looking at a so-called borderline personality," he said eventually. "That's the diagnosis of those who are somewhere between the psychotic and the neurotic. They're often prone to outbursts of rage, and they can be self-destructive."

He cleared his throat.

"This is just to give you a general idea, of course. I can't make a judgment on a specific case without having met the individual concerned."

"I'm aware of that," Thomas said, "but can you help me understand who we're dealing with? How does this kind of personality manifest itself?"

"For the most part, they harm themselves, but sometimes their aggression is turned outward. You could say they 'lock on to' another person."

"Could you give me an example?"

"Men who stalk their ex-wives are frequently diagnosed as border-line. It becomes their mission in life to punish the one who abandoned them. At the same time, they can behave perfectly normal, which makes it more difficult for the ex-partner to be believed. Nobody understands how bad it can get."

This was much worse than Thomas had imagined.

"They can also become paranoid, often due to stress," Larsson went on.

"A persecution complex?"

"You could say that. In serious cases, if a trauma occurs, they can verge on the psychotic, with outbreaks of aggression and violence."

"Could a dramatic miscarriage trigger that kind of behavior?"

"Absolutely."

Thomas closed his eyes. Mats Larsson had just described a police officer's worst nightmare.

The windshield wipers squeaked across the glass. The wind had picked up, and he could see the tops of the trees alongside the freeway swaying in the storm as the last of the leaves were torn from their branches.

He had to ask one more question, even though he already knew the answer.

"Is she a danger to other people, apart from the one she's 'locked on to'?"

"If she believes she's being pursued or is under attack . . ." Larsson fell silent. "You did say she had violent tendencies . . ."

"So the answer is yes?"

"One hundred percent."

Chapter 76

It was almost five o'clock, and the dark clouds covering the sky made it feel as if dusk had already begun to fall. The headlights illuminated the torrential rain.

Thomas was trying to work out how long it would take to reach Korsö. The helicopter could fly them across in twenty-five minutes; there was no time to wait for backup. They had to get there as fast as possible; he could feel it in his bones.

At that moment, his phone rang, just as Margit was about to take the turn for the helipad at Slussen. It was the Old Man; he didn't mince his words.

"We have a problem. The wind speed has increased considerably, and the Swedish Met Office has issued a storm warning for the northern Baltic. There's no way the helicopter can take off in this weather."

Thomas rested his head on the side window and tried to think.

"What about the police launches?"

"I've checked—they're all in the northern area of the archipelago."

Thomas did a quick calculation. The maritime police had three CB90s, three RIBs, and two smaller Skerfe boats. They were designed to cover the whole of the Stockholm archipelago, but the RIBs couldn't cope with the swell in this weather.

"Isn't there a Skerfe boat in town?" he asked.

"No. One's in Berga and the other is on Djurö, and the crew have reached the limit of the hours they're allowed to work and left for the day. We'll have to bring in a fresh team."

"That will take hours."

"I know, but there's no alternative."

"Yes, there is," Thomas said, instinctively reaching into his pocket. He still had a master key for the police launches; no one had asked him to return it when he left the maritime police some years earlier.

"I'll take the boat myself," he said.

There was a long silence at the other end of the phone; the only sound was the rain hammering on the windshield and the swish of the wipers.

"Is that a good idea?" the Old Man said at last.

"I was a maritime officer for eight years." Thomas raised his voice. "You know I can handle a boat even if the sea is a little rough."

"The forecast is storm-force winds, Thomas. It's bad enough already, and worse is coming in over the whole of the east coast."

The Old Man sounded stressed. The situation had slipped out of their control, but Thomas could hear something else in his voice.

Deep anxiety.

He realized that Margit was looking at him. He clenched his fist. *Pull yourself together,* he thought. *Don't lose your temper. We have to get over there, and this is the only way.*

"Do you think I can't handle it? After . . ." He hesitated. "After what happened last winter?"

"I know you're an experienced sailor, Thomas, but you can't even be certain they're on Korsö. I don't want you to risk your life on a hunch."

"She's taken him to the island; I'm sure of it."

Margit swerved to avoid a pool of water in the road. Through the rain Thomas could see the driver of an oncoming car. He let out a silent scream as their vehicles came way too close for a second. Then Margit straightened out their car, and the man disappeared from view.

"I can be on Djurö in an hour."

The Old Man said nothing.

"You'll just have to trust me."

The Old Man gave in. "I just hope you know what you're getting into."

"I do."

Margit turned to Thomas as he ended the call.

"I'm coming with you," she said.

"It's going to be pretty rough."

"I'm coming with you."

CHAPTER 77

The waves were topped with white foam as they drove across Djurö Bridge. The water itself was a deep leaden gray, blending with the color of the sky.

Thomas leaped out of the car as soon as they pulled up outside the locked gates to the harbor. Hunched against the rain, he ran over and keyed in the four-digit code, then continued down the short slope as Margit followed in the car.

As she parked outside the building that also housed the coast guard, Thomas hurried over to the farthest jetty. The police boat was moored at the very end. A few isolated streetlamps spread their glow across the damp asphalt. The ground was treacherous with fallen leaves; Margit slipped in her sneakers but managed to stay on her feet.

Within minutes, both Thomas and Margit were soaked through from the lashing rain. Neither of them was wearing protective clothing; Thomas hoped there would be something on board they could put on.

He could see the boat straining at its moorings; the strength of the wind had increased since he'd spoken to the Old Man.

They clambered down into the boat, and Thomas got out the key. It fit.

With a practiced hand, he switched on the engines, the lights, the radar, and the GPS. The rain messed up the radar, producing echoes that distorted the image, but on a night like this, he was grateful for whatever was available, even though he knew the shipping lanes like the back of his hand.

Quickly he untied the mooring rope at the stern and called out to Margit to do the same with the rope at the prow. He automatically glanced over his shoulder before reversing away from the jetty, but there was no one else in sight in the marina.

Kanholm Bay was waiting off the island of Djurö. The unusually wide and deep stretch of water was notorious among the sailing community. In bad weather, there was no protection from strong gusts of wind, and the waves were high. The sea quickly became choppy and battered the hull, which made the crossing difficult even for a seasoned sailor.

When the wind reached storm force, it was even worse.

However, there was no alternative if they wanted to reach Korsö quickly. The other options would take up more valuable time. Time they couldn't afford to lose.

They had to cross the southern part of the bay. The wind was a northeasterly from Södermöja Bay. It was the worst possible direction, but they were going to have to face it anyway. If they could just get through, they would make it to the island in spite of the weather.

Thomas peered through the windshield. Visibility was poor due to the rain, and against his better judgment, he switched on the searchlight on the roof. That made things worse, and he switched it off again immediately.

Margit stood beside him, trying to see where they were heading.

"Go below and fetch the life jackets," Thomas said. "There should be some sailing jackets down there, too."

After a couple of minutes, she was back with two life jackets and two heavy waterproofs. Thomas let go of the wheel with his left hand and pulled on a life jacket.

"Make sure you fasten it properly," he said to Margit. "Don't forget the safety harness between your legs."

Margit put everything on without saying a word.

Far out to starboard, they could just make out a red flashing light—the radio mast at Stavsnäs. Otherwise the mainland was nothing more than a dark mass.

Time and again, Thomas checked the speedometer. He was traveling as fast as he dared without being reckless. He swore at his own failure to spot the connections earlier.

Why hadn't he checked what Robert Cronwall had said more carefully? He should have realized the role Cronwall had played. Instead he had been unforgivably credulous. If he had been more critical of Cronwall's attempt to play down his contact with Marcus Nielsen, the case might have been solved by now. He hadn't been sufficiently alert; there was no other explanation. The fact that he had just returned from a lengthy period of sick leave was no consolation. It wasn't even much of an excuse.

They were doing almost twenty-seven knots. Thomas kept the boat in the lee of the smaller islands surrounding Långholmen lighthouse; as soon as they reached open water, he would have to drop his speed. Anything else would be foolhardy, not to mention dangerous. He glanced at his watch; the crossing was taking far too long. They still had around twelve nautical miles to go. Would they get there in time?

"How are you feeling?" he asked Margit. She hadn't said much since they cast off.

"Not so good."

In the faint light, he could see that her face had taken on a greenish tinge.

"Do you feel sick?"

"Yes," she almost whimpered. "I think I'm going to throw up."

"Try to lean outside; otherwise the smell will make both of us sick."

Margit pushed open the door and just managed to turn her head so that the contents of her stomach landed on the deck.

As she straightened up, the boat emerged from the protection of Gökskär, and the wind immediately seized the door and tore it from Margit's grip. She tumbled backward as a cascade of water crashed over the rail and gushed into the cockpit.

"Shut the door!" Thomas bellowed. "You have to shut the door!"

"I'm trying!" Margit yelled back.

Thomas didn't dare let go of the wheel to help her; if he did that, anything could happen. He needed all his concentration to negotiate a route between the huge waves crashing over the bow.

So much water was pouring down Margit's face that there was no way she could see properly. She clung to the doorframe with one hand, fumbling for the door with the other. Another huge wave came at them with terrifying speed. The force of the ice-cold water made her lose her grip on the frame, and she hit the table with a bang. When the boat lurched sideways, she slid across the floor and thudded into the wall.

"Margit! Are you okay?" Thomas called out, trying to reach her with his free hand.

Groggily, she grabbed it and pulled herself to her feet. The door was still banging in the wind, and there was so much noise in the cockpit that it was almost impossible to communicate.

Thomas pulled her toward the instrument panel.

"Take the wheel!" he shouted. "Don't let go, whatever you do. You have to hold the course—do you understand?"

He leaned forward and reduced their speed to fifteen knots. He knew that was still too fast, but the thought of Annika Melin drove him on.

"Don't touch anything else!" he roared. "Concentrate on keeping the boat steady."

Margit seized the wheel as Thomas moved toward the doorway. As the boat dropped down between the waves, the door came flying toward him, but he managed to slam it shut. As if by magic, the roaring stopped, to be replaced by a calm that felt unreal.

He bent down to catch his breath, the rain dripping from his forehead. He wiped his face with the back of his hand. The whole cockpit was drenched.

Suddenly Margit let out a yell, and Thomas looked up. An enormous wave towered up in front of the windshield. It was coming at an angle of forty-five degrees, the worst possible scenario under the circumstances. If it hit the bow, they wouldn't stand a chance.

It seemed as if the massive wall of water was just yards away. Margit was still clutching the wheel, frozen to the spot. Thomas pushed her out of the way, took the wheel, and adjusted the speed. He had to steer into the wave and climb over it; if it hit them side-on, the boat would capsize.

The engines roared as he tried to change course so that they would meet the wave head-on.

All at once, the boat lurched. They were halfway across the huge breaker, and it felt as if the bow was hovering in midair.

They were about to turn over in the storm-tossed bay.

Diary:

August 1977

Tomorrow morning the final exercise begins. Two weeks of attacks, carrying out landings under fire, close combat, and live ammunition.

We are to cram into 200-boats, standing tightly packed together so that we don't fall over when the boat beaches, then we will storm ashore like a single body. We will then be expected to use all the knowledge we have acquired during our eleven months in the service of the Coastal Rangers.

And then it's over. Then we leave Korsö.

Only two more weeks until we leave this artificial world and return to our normal lives, an existence where we no longer have to torture our muscles until they scream with exhaustion, where we don't stink of shit and sweat, our nerves always strained to the breaking point with the fear of doing something wrong.

Soon we will escape the sergeant's clutches.

It's as if he understands that he's reached the final chorus. He hits the bottle almost every night. His eyes are often bloodshot in the mornings, and his behavior is worse than ever. He wants to maintain control, but he is losing his grip, slowly but surely.

Soon Andersson will be able to tell his father to go to hell.

It all went wrong. Just as we were about to return to Korsö. It was late in the evening, and we were all lined up, standing to attention. The visiting Finnish commander in chief was to inspect the troops before the exercise came to an end.

Everything had gone well; we had taken our bridgeheads and secured the required areas. We had carried out our missions with great success.

I looked around and felt proud to belong to this group. We were comrades for life, and we were prepared to die for one another.

Kihlberg stood with his legs apart, waiting for the inspection. He saw me glance at him and gave me an encouraging wink that said, We did it! For fuck's sake, we did it!

I nodded back with immense satisfaction.

Then I noticed Andersson. He didn't look good. His stomach had been playing up all week, and he was worn out. Now I could see that his face was greenish white, and he was swaying.

Kaufman was standing next to him, and I gave him a nudge, hoping that he would do something. Andersson mustn't faint during the inspection; he had to hang on for a few more minutes.

The Finnish delegation was approaching, escorted by Swedish officers. The chief of the Coastal Rangers training academy was with the Finnish commander in chief, with the sergeant bringing up the rear.

Just as they were passing Andersson, it happened. It was as if a wave passed through his body; he made a gurgling sound, and out came a cascade of vomit.

Right at the Finnish admiral's feet.

The admiral tried to take a step back, but it was too late; evil-smelling sludge had splashed all over his polished leather boots and the legs of his pants, leaving pale-pink stains.

There was an icy second when no one moved, then the admiral kept walking along the line without a word, followed by his entourage.

Kaufman and Erneskog caught Andersson just as he collapsed. No one dared speak; fear was coursing through our veins. The sergeant stopped in front of Andersson. I swallowed hard when I saw the look on his face.

"Tonight you're dead," he hissed. "Just you wait. Tonight you're dead."

CHAPTER 78

Margit's face was chalk white.

"We made it," she whispered.

Salty water was running down Thomas's forehead and back, and he realized he was soaking wet thanks to a mixture of cold sweat and rain.

"I thought we were going down," Margit breathed behind him.

"Me, too."

The wave had broken at the last second. Without really understanding how it had happened, they had found themselves on the other side of the wall of water instead of being swallowed up by it.

They had survived by a hair's breadth.

Thomas increased his speed. They were protected by Hasselkobben now, and Korsö wasn't far away. They were approaching the Sandhamn inlet, and Thomas ignored the five-knot limit as he passed through the Sound. There were few lights showing along the shoreline, but the Sailors Hotel was lit up as usual. Somehow the familiar sight made him feel better. The wider world, which for a little while had consisted of only dark, ice-cold water, still existed.

The gas station flashed by, and then he was aware of Kroksö on the port side. A small green-and-white lighthouse stood at the eastern inlet for Sandhamn, and as soon as he had passed it, he turned the wheel and set his course for Korsö Sound.

Now he could make out the faint glow of the streetlamps on the quay-side. They helped, but not much. The rain streaming down the windshield made it hard to see properly, and his eyes ached from the effort of trying to distinguish the land from the sea.

With only fifteen yards to go, he braked hard. Before the waves had time to seize the hull, he steered toward the inside of the long concrete jetty in order to reduce the impact of the wind.

A Bayliner was already moored there—the same make as the Melins' boat.

Annika was on the island.

It was almost seven o'clock in the evening, and dusk was falling as they stepped ashore. Thomas stopped and said, "Look at this."

Faint marks were just visible in the white sand. Footprints.

"It must be Cronwall and Melin," Margit panted.

Thomas moved closer; it definitely seemed as if two people had walked along the shore, one in front of the other.

The wind was howling in the treetops, and Thomas had to shout to make himself heard. He tried to assess the situation. It was impossible to see through the dense pine forest that formed a dark wall behind the wide shore, and visibility was even poorer due to the rain. He had visited the island many times, but right now it felt like a totally unfamiliar location.

Annika Melin could be anywhere.

"Let's keep going," he yelled, "but be careful!"

After a few hundred yards, they reached the small open square in the former military community. Thomas paused by a sturdy iron anchor that was embedded in the ground. Everywhere was in darkness, all the doors firmly closed. They could hear the water gushing down the drainpipes on the nearest buildings, and the tall maples above their heads creaked and swayed.

"Follow me." He set off along a narrow track leading to the cabin used by the maritime police as an overnight lodging. Thomas had often slept there over the years.

Suddenly it came to him. The detergent. The washing.

He beckoned to Margit and shouted in her ear, "I think I know where they are. In the sauna down by the shore. We need to turn back."

Rainwater was dripping down Margit's face.

"Come on!" Thomas began to make his way back without wasting any more time, and in minutes, they were there. Margit touched his shoulder and pointed.

"I think I can see a light."

A faint glow seeped through one of the windows. The waves crashed angrily against the rocks, and the treetops whined in the gale.

Thomas checked his gun.

"Let's go!" Hunched against the storm, he ran toward the light. Margit followed close behind, drawing her own gun at the same time.

They stopped when they reached the door. Nothing was moving; only the crack of light suggested that someone must have been there.

Margit removed the safety catch from her gun, and Thomas pushed open the door. They were met by a surge of damp air. Thomas swept the beam of his flashlight around the room: wooden benches fixed to the walls, clothes hooks, duckboards on the floor. The place was eerily silent.

"Can you see anyone?" Margit whispered.

"No."

Thomas put his finger to his lips and walked over to the door leading to the showers. That was where the light was coming from.

He tried the handle.

"On three," he mimed to Margit, who nodded.

He opened the door.

Several of the fluorescent tubes on the ceiling were broken, hence the dim light.

A body was lying in the middle of the floor. A naked man in his fifties.

CHAPTER 79

The phone rang just as Nora was unlocking the front door.

Simon was at his tennis lesson and due to be picked up in an hour.

"Adam, are you home?" she called out. "Can you get that please?"

She fumbled with the key, then remembered that Adam wasn't there either. He was having dinner with Wille's family tonight, so she was home alone for the time being.

Finally she managed to get in, and ran to grab the phone in the living room.

"Hello?" she gasped.

"Is that Nora?"

The line was crackling, as if the person on the other end was far, far away. She immediately knew who it was, and her stomach flipped over.

"Yes."

"Hi—it's Jonas, Jonas Sköld."

It seemed odd for him to say his surname. A few days ago, they had been as intimate as it was possible for two people to be, and now he was introducing himself as if they were no more than fleeting acquaintances.

"Hi, Jonas."

"How are you?"

"Fine, thanks."

She sounded fake, stiff and formal. Why couldn't she just be natural? Adopt a casual tone, as if she hadn't been waiting for this call for three whole days?

She wanted to make him think she had lots of other things going on in her head.

Hi, Jonas, she should have said cheerfully. *Good to hear from you, but I'm kind of busy right now. Can I call you back when I have time?*

The ticking of the kitchen clock penetrated her brain. At least thirty seconds must have passed. What was she supposed to say?

Jonas got there first.

"Maybe you're wondering why I haven't been in touch?"

Should she tell the truth? Tell him she'd wondered at least once an hour since they parted? She had come up with a thousand explanations, then scolded herself a thousand times for caring so much.

She couldn't understand why the short time they had spent together was so important to her. They didn't know each other particularly well; they had just had dinner a couple of times and shared a long walk on the island.

And spent one wonderful night together.

There were so many reasons why they shouldn't see each other again. Jonas was far too young for her. He was her tenant. She was still raw from the divorce, and it was too early to embark on a new relationship. She had almost managed to convince herself over the past few days.

But she couldn't stop thinking about him.

"Yes," she heard herself say in that same stiff voice.

"Would you believe me if I told you I'd left my cell phone in Stockholm?"

"Why wouldn't I?"

She had practically snapped at him; what the hell was she doing? Still . . . surely there must've been other telephones in Thailand, if he was really interested.

"Have you any idea how difficult it is to get ahold of your home phone number from Bangkok? It's not even possible to call information from overseas."

"Why didn't you call the bank?"

Oh God, why had she said that? He was trying, and she was throwing it right back in his face. What was wrong with her?

"I didn't think of that."

"OK."

"Believe me, Nora, I really have been trying to reach you. Eventually I had the bright idea of asking my sister to call information for me."

"You called your sister?"

Nora couldn't help smiling in the semidarkness. He'd been trying to get in touch with her, while she'd been imagining all kinds of nonsense. She wondered what explanation he'd given his sister, and her smile grew wider.

Jonas lowered his voice; his tone was gentler now, more intimate.

"I just wanted to say thank-you for the other night."

She pictured him in the bedroom on Sandhamn, their shadows in the moonlight, his cheek resting on the pillow as he slept. She remembered lying there curled up against his back, the feeling as she ran her fingertips over his warm skin.

Suddenly everything was perfectly clear and simple.

"It was wonderful," Jonas went on. "I'd really like to see you again . . . if that's what you want, of course. I'll be back in Stockholm on Friday—are you free then?"

"I'd love to see you." She hesitated, then mustered her courage. "But on one condition: you have to tell me how old you are."

Jonas laughed quietly. "Do you really want to know?"

CHAPTER 80

It didn't take Thomas long to register Robert Cronwall's familiar features. His heart sank; they were too late.

Margit quickly slipped her gun back in its holster and knelt down beside the lifeless body lying on the ice-cold floor. Cronwall's skin had a deathly pallor, and his hands were secured behind his back with a pair of metal handcuffs. Chafing around the wrists indicated that he had tried to free himself without success. His veined feet were bound together with a length of what looked like washing line, and a thin layer of white scum, partially dried, surrounded his lips.

"Jesus," Margit said.

Thomas felt sick. "Any sign of life?"

"He's stone cold." Margit placed her fingers just below the ear. "No pulse. He's dead." She felt the motionless limbs. "He hasn't been dead for very long; rigor mortis hasn't yet set in."

A white plastic bottle had rolled over to one of the drains, and Thomas moved closer to see what it was. The label came as no surprise: detergent. He picked up the bottle: empty.

"There's a strong smell around his mouth," Margit said. "Do you think she forced the detergent down his throat until he choked?"

"Probably. That would fit the pattern."

"Jesus, drowned in detergent. What a way to kill someone."

"She's sick."

Thomas shined his flashlight over the body and examined it carefully. The right arm bore signs of needle marks, a small blue circle with a tiny puncture mark in the center, just above the elbow.

Annika Melin had drugged Cronwall, just as Thomas had thought. Somehow she had overpowered him, maybe by threatening him at gunpoint, then she had sedated him so that he was incapable of resisting.

However, it must still have required a huge effort to get Cronwall to the place where her brother had died all those years ago.

A will of steel . . . or a deranged mind.

Margit stood up and took out her police radio.

"I'll call it in, tell them we've found Cronwall. We need reinforcements to search for Annika Melin."

Suddenly the ceiling light flickered and went out, leaving them in darkness. Thomas immediately straightened up and stepped back toward the wall, keeping the beam of the flashlight fixed in front of him. With his other hand, he reached for his gun.

"She's here," Margit whispered.

With all his senses on full alert, Thomas listened for a sound that would reveal Annika's whereabouts. There was a faint scraping noise in the distance, then a bang, like a door being slammed at the back of the building.

"Stay here and try to get through to the station," Thomas whispered. "I'll go after her. Keep your gun at the ready. She's dangerous—don't forget that for one second."

Before Margit had time to object, he opened the door and slipped outside.

CHAPTER 81

The wind tore at Thomas; he felt as if someone were slapping him across the face. The storm was still howling in the treetops, and it was hard to stay upright. The few streetlamps looked like a row of abandoned scarecrows.

He followed the track and ran past ghostly, empty barracks. Sheet lightning lit up the sky, and the black roofs flashed in the glare. It happened so fast that the fleeting sight immediately became a memory; by the time the brain had registered it, it was already gone.

There were thousands of places to hide on the former base; how could he possibly find Annika Melin here?

He headed for the old store, where the soldiers used to buy snuff and cigarettes in the days when there were hundreds of conscripts carrying out their military service on the island. He continued up the hill toward the tower. A long-abandoned maypole stood there like an eerie skeleton, and he hurried past a white building that reminded him of a barn.

Now he had reached the top of the hill, next to Korsö Tower. Rainwater poured down its curved façade. The track ran out here, but there was no sign of anyone running as desperately as he had been.

He was beginning to feel the lactic acid; his legs were numb, and he stood perfectly still, trying to catch his breath. An intense pain shot through the toes that were no longer there. Should he carry on looking for her?

At that moment, a heavy branch snapped in the wind; it came flying down and almost caught him on the back of the neck. He jumped aside at the last moment, and it crashed to the ground just inches away. A pine twig whipped him across the face by the corner of his mouth, and suddenly the taste of blood was on his tongue.

His courage failed; he ought to go back to Margit and wait for reinforcements. It wasn't long since he had been at death's door; he mustn't put himself in that kind of danger again. However, when he turned around, he saw a forest path leading to more open terrain. He shuffled past a cairn and emerged on a flat rock, which afforded him a much better view.

The sky was illuminated by another flash of lightning, and ahead of him he glimpsed a shadow moving among the stunted pine trees.

Annika Melin.

She slipped on the moss and almost lost her balance, then continued heading east. The distance between them was manageable.

Thomas stopped thinking and took off after her. He scrambled across the remains of concrete ramparts that had been blown up, the sharp stones rattling and scraping with every step. All at once, his injured foot slipped, and the stones gave way. He slithered down the slope and slammed into the rock. His face was smeared with mud and earth, and he had grazed his cheek. His head was spinning as he dragged himself to his feet, and he had to blink several times before he could see.

When he tried to clamber back up, he was bombarded with flying twigs and small branches.

Another flash, and he saw the silhouette of Annika Melin, considerably farther away. She was heading for one of the remaining fortifications on an outcrop, with a steep rock face behind it.

Limping, Thomas resumed the pursuit. His body was aching, and he was unsteady. As always when he was tired, he had forgotten the new way of walking he had had to learn.

"You have to turn back," he muttered to himself. "It's crazy to try and do this alone. You can't do it."

He thought about his new family, the little life still sleeping inside the protection of Pernilla's body. They must come first, whatever happened. Then he saw Annika again, only fifty yards ahead of him. She was standing perfectly still by the crumbling bunker with the roaring sea in front of her. The waves crashed against the shore, and cascades of spume surged across the rocks.

In the next flash of lightning, Thomas saw that Annika Melin was weeping. Her face was distorted, and the wind tore at her sodden hair, which was flapping up and down on her back like the useless wings of a fledgling trying to escape the nest. He could see her clearly, but there was a deep ravine between them, and there was no way he could get across; he would have to go around in order to reach her.

He began to pick his way over the crevices; when he glanced up, he saw that she had moved forward and was standing right at the edge of the outcrop. The force of the wind made her wobble, but she didn't move. She didn't seem to be crying any longer; her features had smoothed out, and her despair appeared to have lessened.

Thomas was going as fast as he could. He tried to call out to her; he wanted to tell her to wait for him. "You don't have to die, not you as well, enough people have died," he wanted to yell, but he was so out of breath that there was no power in his voice. His words were drowned out by the noise of the waves as they hurled themselves at the rock face, hissing and spitting. He tried to force his legs to move more quickly, just a few more steps; there was still time. It wasn't too late.

Annika held out both arms, as if she were trying to embrace something. Or as if she were preparing to break her fall . . .

Thomas was overcome with panic; he had to stop her.

He hurled himself forward, hoping to grab her legs. His fingers tried to reach the fabric of her pants; he strained his muscles to the utmost, and his fingertips brushed against something wet. But it slipped away, and he was left clutching at thin air as Annika fell headfirst onto the rocks below.

A dull thud reached Thomas's ears—or was he mistaken, confused by the roaring of the sea and the howling wind? He lay there trying to catch his breath.

Time passed. He had no idea how long he had been there, with his cheek resting on wet leaves. Slowly he became aware of the cold. His body was numb; he ought to get up and see what had happened to Annika, but he just couldn't do it.

The drop was at least thirty feet; she must've been dead.

A sob shook his body, and he closed his eyes, trying to fight back the tears.

After a little while, he groped for a sharp stone. He clenched his fist until it cut into his palm. The pain brought him back to life, enabled him to pull himself together and open his eyes.

He rolled over and got to his knees. It took some time for his eyes to grow accustomed to the darkness.

He had to go and check if she was still alive.

Diary:
August 1977

I don't know if I dare write down what happened. I'm just as guilty as the others. I don't know if I have the strength to do it.

I can never tell anyone about this.

Three days have passed since the sergeant woke us in the middle of the night. It was late, well after midnight, and the following day we were heading back to Rindö where we would be demobilized.

He must have come into the room while we were sleeping. We had all gone to bed early, exhausted after the long final exercise. We were spent.

He was standing there with his legs apart next to the bottom bunk where Andersson . . . Pär . . . was sleeping. I was on the top bunk.

I suddenly woke up and saw him. He made an impatient gesture in my direction—not a word, it meant. It was an order, not a request. Automatically I leaped out of bed and stood to attention.

Kaufman and Erneskog were still asleep.

Pär was lying on his stomach, as defenseless as a small child who knows that his parents are watching over him. His right arm was drawn up, his head resting on his hand. His back was bare; he wasn't wearing a pajama top. He looked younger than his twenty years; he was just a boy.

His cheeks were bright red; he was sick and worn out, and he had more or less collapsed as soon as we got back.

The sergeant stood there with a cruel smile playing across his lips. The smell of booze on his breath was unmistakable. He must have been drinking all evening; I had never seen him this drunk before. What was he going to do?

He clenched his fist and punched Pär in the side of the head.

Pär's body jerked, and he opened his eyes. Without saying anything, he took in the figure before him. I will never forget the look on his face at that moment. The fear, the wordless plea.

And then the shame as he remembered what had happened earlier in the day. He cowered as if he deserved to be punished.

The taste of fear filled my mouth, a stale, metallic taste like nothing else. My saliva dried up; I tried to lick my lips, but there was no moisture when I touched them with my tongue.

The sergeant was about to cross the line.

I knew I ought to do something to stop him, but I didn't have the courage. I was so scared I almost wet myself; I tensed my gluteal muscles in an effort to make my bladder behave.

Both Kaufman and Erneskog were awake now, but the sergeant simply silenced them with a gesture. Then he grabbed Pär by the arm and dragged him out of the room, toward the showers.

I stayed where I was for a moment, not knowing what to do, then I followed them down the empty corridor. What the hell was going on?

Pär was lying on the wet floor, naked and shivering, the blue veins clearly visible beneath the white skin. He made no effort to defend himself. He had simply let himself be taken there like a sacrificial lamb, waiting for retribution.

The sergeant turned to me, grinning broadly. I looked away; I didn't want to see the madness in his eyes. I glanced at Kaufman and Erneskog, who had joined me in the doorway. They didn't move either.

By the dim light of a single bulb, we stared at the sergeant as he poured detergent into a bucket and filled it up with water. If only Kihlberg were here, or Martinger, I thought with a lump in my throat. They would have known what to do.

But we were the only ones awake in the entire building. The others were upstairs.

Close, but much too far away.

Kihlberg and Martinger were the strongest in the group. They would have been able to stop the sergeant. They would have stepped in before it was too late.

I looked at Kaufman and Erneskog in despair, praying that one of them would act. Why didn't they open their mouths and let out a roar of protest, anything to bring the sergeant to his senses?

But they were just as cowardly as me.

Earlier in the day, I had thought to myself that we were prepared to die for one another. Now I knew how wrong I had been. Only the rights of the strong counted here. Nothing else. In the true spirit of the Rangers.

I was overcome with self-loathing and closed my eyes. A blast of cold air swept in through the window.

The sergeant crouched down so that his mouth was right next to Pär's ear. He grabbed his head and pushed it into the bucket.

"I'm going to wash out your filthy mouth so that you learn never to throw up on an officer again."

Did Sergeant Robert Cronwall intend to kill Pär Andersson that night? I don't know, but we are all to blame for his death.

We didn't lift a finger to help our comrade, and we kept quiet when the truth was swept under the rug.

We are pathetic cowards who do not deserve to wear the beret of the Coastal Rangers.

CHAPTER 82

Thomas made his way to the edge of the outcrop and saw Annika Melin on the rocks below. Her body was lying at an unnatural angle, like a rag doll that someone had tossed in a corner. One arm was bent behind her back, and her head appeared to be in a deep crevice.

She wasn't moving.

"Annika!" he shouted. "Annika, can you hear me?"

The rain was easing off, but he hardly noticed as he listened hard for any sound from the motionless figure.

"Annika!" he tried again, forming a funnel around his mouth with his hands.

The only response was the howling of the wind.

Could he get to her? He shuffled back from the edge and went over to a clump of dwarf pine trees growing by the side of the slope. He grabbed a branch and pulled it hard. It didn't break, and he tentatively began to inch downward. Suddenly his foot slipped; if the branch hadn't held, he would have fallen all the way to the bottom.

He hauled himself back to the top and sank to his knees.

There was no way he could climb alone in the darkness. If he was going to reach Annika, he would have to return to the tower and walk down the slope on the south side, which would take him to the shore. That was the only safe option.

He crawled to the edge and looked down one last time. Annika still wasn't moving.

If she wasn't already dead, like her brother and Cronwall and the others, she soon would be.

There was nothing more he could do. It was too late.

He was overwhelmed by sorrow at the thought of all those who had already died, and his own inability to save them. All the blood that had been spilled unnecessarily.

How was he going to find the strength to go on after this?

Thomas sank down on the wet rock and pressed his fist against his mouth to stop himself from weeping. It didn't work; a lump formed in his throat, and he began to sob. The tears washed over him like the waves rolling ashore far below, and in the end, he simply gave in.

KORSÖ

The island of Korsö lies by the central shipping lane into Stockholm, just off Sandön, better known as Sandhamn.

During the 1930s, the government wanted to be able to block the shipping lanes in the event of an invasion, and therefore the construction of a robust defense battery was begun on the island. As in most other cases in the archipelago, the Coastal Artillery had to make do with old maritime cannons. Those on Korsö originally came from the warships Wasa *and* Göte.

The Coastal Artillery and later the 2nd Amphibious Battalion were stationed on Korsö from the Second World War until the midnineties. Every spring, the men relocated from Rindö to Korsö, and they didn't return until the end of August.

In 1995, the battery was stripped of its ammunition, and since then, it has fallen into a deep slumber, like Sleeping Beauty. During the fall of 2008, all permanent artillery installations on Korsö were decommissioned. The fortifications were demolished, the guns were broken up for scrap metal, and the tunnels were filled in.

Nothing remained of the archipelago's main defensive battery but crushed stone.

To this day, no one is allowed to go ashore on the island.

ACKNOWLEDGMENTS

The brooding outline of Korsö Tower looms up beyond Sandhamn. As a child, I would gaze at its dark shape and wonder what was hidden there. I never found out, because it was and remains forbidden territory, but as an adult, I recalled the soldiers paddling by in their canoes all those years ago—without making a sound, in full combat gear, their faces covered in camouflage paint.

And that was where this story began.

The Coastal Rangers are surrounded by a kind of mythology. Their dedication and esprit de corps is impressive, and it has been fascinating to read and hear their stories during my research. If we are ever invaded by a foreign power, I cannot imagine a better fighting force to defend us.

I must stress that this entire narrative is my invention, and that all the characters spring from my imagination. However, the incidents, punishments, or "rewards" described in Jan-Erik Fredell's diary are based on actual events recounted in at least one of the following books: *Jag ska bli kustjägare* by C. M. Jönsson, *Man eller monster* by Mats Jacobson, *Kustjägarna 50 år—ett sekel i verksamhet* by the Society of Coastal Rangers' Veterans, and *Sjölunds gossar* by Jan Håkan Dahlström.

I am grateful to many people for answering all my questions: Detective Inspector Sonny Björk from the National Crime Unit; Detective Inspector Rolf Hansson from the Nacka police; Claes Ling-Vannérus, acting team leader with the maritime police; Hans-Jochen Seifert, former company commander with the Coastal Rangers; along with former Coastal Ranger Mikael Hansson and maritime police officers Thomas Eriksson and Patrik Enblad.

Special thanks to my good friend Per Westerberg, a reserve officer with the Amphibious Corps, for all his assistance on military matters.

I also want to thank my family, friends, and colleagues who have read the manuscript and shared their opinions during the journey: Lisbeth Bergstedt, Tord Bergstedt, Anette Brifalk, Helen Duphorn, Gunilla Pettersson, Göran Sällqvist, Katarina Bodén, and Camilla Sten.

Once again, my heartfelt thanks to my publisher, Karin Linge Nordh, and my editor, John Häggblom, who have worked on this novel with such commitment.

Warm thanks also to Emma Tibblin and Poa Strömberg, my brilliant agents at Stilton Literary Agency.

I take full responsibility for any errors which may have arisen, not least if I have misunderstood something relating to the work of the Coastal Rangers, in spite of my enormous efforts to get everything right. I have, however, simplified certain military procedures and titles for the sake of the narrative.

As usual, my wonderful children, Camilla, Alexander, and Leo, have had to put up with a seriously distracted mother occasionally, although this time I did try to do most of my writing in the mornings while you were still sleeping!

You know I love you more than anything in the world.

Lennart, you're the best. In every way. Congratulations on our bronze wedding anniversary!

Sandhamn, February 2011
Viveca Sten

ABOUT THE AUTHOR

Photo © 2016

Since 2008, Swedish writer Viveca Sten has sold almost four million copies of her Sandhamn Murders series, which includes *Still Waters*, *Closed Circles*, *Guiltless*, *Tonight You're Dead*, *In the Heat of the Moment*, *In Harm's Way*, and *The Price of Power*. Published in 2014 and hugely successful, *The Price of Power*, Sten's seventh novel, cemented her place as one of the country's most popular authors, one whose crime novels continue to top bestseller charts. Set on the tiny Swedish island of Sandhamn, the series has also been made into a Swedish-language TV miniseries seen by thirty million viewers around the world. Sten lives in Stockholm with her husband and three children, yet she prefers spending her time in Sandhamn, where she writes and vacations with her family. Follow her at www.vivecasten.com.

ABOUT THE TRANSLATOR

Marlaine Delargy is based in Shropshire in the United Kingdom. She studied Swedish and German at the University of Wales, Aberystwyth, and taught German for almost twenty years. She has translated novels by authors including Åsa Larsson, Kristina Ohlsson, Helene Tursten, John Ajvide Lindqvist, Therese Bohman, Ninni Holmqvist, and Johan Theorin, with whom she won the Crime Writers' Association International Dagger for *The Darkest Room* in 2010.

Made in the USA
Monee, IL
06 January 2024

51039048R00246